Praise for
The Invitation

'Veronica Henry captures the period so beautifully. Romance, heartbreak and secrets. I loved it!'
FERN BRITTON

'Pure joy! 1950s London and Somerset, the Savoy, a countryside Manor House, family secrets, love and loss'
LIBBY PAGE

'Veronica Henry incorporates a richness of character and place that colours every one of her books a must-read'
SUE MOORCROFT

'A heart-breaking tale with a wonderful post-war country house setting and a cast of vivid characters, *The Invitation* is a novel to cherish and delight in'
RACHEL HORE

'Beautifully romantic. Veronica really is the queen of writing family dramas. Like a glorious banquet, it left me full, happy and a little giddy and still wanting more'
JO THOMAS

'Suffused with Veronica Henry's trademark warmth, generosity and elegance, it's a treat from start to finish. I loved it'
EMYLIA HALL

'Enchanting. I threw myself at it knowing I was in for a delicious treat – and I was. It was terrific!'
ELIZABETH BUCHAN

Also by Veronica Henry

One Night at the Château
The Secret Beach
Thirty Days in Paris
The Impulse Purchase
A Wedding at the Beach Hut
A Home from Home
Christmas at the Beach Hut
A Family Recipe
The Forever House
How to Find Love in a Bookshop
High Tide
The Beach Hut Next Door
A Night on the Orient Express
The Long Weekend
The Birthday Party
The Beach Hut
Marriage and Other Games
Love on the Rocks
An Eligible Bachelor
Wild Oats

THE HONEYCOTE NOVELS
A Country Christmas
(previously published as Honeycote*)*
A Country Life
(previously published as Making Hay*)*
A Country Wedding
(previously published as Just a Family Affair*)*

A Day at the Beach Hut (short stories and recipes)
A Sea Change (Quick Read)

The Invitation

Veronica Henry

ORION

First published in Great Britain in 2026 by Orion Fiction,
an imprint of The Orion Publishing Group Ltd
Carmelite House, 50 Victoria Embankment,
London EC4Y 0DZ

An Hachette UK company

The authorised representative in the EEA is Hachette Ireland,
8 Castlecourt Centre, Dublin 15, D15 XTP3,
Ireland (email: info@hbgi.ie)

1 3 5 7 9 10 8 6 4 2

Copyright © Veronica Henry 2026

The moral right of Veronica Henry to be identified as
the author of this work has been asserted in accordance
with the Copyright, Designs and Patents Act of 1988.

All rights reserved. No part of this publication may be
reproduced, stored in a retrieval system, or transmitted
in any form or by any means, electronic, mechanical,
photocopying, recording, or otherwise, without the
prior permission of both the copyright owner and the
above publisher of this book.

All the characters in this book are fictitious, and any resemblance
to actual persons, living or dead, is purely coincidental.

A CIP catalogue record for this book is
available from the British Library.

ISBN (Hardback) 978 1 3987 2413 6
ISBN (eBook) 978 1 3987 2415 0
ISBN (Audio) 978 1 3987 2416 7

Typeset at The Spartan Press Ltd,
Lymington, Hants

Printed and bound in Great Britain by Clays Ltd,
Elcograf S.p.A.

www.orionbooks.co.uk

In memory of my grandfather
Hubert Victor Stallabrass 1904–1998.
He was a sergeant in the Metropolitan Police and was
stationed at Richmond, Surrey, during World War II.
This is for you, Grandpa x

The Invitation

Foxwood, November 1953

There was a towering stack of them. On one side was a jolly Father Christmas sitting with his legs spread out in front of a fireplace, a glass of port in one hand and a dreamy smile on his face. And on the other side, in shiny black letters embossed onto pristine white card, were the words that had been the same for as long as anyone could remember:

> ON THE LONGEST NIGHT OF THE YEAR
> THE PLEASURE OF YOUR COMPANY
> IS REQUESTED AT
> THE SNOW BALL
> FOXWOOD
> NR BREVERTON
> SOMERSET

The twenty-first of December. Always the twenty-first of December. People for miles around kept the date free, hoping to find one of the coveted envelopes pushed through their letterbox. No one knew quite how you got on the guest list, but if you were lucky enough to be invited, you would think of nothing else until the longest night arrived.

She looked at the list of names she had drawn up for this year. In consultation with the rest of the family, in theory, but of course she had the final say. It was always a mix of stalwarts and surprises. You didn't want it to be the same every time. You had to keep it fresh and ring the changes. That was the art of being a good hostess.

She unscrewed the lid of her Waterman and filled it with ink. Her husband couldn't understand why she didn't give the job to his secretary, but he must know by now she was a perfectionist? Every detail mattered, from the dotting of an 'i' to the elaborate flourish on a guest's name.

As she began her task, painstakingly blotting her work to avoid smudges, she began to picture the evening in her mind. She could smell the resin of the Christmas tree, the waft of spices from the kitchen, the mingled perfumes of the guests. She could hear the rustle of silk, the faint arpeggio of a distant piano, the ringing of dress boots on the flagstones. Cold cheeks ready for a kiss of greeting; the warmth of a fur coat removed by a servant. The frantic tooting of a horn as an excited party arrived in an overcrowded motor car, a hip flask passed from guest to guest in the back seat.

There was so much to do to make it perfect.

And all the while she wrote, there was one name conspicuous by its absence that repeated itself over and over in her head, a metronome that might eventually drive her so mad that she would relent, perhaps against her better judgement. But for now, she was determined this particular guest would be left off. If anyone else noticed her omission, there would be puzzlement, for why on earth would she leave him off when he was such a close and dear friend of the family?

There was such a thing as too close, she thought. And perhaps he would come anyway, assuming his invitation, not needing his inclusion to be confirmed in writing. He had that kind of confidence. Some might call it arrogance. So maybe she should include him after all? Would she even notice him amongst all the other guests?

She decided not to, for now. There was plenty of time to add him later if she had a change of heart.

Nearly an hour later, the invitations were all addressed, sealed and ready to be taken to the post office for a crimson stamp, then whisked away in a hessian sack for each to begin their journey, perhaps to a sprawling country manor or an elegant London townhouse or a cottage on the outskirts of Breverton.

She screwed the lid back on her pen, stared at the one remaining invitation, then picked it up and put it away in the bureau drawer which she locked with a tiny key.

I

April 1953

So this was what it was like, Alfie thought. Falling in love. He was falling in love in the American Bar at the Savoy, on a powder-soft evening in spring, the delicate warmth of the April sun still clinging to the pavements, the clouds drifting away like theatre goers as night fell.

Later, he would shudder as he remembered how close he had been to leaving.

It was an engagement party, and he wasn't keen on engagement parties. They seemed superfluous and a little bit smug. Tonight, everyone was drinking fast, and the air was thick with idle gossip, shrieks of laughter and a pall of cigar smoke. He wasn't in the mood. He'd have one more drink and hop it.

And then he saw her. She wore a black velvet beret on her dark curls, and on it was pinned a diamanté spider, a little flash of bejewelled wit that was quite at odds with her demure tea dress, and if Alfie was intrigued by anything, it was contradictions. She was raking the crowd with her eyes, presumably working out if there was anyone there she knew, or liked, and then Alfie saw her eyes narrow as Johnny Mullinger bore down on her. Johnny saw every woman in London as a personal challenge. With raven hair and Malteser eyes, he was a practised seducer and rarely met resistance. Alfie snatched up one of the cocktails lined up on the bar and swept across the room.

'There you are, darling,' he said, cutting right in front of Johnny and pressing the glass into the woman's hand. 'A French 75. Shall we go and sit down?'

She flicked a glance at Johnny, who was looking both thunderous and lecherous. 'Just the ticket.' She smiled at Alfie. 'Thank you.'

And without another word she followed him to a nearby table and they both sat down, leaving Johnny to scowl and slink away with his hands in his pockets.

'I knew the service here was good,' she said. 'But to have my favourite drink brought to me before I've even thought about what to order is quite something.'

'Chin chin,' he said in reply, and they clinked glasses.

He tried to work out what colour her eyes were. He ran through the possibilities: sky was too light, navy too dark. Teal too green; turquoise too bright. Petrol was a bit murky. Was there a sea-blue? Though that wasn't right either. He should know, given that colour was in his blood, even if he was trying to avoid the family business and stay in London as long as he could. Duty to Arbutus Paints would call in the end, and he would have to return to his beloved Somerset eventually, but in the meantime, there was fun to be had.

Sapphire, he decided in the end. Her eyes were like sapphires, deep and sparkling. As he gazed at her across the table, he felt the same familiar warmth as when he rounded the final corner of the drive to Foxwood on a Friday evening, when the house stood square and splendid and welcoming in front of him, the windows ablaze, the front door ajar, the dogs quivering with excitement on the top step.

'Do you have a name, by the way?' she asked, breaking into his thoughts.

'Oh. Gosh. Sorry. Yes. Of course. Alfie.' How crass, not to introduce himself.

'I'm Clementine,' she said.

He wanted to say her name over and over again, to see how it felt in his mouth, but he said it once for now.

'It's very nice to meet you, Clementine.'

'I need this,' she told him, holding up her glass. 'You won't believe the day I've had. I only just stopped a client's Pekingese from cocking its leg on our most valuable painting. Although, to be honest,' she leaned into him, laughing, 'some might say it would have improved it.'

He joined in her laughter, for it was infectious. Her voice was surprisingly gruff, and she struggled to pronounce her r's: she had what his family had always fondly called a howwid wabbit. It was utterly entrancing.

'So what do you do?' He took a sip of his Martini, the icy molten silver stinging his lips.

'I work for my half-brother. He's an art dealer. Benjamin Bell?' She looked at Alfie to see if he recognised the name, but he shook his head. He wasn't going to give too much away just yet. 'If I've told him once not to prop paintings up against the wall, I've told him a thousand times. But he doesn't listen, because I boss him about from dawn till dusk, poor thing.'

'*Are* you bossy?' asked Alfie, who had known enough bossy girls in his time to know it wasn't a quality he was looking for.

'Dreadfully,' she said. 'But only with Ben, because he's hopeless. I wouldn't boss you about. Probably. You don't look as if you need bossing.'

'Only sometimes.' He thought perhaps he wouldn't mind her bossing him.

'So how do you know the happy couple?' Was there a hint of irony in her voice? There was certainly a glint of mischief in her eye.

'I know Nigel from school. We were in the same house. You?'

'I share a flat with Henrietta and another couple of girls. She's a darling but she does bang on. She even talks in her sleep, you know.'

Alfie had met Henrietta a few times now. He liked her but she did talk too much. He wasn't sure how Nigel put up with the constant monologue of non-sequiturs and information about people he'd never met mixed in with a barrage of instructions.

'Does she?' For a moment he imagined waking up next to Clementine. Finding her curled against him, warm and soft and smelling of that delicious scent, the one that was driving him mad wondering where he had smelled it before. Honeysuckle, he realised. The honeysuckle around the loggia at Foxwood.

'So why haven't I met you before?' she asked, breaking into his day dream. 'Where have Nigel and Henrietta been hiding you?'

'I suppose I'm so busy with work I haven't had time to socialise.' It was true. Christmas and New Year had been frantic, and now they were gearing up for the onset of the summer season.

'What do you do?'

'I've got a business with another chap from school. Freddie Lambert? Do you know him?' She shook her head. 'It's called Coupe. We started it as a bit of fun after National Service, but it's taken off. We supply wines and spirits to balls and parties and weddings.'

'That sounds great fun.'

'Oh, it is. But it's harder work than you think. A lot of shifting boxes around.'

'It's the same with art. Endless wrapping up of paintings and making sure they don't get damaged.'

Was now the time to mention that he knew, only too well? He didn't want to sound like a know-it-all. There was nothing worse. So he nodded and smiled. But the connection cemented the draw he was feeling to her. Few people he knew understood the world he had once been on the edge of. He'd only had a glimpse inside, but it had been thrilling and exciting to a teenage boy.

For a moment, he imagined Edwin's nod of approval at his companion. It spurred him on.

'We're thinking about getting our own shop,' he told her. 'With a cellar underneath. But it would be a big investment.' He mustn't talk about himself too much. 'What about you? What kind of art do you sell?'

'Contemporary. Young artists, mostly. Some of it's abstract and makes people furious.' She laughed. 'But some of it you'd have on your wall. A mix, really. It's good to be provocative but at the same time, we have to make a living.' Clementine held out her empty glass with a smile. 'Oh dear. I seem to have drunk that awfully fast. Would you mind getting me another?'

'As long as you promise to stay right there.'

She sat bolt upright and feigned stillness. 'I shan't move an inch.'

'So – you've met the delightful Clementine?' said Nigel as he joined him back at the bar. The two of them had been at Haileybury together, which in general turned out good eggs with impeccable manners and none of that careless arrogance that can give public school a bad name. 'She's unencumbered, you know.'

'She's fabulous,' said Alfie.

'Bloody hell,' said Nigel with a wink. 'Alfie Arbutus finally shows a chink in his armour.'

Alfie grinned. He was used to being teased about his bachelor status. But he was surprised to feel a sudden urge to run out into the night up to Bond Street and bang on the door of Mappin & Webb, then rake through the jewels on the black velvet pads until he found a ring that matched her eyes. You probably shouldn't ask someone to marry you after three Martinis, he thought. But he wanted to know more.

'What should I know about her?' he asked Nigel. 'She says she shares a flat with Henrietta.'

'Yes. Henrietta says she's quite a girl. Gets furious if the others leave their knickers drying in front of the fire or don't do the washing-up. But fun. Don't be fooled by the demure act. There's more to her than meets the eye.'

Alfie was quite happy with what met his eye. But he was a little curious as to why someone as appealing as Clementine was unattached. Perhaps she felt the same as he did? Unwilling to settle for second best. Marriage was, generally speaking, for life, so you had to be careful. Although of course, the longer you left it, the less choice there was. He'd been to six weddings in the past two years.

He'd had some very jolly girlfriends. Mostly they were great company, easy-going, kind (to Alfie's mind this was the most important quality in a human being) and full of go. But he'd never gone to sleep dreaming of them, or woken up with a longing to see them. And he'd never taken one of them home to Foxwood. He knew that frustrated his mother. Elizabeth was never interfering, but he could tell she was longing for him to find someone.

As he carried Clementine's replenished glass carefully through the throngs, he saw Johnny Mullinger had slithered into his seat next to her. Alfie stood still for a moment, shocked by the rush of adrenalin that made spots dance in front of his eyes. The last thing he wanted was a confrontation. Fisticuffs at the Savoy would not be a good start to the evening. But he had to do something.

'That's my seat,' he said to Johnny, who raised a dark eyebrow.

'I don't think there's a *placement*,' he replied. 'Everyone's sitting wherever they like. And I like it here.'

He leaned back and looked down at Clementine's legs with a leer.

'It's my fault,' said Clementine. 'I should have told you Alfie was sitting there.'

Johnny spread his hands and gave a shrug.

Alfie's grip tightened on the stem of the glass. He didn't want to make a scene, but he could see Johnny was taking huge pleasure in the situation. He hadn't been to Haileybury. He was no gentleman. There were two spare seats at the adjoining table, next to a gaggle of Nigel's friends from his office. He was going to take a risk.

He indicated the two seats. 'Shall we?' he asked her.

Her eyes flickered over and she understood immediately.

Was it ungentlemanly of him to force her into getting them out of an awkward situation? Johnny was smirking, quietly confident. It was only a split second but it felt like a lifetime before Clementine jumped up.

'Oh perfect! Will I bring your drink? There.' She patted Johnny on the shoulder. 'You can sit there as long as you like. It was lovely to meet you.'

Alfie was almost speechless with admiration as she whisked away his half-drunk Martini and hopped over to the next table. Somehow, she had managed to execute the manoeuvre without humiliating Johnny in the least.

'Thank you for rescuing me,' she murmured as she settled herself down. 'I don't know about wandering hand trouble, but he definitely has wandering eye trouble. Ugh.'

She gave a little shudder. Alfie felt his heart rate subside. He could sense Johnny's ire from where he was sitting. It was probably time to make a sharp exit. He leaned forwards.

'Would you like to go somewhere for dinner?'

Her face brightened. 'Oh yes! I'm starving, and a girl can only eat so many peanuts. I had a ham sandwich at about midday and that does not bode well for drinking cocktails. I'll be talking gibberish by the end of this.' She raised her glass and began to sip.

'How about Wilton's?' he asked. Normally he'd go somewhere much more lively, but he wanted to focus on her.

'Oh perfect. You clever thing. Not too noisy. I'm a little deaf.' Her face clouded with this confession. 'Only in one ear. Measles.'

'Oh. I'm sorry.'

'It's fine. I just prefer quiet. Especially if I'm trying to get to know somebody.'

Her sapphire gaze met his grey one and they stared at each other for a moment. It felt momentous. He would remember this night for as long as he lived, he thought.

'Should we say goodbye, do you think?' she asked. The crowd was getting louder and more boisterous. 'Or just slip away?'

'Slip away, definitely. It would take too long otherwise.'

'Well, quite. And we don't want anyone tagging along.' There was a little pause. 'Do we?'

He revelled for a moment in the glow of their complicity. 'We do not.'

She put her unfinished drink on the table, leaned in and whispered in his ear. 'Then let's go.'

His heart gave a little bump. How could someone you'd only met half an hour ago make you feel as if you were falling, falling, falling into the softest feather bed?

The sun was thinking about setting as they came out of the hotel onto the Strand. A row of black cabs lined up like beetles. Alfie wasn't inclined to take a taxi usually, not because he was mean, but because he loved meandering through the streets on the way back to the family flat in Pimlico at night. He relished the way London was coming back to life at long last, the music and laughter that drifted from the bars and clubs, clusters of girls dressed up to the nines, coquettish and carefree, eyeing up the sharp-dressed men. The barrage balloons had gone from the skyline, replaced by cranes breathing new life into the ghosts of bombed-out buildings. And the terrible smog that had hung over the city last winter, needling its way into people's lungs, had finally drifted away. The city felt sweeter, full of hope.

He was, however, happy to invest in a cab for Clementine.

'Taxi, or would you prefer to walk?'

'Oh gosh, walk. I need to clear my head. And it's a wicked waste to get a taxi unless it's very late or you're completely footless.'

She tucked her arm in his, quite unselfconscious about close contact. Alfie couldn't believe how right it felt, the warmth of her against him. He felt as if he was floating along the pavements as they headed towards the Embankment, watching the sun sink into the Thames as if it, too, was in a cocktail haze, a little woozy.

He loved April. Its promise of the next season to come. The first cut of lawn. Cardigans sliding off bare arms and loosening ties. Pimm's on the terrace. For a moment, he longed for Foxwood, which would soon be shimmying into summer clothing, the first rose buds flashing pink. The cuckoos would be calling, the swallows swooping –

Suddenly they were turning into Jermyn Street and the familiar facade of Wilton's was in front of them. It wasn't Alfie's usual kind of haunt for a date – he preferred a more casual trattoria – but it was a family favourite and for some reason he wanted the security of formality. It wasn't that he wanted to impress Clementine, but he wanted to concentrate on her and not be distracted by high jinks and shenanigans.

Their coats were taken, and the maître d' led them to a discreet corner, where the head waiter greeted them.

'Good evening, madam.' He turned to Alfie. 'Mr Arbutus.'

Alfie saw Clementine's eyes flicker with interest as she heard the name.

'Good evening, James,' answered Alfie as they sat down and opened their menus. 'What do you recommend tonight?'

'The asparagus is exceptional.'

'Of course.' The asparagus season was just beginning. He could imagine the bunches on the table in the kitchen at Foxwood, freshly cut, Daisy snapping off the woody ends, whipping up a buttery yellow sauce.

'And the Dover sole. Your favourite, I think?'

'Everyone's favourite,' chuckled Alfie. 'What do you think, Clementine?'

'Both of those sound absolutely perfect. I don't need to look any further.'

She shut her menu decisively.

'Asparagus and Dover sole for two, then, please, James. And a bottle of . . .' Alfie ran his eye down the wine list. 'The Pouilly Fuissé.'

'An excellent choice, sir.' The waiter took the menus from them.

Once they were alone, Clementine looked at him.

'Arbutus,' she said softly. 'Are you related to Edwin?'

'Yes,' he said. 'He was my brother.'

To Alfie's surprise, her eyes filled with tears. She put out her hand to cover one of his and squeezed it. He felt a lump in his throat, moved by her perceptiveness, her openness, her compassion.

'You have the look of him,' she said.

Their family resemblance had always been striking. Alfie and Edwin both looked like their father, with that sweep of thick hair springing from a widow's peak, combined with pronounced cheekbones and a full mouth. Edwin had had their mother's colouring – burnished gold hair and green eyes – which made for a dazzling combination. Alfie was a more subdued version – light brown hair; grey eyes.

'Perhaps a little,' he said now.

'You do,' she insisted. 'I've seen photographs. The ones in the paper.' She squeezed his hand again. 'I'm so sorry. The beastly war.'

'We weren't alone in losing someone.'

'I know. But it doesn't make it any easier, does it? My mother lost her first husband in the Great War. She's never really got over it, though she adores my father.'

He could see there were tears in her eyes. They made the blue even brighter.

'We miss him,' was all he could think of to say.

'It must have been a big honour, to be chosen as a war artist. Your parents must have been very proud.'

'Yes.' He thought his mother had been more relieved than anything. Not that being a war artist was a safe option, for they were commissioned to capture the reality of war as far as they could, which often meant being in the thick of it. But drawing or painting the sweat, blood and smoke somehow felt safer than fighting.

Alfie was fifteen the last day he had seen his brother. Edwin was ten years older than him, allocated to the Admiralty, home on leave before setting off for Iceland to capture the Allied occupation on canvas. He had thrown his arms around their mother, kissing the top of her head as nonchalantly as if he was heading off to the Trout Inn for a bitter shandy before dinner. He'd waved an arm in the air before galloping down the steps and into his yellow soft-top Alvis where his kit bag and artist's materials were already in the boot. Alfie had moved towards his mother to put an arm around her shoulder, but Elizabeth had stepped away from him, turned and fled up the staircase, leaving Alfie to watch Edwin's car disappear off down the drive, paralysed with uncertainty as to what to say, or do, or feel. That was the trouble with war. It was overwhelming but you had to put on a brave face and pretend everything was normal, no matter how you felt.

'It's good of you to talk about him,' he told Clementine. 'People usually avoid mentioning him as much as they can.'

She frowned. 'You don't stop talking about someone just because they've died, surely?'

'They do, I'm afraid.' His own friends. His own *family*, sometimes. His father, certainly, rarely spoke about him. But Edwin was always there. The golden ghost.

He looked across at Clementine and sensed he had found something precious. He had waited long enough. Sometimes, he had thought he would never find anyone to melt his frozen heart. That he would just have to find someone to marry whom he could tolerate, rather than adore, which wouldn't be fair on them, because no one wanted to be merely tolerated. But here his heart was, beating away deep inside him, pumping blood around his veins, reaching every corner of him, like warm treacle, melting away all those chips of ice.

As James brought them their wine, he held up his glass to her.

'Well. Here we are. Wilton's on a Tuesday.'

'I know,' she sighed happily. 'Isn't it bliss?'

They chatted easily, offering each other titbits of

information so they could put each other into context. Alfie told her about his family's paint factory, and how they had made specialist paint during the war: anti-glint paint, to stop glass from catching the enemy's eye; fire-resistant paint to coat the rafters of buildings; black-out paint for windows, and a special kind of gloss that held shattered glass together if a building was bombed.

'We made a lot of money, but we saved a lot of buildings and a lot of lives.'

'That's how we won the war. People thinking on their feet and making sacrifices. Not being afraid to change.'

'Yes.' He was glad she understood. He gave a wry grin. 'And now we're back to normal, churning out common or garden paint for people's homes. Anyway, enough about that. Tell me about you.'

Clementine told him about her work at the gallery. She was more than just her brother Ben's assistant. She was charged with keeping her eye out for new artists for them to exhibit.

'I've found this incredible young Scottish artist I'm very excited about. I'm hoping Ben will agree to an exhibition later this year. His work's very intricate and delicate but quite challenging. Visceral. I can feel it here.' She put a fist on her solar plexus.

He loved the way her eyes shone when she spoke about her protégé. He could see how deeply she cared. He knew a bit about her world through Edwin, of course, so was able to show more than polite interest. She had so much more spark than most of the girls he knew, who thrived on gossip and speculating how much money people had.

Suddenly, the Pouilly Fuissé was drained and little

bowls of lemon soufflé were empty in front of them. He didn't want the night with her to end, but end it must.

Alfie insisted on taking Clementine back to her flat in Kensington in a taxi even though she told him she'd be all right on the bus. They stood outside on the pavement, under a flowering cherry which filled his head with its glorious scent. The taxi was waiting on the other side of the road to take him on to Pimlico, engine idling, and the driver spread his newspaper out over the steering wheel. He was used to prolonged farewells. It was an occupational hazard.

'Thank you for a lovely evening.' Clementine was gazing up at him. 'I think it might be the nicest I've ever had.'

'Wilton's is always good.'

She nudged his arm with her elbow. 'I didn't mean the food, though it was delicious. I meant the company.'

'Oh.' He went pink with pleasure.

The taxi driver pipped his horn, making them both jump.

'You'd better go. The meter's running.'

He didn't want to, but she was right. He hesitated, not sure what to do, whether to lean in to kiss her cheek politely or offer his hand or put his hands in his pockets and shuffle off. He wasn't usually so reticent. Kisses were easily obtainable these days, yet something was holding him back. What if she didn't want to be kissed? The thought of rejection was too much to bear—

Suddenly he felt her arms around his neck, and her warm mouth on his. He'd been so lost in his dilemma, she must have tired of waiting for him to make the first move. Her kiss was fleeting, yet underpinned with urgency, just long enough to be a promise of something more. Nigel had warned him, he remembered now, not to be taken in by Clementine's demure exterior. Clementine's kiss was... breathtaking.

She disentangled herself, laughing at his startled expression.

'Go! Or the cab fare will be more than the dinner bill.'

He didn't care about the fare. He grabbed her, pulled her close, wrapping her up in his arms. She gave a squeak of surprise just before he put his lips on hers again, taking control, gentle but fierce. After a few moments their kiss became languid, exploratory, a kiss that could last until the end of time. She pressed herself against him and he could feel their hearts crashing together and he thought maybe, just maybe, everything was going to be all right, and he didn't have to spend the rest of his life pretending after all.

'You'll know, when it happens,' Edwin had once told him. 'If you have to wonder, it's not the real thing. But when it does happen...' he searched for the words – 'it's overwhelming. Everything joins up. Your mind, your heart, your soul, your body. It's like being electrified.'

Alfie was riveted but wasn't sure he entirely understood. He'd still been a gangly teen, with little access to female company because of the war, but of course the whole subject of women and what they did to you, intentionally or unintentionally, was intriguing, and Edwin was his only access to information.

The funny thing was, Alfie didn't think Edwin was talking about his fiancée when he talked about being electrified. Meg was the daughter of one of their father's friends from Oxford, a Rhodes scholar and now a wealthy businessman in New York. Meg and Edwin had fallen in love when she came to London on holiday one summer and his parents had offered her a room in the family flat. Their wedding had been postponed when war broke out, and nobody knew when it would be rearranged, of course, because no one knew when it was all going to end, and Edwin hadn't seen Meg since the August before the beginning of the war. The last time Alfie had seen them together, Edwin hadn't looked like he did now, eyes shining, almost fizzing with some kind of energy. He didn't like to quiz him further, for he wasn't sure what to ask, and it unsettled him.

He had wondered, after that illuminating conversation, if Edwin had met someone else? It wasn't unlikely. He was still living at the family flat in London, in between postings. Being a war artist had a certain cachet, and Alfie knew enough about women to know they might not find the presence of an American fiancée an obstacle.

He knew the truth now, of course, but he always pushed it to the back of his mind, for he was the only one party to his brother's secret. And now he understood why Edwin had been able to describe the feeling in such detail, for he felt exactly the same. Electrified.

Clementine had set his blood on fire. When he looked in the mirror, he saw the same slightly dazed and completely bedazzled expression he'd seen on Edwin. And when he touched her, it turned him inside out. Did she feel the same? He thought perhaps. They had met nearly every day since their dinner at Wilton's three weeks' ago, unless she had a private view or he had an event. At lunchtimes, they sat on a bench by the pelicans in St

James's Park, because it was halfway between her brother's gallery and the dusty old cellars he and Freddie were renting on Pall Mall.

'We Arbutuses love a pelican,' Alfie told her. 'It's our family crest.'

He showed her the signet ring on his little finger, which bore the crest of a mother pelican pecking her breast to draw blood to feed her offspring.

'It looks a bit gruesome, but it's to show her loyalty to her children,' he explained.

'I love it,' said Clementine, admiring the bloodstone, tracing her finger over the engraving, pressing it into her flesh to see if the image would print itself on her skin.

'It's my birthday in two weeks,' Alfie said, on impulse. 'Would you come to Foxwood? I always have a birthday tea in the garden.'

He'd never taken a girl back to Foxwood before. It was his haven, and he was very possessive of it. Protective, even. Girls were for London, for gallivanting and larking about. Foxwood was for his more reflective side, for it was still full of shadows, of memories, and the thought of taking someone there and having to pretend that it wasn't was daunting. But he could already imagine Clementine lying on a rug on the lawn, eyes half closed while the clouds scudded about above her. Somehow, he thought she would understand, without him having to explain, that even though Foxwood was everyone's idea of the perfect English country house, and everyone in it seemed gilded, it held heartache in its walls. But it was still special. He could never turn his back on it. And he knew it was where he belonged, ultimately. Dancing the night away at the Astor Club, rife with dukes and gangsters, or the jazz-filled Flamingo, was a rite of passage. They were places you passed through on your way to real life.

'I'd love that.' She squeezed his hand, as if to say, 'I know how much this means', and they sat there in the sunshine, each of them privately wondering what on earth would have happened if they hadn't turned up to the engagement party they'd each had no desire to go to.

2

Thank goodness for May, thought Stella. She was still lying in bed at nine o'clock, enjoying the luxury of a lie-in on a Saturday morning, with no need to jump up and relight the fire. The early morning sun was trickling through the weeping willow above, and occasionally she caught the jewelled flash of a dragonfly. Outside on the deck, Ted lay on his stomach, lining up his soldiers, meticulous, thoughtful, his mind full of some sort of elaborate battle plan. In a moment, there would be the noise of gunfire, the noise that only small boys can make – *peow peow peow*.

May meant they had turned the corner, for April could be fickle, its promises of warmth snatched away by a stiff breeze or a sudden squall. May meant you could make plans, leaving behind the memories of winter, the ice on the inside of the windows and frozen pipes and a mist that seemed to be made of icicles hovering over the canal each morning. And it meant adventures for Ted, and hopefully farewell to the nasty cough that made its way unbidden into his chest every time he got over-tired or came home from school with a cold.

Life was tough over winter, for the two of them, for although he was a good boy, the *best* boy, she couldn't just leave Ted alone on the boat, ever, to do the things she needed, so he had to come along, if she went shopping in Breverton, or to the doctor's, or to a meeting at the magazine in London, which meant him missing school if it wasn't the holidays and coming with her on the train. And he needed a bed of his own, a room of his own, not to have to curl up at night in the bunk with his mother, although they'd built a wall of pillows in between them because he kicked, endlessly, and she needed her sleep.

Winter was about survival, clinging on, trying to keep warm, her frozen fingers stiffening until they could barely press down the keys on her typewriter. It was all she could do to finish the stories she had to post off every week, the ones that kept the wolf from the door. But now, with the longer days and the promise of a reliable sun, she could turn her mind to her escape plan. After all, if children all over the country waited with bated breath for her weekly instalments, surely they would welcome a whole book by her?

Producing an illustrated story every week for *Roundabout* magazine was never going to make her a fortune. But it meant she could work at her little table on the boat, typing during the day, then drawing late into the night when Ted was asleep. She posted her endeavours off every Tuesday morning to be edited and sent off to the printers ready for children to collect from the newsagents two weeks later. She loved the thought of them burying their noses in the adventures of the Ditch Babies, mischievous little creatures who lived on the side of the road who might, if the mood took them and you deserved it, let down your bicycle tyres, steal sixpence from your purse or swap round the washing on your washing line. They were hugely popular because although they were naughty they were never malevolent, and they did good deeds as well as bad ones, making sure justice was done and everyone got what they deserved.

Living on the canal had opened Stella's eyes to a whole new world and it had given her the inspiration for an illustrated children's book. It seemed the perfect setting. After all, most people lived not too far from a canal, so she'd created a magical world inspired by her and Ted's life, and the creatures that surrounded them, capturing the same sense of mischief and fun that she'd threaded throughout *The Ditch Babies*. Children loved a bit of anarchy and a bit of rebellion. Perhaps even more so after years of being told to keep quiet during the war and making themselves invisible. The world was there for the taking now, and with *The Towpath Gang*, Stella was determined to show the next generation of children the joys of the countryside so they could explore it for themselves. She hoped to give them a spirit of adventure. The same spirit Ted had, for in summer he roamed for hours along the canal, fishing and building dens and climbing trees. It was sad, she thought, that he didn't have a brother or a sister to roam with, but that was always going to be the case. The last thing she wanted was someone else. The very thought made her shudder. There was only one man she wanted, and he was gone. For ever.

She opened half an eye. Ted was still embroiled in his soldiers, so perhaps she would allow herself to think about him, something she only allowed herself to do for fifteen minutes a day. Sometimes she divided those minutes up into three lots of five. Sometimes she saved them all up until she climbed into bed at night. It depended what she was doing and how busy she was. When her mind wandered towards him, sometimes she would tell herself off, like a nanny slapping the hand of a child reaching for a forbidden biscuit. *Not now. Not yet.*

If she thought about him too much, her mood plummeted, which was how she'd come to ration her daydreams. After all, they were used to rationing, even though it had officially ended now. How long it was taking, she thought, to disentangle themselves from the aftermath. War didn't just end, with life going back to normal the next day. There were scars.

'I think rationing's quite good for you, actually,' he'd once said. 'Not being able to have things you like. It makes you enjoy other things more.'

'Like what?' she'd teased him. 'Fresh air?'

'Yes. Fresh air. Birdsong. Whistling. Morning dew. The top deck of the bus.'

'You can't eat any of those.'

'True.'

'All I want,' she said, 'is a Chelsea bun. A big fat Chelsea bun covered in sugar.'

'As soon as it's all over, you shall have one every day. I'll bring it to you for breakfast, on a silver platter.'

He mimed whisking off a dome and presenting her with it.

Remembering their exchange, she smiled. She still hadn't had a Chelsea bun, even though they were readily available, because she couldn't bear the thought that, now, he would never bring her one. She shut her eyes against the glare of the sun, to relive the first time she saw him.

Stella had been ticking off the new paints against a pro forma when the bell had tinged more forcefully than usual, startling her, and a man bowled into the shop, his shirt sleeves rolled up, his hair dishevelled, bringing in a restless energy.

'I've run out of Cadmium Orange,' he announced. 'You can't paint an Italian sunset without Cadmium Orange. I tried mixing but there's no getting away from it.'

Stella put down her paperwork. 'Any one in particular?'

'Old Holland,' he said, in a tone of voice that suggested there was no other choice. 'Please.'

Stella made her way over to the Old Holland stand and ran her fingers along the tubes until she found the right one. She turned and jumped to find the new customer standing right behind her. He smelled of linseed and burnt toast and Pears soap; a combination that was both comforting and exciting. It made her want to step closer to him, but girls like her didn't belong with someone like him. For underlying the toast and linseed and soap, she could also smell money.

Instinctively, she stepped away.

As soon as she did, he realised he'd come a little too close and put his hands up in apology.

'Sorry – I just wanted a look at the other paints. I'm a bit low at the moment. I might as well stock up while I'm here. There's nothing more aggravating than running out while you're in the middle of something. It's hard to get back into the flow. Scarlet Lake, Purple Madder, Winsor Emerald.' His face was screwed up as he tried to remember. She picked them out as he recited. 'Thank you.'

He stared down at her, smiling. She held the paints in her hand and stared back, hypnotised.

'I'll wrap them for you,' she managed eventually.

He frowned.

'Have you worked here long? I haven't seen you before. I've been away in Italy, trying to get a bit of warmth into my bones before bloody Hitler puts a stop to it all.' He followed her back to the long pine serving table where she began to roll the tubes up in tissue paper. She was filled with envy. Hopefully, it wouldn't be long before she could afford to buy herself some paints of her own.

'I've been here two weeks,' she told him.

'Well, you've certainly transformed the place.' He looked around with approval. 'Is this all your handiwork?'

She laughed. 'I couldn't find anything. So I tried to put it all in order.'

'You've done a great job. And this is a wonderful place to work. Old Corbières is a good egg. I've had some of my best evenings with him, on the grog. He's had a pretty colourful life.'

'He's quite a character,' she agreed. 'Though I barely understand him half the time.'

'Nobody does. Right, what have I got to cough up?' He reached into his pocket and pulled out a couple of grubby notes and a few coins. She counted up his change and put the paints in a brown paper bag with *Corbières Fine Art Supplies* printed in green across the middle.

He was staring at her as he took hold of the string handles.

'I expect people ask you this all the time,' he said, 'but would you consider sitting for me?'

She sighed. 'Mr Corbières has told me to tell him if

anyone asks that. And they won't be allowed back in the shop.'

His face fell. 'Oh God. I hope you don't think I meant anything other than... I'd like to paint you. Just because Mr C staggered around Paris with all those absinthe-soaked reprobates doesn't mean we're all like that.' He seemed genuinely upset.

'I didn't think you were. I'm just not sure about being painted.'

'But people must ask you all the time. Your hair. It's extraordinary.'

Stella made a face. 'Just don't say Pre-Raphaelite,' she said. 'Or mention Lizzie Siddal. Or Ophelia.'

'Oh. Do people say that to you all the time? Am I a cliché? I'm so sorry. I can't bear the thought.'

She sighed. 'I suppose I'm in the wrong place if I don't want to be endlessly compared. I should have stayed in Wanstead. No one there has a clue who the Pre-Raphaelites are. They just call me Ginger Nut. Or Bryant and May.'

He laughed at that. 'So what *is* your name?'

'Stella.'

'Stella. As in star?'

She shrugged. 'As in my gran.'

'It's beautiful. And it suits you. Your eyes are the colour of stars.' He was gazing at her. Most men she came into contact with back home found her too overwhelming – she could see it in their faces, a mixture of fascination and repugnance at the match-red flame of her long mane of hair, her pale skin and almost silver eyes. They liked their women to fade into the background. Here, in the middle of the city, she had aroused more interest than she'd ever had in her life.

And this man, in particular, seemed enthralled. She stared back at him, taking in the mop of sandy hair that needed cutting, the faint stippling of stubble on his jaw line and the blue circles under his eyes. He was scruffy and dishevelled, his hands covered in paint, his nails ragged and chewed, indicating nerves, but the dirt on him wasn't engrained. It was the kind of dirt that would float away in the scalding hot bath he'd no doubt be able to draw for himself this evening. He would scrub himself with the delicious soap she could smell on him, emerging pink and clean, then pull on a snow-white shirt...

'Well,' he said. I'm Edwin.'

She started at his voice, at his breaking her reverie –

'*Peow peow peow!*'

Just as she predicted, the gunfire started and her daydream was shattered, pulling her rudely back into the present. She didn't chastise Ted for startling her, or for the apparent violence of his game. It was just what boys did, which was hardly surprising, given that the war, although it was over, was a not-so-distant memory. She rolled out of bed and climbed the steps that took her out onto the deck. The entire platoon was scattered all over it.

'Careful they don't end up in the drink,' was all she said by way of admonishment. 'Fancy a cup of tea?'

She put her hand over her eyes to check where the sun was. She'd have to see what she could scrape together for lunch later: a boiled egg and some bread and dripping, and an apple. Was that enough for a growing boy, or should she walk into Breverton for a tin of corned beef?

She hated this time of the month, when her money was dwindling and everything had to be eked out. Payment for her last lot of stories should arrive on Thursday and she could put the cheque into her post office account and with luck it would have cleared by the next week. Is this what they meant by living hand to mouth, she wondered?

Three chapters, she told herself. When she'd done three chapters she would have something to show a publisher and then perhaps their luck would change.

3

If it wasn't for the flowers, Elizabeth often thought, she wouldn't be able to get through the day. Even now. But they gave her hope. From the first drift of snowdrops under the oak trees in January, they gave her purpose, for the garden at Foxwood was a full-time job. More than a full-time job, for it kept Joey busy all year round, and they got another lad in too, Maurice, for the lawns in the height of summer when everything ran away, as it was about to. May was bursting with enthusiasm as it hurtled towards June, eager to show off, the wisteria hanging heavy at the front of the house, always at its best for Alfie's birthday, and the garden smelled divine, making her head swim and the bees lurch drunkenly from branch to branch.

Thank goodness for the flowers.

She was walking through the hall with an armful of peonies just as the telephone rang. She stopped short. There was never a time when she didn't remember its shrillness breaking into their Sunday that evening. Every time it rang she felt a momentary ripple of panic before remembering that she didn't have to worry anymore because the worst had happened. The thing she had feared the most.

So who might it be? Not *him*, especially not at the weekend, with Michael still sitting in the dining room. It was probably the Reverend Elphick, who was always particularly annoying on a Saturday. He wrote his sermon on a Friday, and it left him dangerously unoccupied until Sunday, so it was Saturday when he chased people who'd promised him things. Elizabeth found it increasingly difficult to be civil to him. He was so smug, so convinced that he provided her with comfort and succour and guidance, when all she wanted to do was shout at him, tell him she didn't believe in God, how could she, after the bloody war, after bloody Hitler, after Edwin . . . But she couldn't, because she was Elizabeth Arbutus of Foxwood, and she had a duty to set an example to his parishioners.

The bell shrilled on. It *could* be the vicar, about the fête, always held in the grounds of Foxwood and ominously close, or perhaps Marigold Dempster asking them for one of her awful suppers, or Alexandra with some envy-inducing London gossip. There was only one way to find out.

'Breverton six four two.' Her voice went up at the end, as if she was querying herself.

'Mumma.'

'Alfie!' She smiled. 'Happy birthday, darling. You are still coming?'

She hoped so. Daisy had already put the scones into the oven, plump with sultanas.

'Of course. But I'm bringing a friend. They're keen to see the garden. I said it was the very best day of the year to see it.'

'Well, of course. That's lovely.'

'We'll be there around half past two.'

'Does your *friend* have a name?' Her tone was teasing.

There was a smile in his voice as he answered. 'She does. Clementine.'

'Clementine. How pretty.'

'*Very* pretty.'

Was he talking about the girl, or her name? Elizabeth was already imagining her, racking her brain for any Clementines she knew of.

'We'll see you just after lunch, then. Will you be staying?'

'I think that would be nice. Make a weekend of it. I'll ask her. If that's all right?'

'Of course.'

She put the phone back in its receiver with a smile and a raised eyebrow, pondering what she'd just heard. Then she picked up the receiver again and dialled a number.

'For God's sake,' said a weary voice eventually. 'What time do you call this?'

'It's half past nine,' said Elizabeth crisply, staring at the fat-cheeked face of the sun in the grandfather clock. 'I've been up for hours. Listen, do you know of any Clementines? Alfie's bringing a Clementine for his birthday tea.'

'Only that ghastly Clemmy Horrocks. She's a terrible drip. She wouldn't be Alfie's type.'

'But we don't know what Alfie's type is. Do we?'

'No, I suppose we don't. How intriguing. This is almost worth getting up for. I might drive down.'

'Why don't you?' The weekend was always more fun with Alexandra around. 'After all, you are his godmother.'

'Oh yes. I'd better get him something. Oysters. I could bring oysters from Fortnum's.'

Elizabeth knew it would take Alexandra at least three hours to get ready. Throwing oysters into the picture would mean she wouldn't be here till dusk.

'Forget oysters. We've got mountains of food. Daisy's been beavering away for days. Just jump in the car.'

'Oh God, I can't. I've got to make myself look human first. I look an absolute hag. Honestly, it's terrifying.'

Elizabeth rolled her eyes. Alexandra didn't look a day over thirty, even if she'd been up all night, which she probably had.

'It's only us. We don't care.'

'I care. And I don't want to frighten *Clementine.*'

Elizabeth wondered for a moment if it was a bit cruel to inflict Alexandra on their new guest, but decided the chances of her getting here in time were remote, so it didn't matter.

'See you when we see you.'

She put the receiver back for a second time, holding her hand on it for a few seconds as if she was about to pick it up again, then thought better of it. She ran through guest numbers quickly to assess if a dash into Breverton was necessary, but she didn't think so. She'd have to tell Daisy straight away though.

'Daisy! Red alert. We have extra guests for tea,' she sang as she headed back into the kitchen.

Daisy looked up from sliding her scones off the baking tray and onto the cooling rack. 'Oh?'

'Alfie's bringing a friend. Clementine.'

'Oh!' The cook's eyes and smile widened.

'I know. And Alexandra's coming.'

'Is she now?' Daisy looked less impressed at this news. Alexandra meant chaos and cocktails and breakfast trays. But Elizabeth knew Daisy didn't mind really. She was happiest when the house was full.

It was hard to imagine life before Daisy. She'd come to them as a live-in maid after losing her fiancé in the war. She'd quickly made herself indispensable and when their old cook, Mrs Prosser, had retired, she had taken over. Mrs P had taught her everything she knew, and over the years Daisy had grown ever more confident until now she ran not just the kitchen but the whole household as well, with the help of a couple of maids and a cheery unflappability. She had given the house structure and momentum. She made them all feel secure, but wasn't afraid to speak her mind when things weren't being run quite how she thought they should be. Elizabeth's biggest fear was that Daisy would find someone to marry and would leave them. Though at the same time, she wanted her to find love and happiness. Of course she did.

The bloody, *bloody* war.

'Do I need to go into Breverton?' Elizabeth asked. 'Speak now.'

Daisy ran through everything in her head. 'I can do another batch of scones. And I've done a Victoria sponge for his cake, but I can add an extra layer. Perhaps we could do with another loaf? Or two, even.' There would be breakfast tomorrow. 'And perhaps some more bacon? Will they be staying?'

'I think they probably will... Alexandra will stay, of course. I'll put her in her usual room and could you make up the little room for Clementine. I'll go and get some more bread and bacon.'

'And cucumber. Another cucumber. And perhaps a bit more butter, if I'm doing all this extra baking.' It was a joy, to be able to bake with abandon, now that sugar and butter were no longer rationed. It still felt a bit wrong, a bit unpatriotic, to be so extravagant, but Daisy didn't care. Not today, on Alfie's birthday. Clementine, whoever she was, was a lucky girl.

Elizabeth picked up the wicker basket kept by the kitchen door. 'I'll be back in half an hour.' She stood for a moment in thought. 'Perhaps a chicken, in case everyone is here for Sunday lunch? We've got masses of new potatoes and runner beans.'

Daisy waved a set of floury hands in approval. Elizabeth slipped out of the kitchen and made her way to the dining room.

There was Michael, her handsome husband, sitting at the head of the table, the bay window behind him, sun streaming in. *The Financial Times* and a silver pot of coffee were in front of him, and he was in his usual Saturday outfit of Tattersall shirt and a Paisley cravat with moleskin trousers. Elizabeth glided over and dropped a kiss on his head. She'd been up and dressed and making herself busy long before he was awake. She'd come to hate seeing the look in his eyes when he woke, the dull stare of realisation, so she tried to avoid it.

'Guess what?' she said now, her voice filled with excitement.

'Well, I can't,' he said. 'That would be impossible.'

She tutted, but she smiled nevertheless. 'Alfie is bringing a girl for his birthday. Clementine.'

Michael raised his eyebrows. There was one bright white hair amidst the darker ones that Elizabeth itched to pull out, but now wasn't the time. Instead, she reached for the coffee pot and poured him another cup.

'Do we know her?' he asked, knowing he was supposed to ask.

'We couldn't think of anyone it could be. Alexandra's coming to inspect.'

'Well, I hope you'll be gentle with the poor girl.' Michael shook out the paper before folding it back up neatly into four and smiled at her.

He knew Elizabeth and Alexandra only too well. They wouldn't mean to overwhelm, but they were quite a force to be reckoned with, the pair of them. They had been, ever since they'd arrived at St Mary's Calne together, and Alexandra had let Elizabeth share her pet mouse, which was her clever way of getting her to feed the animal and clean out its cage. Elizabeth had been fully aware she was being exploited but she didn't mind. She'd loved the mouse, and she'd loved her new friend.

She still adored her. Elizabeth didn't know what she would do without Alexandra, and would forgive her everything, even her being endlessly, maddeningly late and sometimes rude.

'I'm just honest,' Alexandra would say, and it was true.

'I'm going into Breverton for extra provisions. Do you want to come?'

'No, I'm going to the factory to go over some figures. It's too hectic during the week.'

'Mmm.' Elizabeth looked at her husband thoughtfully. He was working too hard these days. She couldn't pretend that didn't suit her, but she also worried about him. 'Alfie will be here about half past two. We'll have tea at three.'

Michael nodded. 'Shall I ask Maurice to mow the top lawn again?'

Elizabeth gazed out of the window. She had wondered that. It had been mown on Monday and was already sprouting daisies. And there was nothing more delicious than the scent of freshly cut grass. But it would add another layer of frenetic activity to the morning and she wanted to enjoy the preparations, not get herself worked up.

'I think it's the perfect length, actually.'

Michael's eyes followed her gaze. 'Yes. Yes, I think you're right.'

How brilliantly expert they were, she thought, at navigating life on the surface.

The little town of Breverton was buzzing, mellow in the May sunshine, light bouncing off the diamond-bright windows, the river shimmering, the lime trees providing much-needed shade for wilting dogs. Elizabeth parked on the high street and galloped in and out of the shops, accumulating everything she needed and some things she did not – some new soap for the possible guest, a bottle of sherry, clotted cream, even though it was too early for raspberries but an apple Charlotte would be nice for lunch tomorrow. At last her basket was full to the brim and she couldn't possibly stuff in anything more. She made her way back to the car and set the basket on the front seat.

Then she walked down to the bottom of the high street. Outside the Breverton Arms was a red telephone box. She felt in her pocket for the coins she already knew were there. She could fool anybody but herself that this hadn't been her plan all along.

If anyone saw her and thought it strange that Elizabeth Arbutus was using a public telephone box, she would say she was asking Daisy if they needed lard. The important thing was to look composed, not as if her heart was about to burst. She put on her serene expression, the one she used when the vicar was at his most tiresome, picked up the receiver and asked to be connected. The coins were in her right hand, ready to be pushed in as soon as he answered.

Only he didn't. With every ring, her heart sank a little lower. And, of course, all she could picture was him tangled up in his sheets, smoking a cigarette, with one arm around some girl, her head resting on his chest, staring up at the ceiling in post-coital wonder. She would be able to feel his heartbeat, feel his fingers winding themselves amidst her silken strands of hair –

She slammed the receiver back down, bit her lip so sharply she could taste blood, and told herself she had no right to be jealous. Then congratulated herself that at least now he wouldn't know she'd called. She hated him seeing her vulnerability – sometimes, she thought he liked it when she was in a state of agitation.

As she headed back to the car, she felt much happier knowing he hadn't answered the telephone. That would have unleashed all sorts of unknowns. Now she could focus on Alfie's birthday tea, which was much more important. She slid back into the driver's seat and took a few deep breaths to calm herself. What on earth had she been thinking?

4

'No! No, no, no! Absolutely not.'

'But it's my favourite.' Clementine twirled around and looked winningly over her shoulder, smiling at her friend. 'And it's not too anything.'

'It's too white, is what it is. One blob of raspberry jam and you'll be done for.'

'I'm not six. I don't drop my food. And they'll have napkins.'

'I wouldn't risk it.' Henrietta shook her head disapprovingly from her place on the sofa. She was in her dressing gown, dunking endless digestive biscuits into a cup of tea. Their fellow flatmates were still slumbering. 'What about your blue silk?'

'That's too formal for a birthday tea.'

'You could borrow my yellow sundress.'

'It'll be far too long and I don't have enough bosom. I should have got something new.'

'No. Never invest too early on. It's bad luck.' Henrietta brushed crumbs off her lap.

'I haven't got time to try anything else. I'll just have to avoid jam.'

Clementine smoothed down the cotton piqué of her dress. It was sleeveless, with an open collar and covered buttons and a full skirt. She tried to bury any doubts. Clothing panic was new to her. Normally she knew exactly what to wear for every occasion and had just the outfit, but she wasn't sure quite what to expect at Foxwood.

Henrietta had given her a potted rundown on Alfie's family when she'd told her about her invitation.

'His mother's very glamorous, but not in a showy way. One of those people who looks good in anything. Nigel says she always got the Magna Mater prize when she turned up at Sports Day.'

'The Magna Mater prize?'

'Oh, you know. The mum they'd most like to...' Henrietta waggled her eyebrows.

'That's disgusting.'

'That's boys for you. Anyway, his father's got a very successful business. A paint factory. They made a packet during the war, providing all the paint for camouflage. I expect Alfie will have to take it over. So there's that to bear in mind. You'd have to move to deepest darkest Somerset.'

'You're going a bit fast. We've barely known each other a month.'

Henrietta gave her friend a look.

'You can't hang around much longer, Clementine. I thought I was leaving it late.' Henrietta was getting married in June and would insist on making Clementine feel as if she'd missed the boat. 'Think about it. A lovely house in the country. I'll be in Berkshire, which isn't a million miles away.'

'Mmm.' Clementine wasn't sure about Henrietta's view of the next phase of life, a life where these sorts of conversations and dilemmas would be a thing of the past, where you'd never run out of milk or resort to a rusty old tin of pilchards for supper because your role would be to make sure life was beautifully organised and your husband was happy. That wasn't what she wanted. Clementine loved her job. Working for – *with* – Ben was fulfilling and exciting and fun. It would be a lot to give up. And actually, she didn't think Alfie, if this came to anything, would be the sort of man to *want* her to give it up. She wasn't going to let that slip to Henrietta. Her friend had little ambition. She couldn't *wait* to be entirely dependent on Nigel. Clementine knew there was no point in trying to explain to her that times were changing.

Despite Henrietta's misgivings, she felt cool and confident and comfortable in her outfit. It was a rare dress that gave you all those things. She picked up her overnight bag, pushed her feet into her sandals, threw her arm around Henrietta's neck and gave her a hug then ran for the door. She felt a rush of excitement as she flew down the stairs, as if she was tobogganing down a steep hill on a tea tray. She was on her way to Foxwood.

There he was, parked on the pavement in a yellow Alvis, the top down in honour of the sun. He looked up as he heard the door slam behind her, then jumped out and ran around to open the passenger door for her.

'Hello!' she gasped, smiling as he bent his head forwards to brush his cheek against hers in a gesture that was both chivalrous and intimate. 'What a gorgeous car.'

'It was Edwin's,' he said as she climbed in. 'He loved it so much, it seemed a shame to sell it. It's a bit flash for me, but...' He gave a shrug, closed her door then headed round to the driver's side.

'Happy birthday!' she said, digging into her handbag and handing him a small parcel.

'You shouldn't have!' he said, but he was smiling. 'Shall I open it now, or when we get there?' He was turning it over in his hands.

'Well, you can probably guess what it is.'

'Soap?' he said, feigning a puzzled frown. 'Whisky?'

She nudged his arm, laughing. 'It's the very latest thing, I'll have you know.'

'Well, I don't think I can wait, in that case.'

He pulled at the ribbon and peeled back the paper to reveal a book with a grey cover, with nine red hearts laid out like a playing card, and a wreath in which were entwined the words A WHISPER OF LOVE, A WHISPER OF HATE.

'*Casino Royale!*' Alfie exclaimed. 'Ian Fleming. John Betjeman gave it a jolly good write up in the *Telegraph*. How thoughtful. Thank you. I shall enjoy that.'

He looked genuinely thrilled.

'By all accounts, it's a page-turner. People rip through it in no time. And I believe it's quite racy.' The assistant in Foyles had told her they were selling like hot cakes.

He chuckled.

'I'll let you know. Thank you. It's perfect.' He wrapped the book back up carefully in the paper and stretched over to put it on the back seat. 'It's a good three and a bit hours to Foxwood,' he said as he turned the key in the ignition. 'But I've brought sandwiches and a flask of coffee so we can stop on the way. There's a rug on the back seat if you get cold. It's one of those funny days when, if the sun goes in, it could be nippy.'

As they whizzed through Kensington, she leaned back in her seat, looking at Alfie's lightly tanned hands on the steering wheel, the cuff of a pale-blue shirt peeping out from the sleeve of his sports jacket. He turned sideways to her and smiled, looking straight into her eyes for a moment before turning back to the road, and she was yet again struck by how strong her feelings were for him.

She thought of all the men she'd had romantic entanglements with over the past few years. She'd managed to extricate herself from every single one without a modicum of regret. Some of them hadn't taken it well: they usually didn't see it coming, and she had to listen to their protests, their indignation, their despair, and suffer endless telephone calls and ringing of doorbells at unearthly hours, but she'd got the hang of being quite firm in the end. Henrietta told her she was cruel, but Clementine thought it was much kinder in the long run, not to give false hope.

'If I know I'm not going to marry them, what's the point?'

'To have fun? Surely it's more fun to be taken out for dinner or to the flicks than to be stuck in on your own?'

'I like my own company!' Clementine laughed at her friend's outrage. 'And I've always got Ben.'

It was true. Ben was always there, if she wanted a night on the tiles. And he took her to the very best places. Lively restaurants where the wine and laughter flowed, chaotic jazz clubs, sultry candlelit bars where people had clandestine assignations safe in the knowledge that all secrets stayed within their walls. Clementine lived in hope that one day Ben would find someone special. He needed a free spirit who wouldn't blanche at his bohemian ways and his insouciant love life. It was his reaction to the end of the war. Since he'd left the Intelligence Corps, he'd gone a bit wild.

She thought that Ben would approve of Alfie. Something shone out of him. It was more than charm – she knew plenty of men who could turn that on and make you feel a million dollars for as long as they wanted. It was more solid than that. And although the sight of him gave her butterflies, they weren't the fizzy, fluttery ones that unsettled you, more the kind you had when you woke up on your birthday knowing the day was going to be a special one.

After they'd stopped for lunch, the heat of the sun and the thrum of the engine meant she fell asleep until Alfie nudged her and she woke to find they were needling their way through velvety fields alternating with rolling orchards. The hedgerows were overflowing with hawthorn and cow parsley while stumpy apple trees sported palest pink. Globes of mistletoe hung in the poplars, watched over by a flock of rooks. The air was sweet with blossom and dairy cows and hay.

'It's beautiful!'

'Welcome to Somerset. The land of cheese.' He grinned. 'And ciderrrrr.'

Eventually they turned off into Breverton high street. It was the dearest little town, she thought, row upon row of pale stone houses, a bridge over a burbling river, bustling with people making their last-minute purchases – a vital lettuce or some beef dripping – for the shop owners were ruthless about shutting on a Saturday lunchtime, the shutters and blinds coming firmly down and the doors closing.

'Shall we stop?' said Alfie. 'I could do with some cigarettes. We'll pop into the Breverton Arms.'

Clementine freshened up in the ladies' cloakroom, dragging her comb through her windswept curls and reapplying her lipstick. She was glad they'd stopped, for she didn't want to arrive at Foxwood bursting for the loo and looking as if she'd been dragged through a hedge backwards. It was so thoughtful of Alfie. She suspected he didn't need cigarettes at all, just guessed that she would appreciate the chance to gather herself.

Her dress was still crisp, and the sun on the journey had brought out her freckles. They made her look even younger, for she barely looked her age as it was – twenty-three! How had that happened? How had she been out in the world for nearly five years, standing on her own two feet, navigating city life and earning her own money? She could sense change coming. With Henrietta's wedding on the horizon, life would be different. The flat wouldn't be the same without her. Clementine couldn't imagine a replacement, though one would have to be found. Was today going to herald an even bigger change? There was a sharpness and a sweetness inside her, like a lemon sherbet. Anticipation and excitement. A delicious mix.

Just outside Breverton, the car left the main road, plunging into woodland, the trees whispering above them, bright with new foliage, and the air thick with the scent of wild garlic. They wound their way through, the little lane twisting and turning further and further into the depths until it became quite dark, and Clementine shivered. Alfie put out a hand and touched hers reassuringly.

'Nearly there,' he said.

He dropped the car down a gear and roared up the final hill. 'This is my favourite bit of the journey,' he shouted above the roar of the engine. She thought they might fly off into the air when they reached the top, he was going so fast. But as they roared down the other side, the trees cleared and a magnificent view of a rolling valley appeared in front of them. They turned a corner and there, there was a set of gates made from the same pale stone she'd seen in Breverton, a statue of a fox on top of each one, sitting demure but watchful, coiled ready to spring.

Foxwood.

Alfie didn't stop as he drove through the gates. Nestled at the top of the valley, with views over undulating fields and a ribbon of winding river in the near distance, Foxwood was set back from the road behind a mossy stone wall. It had a facade the colour of set honey and a slate mansard roof with a row of dormer windows hovering over two rows of sash windows draped in loops of pale blue wisteria. Shallow steps led up to a yellow front door. Drifts of box softened the frontage, and the sweeping lawns either side were studded with daisies. It sat there, quite sure of its position as the most beautiful house for miles around. Yet it wasn't showy. It looked like a home.

As Alfie drew up and stopped the car, two dogs shot out of the front door. With their pale ginger coats they were the perfect match for the house.

'They're like teddy bears!' cried Clementine.

'Irish terriers. My mother's pride and joy. Hello, Oscar. Hello, Joyce. Named after Oscar Wilde and James Joyce, of course.' He rolled his eyes with a grin. 'They are absolute menaces and they'll want to sleep on your bed.'

She looked around her, digging her fingers into the dogs' soft coats as they nudged at her, marvelling at the scene: could there be anything more perfect than an English country house in May?

'How do you ever want to leave?' she asked.

'I don't,' he said, and they headed for the front door.

Inside, the house was quiet and cool. As she stepped into the hall, Clementine gave a gasp of pleasure. The walls were buttercup-yellow, like the door, and smothered in paintings. She recognised the artist straight away.

'We emptied his studio after he died,' said Alfie. 'My parents didn't want to sell a single picture. It's a bit of a shrine.'

Clementine took in every detail. It was as if Edwin Arbutus had tried to paint everything he came across in life, seeing beauty in the most mundane object. There was a pair of riding boots, shining conker-brown and captured so perfectly you could smell the leather. A wine bottle and two half-full glasses next to a plate of cheese. A dog just like Oscar and Joyce stretched out in front of a fire.

'That's Oscar's mother,' Alfie told her. 'Clodagh.'

'I can almost see her breathing.'

'I know.' Alfie sighed. Clementine put a hand on his arm. It must be hard, to have such a vivid reminder of the person you'd lost. It was probably easier if you lived with them; went past the paintings every day, rather than being reminded every time you came back. She could see a muscle twitch in his cheek as he looked at them, and his eyes were blinking rather fast. She felt her heart fold over, overwhelmed by the strength of her feelings: a kind of warmth, a tenderness, a compulsion to make everything all right, but she didn't know what to do. It was so quiet and still in the hall it felt like a museum, as if any moment now a guard might appear, to ask for a ticket.

Alfie shook his head and stepped away. 'I wonder, where is everyone? In the garden, no doubt. Come along.'

She could barely keep up as he swept through a half-open door and led her through a room with periwinkle-blue walls and a cluster of flowery sofas. Alfie headed to the French windows, standing back to allow her through first. She stepped outside, blinking at the brightness of the May sunshine.

On the terrace beneath a loggia running along the back of the house, a long table had been laid with a white embroidered cloth. A woman standing with a tray of tea things was the first to spy them. Her face split into a radiant smile.

'Mr Alfie!'

She must be Daisy. The cook. Alfie had run through everyone in the household for her. At her cry, everyone turned around to look at them. Clementine composed her features: she didn't want to grin too inanely, but she wanted to seem pleased to meet everyone. There were two men, a watchful creature with strawberry-blonde hair who must be Alfie's sister, Diana, and from the foot of the table, a woman who rose and began to glide towards them, arms outstretched. Alfie's mother. Clementine remembered Henrietta's description, and decided she had played her down, rather.

Elizabeth Arbutus wasn't technically beautiful. Her eyes were slightly hooded, her nose rather Roman, her mouth a little too wide, but her cheekbones were exquisitely sharp and as she drew closer Clementine saw her eyes were a shimmering green set off by a fitted dress in jade brocade. Her outfit made Clementine feel immediately underdressed, although Diana seemed to be in an Aertex with grubby jodhpurs and Alfie had repeatedly assured her that she was to wear whatever she felt comfortable in.

'Clementine. It's so lovely to have you here.' Clementine felt the icy metal of a cluster of rings as Elizabeth slid a cool hand into hers and led her to the table. 'Come and meet everyone. This is Michael. Alfie's father.' She put her hand on the shoulder of the man at the head and Clementine was struck by the family resemblance between him and his sons: he was tall and slender with thick grey hair that swept back from his forehead. Handsome, she thought, the archetypal English country gentleman.

Elizabeth waved an airy hand towards the others. 'And these are Diana and Rory, Alfie's sister and her husband.'

Diana gave her a smile that didn't reach her eyes as she lit a cigarette. Rory beamed.

'Hello, Clementine.' He had the eager air of an unwanted puppy that was only too aware it was a mongrel and was on borrowed time.

'And let's not forget Daisy, the most important person in the house,' said Elizabeth, sliding an arm around the cook's shoulders.

Daisy rolled her eyes and shook her head at the hyperbole, but she looked pleased. She seemed much younger than Clementine had imagined when Alfie described her as the lynchpin of the household, the provider of three square meals a day – four, if you counted tea. She was in a flowery overall and flat brown lace-up shoes, and her fine brown hair refused to stay in its ponytail, but there was a wisdom in her eyes, a self-assuredness that wasn't always present in household staff.

'You must be thirsty after that drive,' Daisy said. 'I'll get you some lemonade before you have tea.'

'That would be so kind.' Clementine made her way around the table, shaking hands. The men had got to their feet. Diana remained seated, gazing at her coolly with a rather fixed smile.

'Sorry. I can't get up.'

She nodded down at a small Jack Russell in her lap. Clementine could feel the wariness rolling off her. Was it simply sisterly protectiveness? She couldn't blame her for wanting to protect Alfie.

'Here. Sit next to my father.' Alfie pulled out a chair, and as Clementine sat down, she assured herself her dress was just right, somewhere in between Diana's dowdiness and Elizabeth's elegance.

'How's business?' Alfie asked Michael, who gave an uncertain shrug.

'There seems to be a bit of a boom now the war is truly behind us,' he answered. 'People are starting to take an interest in their homes again.'

'There wasn't much point for a long time,' said Diana. 'Not when you thought a bomb might drop on your house any minute.'

'A boom's good, though, isn't it?'

Michael grimaced. 'In theory, but it's got very competitive. Everyone's getting in on the game.'

'It's the women you have to fire up. Everyone knows it's the woman of the house who makes the decisions.' Diana looked meaningfully at her mother.

'Oh, absolutely,' said Elizabeth.

'Personally, I couldn't care less about the colour of my walls,' said Diana. 'But trust me, the women are the key.' She pointed her cigarette towards her mother to emphasise her point.

'Well, maybe I should ask your mother to come and advise us.' Michael looked over at his wife. 'You're always saying you have too much time on your hands.'

'Oh, not now the garden's in full bloom. I couldn't be busier,' said Elizabeth.

Diana narrowed her eyes and stubbed her cigarette out next to a half-eaten scone.

'Darling, that's not an ashtray,' Elizabeth chided her.

There was a momentary pause as the wind rustled in the wisteria.

'Anyway, Clementine doesn't want to listen to us talking business.' Elizabeth picked up a plate. 'Clementine, have a cucumber sandwich and tell us all about you. Where are you from?'

Clementine knew that this was not a geographical question. It was much more loaded than that. But she knew exactly how much to give away, and what to say to reassure Elizabeth and Michael that she was suitable.

'I'm from Salisbury.'

'Oh.' Elizabeth pondered her reply. 'The cathedral. That's all I know about Salisbury.'

Clementine laughed. 'That's all anyone knows. My father's the bursar of a girls' school. It's where he met my mother, after she was widowed in the first war. She was the Latin mistress.'

'A brain box. How marvellous.' Elizabeth looked impressed.

'*Amo, amas, amat,*' intoned Michael.

'*Gallia in tres partes divisa est,*' said Rory.

'I don't see the point of Latin, unless you're looking at tombstones,' said Diana.

'That just makes you a savage, darling.'

Diana scowled at her mother. Clementine sensed the antagonism between them bubbling up again. She ploughed on, hoping to smooth things over.

'I was useless at it, even though my mother was the teacher. But they're jolly important, the Romans, when you think about it.'

'Quite,' agreed Michael. 'We wouldn't have roads, or plumbing, or a legal system. Or wine.'

'We'd have worked it all out eventually,' said Diana.

'Peas,' said Rory brightly. 'They brought us peas. Where would we be without peas?'

'Poor Clementine,' said Elizabeth. 'She came here for a lovely birthday tea, not to be grilled about what the Romans did for us.'

'I'm quite used to it.'

'Anyway, you live in London now?'

'I do, yes. In Kensington. And I work in Soho. For my half-brother. Benjamin Bell.'

Everyone looked blank.

'He's got a small art gallery. He's very good at discovering new talent.' She wondered if she should go on to tell them about what an admirer of Edwin Ben was, but noticed a look of utter horror on Elizabeth's face. Was talking about paintings dangerous territory? She didn't want to upset anyone. Had she made a terrible faux pas? Then the look disappeared as quickly as it had arrived, and Clementine turned to see a man striding around the corner of the house. In a pale linen suit with a Panama hat and dark glasses, he looked as if he belonged in the heat and dust of Havana or Singapore or Bombay.

'Jasper!' Alfie's obvious delight was in total contrast to Elizabeth's reaction. Clementine watched as the two men clasped each other.

'Many happy returns, old boy,' said Jasper, untangling himself and heading towards the table. 'Michael.' He held out a hand to be shaken. 'Diana.' He dropped a kiss on her head then ruffled her hair. Diana went beetroot, with what Clementine couldn't be sure. Confusion? 'Elizabeth.'

Elizabeth held up a cheek to be kissed.

'I thought Alfie said you were otherwise engaged.' Her voice sounded tight. She didn't look pleased.

'I am. I'm on my way down to sail in Dartmouth with friends, so I thought I'd drop by. Hello, Rory.' Once he'd shaken Rory's hand he turned to Clementine. 'And who have we here? I'm Jasper Stone.'

'This is Clementine,' said Alfie. 'Jasper is – was – is, Edwin's best friend and partner in many crimes. He's one of the family, really.'

'How lovely to meet you.'

As she took Jasper's hand, Clementine felt disconcerted. Not because of any effect he had on her. She'd met enough of his ilk not to have her head turned by superficial charm and dazzling good looks – Johnny Mullinger at the Savoy the other evening, for a start. But underneath everyone's apparent delight at Jasper's arrival, she could feel an undercurrent. A ripple of unease, like a fly landing in a bowl of raspberry jam.

From nowhere, Jasper produced a bottle of champagne. 'Glasses, Daisy. We'll need glasses.'

Daisy nodded. 'I'll get some. And shall I bring the cake?' She deferred to Elizabeth, who smiled. She seemed to have recovered her composure.

'Yes, bring the cake. Why not?'

'And here.' Jasper dropped a brown paper bag in front of Alfie. 'Signed by the man himself, I'll have you know.'

Clementine knew what was going to be inside the bag before Alfie had a chance to open it. Moments later, he drew out a book.

'Oh,' said Alfie. '*Casino Royale*. I've heard all about it. What a marvellous present. Thank you.'

'Hang on to it. It'll be worth something one day.' Jasper had fetched himself another chair from across the terrace, and folded himself neatly into it.

'I shall.'

Clementine took a gulp of her lemonade. Alfie caught her eye and gave a gentle smile of apology. She gave the tiniest shake of her head together with her own smile to assure him it didn't matter in the least.

When Daisy brought out the cake, three layers with white icing on the top, Jasper leapt up to help her light the candles. As Alfie blew them out, to a rousing chorus of 'Happy Birthday', Clementine marvelled how a few weeks ago she hadn't even known this man existed, yet it felt as if she'd known him all her life. As he slid in a silver knife to cut the first slice, everyone urged him to make a wish.

'Don't you worry,' he said. 'I've made one already.' He caught Clementine's eye again.

'I always wish the same thing,' Diana announced. 'For Edwin to come back. To walk round the side of the house like you just did, Jasper, and surprise us all.'

There was an awkward silence. Diana looked defiant.

'What?' she said. 'Are we not supposed to talk about him?'

'Of course we can talk about him, darling,' said Elizabeth, but she looked upset.

Clementine remembered Alfie saying Edwin was often an awkward subject. She tried to imagine how her family would react if Ben died. It would always be difficult, she supposed.

'In fact,' said Jasper, who meanwhile had opened the champagne and filled up all the glasses, 'let's drink to him. I know it's Alfie's birthday, but he's definitely here in spirit. To Edwin.'

'To Edwin,' everyone murmured, including Clementine. She noticed Michael look away, across the lawns, his jaw clenched, and her heart broke for him.

The cake was cut up and everyone was given a piece.

'This is absolutely splendid, Daisy,' said Alfie, digging his fork in. 'You've done me proud.'

Before Daisy could reply, another figure stepped out of the French windows.

'Here you all are,' said a languid voice.

'Oh, Christ,' said Jasper, sotto voce.

'Alexandra! You made it,' said Elizabeth.

All the men except Jasper stood up as the most extraordinary creature made her way across the terrace. Her head was wrapped in a fringed scarf from which peeped tufts of raven-black hair, a colour God definitely had not given her, and she was draped in what looked like a man's dressing gown, but somehow she made it look the height of fashion. She was heavily made up, and as she fell into the nearest empty chair, Clementine breathed in a dangerous scent that reminded her of an opium den. Not that she'd ever been to one.

'Ooh,' said Alexandra, catching sight of her. 'You look far too sweet to be with Jasper. He only likes fallen women. Tell me you're with Alfie.'

'I am.' Clementine smiled.

'Marvellous. Though I'm afraid you'll need my approval if things are going to go anywhere.'

'Leave her alone.' Alfie strode round the table to give her a hug. 'I don't want you frightening her off.'

'I take my godmotherly duties very seriously.' She sat back in her chair and turned her face up to the sun. 'Bliss. London's such hell when the sun comes out. All those armpits.' She wrinkled her nose.

There was a faint look of alarm on Daisy's face.

'That'll be eight for dinner, then,' said Daisy. 'I'd better go and magic up some more lamb chops.'

5

'What the hell are you doing here?' Elizabeth hissed, half an hour later. Jasper had left the table, ostensibly to get some cigarettes out of his coat pocket, and she'd followed him into the hall, cornering him by the grandfather clock.

Jasper put up his hands and shook his head in mock confusion. 'It's Alfie's birthday. I wanted to wish him many happy returns. It's only a short detour.'

She felt tears prickle the back of her eyelids. 'You should have told me you were coming.'

He gave a sigh that was half exasperation, half despair. 'How? You've banned me from telephoning the house. Anyway, I thought you'd be pleased.'

'Don't do this to me, Jasper. It's not fair.'

'But you want me here.'

'I do not.'

'Then why did you phone me this morning?'

She stared at him. 'I didn't.'

'You absolutely did. I know it was you. I can tell by the ring. It sounds different when it's you.'

'That's rubbish.'

He stepped closer to her. Put his hands on her shoulders. 'Look at me and tell me you didn't ring. Look at me and tell me you don't want me here.'

She shut her eyes tighter. She was not going to cry. His fingertips were burning through the brocade of her dress. She wanted to feel them on her skin. It was how he got her, every time. When he wasn't there, she could convince herself she could live without him. But when he touched her, it was all that mattered.

'You're enjoying this, aren't you? You can be very cruel, Jasper—'

'Shhh.' He put a finger to her lips. 'I'm not cruel. I'm in love with you. I'm in love with you, Elizabeth. I wanted to see you.'

'Stop it.'

'I can't.'

'I can't go on like this. Lying and living a double life.'

'You know what to do.'

'I've told you. I won't. Not ever!'

He blinked at her ferocity. 'But it's simple mathematics. If things stay the same, we're all unhappy. All three of us. If you leave Michael, then at least two of us will be—'

She pushed him away. 'You're impossible. I'm going back outside. Please, Jasper, if you really love me, leave right now. I want to concentrate on Clementine. I don't want to be distracted by you. I mean it.'

She turned, and made her way back towards the drawing room. Jasper drew a cigarette out of the packet and tapped it before putting it to his lips and sinking into the chair by the telephone. He crossed his legs, resting one elegant ankle on the other knee and blowing three perfect smoke rings into the air, one after the other.

*

Even though she was hard of hearing, Clementine caught every word of their exchange through the cloakroom walls. She was mortified. She didn't dare leave. She held her breath as she waited, not daring to run the taps. Eventually, she thought Elizabeth had left the hall, as she heard her heels on the tiled floor, but she had no idea if Jasper was still lingering there. She had to do something, because Alfie would be wondering where she was.

This was awful. Her cheeks were still burning with embarrassment at what she had heard. Alfie's mother and Jasper were having an affair. She could absolutely see why. They were well-suited, with their good looks and glamour. Not that Alfie's father wasn't attractive, but he didn't have that glittery edge Elizabeth and Jasper both had; the quality that had probably drawn them to each other. No doubt Michael was content to be at home, to run his business, to have his family around him and his friends from time to time. Perhaps that wasn't enough for Elizabeth?

She wasn't going to judge, for grief did strange things to people. But she felt awkward at being party to their secret. They obviously hadn't realised that when she'd taken the cake plate back to the kitchen, she had come back via the cloakroom in the hall. And now she was trapped. The window was far too small to climb out of.

She decided she would just have to leave. Jasper wasn't going to loiter in the hall indefinitely. She turned the key in the lock slowly, so it didn't make a noise, then twisted the knob carefully and pulled the door towards her before tiptoeing out.

He was still there, sitting sprawled in the armchair that was positioned next to the telephone, smoking a cigarette.

'Oh, hello, Jasper,' she said, bright as a button, as if she was surprised to see him. 'What a lovely afternoon it's been.'

Her skin prickled as his eyes roamed over her.

'I wouldn't miss Alfie's birthday for anything,' he said. 'I always promised Edwin I'd look after him if anything happened. He's like the younger brother I never had. He's very important to me. The whole family is.'

His dark eyes burned with intensity. He must be calculating whether she had heard. She could easily not have. The cloakroom walls were thick. She hoped her insouciance would allay his fears. Clementine wasn't the best at obfuscating, but she was desperate for him not to realise she knew their secret.

'I'm sure he appreciates you making the effort.'

Jasper didn't answer. He was surveying the pictures on the wall around him.

'What a bloody waste.' His voice broke. 'It still kills me every time I look at them.'

His face seemed to have collapsed – the vivacity she'd seen earlier had melted away, and all that was left was despair.

'I'm so sorry,' she replied. 'He must have been a very special person.'

'Yes,' said Jasper. 'He brought me back to Foxwood from school when my mother died. I was thirteen, and I wasn't supposed to cry. He knew what I needed. To muck about in the woods pelting conkers at each other, then loll on the rug by the fire eating crumpets and not have to think about Latin prep or rugby trials.' His smile was wintry. 'They made me feel like one of them from that day on. My father got remarried six months later.'

She stepped forward to put a comforting hand on his shoulder, but he moved away from her, leaning back into the chair, screwing his eyes tight shut. The grandfather clock went *tick tick tick*, managing to sound both comforting and ominous. Then he spoke.

'Sometimes I come here and I drive up the drive and I think – what if he's there, this time, by some miracle, sitting at the table, making everyone laugh. Making everyone happy. He was one of those people who light everything up without even trying. You can see it, can't you, in his paintings?' He waved his hand around the walls. 'They're so alive. And how can they be, when he isn't?'

Clementine nodded as she looked more closely at all the pictures. Jasper was right. Even the still lives had a kind of energy. The riding boots looked as if they still held the warmth of whoever had worn them, as if they'd just been slipped off. 'They're wonderful.'

He looked up at her. He seemed exhausted, as if the emotions he was feeling had drained him.

'She's the closest I can get to him.'

His voice was soft, so soft she almost thought she had heard him wrong, but when she looked into his eyes she knew she hadn't. He was defiant, desolate, despairing.

There was no point in pretending she didn't know what he meant. Clementine could think of nothing to say but, 'Oh. I see.'

The grandfather clock ticked on. Jasper ground out his cigarette in an ashtray.

'It would help enormously,' he said, 'if you didn't say

anything to anyone. Elizabeth has been through enough. Everyone has been through enough.'

'It's none of my business.' Clementine tried to keep her tone light. 'And I won't say a word.'

'Thank you.' He looked genuinely grateful and a little beaten. And despite what she knew, Clementine felt disarmed.

When she got back to the tea table, Alexandra's eyes lit up as she approached.

'There you are. We were beginning to think Jasper had seduced you in the downstairs loo. Did you see him on your travels?'

'Um . . . no.' Clementine wasn't good at lying, but it seemed easiest to deny all knowledge of his whereabouts. Everyone seemed satisfied with her answer. She sat down next to Alfie, and he reached a hand out to pat her arm, as if to indicate he'd missed her. It felt reassuring. After everything she'd heard, she was unsettled.

Alexandra leaned forwards. 'Now, I want to hear everything about you. In particular, why on earth you're not married yet when you're so pretty.'

'Alexandra!' Elizabeth rolled her eyes and chided her friend. 'I'm so sorry, Clementine.'

Clementine laughed. 'I suppose I haven't found anyone worth marrying.'

'Good for you.' Alexandra nodded her approval. 'I don't know why everyone rushes into it, I'm sure. But when the time comes, don't forget the snore test.'

'The snore test?'

'Spend the night with them as early as you can, to make sure they don't.'

'I see.' Clementine felt herself blush. Were they all wondering what stage her relationship with Alfie had got to? They didn't need to know she'd already spent more than one night at the flat in Pimlico.

'Snoring can be the sign of a lot of other problems.' Alexandra widened her eyes in faux horror.

'I don't know why you're giving her advice, Alexandra,' laughed Elizabeth. 'You've never been married.'

'No, but I've listened to enough complaints from disillusioned wives to know the pitfalls.'

'Not from me.'

'No, not you, darling. You're the happiest wife I know. And who wouldn't be?' Alexandra looked over at Michael. 'God knows I've tried to lead him astray often enough.'

Michael put his hand over Elizabeth's and squeezed it.

'I know how lucky I am, Alexandra. I wouldn't jeopardise our marriage for the world.' His tone was dry, but he was smiling. He was obviously used to Alexandra teasing him.

Elizabeth pulled Michael's hand up to her mouth and kissed the back of his fingers in a gesture that was both proprietorial and intimate. 'It always infuriates Alexandra that you're never tempted to stray.'

Clementine wasn't sure how Elizabeth had the nerve, given what she'd overheard in the hall. She was leaning against her husband, laughing, looking like love's young dream.

'Why on earth would I?' Michael asked, gazing down at her.

'Wedded bliss,' sighed Alexandra. 'It's a rare and beautiful thing.'

'It's never too late,' Elizabeth told her friend.

Alexandra shook her head, her earrings jangling. 'Oh, it is. I'm beyond hope. And I'm far too set in my ways. And there's not much point in getting married, if you're not going to have children. Which I'm obviously not.'

Diana had looked unimpressed all the way through this exchange. She stood up, ejecting the Jack Russell from her lap. 'Well, it's been lovely, but I think we're going to push off.'

'Are we?' Rory looked startled.

'Aren't you staying for supper?' Elizabeth frowned.

'I've got to get the horses in.'

'What a shame,' said Alexandra.

Diana glared at her. 'Heel, Bingo. Come on, Rory.'

She spoke to her husband and her dog in exactly the same tone.

Rory put his hands on the arms of his chair. 'I was looking forward to lamb chops.'

'There aren't enough anyway. Even Daisy can't magic lamb chops out of thin air.'

'Have we got something at home?'

'There's some mince left over.'

Rory didn't look thrilled at the prospect, but there was no point arguing with Diana. Everyone knew that. So he got up out of his chair and followed her dutifully, with Bingo bringing up the rear.

'And then there were six,' said Alexandra. 'Although where on earth has Jasper got to?'

'I'm here,' said Jasper, appearing in the French windows. 'Though I'm off too. Just a fleeting visit.'

'Oh,' said Alfie. 'I fancied a birthday pint at the Trout.'

Jasper looked at his watch. 'I'm due in Dartmouth for dinner. Why don't we catch up in town next week?

Cheerio, everyone. And it's very nice to meet you, Clementine. Look after the birthday boy for me.'

He pointed a finger at Alfie and gave her a wink. She smiled at him.

'Don't worry, I will.'

Clementine felt relieved as she watched Jasper walk away. She really couldn't make head or tail of the relationships around the table. Was it because of what she had heard that she felt some of the remarks had been loaded? Did anyone else suspect Jasper and Elizabeth? She wished she hadn't heard anything. It made her feel very uncomfortable.

Alfie didn't seem to think anything was amiss.

'That was good of him, to drop by.'

'You know how fond of you he is,' said Elizabeth. 'Clementine, why don't I show you up to your room? You might want a lie-down before dinner, after that journey.'

Clementine had to admit she did feel rather exhausted by it all.

Clementine followed Elizabeth up the curved staircase above the hall where so much had already unfolded.

'We're not terribly formal here, so don't worry about changing for dinner,' said Elizabeth. 'But if you'd like to borrow a cardigan, I have plenty.'

She opened the door of a small bedroom with a high brass bed and a crewel-work eiderdown. It smelled of beeswax and the blossom from a jug of anemones on the chest of drawers. There was just one painting, over the fireplace. It was of Elizabeth, sitting in a wing-backed armchair, smiling up at someone, a coupe of champagne in her right hand. She was wearing a long black silk dress with a shawl collar, and the fabric shimmered in the light from a candle on the side table.

'Oh,' said Clementine, delighted. 'How wonderful.'

Elizabeth gazed at it. 'It's my favourite thing in all the world,' she said eventually. 'But I find it hard to look at, so I keep it in here.' She swallowed. 'Everything was all right then.'

Clementine felt a lump in her throat. There was a tenderness to the painting that demonstrated just how very much Edwin must have loved his mother.

'I'm so sorry,' she said. 'It must be terribly hard for you.'

'It is. But we mustn't complain. We're not the only ones to have lost someone.' She gave a bright smile. 'Now, there's everything you might need in the bathroom, and a towel. You'll need a hot-water bottle – Daisy will do you one. It might be May, but it can still get cold...'

'This is all lovely. Thank you so much. What a pretty bedroom. The whole house is beautiful.' Clementine hoped she wasn't gushing.

'We're very happy to have you here. Very happy.' Elizabeth put out a hand and squeezed Clementine's arm. There was a warmth in her eyes that lit her up from the inside. Or was it just the late afternoon sun slanting in through the window? Clementine thought she was being genuine. She was a good judge of character, adept at observing what people did rather than what they said. Elizabeth was complex, that was certain, but she wasn't going to let what she knew about her colour her judgement just yet.

There was a lot to uncover at Foxwood. It was very apparent that the Arbutus family were still living in the shadow of Edwin, whilst doing their best to pretend everything was all right. Clementine knew from her mother that you never really got over losing someone you loved. Although you could make a new life for yourself, you never forgot them.

Even though she'd never met him, Clementine was very conscious of Edwin's presence. He was still here, on the walls of the house, in everyone's memory, in everyone's heart, his spirit drifting in and out of every room. He would be there at the table tonight, hovering, taking charge of the conversation without even being there. It was a little unsettling.

But to offset that, there was the solidity of Alfie. Amidst the glamour and the undercurrents and simmering rivalries that flashed under the surface, he'd been calm, unflustered and stalwart, making sure she felt comfortable and welcome. Everyone loved him. You could see by the way they looked at him. Even Diana, who didn't seem to like anyone much.

She thought of Henrietta's words, how Alfie would eventually take over the paint factory. If things carried on the way they were, might she one day be mistress of Foxwood? When she'd pictured her future, it had never been this grand. She'd imagined a comfortable house not unlike her family home, with a large garden rather than grounds. Maybe some daily help, but not live-in staff. Certainly nothing on this scale. She wasn't sure she could imagine herself in Elizabeth's place.

Steady on, Clementine, she told herself. You've only known him five minutes. Hold your horses, girl.

6

After showing Clementine her room, Elizabeth made her way down the corridor to her own bedroom to gather herself. Seeing Edwin's painting always unsettled her. As if Jasper's untoward appearance hadn't rattled her enough. She wasn't sure how she was managing to remain serene when all she wanted to do was scream. At the injustice of it all, and her own weakness, and the mess that was her life.

She sank onto the stool in front of her dressing table and stared at the photograph of Edwin she kept by the mirror. She looked at it every time she sat there; a portrait taken on his eighteenth birthday. She tried never to think about how old he would be now, or to picture what he might look like. It was hard enough to remember every single thing about him, his every feature, his laugh, his voice, his smell, even. Every time she conjured him up, the pain ripped through her anew. She felt it in her heart, in her belly where she'd carried him, in every vein as the blood pumped the agony around her body. Would it ever bloody stop?

With a slightly shaking hand, she retouched her lipstick

and dabbed some rouge on her cheeks, then tipped some perfume onto her wrists and rubbed them together. Thank God Jasper had respected her wishes and made himself scarce. He had known that was the gentlemanly thing to do, but she couldn't always guarantee his chivalry. His frustration with the situation sometimes made him behave badly, although he was always sorry afterwards.

'I sometimes think I'll go mad with it,' he said.

It *was* madness, how it had all begun.

When they left school, Jasper and Edwin had racketed about London, meeting the great and the good, dancing with ravishing girls and breaking their hearts, the pair of them, endlessly photographed in *Tatler* and *Harper's Bazaar* and the gossip columns. Jasper was extremely eligible, having come into a substantial amount of money left to him by his mother, and Edwin was making a name for himself.

Edwin had brought plenty of girls home to Foxwood, all perfectly charming, and all enchanted by the house, of course. Elizabeth could see the hunger in their eyes, saw each of them imagining herself in Elizabeth's place one day. She could see them planning the wedding, the subsequent christenings, the parties, the croquet matches. And, of course, there was the Snow Ball, where legions of them jostled for prime position and Edwin danced with all of them, seemingly oblivious to their charms. Until Meg, of course. Poor darling Meg, his fiancée, who hadn't been able to come to Edwin's memorial because of the war. No one had expected her to come all the way from America.

It had been overwhelming, the memorial, brimming with memories and meaning, and by the end of it she wasn't sure if she felt better or worse, although the vicar (it had been dear old Reverend Cartwright then, not the ghastly Reverend Elphick) had told her it would help her heal, that it would give her a certain peace of mind.

It was Jasper, on leave from fighting in Egypt, who had stepped in, without hesitation, when Michael had broken down the night before and declared he couldn't go through with the eulogy. He had walked up to the lectern, squaring his shoulders for the biggest challenge of his life so far – and he'd had a few of those in combat. She had seen his hand shaking on the notes, hastily written with her help, but he'd done a wonderful job, making them all laugh with his memories of Edwin's antics, his voice only breaking towards the end when he urged them to take a moment to remember the man he called 'the brightest flame on the London art scene, an artist who never painted the same thing twice, who brought his eye for beauty and detail to every single painting'. It was then Elizabeth saw a gravitas in Jasper that made him go up in her estimation. She didn't admit to herself that Michael had gone down.

Jasper had telephoned, a year or so after the war ended, having been demobbed, to see how she was and to invite her for lunch.

'I've found something I think you should have,' he told her.

She took the train up to London from Breverton, the first time she'd been since Edwin died, for she had no heart for shopping or meeting friends even though the war was over. Jasper was lean and tanned from his time in the desert. He had taken her to a funny little Italian in Soho, plied her with pale gold Soave that made her relax after just half a glass and talked to her, properly talked to her, about how she felt and what she was going to do with her life. For the first time in a long time she felt like a person in her own right. She and Michael hadn't yet found a way to *be* with each other. He was closed up, frozen, would never talk about Edwin although she longed to.

'I have no idea how to live,' she told Jasper. 'Nothing seems to have any point. There's the garden, I suppose...'

She shrugged and took another sip of her wine.

'Edwin would want you to be sad, because he was a vain bugger,' he said. 'But not for ever. What can we find for you to do, I wonder?'

He looked at her and her cheeks went warm and her head swam. It must be the wine, she thought, so she put her glass down. And he suggested coffee at his flat, so he could show her what he had found.

'It was in a pile of paintings Edwin had been working on,' Jasper explained once they were back in his living room. 'He left them here and it's taken me this long to find the courage to look at them. Most of them are of no consequence but this one...'

He held it up.

She gasped at the sight of it. It was a portrait of her, full length, sitting in her favourite chair in a black silk moiré evening dress, holding up a coupe of champagne. When – how? – had he painted it? He must have painted it from memory for she had never posed for him. He had captured every single feature with startling clarity, the curve of her lips, the light in her eye, each lash, each strand of hair. There was no clue as to the occasion. It could have been one of many parties they'd had at the house.

Overwhelmed, she put her face in her hands, and began to sob.

Alarmed, Jasper came over to her, putting his hands on her shoulders. 'I'm so sorry. It was supposed to be a comfort. How careless. Forgive me.'

'It is a comfort. It's wonderful,' she managed between sobs. 'But oh . . .' She couldn't articulate the pain. Instead, she leaned in to Jasper, falling against his chest, then felt his arms go around her as he pulled her tight.

'Shhhh,' he said. 'Shush. It's all right.'

He stroked her hair and rocked her until she stopped. And then she looked up at him, and it seemed the right thing to do, to kiss him, because she wanted to feel anything other than cold, hard, numbing grief, so she slid her hands into his hair, pulled his face towards hers and kissed him, properly kissed him, tasting Soave and cigarettes and bitter black coffee and *him*.

'I didn't mean for this to happen,' he told her as they drew breath. 'This wasn't my intention.'

He looked genuinely remorseful.

'Of course not,' she said, and kissed him again. A sweet energy was pumping through her that made her feel almost reborn. It was sharp, urgent, compelling. 'Take me to bed.'

'Really?' His dark eyes were troubled. 'I don't want us to do something we'll regret. Something reckless.'

'That's exactly what I want,' she replied. 'I want to be totally, utterly and completely reckless. Now.'

She followed him into the bedroom with no thought for the consequences.

What surprised her was not how good in bed he was – she had taken that for granted – but how tender and kind he was, more thoughtful than passionate, taking it so slowly and gently she fell into a place of unadulterated (though that was hardly the right word – this was definitely adultery) bliss followed by the kind of deep, dreamless sleep that her body and mind had craved for months.

All these years on, how on earth was she supposed to stop the affair with Jasper? Elizabeth thought. She and Michael had reached a kind of impasse, circling around each other politely, all passion spent. They loved each other, but grief had eaten away any ardour. Their marriage felt like duty. They still shared a bed, but every time they reached for each other, it was silent, and felt automatic, like something they had to go through because it was expected, with no hint of the heat there had once been between them. And she had never had any idea what he was thinking, whether he was longing for her touch, or dreading it. Whether he truly loved or simply tolerated her. His declaration to Alexandra earlier, that he wouldn't jeopardise their marriage for the world, was probably true enough, for there was too much at stake. Foxwood, the factory, the family. But otherwise, they had reached stalemate.

They could stumble along like this until the end of time, she supposed, but it felt wrong. And sad. She knew it was up to her to change things. Men were far too accepting of the status quo in a marriage. It was always the women who took charge.

She tensed as she heard a light tap on her door.

Tippity-tip. Was it Clementine? Had she overlooked some essential? Elizabeth was proud of her reputation as the perfect hostess.

'Come in!'

It was Alfie. Dear, darling Alfie, with a rather sheepish smile on his face.

'I just wondered,' he said, ambling in with his hands in his pockets, 'what you think of Clementine?'

'I think she's a delight. From what I've seen so far. Charming, and confident, but not full of herself.'

Elizabeth felt a rush of fondness for her youngest son. It must have been hard for Alfie, being first in Edwin's shadow, then in the shadow of his death, but he'd handled both with his characteristic grace. She was so very proud of him, and it was a joy to see his eyes shine when he spoke about Clementine. Elizabeth's assessment of the girl was genuine, and she chided herself for not being more focussed on her. Bloody Jasper, stealing her attention.

'I feel as if I've known her all my life,' Alfie was saying. 'Not just five minutes. Is that usual?'

'I think it's a very good sign. When everything's right, it's sort of a comforting feeling, more than anything.' That had been true with Michael. She felt the needling flash of guilt again.

'That's exactly it! I can imagine everything with her. It's extraordinary.'

'It's what you deserve, darling.'

'I just wanted to make sure I wasn't completely delusional.'

Elizabeth knew it was important for people, especially your children, to make up their own mind about things. She had never been interfering, either as a wife or a mother. You gave them your opinion and your advice, then let things run their course, and made sure you were there to support whatever decision was made. But she had liked Clementine from the moment she'd walked out onto the terrace. She was perfect for her boy. Pretty but not too pretty, clever but not too clever, kind, thoughtful (she had helped Daisy with the clearing away, and that showed she didn't think too much of herself) and charming. Charm was very important in life. It got you through most things.

'You have my seal of approval. And, I think, Alexandra's, which is even more of an achievement.'

Alfie laughed. 'Almost an impossibility.'

Elizabeth turned back to her dressing table. To the left was an ivory jewellery box inlaid with mother-of-pearl. She lifted the lid and rummaged until she found a small satin pouch. She held it out to Alfie. 'This was my mother's. It was her engagement ring. You might like to keep it for the right moment. When it comes.'

Alfie opened the pouch. Inside was a square-cut sapphire ring. He held it up to the light, admiring the brilliance of the cluster of diamonds surrounding the large blue stone. The very colour of Clementine's eyes.

'Thank you. This means the world.'

'It would have meant the world to Granny, for you to have it,' she told him.

Alfie slipped the ring back into its pouch.

He gave her a look of such gratitude and appreciation, it made her feel uncomfortable. Would he be so appreciative if he knew the truth? Her betrayal of his father? Michael, after all, had done absolutely nothing to deserve it, not really. Far from it. He was kind and loyal and protective and generous. Elizabeth watched Alfie put the pouch in his trouser pocket. All she wanted for Alfie was a happy, uncomplicated marriage that wouldn't lead either him or Clementine to make the same mistake she had. And if they did get married, it would herald a new phase in their lives. All the more reason for her to leave the old phase in hers behind. There were more important things on the horizon.

7

It had been a good day, thought Stella. She had walked Ted into Breverton where the dad of one of his schoolfriends had umpired a football match on the village green. There'd been squash and jam sandwiches afterwards, and an invitation for Ted to come back and play tomorrow, and now Ted was spark out in the bunk and she was enjoying the last of the sun up on the deck with her sketchbook. Everything on the canal had grown almost overnight. May overtook everything with her verdant stealth, with ranks of bulrushes and trailing willow, broken up with the bright yellow of buttercups and irises. The mother moorhen was out with her young, dabbling away. She closed her eyes, relishing the warmth and the peace. Although her fingers were gripped around a pencil, she wasn't ready to work just yet. She let her mind drift back to where she had left it that morning, to just before the war.

She'd been barrelling her way out of the Underground station, a few months after she'd first met Edwin in Monsieur Corbières' shop, when she saw the poster. Plastered on the wall, smack bang in front of her. Lifesize.

If she stepped into it, she would match it, limb for limb. Her mouth fell open. He'd stolen her, every inch of her, from her dark green coat to the flowery dress that peeped out from beneath the hem to her T-bar shoes – she could even see the scuff marks on the back of the heel where she'd caught them on the kerb. And her hair was unmistakable – that unruly tangle she had stopped trying to tame. He had captured every coppery corkscrew strand.

And who on earth was it she was supposed to be kissing? There was hardly anything of the man visible, just a pair of shoulders in a dark overcoat, and a hat. Nevertheless, there was an intensity in the portrayal of their kiss. You could feel the heat rolling off it.

She had never hung around anyone's neck like that, or kissed them as if the end of the world was nigh, but she felt a swirling in her belly as she took in the scene, and the words underneath it: *WHO KNOWS WHERE IT MIGHT TAKE YOU?*

It wasn't her, and yet it was. Undeniably. *How dare he?*

She knew it was Edwin behind it, because he'd told her about his commission the next time he came into the shop. A series of posters called London Lives, encouraging people to travel on the Underground. She had no idea that he'd intended to use her. How had he captured her so perfectly? Had he followed her? Taken a photograph without her knowing? He couldn't do that. He couldn't just steal her, and put her into a story that was completely made up.

Yet at the same time, she wanted the story to be true. It made her pulse race, the thought of being so close to someone. And she knew, by looking at it, that everyone who saw it would feel the same. It was brilliant.

'Is that you, love?'

A man was standing next to her, his eyes moving from the poster to her, roaming over her coat, her hair.

'No,' she said. 'I've never seen it before.'

'It's the spit of you,' he said, unconvinced.

She turned and walked away. She felt as if everyone's eyes were upon her. She felt *seen*.

Edwin came into the shop again a week later. She'd spent the week travelling with her hair in a thick plait stuffed under her coat to keep herself incognito, after more than one person asked if she was the girl in the poster. She was confused, and suspicious.

He strolled in as if he was guilty of nothing. She marched up to him in a fury.

'You can't do that. You can't just *steal* me.'

'What?' He was laughing at her as she pushed him in the chest. 'Who says it's you?'

'It is me. It's my coat. My dress. My hair.'

'It's not you,' he protested. 'It's a character I invented. Her name's Angela. You might have given me a *tiny* bit of inspiration but she's just made up . . .'

'It's embarrassing. People keep asking if it's me.'

'Well, you can tell them it's not.'

She glared at him. He seemed totally unrepentant.

'How did you do it?'

He tapped his head. 'I remember everything I see. I can draw people from memory.'

'You should have told me. You should have *asked* me.'

She was trembling with emotion, unable to contain herself. He stared at her and it was as if he was only just realising the impact of what he had done.

'If you're really upset,' he said, 'I'll get them taken down.'

'How many are there?'

He shrugged. 'I'm not sure.'

'There's one at Russell Square. And one at Oxford Circus.' She'd gone home via another station to avoid it, but there she was, plastered over a wall in Argyll Street. 'There might be one at every station.'

'*Qu'est-ce qui ce passe?*' At the sound of their voices, Monsieur Corbières came bustling in from the stock room, demanding to know what was going on.

Stella turned to him, indignant.

'He's done a picture of me. It's all over bloody London.'

'It's a poster, Mister C. To encourage people to take the Underground.' Edwin pulled a rolled-up copy from behind his back. 'Here. I brought you one to put up in your room.'

He unfurled it with a flourish.

'My room?' She looked at him witheringly. She couldn't imagine for a minute her landlady letting her pin that up on the wall. She'd drum her out of the house.

Monsieur Corbières peered at the poster. 'It's *magnifique*. And who is that?'

He jabbed a finger at the man.

Edwin shrugged. 'They're both figments of my imagination. Jack and Angela.'

Monsieur Corbières gave him a beady stare. 'You should take her for dinner. To say thank you.'

'I don't want to go for dinner,' Stella said, her voice shrill. The very thought made her heart race and she wasn't sure why. 'You can't *buy* me.'

She was trying very hard not to seem hysterical. It was

hard to stay calm, though, because Edwin was looking at her in a way that was confusing. A combination of concern and admiration and amusement.

'I wouldn't be buying you,' he said. 'I'd love to take you for dinner.'

She'd never been out for dinner with anyone in her life. And certainly not someone like him. She cringed at the thought of how overwhelming it would be. She imagined chandeliers and champagne and snooty waiters. It would be torture. He would soon see her for what she was. A butcher's daughter who had delusions, not of grandeur exactly, but of bettering herself, of becoming someone. She would have to sit opposite him and try not to stare. She was trying not to stare now. He was so distracting, with those green eyes that kept laughing at her.

She wasn't ready yet. She wanted out of her world, but she wasn't ready to step into his. She needed to inch her way up the ladder, gaining confidence and experience and knowledge. Working for Monsieur Corbières and getting her own digs had set her on the first rung, but if she scrambled up too high too quickly she might find herself back at the bottom.

She gave him the only answer she could think of that would stop him asking her again.

'Thank you, but my boyfriend wouldn't like it.'

'Oh.' He looked crushed, the disappointment clouding his face. She suspected he was someone who didn't come across disappointment very often.

Monsieur Corbières raised his eyebrows. He knew very well she didn't have a boyfriend. She avoided looking at him.

'And I don't know what he'll say when he sees one of

those posters. I don't suppose he'll be very pleased.' For a moment, an image of her imaginary boyfriend came into her head, burly, scowling, fists balling at his side, overprotective. Exactly the kind of boyfriend she didn't want.

Edwin made a pained face. 'I didn't think of that.'

'No. Well. You should think about things. Before you go slapping up posters all over London.'

'I am sorry.' He seemed genuinely contrite.

Stella had never felt so many emotions all at once. A curdle of indignation, fear and doubt, but also fascination and something she thought might be pleasure. Pleasure at being the focus of his attention. At the thought of him sitting at his easel, or wherever he did his painting, recalling every inch of her.

'It's all right,' she managed eventually.

He nodded. He seemed to be about to say something, thought better of it, wrapped his voluminous black coat around him and left the shop with his head down. Monsieur Corbières looked at her.

'Don't push him away,' he said.

Stella looked down, at the very shoe he had recaptured on the poster. A boring brown serviceable shoe worn by shop girls like her all over London. 'I don't belong in his world.'

Monsieur Corbières looked thunderous. 'You will never become an artist if you think like that. You must not be afraid of people and what they are.'

Stella looked at the man she had already become so fond of in the time she had worked for him, with his grey whiskers and his immaculate but faded clothes. He was French. Of course he wouldn't understand. You only had to listen to Edwin's cultured, languid tones and her East

End twang to know that they could never be a match, not in a million years. Mr C didn't understand the English way. You didn't mix with people out of your class unless you wanted an unhappy ending. You might get a bit of fun between the sheets, but you'd never get taken seriously, let alone get a ring on your finger.

Not that Stella was after a ring. She had her sights set much higher than that. She wanted a career. Something that was even more difficult for someone of her background.

She sighed and turned away, heading towards the counter to indicate the conversation was over, tidying the sheets of paper they used to wrap things. She didn't want to argue with Monsieur Corbières. She needed him. And he needed her, too, so they shouldn't let anything come between them.

Her parents still didn't understand what she was doing working here, and why she had moved out to live in a grotty room in a boarding house in Bayswater.

'You get the same money here, and you don't have your rent to worry about. You're wasting money and time,' her mum had said.

The thought of being elbow deep in sausage meat for the rest of her life, stuffing cases for the bangers her father was so famous for, or mixing up the filling for the steak and kidney pies, made Stella shudder. She'd been squirrelling away her wages for ages without telling her parents her dream of going to art school one day, for they'd laugh like drains at the notion. But drawing was her escape. Painting, too, when she could afford the materials. That was how she'd ended up here. She'd had a little bit of birthday money so had headed up to the West End to a tiny cobbled street and a shop with a dark green door, the name *Monsieur Corbières* in gilded capitals over the double-fronted window. As soon as she stepped over the threshold, she felt butterflies in her stomach and a peculiar tingling in her fingers. Her brain started racing with all the possibilities. How on earth could she choose what to spend her money on?

Inside it was a glorious muddle of shelves and tables and cabinets piled high in the most haphazard fashion. Paint tubes, bulging with slick, oily colours ready to be squeezed out: cobalt blue, regal magenta, vibrant scarlet. Brushes, some as fine as an eyelash, others as thick as the one her father used to shave each morning. Bundles of pencils, ranging from pin sharp and hard to blunt and caressingly soft. And reams of deliciously blank paper, from smooth and shiny to thick and bumpy and rough. There seemed to be no rhyme or reason to how it was displayed. You just had to search for what you wanted, hoping you might come across it somewhere amidst the mayhem. There were easels, palettes, stacks of art books, some left open, as if the reader had wandered off in the middle. Everywhere seemed covered in a fine layer of dust. It was a treasure trove.

Stella spent a happy hour wandering around, looking, touching, stroking, absorbing it all. It was like a sweet shop to her, as mouth-watering as jars of bullseyes and liquorice all-sorts. The shop was quiet, with an elderly gentleman who pottered in and out. He was small and round and dapper, and seemed to be busy doing nothing, but not once did he put her under pressure, just gave her an absent-minded nod. Gradually, she gathered up the things she wanted. A sketchbook, a clutch of pencils, a sturdy rubber, a small box of watercolour paints and, finally, a magnificent squirrel hair brush that finished in a satisfying point. As she walked to the counter, she realised she didn't want to leave.

'All of these, please,' she said to the man.

'Very good,' he said, with a pronounced French accent.

She stood at the counter while he added up the tally and her purchases were wrapped, daydreaming about her next day off, how she would jump on the train to the countryside armed with a cheese and tomato sandwich and her newly acquired purchases.

And then her eyes fell upon a handwritten notice pinned up on the wall.

SHOP ASSISTANT WANTED
FIVE DAYS A WEEK
KNOWLEDGE OF ART MATERIALS AN ADVANTAGE
PLEASE ENQUIRE TO MONSIEUR CORBIÈRES

She stared at it for a full half a minute. She knew she didn't want to stay at the butcher's shop for much longer. If she carried on, she would be swallowed up by blood-soaked sawdust and would never escape the sweet, metallic tang that hung in the air. She could be here instead, breathing in paint and turpentine and pencil shavings, mixing with people who understood the urge to put the images inside their mind onto paper.

As Monsieur Corbières wrapped the final box with a flourish, Stella cleared her throat. This was the first time in her life she'd been presented with a chance to step out of the world she knew so well, and into another.

Surely it couldn't be that easy? She had to get it right. She indicated the sign.

'Are you Mister Corbières?'

'Monsieur,' he corrected her.

'Are you still looking for someone? To help in the shop.'

He looked at her with the gaze of an artist who took in every feature, every detail, as if appraising her, before he decided on his reply.

'I am.'

'How do I apply?'

'Well.' He put the five packages inside a bag. 'We talk. I decide if I like you.'

'Oh.' She smiled. 'Fair dos.'

He put his hands on the counter top. 'Tell me why you want to work here.'

'Because . . .' She looked around for a moment. 'I've never been here before, but it feels so full of possibility. Full of pictures that have never been painted. What could be more wonderful than that?'

He looked surprised by her answer. 'And where do you work now?'

Stella took a deep breath. He might take some convincing.

'I work for my dad. In his butcher's shop. Me and my mum make the sausages and the pies, and we sort out the bills. So I'm good at maths, and dealing with people. And I can drive – I do the deliveries sometimes. But honestly, I'll go mad if I stay there much longer. There's more to life than sausages.'

'It is a good trade, the butcher.' Monsieur Corbières patted his stomach. 'It is important to eat.'

'Oh yes, but I want to learn how to *think*.'

He chuckled. 'You are crazy if you think you will learn the answer to anything in here. Artists drive you mad. They forget to pay their bills—'

'Oh, I could sort that out. That's another one of my jobs – chasing payments. I'm never afraid to ask for money.' She was building in confidence as she spoke. Her eyes darted around the shop. 'And I'm good at keeping places clean and tidy. You can't have a filthy shop when you're a butcher. You'd be out of business in minutes.'

'You think it is filthy in here?' He seemed surprised, as if he hadn't noticed the chaos.

'No! No, no, no.' She panicked she had offended him. 'But it could do with a little reorganising.' That was saying something.

'Hmm.' Monsieur Corbières looked at her. 'You must understand, I'm getting old. I forget things. I get cross with people. I get tired too. But I want to stay here until I die. So, I need someone who knows where everything is, what to order, what each customer wants.'

Stella grinned. 'I could do that, easy.'

'Can you make proper coffee?'

'No. We only drink tea at home. But I could learn.'

'And your name?'

'Stella. Stella Knight.'

'And do you paint, Stella Knight?'

She shrugged, embarrassed. 'I do when I can. I love it.'

'You must let me see.'

'I couldn't.' She was half-laughing. 'I've never had any proper lessons. We didn't even have an art teacher at my school. So I'm pretty terrible.'

'It is much better to think you are terrible. It is the only way to improve.' He leaned in. 'The worst artists are the ones who think they are great.'

'Oh. I've never thought about it like that.' Stella looked at him thoughtfully. She might learn rather a lot from Monsieur Corbières if she played her cards right.

'Can you start... tomorrow?' he was asking.

Stella swallowed. Her parents weren't going to like it one bit. But she knew this was a chance she couldn't let slip through her fingers, that it was a stepping stone, that if she didn't fight for it she'd be stuck stuffing sausages until the end of time.

'What about Monday?' she said, for she was pretty certain Monsieur Corbières didn't have anyone else up his sleeve.

His black eyes gleamed with pleasure and he held out a plump little paw for her to shake.

And now, here she was, his right-hand girl. Order had been restored. It had taken her a while to organise the shop, but she had pulled everything out, dusted and polished, and put everything in a logical place, in pleasing rows and serried ranks. She could put her hand on whatever anyone wanted straight away, instead of sifting through the entire contents. There was a system for ordering so they never ran out of anything.

'You are a miracle,' Monsieur Corbières had murmured. 'What if you had never come here?'

'It doesn't bear thinking about, Mr C,' she told him, and she meant that, because she had never been happier.

Today, though, she felt slightly off kilter. What had happened had shifted her view of the world somewhat. Confronting Edwin about the poster had made her realise that people could do things that affected you and there was nothing you could do about it. Of course, she knew that you couldn't control everything in the world – the ominous rumblings in the news about war with Germany were becoming even more urgent – but until now she had been in charge of her destiny, making her own choices, calculated decisions underpinned by logic and practicality and simple maths.

What with the posters, and Edwin's reaction to her reaction, and her reaction to him asking her out to dinner – not the one she'd shown him, but how she'd felt inside – she sensed a little bit of power slipping away. And she panicked. If you let your heart rule your head, that's when the trouble started.

When she walked past the poster on Russell Square that evening, and saw herself in the arms of the man she didn't know, she wondered if it was Edwin, if he'd painted himself into the picture. She knew a part of her hoped he had. She blushed as she hurried down the steps into the Underground, then squashed herself into the carriage with all the other passengers. She shut her eyes and let herself wonder what would have happened if she'd said yes to dinner. If that was how the evening would have ended? Was that his fantasy on the poster? Or was it quickly becoming hers?

Next time, she decided, she would say yes to dinner. If he asked her.

Stella sighed, and flipped open her sketchbook. She'd spent long enough reminiscing. It went in phases, her need to remember him, and it was particularly intense at the moment, for some reason. If she was going to meet the deadline she'd set herself, she couldn't spend her spare time day dreaming. She would visit his memorial tomorrow, while Ted was at his friend's. That might bring her some comfort, but for now, she needed to work.

She gazed at the opposite bank, and let her imagination wander, to a boy in a striped jumper and baggy shorts straddling the thickest branch of the willow tree opposite, grinning from ear to ear. The leader of the Towpath Gang. She could see his grubby knees and his fat little toes in her mind's eye, and she began to draw, her pencil skating over the paper as lightly and swiftly as the iridescent damselflies scudding along the surface of the water.

8

After Sunday lunch, before they drove back to London in the early evening, Alfie took Clementine down to the village church to see Edwin's memorial. Foxwood lay in the tiny hamlet of Popplewell, just half a mile out of Breverton, and because the church was particularly picturesque, it was popular with those who found the large, square church in Breverton too austere.

They walked down, hand in hand, Clementine in a wide-brimmed straw hat Elizabeth had lent her, for today was even hotter than the day before.

'I hope you don't think it's morbid,' he said.

'Of course not,' she said.

'It's not a grave,' he said. 'Because they never recovered his body so we couldn't have a proper funeral. And all we've got is a tree, to remember him by.'

The way he said it, so casually and matter-of-factly, made her wince. Even now, you heard about things people had gone through that you couldn't fathom.

Clementine said nothing, just slipped her hand into his and squeezed it. He led her through the graveyard, centuries of grey tombstones spattered with bright green lichen lying amidst the freshly mown grass. The names of some of the deceased had almost completely eroded, ghostly letters only discernible if you really tried hard to make out who had died in 1822. And then there were the more recent graves. Even a village this small had lost men in the war. There was a cluster of them, most with recent bunches of flowers. Clementine's heart ached for them all. Had they lived their dreams before they died? Found love?

Sometimes, she felt guilty that her own war had been uneventful. The worst she could say about it was that it had been dull. Salisbury had escaped unscathed, for it was said the spire of the cathedral was a useful landmark for enemy bombers, so it had never been a target. Her father had been too old to be called up, and had carried on at the school. They had never been at any great risk.

Yet underlying everything was the reminder that her mother had lost her first husband, Ben's father, in the first war. It had made Ruth very protective of Ben, who was old enough to be called up when war on Germany was declared for the second time, and Ruth had been limp with despair.

'I know it's selfish,' she had wept to Clementine's father, Jeffrey. 'But I can't lose him too.'

So although Clementine didn't have any direct experience of losing someone, she had lived with her mother's fear of history repeating itself, and her heightened anxiety as they listened to the wireless every night. As she was the offspring of her mother's second, later marriage, her school friends had much younger parents, who were almost blasé and seemed to carry on life with nothing but a few grumbles about rationing and blackouts.

They stood in the shadow of the church and she stared at the plaque nailed to the tree planted in Edwin's honour. It was an Irish yew, much narrower than a normal yew, and it stood up straight and tall and slender.

IN LOVING MEMORY OF
EDWIN MICHAEL ARBUTUS
1919–1944
A BELOVED SON AND BROTHER

'We all come down and talk to him, even though we know he's not here,' said Alfie. 'My mother used to come here every day. Maybe not so often now.'

He fell silent for a moment. Clementine shivered. How, as a mother, did you decide to stop visiting your child's grave so often? She put out a hand to touch the deep green foliage.

'His poor fiancée,' she said.

'Yes.' Edwin sighed. 'Meg couldn't come to the memorial service. Her family wouldn't let her travel because of the war.'

'She must have been heartbroken.'

'Of course. But she's married someone else now, so I guess...' He shrugged. 'The family have always kept in touch. Her father was a Rhodes scholar – he met Dad at Oxford, and they stayed friends. He's enormously wealthy. I sometimes wonder...' He paused for a moment. 'I sometimes wonder if Edwin felt it was his duty to marry her. Not that my parents would have put him under any pressure. But the money...' He gave a wry smile. 'The factory was struggling before the war. Ironically, it was the war that turned it around.'

Clementine remembered him telling her, that first night, about everything they had done. Alfie cleared his throat. He suddenly seemed awkward; was looking down at the ground, tracing the toe of his shoe in the gravel of the path.

'And things are getting tough again. The industry's very competitive, everyone jumping on the bandwagon now everyone's interested in their homes again. My father's struggling to keep on top of everything because we're having to expand...'

Clementine frowned. She had a feeling this was leading somewhere, but she wasn't sure where.

'Go on,' she said.

'My father asked me to come and work for him last night,' he said suddenly. 'Before dinner, while you and my mother were upstairs.'

'Oh.'

'It's always been understood that I'd take over from him at some point, when he retires. But he needs someone to work alongside him now, so he gave me first refusal.'

'And do you want to?'

Alfie didn't answer for a moment.

'I couldn't sleep last night thinking about it,' he said eventually. 'At first I thought I didn't want to leave London. Not yet. I told you me and Freddie were hoping to open a shop. He's got a couple of places lined up for us to look at.'

'I'm sure your father would understand.'

'He made it very clear that he wasn't putting me under pressure.' Alfie cleared his throat. 'But I feel so torn. It's wonderful here, and it's where I belong. But I'd feel bad letting Freddie down, and I'm proud of Coupe and everything we've done...'

'Of course you are. It's been a huge success. And you've got such exciting plans.'

'Yes. And part of me wants to prove I can do something on my own. But on the other hand, it's my duty to step into Edwin's shoes and help my father.'

'You don't have to be Edwin, Alfie. You don't have to sacrifice yourself.'

Alfie sighed. 'Coupe's fun and exciting but it's not for ever. It's not a legacy, with hundreds of years of history. I'm proud of Arbutus Paints, and my future in it. I'm just not sure I'm ready yet. But –' he paused for a moment, shutting his eyes – 'I'm not sure how to say this.'

'Go on.' Clementine nodded her encouragement.

'If you were with me, I wouldn't think twice.'

'What?' Clementine was startled. This wasn't what she was expecting.

'Clementine,' he said, 'if Edwin's death taught me anything, it's to be bold, and grab what you want. And to trust your instincts. Since I've met you, a light has come back into my life. I wake up and the first thing I think of is you. I can't imagine my life without you in it. Edwin always used to say when you know, you know – and I've never been more sure of anything. And so I hoped, I wondered –' He took both of her hands in his. 'Would you marry me?'

Clementine gazed at him in shock, not sure she had heard correctly.

'Alfie... Oh my goodness. I mean... I feel the same. And I can't think of anything more lovely than marrying you. But you need to know... I couldn't just leave Ben and come and live in the country. I'd have to carry on working. I'm not someone who's going to be happy arranging flowers and having coffee mornings like Henrietta. I need more.'

'Of course,' he said. 'And that's why I love you. I don't want you to change at all. We'd still have the flat. You could stay in town whenever you wanted.'

Clementine tried to take it all in. She was usually very good at making up her mind quickly, but this was momentous, and she didn't want to make a promise she regretted. For a moment she was distracted by a figure on the other side of the churchyard, a young woman slipping behind a gravestone, probably here to pay her respects to someone else lost in the war.

'I'll do whatever we need to do to make it work,' Alfie said. 'What do you think?'

Alfie was squeezing her fingers and she realised she had to put him out of his misery. She wasn't going to be seduced by the glamour of Foxwood, the status of the family, the gracious country living. She was making up her mind based on the fact that she loved this dear, wonderful man with all her heart.

'I think,' she said carefully, 'we could make the best of both worlds, you and I.'

'In that case,' said Alfie, putting his hand in his pocket and taking out the little silk pouch his mother had given him. 'Let's do this properly.' He pulled out his grandmother's ring and dropped to one knee. 'Clementine, would you marry me?'

'Yes!' she said, laughing as he slipped the ring onto her finger. 'Oh, yes!'

He jumped up with a roar of delight, taking her in

his arms. She held up her hand to show him the ring. It caught the late-afternoon light, flashing with brilliance. And they held each other tightly as the sun slipped down behind the church spire, in the shadow of Edwin's yew tree.

9

Stella was very careful about when she came to the churchyard. Usually it was after she had taken Ted to school, stepping through the graves in the morning mist, the grass crisp with frost if it was winter, skirting daffodils and serenaded by the twitter of excitable birds in the spring. There was rarely anyone afoot at that time of the morning. Occasionally there was a posse of gravediggers, and once a gaggle of women armed with flowers and sheaves of greenery had thundered up the path and disappeared inside the church, but none of them showed any interest in her, and she made sure she had a decoy grave to scuttle over to if ever she was taken unawares. The last thing she wanted was to be caught lingering by a member of the Arbutus family, for what would she say to them? How would she explain herself?

Her daydream of Edwin yesterday evening had been so vivid that she had dreamt of him all night and had felt compelled to come and visit his memorial today. Even though she knew there was nothing of Edwin here, that the tree was merely a symbol, it made her feel close to him. The closest she could ever get. And although she had no idea what she believed, and certainly wasn't going to ask the vicar of here or anywhere else for guidance, she nevertheless offered up her own kind of prayer that wherever he was, whoever he was with, he was at peace and being looked after.

Somehow, she had found the courage to go to his memorial service when it was announced in the paper. She'd had the perfect excuse, after all. Monsieur Corbières had asked her to chaperone him, so she had aroused no suspicion. They had come down on the train and everyone assumed she was Mr C's chaperone, as she held his arm and led him into a pew at the back of the church. No one noticed that it was Mr C gripping *her* hand to give comfort during the service, rather than the other way around.

So this afternoon she was startled to see two figures by Edwin's tree, backlit by the setting sun. A young man and woman. She backed away hastily, taking cover behind a large tombstone that would completely obscure her if they turned around. She knew straight away who the man was, for he was facing her, and there were enough similarities for her to realise it must be Edwin's younger brother, Alfie. He was slighter than Edwin, and his hair was darker, but his bone structure, the set of his shoulders, his profile, that sweep of hair, were all strikingly familiar. It made her want to reach out and touch him, feel the warmth of him in her fingertips, someone made from the same two people as the man she had loved with all her heart.

She remembered Edwin talking about his brother with such affection, such fondness. She couldn't see the woman clearly, for she had her back to Stella, and, besides, she was wearing a straw hat that covered her hair and her face. Their conversation was intense, but she was nodding agreement to something.

Stella watched, spellbound, as Alfie dropped to his knee, took the woman's hand and slid a ring onto her finger. She felt a jolt as she looked into the future. A wedding. Perhaps even here, in this church, though more likely at the bride's home. And would she then be brought to Foxwood, to step into a life of comfort and grandeur, of English country ways, of tea on the lawn and house parties, sherry at six and dressing for dinner and cut flowers from the garden? Stella had never been to Foxwood, but Edwin had described it often enough, and drawn it for her too, that house of golden stone with more windows than there were in the street where Stella had been brought up.

When Edwin spoke of Foxwood, when he'd talked about them living there one day, she'd protested that a girl like her did not belong in a house like that.

'Unless I was in the kitchen, peeling potatoes.'

'You're being ridiculous.' He'd nudged her with his elbow fondly. 'You would love it, and it would love you. I can see you there, holding court by the fireplace. Or at the dining table – just think of the feasts we would have!'

She had almost come to believe his dream. And it had almost come true. It had been so close. He'd had a plan. He'd started to put it into action. And even though they both knew it would take time for everyone to come to terms with the change, he assured her that it would be worth it in the end.

'You'll be one of the family,' he assured her. 'They will love you as much as I do.'

But fate had intervened. The timing had been all

wrong. There hadn't been time to put the final pieces of the puzzle into place. And as a result, she was still an outsider, with no chance of stepping into the picture. Stella pressed her back against the rough stone and shut her eyes to stop the tears escaping. Then she turned and hurried away through the churchyard before the couple looked up and noticed her.

10

'I'm delighted for you, Clem. I was starting to worry that there wasn't a man good enough for you in the whole of London.' Ben stretched his legs out in the back of the taxi and stretched his arms over his head, grinning.

They were barrelling their way through London towards the Imperial War Museum, where Ben had promised to show Clementine what he considered to be Edwin's best paintings. Her visit to Foxwood had made her even more intrigued by him, and she wanted to find out everything she could about the man who could have been her brother-in-law.

'Me too,' she laughed. 'Although I wasn't crying into my pillow every night convinced I was going to be a spinster. I knew someone would come along eventually. And even if they hadn't, so what? Getting married isn't the be all and end all.' She grinned. 'I'm secretly quite excited. Prepared to be bored rigid by wedding talk.'

'I'd better start advertising for your replacement.' Ben made a face.

'Don't you dare.' Clementine slapped her half-brother on the leg. 'We're staying in London for the time being.

He's not starting at the factory until after Christmas. And even then I'm not giving up work.'

Ben raised his eyebrows. 'Is Alfie happy about that?'

'Of course. I made it clear that's the deal.'

Ben laughed. 'He's got no idea what he's taking on, has he?'

'Oh, come on. I'm a pussy cat. You know that.' But Clementine was smiling. 'Anyway, he's very progressive. He doesn't want me barefoot in the kitchen. And he knows how important the gallery is to me. So you're stuck with me for the time being.'

'Well, I'm glad. I don't know where I'd find another you. And by the way, congratulations.'

She glanced at the ring on her finger. She still wasn't used to seeing it there, but she had to admit it was perfect. Even Henrietta had been impressed, declaring it very pretty and just the right side of flashy.

'You don't think I've made a mistake, then? You don't think it's too sudden?' she asked now, suddenly not so sure of herself.

'Come on, Clem. If you've got anything, it's a good gut. You've got a sixth sense about people. You're the one who tells me which artists to work with; the ones who are going to be tricky. And you can always spot the clients who are going to be difficult. I'd trust your judgement entirely.'

'Oh.' Clementine was pleased with this assessment. 'Good.'

'You do know the gallery wouldn't be half the success it is without you, don't you? You're my sounding board. I never make any decisions without asking you first.'

'Really?'

Ben stared hard at her through his thick-rimmed glasses. His curly hair looked as if it had never seen a comb, and his green velvet suit looked as if it had been slept in. It probably had. They made a great team, she thought. He had such a brilliant eye, and was a consummate risk-taker, happy to gamble on someone he thought might be a success. And she was skilled at corralling his genius, imposing order on the chaos of the crazy social life that went with running a gallery, as well as looking out for newer talent.

'In fact,' he said. 'I was hoping to make you a partner one day. If you'd be interested.'

'A partner?' She couldn't help laughing.

'Bell and Bell. It has a certain ring to it, don't you think?'

She groaned at his play on words, but she was smiling. 'That would make me so proud. And Mum and Dad would be tickled pink.'

Her father Jeff had adopted Ben when he'd married her mother, and Ben had taken on his surname when he was eleven, keeping Renfrew as his middle name, which had touched Jeff no end. To think of both their names over the gallery door one day made her glow with pride. She was so lucky, thought Clementine. A wonderful husband-to-be. A wonderful brother – there was nothing half about him. They'd shared everything when they were growing up, even though they were far apart in age. He'd shown her the ropes when she came to London. She thought the world of him.

'Tell me more about Edwin,' she said to him now. 'I'm completely fascinated. I keep picking up little bits here and there about what he was like, but of course I can't be too nosy. I feel as if there was more to him than meets the eye.'

As the cab wended its way from Soho to Southwark, Ben told Clementine what he knew. He'd heard lots of gossip over the years, from artists who'd known him, who'd drunk with him in the haunts around Soho and the clubs of Mayfair he frequented.

'Apparently, he could have had any woman he wanted. They threw themselves at his feet. But he was engaged to some American.'

'Meg. Meg Engadine.' Clementine nodded.

'That's it. Anyway, everyone seemed to like him. He was always resolutely cheerful and upbeat, not like most artists. You know what a thundering nuisance they can be. He didn't seem to suffer from self-doubt, or torture himself about his art, or drink himself into oblivion.

'If only they were all like that.' Clementine did her fair share of reassuring their clients.

She mulled over his words as they headed into the East End. The scars of war were much more evident here than in the West End, as they weren't as far on with the restoration. Sometimes, in the middle of London, you could forget it had ever happened. And then there it was, the grand facade of the Imperial War Museum, standing proud despite taking a hit forty-one times at the height of the bombings.

Ben led Clementine at a smart pace through endless galleries, underneath a First World War fighter plane and cases full of memorabilia that she didn't have a chance to examine before stopping in a room full of paintings depicting scenes from the war.

'I know it sounds strange, but this is one of my

favourite places to come, when I want to think,' he told her, his voice filled with awe. 'All these moments, captured so we couldn't forget.'

They wandered through the exhibition. A cherry-picked selection from the nation's war artists, from Edward Ardizzone to Henry Moore to Laura Knight. Service men wandering through Hyde Park, clusters of people tucked up in the Underground for the night, buildings razed to the ground in front of St Paul's. Factory workers heading down the escalator to a secret underground factory. An evacuation train filled with nurses. Tiny scenes of intimacy and huge apocalyptic landscapes. Camaraderie and solidarity, despondency and determination, terror and bravery, the everyday and the extraordinary – it was sobering, a salutary reminder of what had happened, but also inspiring, to think that a human being could capture such intimate moments either from memory or from being at the scene, pulling the observer straight into the heart of the story.

Sometimes it was the humdrum scenes that held the most impact, small domestic details that tugged at the heartstrings. In a short space of time, Clementine felt she had relived the whole of the war, from a hundred different perspectives. It was exhausting, yet she felt honoured to have seen it.

It was one of the few times Clementine had seen Ben subdued. He was so overcome with emotion, both at the subject matter and the talent, that at one point there were tears rolling down his face.

'Hey,' she said. 'It's over.'

'Not for everyone,' he told her, and he was right, of course, for so many people were still suffering the loss of a loved one or a home or sometimes both. And it must be a reminder of how he'd lost his own father in the previous war, a man he couldn't even remember, for he had been tiny.

Clementine hooked her arm in his as they stood in front of three paintings by Edwin: a looming warship, a trio of Spitfires, and a flotilla of Walrus seaplanes floating up a river. His style was unmistakable: everything was drawn with a draughtsman's precision, depicting the gargantuan machines of war with a keen accuracy, yet he gave them his own spin, using pale colours and intricate crosshatching that took the menace out of what he was drawing.

'I think he was one of the best,' sighed Ben. 'There's no drama to hide behind in his work. Just pure majesty and stillness. The calm before the storm. What a waste of talent.'

'What a waste full stop,' said Clementine. 'I can't tell you how much his family still miss him. You can feel him everywhere in the house. You can see it in their eyes. You can see them looking for him. As if they expect him to walk back in at any moment.'

'Still?'

'I suppose you don't get over it, do you?'

'Doesn't it make you feel out of place?'

'No. Not at all. They're all very nice to me. Well, except his sister Diana. I don't think she likes me. I think she thinks I'm trying to take over.'

'Take over what?'

'Well, exactly.'

She didn't tell him about Elizabeth. She kept that secret to herself, for she felt a strange kind of loyalty to her future mother-in-law. Just because someone had suffered didn't mean they could behave how they liked, but there was something fragile, something vulnerable about Elizabeth that made Clementine feel protective. She had been so kind since meeting her. She hoped in time they might become quite close.

'Thank you for bringing me here,' she told Ben. 'It's given me a bit more insight into who Edwin was.' She sighed. 'I'd love to have known him. But I've got Alfie, which makes me the luckiest girl in the world.'

After much debate, Alfie and Clementine decided on a very small wedding. They both agreed that if they were going to get married, they should get on with it, and keeping things simple was the easiest way. Clementine was going through the horror of vicariously organising Henrietta's; her friend was getting married any minute now at her family home in Berkshire. It was an elaborate affair, with over a hundred guests.

'Honestly, it's fraught with problems,' Clementine told Alfie. 'What size gravy boat to put on the wedding list? Who to choose as a bridesmaid? As for the dress fitting – it's a three-act drama. I think a small wedding is rather smart. Everyone will thank us for it. No one wants to spend hours and hours sitting next to someone they don't know and never want to see again.'

Alfie was worried that if they had it at Foxwood, it would get out of control, with more and more guests added to the list.

'Too many people would be offended if they weren't asked.'

'Why don't we get married in London?' suggested

Clementine. 'My parents won't mind me not getting married from home. In fact, they would probably be relieved. My mother really isn't the organising type. She'd find it completely overwhelming. She and my father would much rather turn up on the day.'

Her parents had been quietly pleased when she told them about marrying Alfie. They didn't question her haste at all. Like Ben, they trusted Clementine's judgement. They'd always treated her like a mini-adult as a child, letting her make her own choices and decisions, with a kind of fond distance, almost as if she didn't have anything to do with them, but was something rather delightful they'd found in the house one day.

They plumped for a ceremony at St James's on Piccadilly, then lunch for twenty at the Savoy, as it was where they had met. They booked rooms at the hotel for both sets of parents, and Diana and Rory. Michael insisted on paying for a suite for the happy couple as part of their wedding present.

Apart from family, the only other guests would be Henrietta and Nigel, Freddie and his girlfriend Camilla, and Ben and Alexandra and Jasper.

'I feel as if there's more of my side than yours,' Alfie worried.

'I don't mind. Your family's bigger than mine. And we don't want any more guests, do we?'

Alfie looked again at the list they'd drawn up.

'I think twenty is the perfect number. My idea of hell would be a big wedding. I've done enough of them, I can tell you, both as a guest and as a client. The bigger they are, the more can go wrong.'

'Nothing's going to go wrong,' said Clementine.

The only thing they disagreed on was the best man. In fact, they almost had their first argument when Alfie said he was going to ask Jasper.

'He did a brilliant eulogy for Edwin, so I know he'll do a good speech.'

'But surely you want Freddie? He's your best friend. And won't he be very hurt?'

'Of course not. He understands that Jasper is my surrogate brother. He stepped up when Edwin died. He was always there, to do all the things Edwin used to do. Give me advice, take me out on the town, remind me when it was Mum's birthday...' Alfie looked upset. 'I don't know what I'd have done without him. And Edwin would have been my best man, if he was still here. So of course I'm going to ask Jasper.'

Clementine went very quiet. There wasn't much she could say.

'I don't understand your objection.' Alfie could sense her disapproval.

'I haven't got one. Not really. It's just... I don't know. Ignore me.' Clementine knew if she said anything more, she would ruin the wedding. She would ruin everything. 'I think I'm tired. There's too much whirling around in my head. Of course you should ask Jasper. I'm sure he'll be wonderful.'

11

Towards the end of July, Stella was in the grocery shop in Breverton. She'd been to the post office to post another batch of stories off, then had nipped in to get a few provisions and perhaps a weekend treat for Ted. The woman in front of her was buying icing sugar, three bags of it, and was chatting away to Margaret behind the counter.

'I didn't get much notice for the cake so it's not been fed much brandy. I've just got to ice it now. I'm hoping it's going to look all right. They insisted they wanted me to do it. "You're our cook, Daisy – why would we want someone else to make it?" Mrs A said, but I'm not a professional cake maker.'

Margaret looked anguished. 'Oh, that would give me conniptions. I couldn't take the strain.'

'They only want it simple. A few little rose buds on the top. And it's not a big one. Just a single layer. There's only twenty guests.'

'I wouldn't have thought they'd have such a small wedding.' Margaret pursed her lips.

'I know. I thought they'd do something big at Foxwood.'

Staring at the tinned veg, Stella froze.

'But maybe... what with the son...' Margaret shrugged.

Daisy sighed. 'Yes. I suppose that's what's behind it.'

Edwin. They meant Edwin, thought Stella. And they must be talking about his brother; the couple she'd seen in the churchyard. Alfie and Clementine. She'd seen the engagement announcement in the *Breverton Weekly News* a few weeks ago. Seeing it in black and white had chilled her. Not that she wasn't happy for them, but it brought it all back, everything that had slipped through her fingers, and she'd sobbed herself to sleep as quietly as she could, so as not to disturb Ted.

'You'd think it had been long enough.' Margaret was piling the sugar into Daisy's basket.

Daisy looked anguished. 'I don't think they'll ever get over it. Though perhaps things will change after the wedding. They'll both come down to live at Foxwood, I expect. Mr Alfie will be working at the factory. And I suppose Clementine will be having babies before we know it.'

Stella shut her eyes. That could have been her. He'd painted her the picture so vividly, she had almost believed it was going to happen.

'It'll be nice to have babies at Foxwood.' Margaret nodded her approval.

Daisy's face lit up. 'Oh, it will. It's just what it needs. A bit of new life.'

Stella bent her head and stared at her list. She should get some jelly. Ted loved jelly. Or what about some custard powder? If she watered it down it would last a few days. One day, she thought, she might have enough money to buy jelly *and* custard, and make a magnificent trifle, with Swiss roll and tinned fruit and whipped cream.

She could be asking this very cook to make a trifle now.

Something bubbled up inside her. She felt her throat tighten, and her chest. Oh God, here it was. She turned and fled the shop. Sometimes she thought her grief had finally left her, sliding away in all its smugness, but it grabbed her when she wasn't looking, pulling her down into a pit of despair that felt as overwhelming as the very first day she'd heard the news.

At the bottom of the high street, by the bridge over the canal, she stopped, took in deep breaths to calm herself, told herself she needed to pull herself together. She wouldn't let the grief win. It wasn't real. It was like ectoplasm, an other-worldly fog insinuating its way inside you, trying to take over, but you didn't have to let it in. She'd go back to the shop and buy the jelly. There was a white ceramic jelly mould on the boat. She couldn't imagine what use Edwin had once had for it, but the thought of Ted's face as she turned a pink, wobbly rabbit out onto a plate spurred her on.

That was what life was about. Rabbits made from raspberry jelly, not grey, suffocating grief.

12

At ten o'clock on the morning of the wedding, Clementine was ensconced in Diana and Rory's room at the Savoy. Clementine had worried it was a bit of a cheek, taking it over, but Elizabeth reassured her.

'You don't want to mess up the honeymoon suite,' she said. 'Save it for tonight. Diana and Rory won't mind.'

So here she was, in front of the dressing table in rollers and her wedding underwear, a glass of champagne at her elbow, patting powder onto her face and hoping she wouldn't look too shiny by the time she got to the altar, for it was seventy-four degrees already and set to be in the eighties by lunchtime. Her wedding dress was hanging on the front of the wardrobe. She thought it was perfect and she was proud that she'd been able to buy it off-the-peg from a shop in Knightsbridge, for although she wanted to look the part, she didn't see the point in spending vast amounts on something you might only wear once. It fitted very well, the hem only needing taking up an inch and the bodice letting out a touch. Elizabeth was coming back at half past ten to fasten her into it. Then she would go down to the foyer where her father would be waiting, for a glass of champagne – another one; she must be careful, for people kept pouring it for her – before getting into the taxi for the short drive to Piccadilly.

She was blotting her lipstick with a tissue when the door flew open and Diana barged in.

'Oh. Sorry. I'd have thought you'd be gone by now,' she said.

'I'm only going to be another ten minutes. Your mother's coming to do my dress up in a moment. Do you want to get changed?'

'No,' said Diana. 'I'm ready.'

Clementine reddened. Diana was never one for dressing up, but even so, her beige trousers and plain white blouse were a little drab even for her. She probably wanted to freshen up.

'Do use the bathroom if you want. I'm so sorry – I've taken over rather.'

'It's all right. I'm used to it.'

Diana was standing in the middle of the room, swaying slightly. Was she drunk? That would explain the redness of her face and the slur in her words.

'I shan't be long. And I'll clear everything up before I go.'

Diana didn't seem to be listening. She was looking around the room, at the champagne on ice, the pots of make-up, the circlet of fresh flowers ready to be put on last.

'Do you know, Mummy never bothered to come and help me on my wedding day?'

Clementine remembered seeing one or two photos of Diana's wedding at Foxwood. She hadn't taken to the role of bride naturally. Her smile was fixed as she held on to Rory's arm, and she looked as if she'd rather be anywhere else. Her dress was quite ordinary, and there was no head-dress or veil. What she had just said was probably true. It didn't look as if Elizabeth had had any hand in the preparations.

Clementine was at a loss as to what to say. Now really wasn't the best time for Diana to be airing her grievances, but she didn't want to say as much.

'I'm so sorry.'

'She's just not interested in me.'

Clementine swallowed, flicking a glance at the clock. Time was ticking by. She should be downstairs in fifteen minutes. Where was Elizabeth?

'Maybe we could have tea or something, when this is all over? Have a good chat?' Perhaps if they got to know each other better, this antagonism would dissipate and she could reassure her sister-in-law.

Diana didn't answer. She was staring at Clementine's wedding dress. It was pale cream dupion, with a hint of Dior's New Look: a fitted jacket sporting tiny covered buttons, an extravagant bow at the waist, then a full skirt that reached the floor.

'Your dress is lovely,' said Diana, her face crumpling. She suddenly seemed vulnerable and small.

'Thank you,' was all Clementine could think of to say.

Then Elizabeth swept in, striking in pink-and-white striped silk with a huge hat. She glanced at her daughter and frowned.

'Diana, darling, you need to get ready. You're leaving for the church in ten minutes.'

Diana put her hands on her hips in a defiant stance. 'I am ready.'

Elizabeth's gaze swept her up and down, judging, assessing, deciding. There was no time to argue. There would be no time to find an alternative outfit. A fuss would ruin everything. She gave a tight smile.

'In that case, go and make sure the boys are ready, would you?'

'Boys?'

'Daddy and Rory.'

'They're down in the bar. With Jasper. The *best* man.' Diana's tone was mocking. Was her remark deliberately loaded? For the second time, Clementine wondered if Diana had also uncovered Elizabeth's secret affair.

Elizabeth didn't flicker. 'Why don't you go and join them?'

'I know when I'm not wanted.' Diana put her hands up. 'See you all in church.'

She melted away, humming 'The Wedding March' loudly and tunelessly.

When she was gone, Clementine saw rather than heard Elizabeth's sigh. Was it resignation or relief? It was strange, how Diana always seemed to be so out of place, and to go out of her way to be difficult. Clementine supposed it was because she was unhappy. She had assumed she was perfectly content, with Rory and the farm and her horses, but perhaps not.

'Right, let's get those rollers out. Then we'll get the dress on.' Elizabeth clapped her hands and brought her attention back to the matter in hand.

The next moment she was pulling out pins and unwinding Clementine's curls. Clementine picked up her glass of champagne and took a gulp. This family was even more complicated than she'd first thought. But Alfie wasn't, he was robustly straightforward, and she was marrying him, not them, so with luck everything would be all right.

*

St James's at Piccadilly had recently regained its dignified grandeur, lovingly restored after a hit during the Blitz. The gentle strains of Bach floated from the organ pipes as the guests arrived and the sun slanted in through the stained glass, lighting up the nave and the carved marble font.

As mother of the groom, Elizabeth took her place in the first pew on the right, with Michael next to her by the aisle. She always felt overwhelmed in church nowadays, no matter what the occasion. She thought it was perhaps her quiet fury at the God she didn't believe in. She wanted to hurl her hassock at the vicar. Scream at the congregation to wake up to the hypocrisy of organised religion. It didn't change anything. It certainly didn't make anything better. But she was far too well brought up to do anything more than arrange the most beatific of smiles on her face and wait for the ceremony to unfold.

She tried not to think about the wedding that never was, between Meg and Edwin. She tried not to look at Jasper, standing next to Alfie at the altar, his best man by default. She tried not to look at the back of his neck, the neck she had kissed so many times, or his lithe frame draped in an immaculate tailcoat, the grey cloth dropping away to a sharp point. She hadn't seen him alone since Alfie's birthday, for there had been far too much going on, and she missed the tangle of their limbs, the scent of him on her skin, the delicious quiver that went through her when he brushed his lips along her collarbone.

Or did she? The past few weeks had been rather filled with joy, as their lives had recalibrated to welcome Clementine, and the wedding had given her, and

Foxwood, a fresh purpose. And she certainly hadn't missed the subterfuge, the needling of her conscience, the eternal sick guilt in her stomach. The preparations had brought her and Michael together as they went up to town to meet Ruth and Jeffrey for the first time, discussed what they would give Alfie and Clementine as a wedding present, and shopped for a new morning suit for him and the perfect outfit for her. They'd even gone for a celebratory lunch at Quaglino's. She couldn't remember the last time she and Michael had come to London together, and she resolved they must do it more often. The Pimlico flat was there to be used, after all, with plenty of room even if Alfie and Clementine were in situ.

She sighed and hooked her arm in Michael's, and her husband turned to her, surprised at her sudden display of tenderness. He smiled, and she slipped her hand into his and squeezed it. He squeezed back and tapped her knuckles gently with his thumb, a tiny gesture that said, 'I know. I miss him too.' She rested her head against his shoulder for a moment, overwhelmed, then sat up straight as the organist segued into the jaunty twirls of Handel's 'Arrival of the Queen of Sheba'.

As she watched Clementine walk down the aisle on her father's arm, Elizabeth felt something shift inside her. She couldn't have asked for a more perfect choice for Alfie. Clementine was strong-minded but not stubborn. Fun but not frivolous. Independent but not distant. Even her dress met with Elizabeth's approval – it was elegant and simple and timeless. She couldn't see trouble on the horizon, or the two of them locking horns the way she did with Diana. She was still furious with her daughter for turning up in an outfit Elizabeth wouldn't even be seen gardening in. She had done it on purpose, but to get at whom Elizabeth wasn't sure. She could never fathom Diana's never-ending need to provoke, but she had learned not to rise to it.

Afterwards, as they all streamed out from the church and into the courtyard that looked out onto Piccadilly, she shook her little box of confetti and threw it all over the newlyweds as they emerged. Tiny tissue horse-shoes fluttered through the air as crowds of people clustered on the pavement and clapped, some of them wiping away a surreptitious tear. For a moment, Elizabeth was taken back to her own wedding day. No one said their vows imagining that one day they would break them. She still couldn't believe she had. On the outside, she and Michael didn't look so unlike the young people they had been, over thirty years ago. A little greyer, a little thinner in the face and thicker in the middle, perhaps. But inside, oh, how they had changed. She felt a squirm of shame.

There was just the lunch to get through.

She held her cheek to Jasper's in the receiving line at the Savoy. She tried not to jump at the touch of his skin on hers, smiling and moving on to the next guest. She had done her best not to interfere with any of the arrangements and had prayed to the god of seating plans that they were nowhere near each other, and they weren't: Jasper was flanked by Camilla and Diana at the bottom of the table, while Elizabeth was at the top in between Clementine's father and Alfie. She raised her glass to her lips and took the tiniest sip of champagne, for she knew that if she had too much, she would have the urge to get him on his own and slide her hand inside his shirt. Would there be anything more unseemly?

*

'Clem, you are so clever!' Henrietta was fanning herself with the lunch menu that had been put on each plate. 'I don't know why I didn't think of it. A wedding lunch at the Savoy. So elegant.' She stopped fanning to read the menu. 'Crab beignet with a mousseline sauce. Rack of lamb with new potatoes and green beans. Galettes aux fraises. Divine!'

They were in the Pinafore Room, with its Art Deco panelling and large window overlooking the Embankment and the Thames beyond. There was just one large table, seating ten down each side, with a pristine tablecloth, huge silver vases spilling out white hydrangeas and ice buckets filled with champagne. A glittering chandelier hovered over the proceedings.

'Your wedding was lovely too,' Clementine reassured her friend.

'I know, but this is so intimate. And you get to enjoy your guests. I spent all day running from person to person and I don't remember a single conversation.' Henrietta sighed. 'This is perfect.'

'It just seemed right. It's where we met.'

'At our engagement party. I know.' Henrietta's eyes slid around the table. 'Here, your sister-in-law is a bit of a sour puss. And what is she wearing? Did she come straight from the stables?'

'Ssh. Clothes aren't Diana's thing.' Clementine tried not to laugh. 'I feel a bit sorry for her, actually.'

'Hmm. She could have made a bit of an effort. Is she jealous of you, do you think? For stealing her baby brother?'

'I don't think so.'

Henrietta's gaze settled on Jasper, with his perfectly cut suit and immaculately knotted tie. He was flirting openly with Clementine's mother Ruth, making her laugh, waving his glass of champagne to accentuate whatever tall tale he was telling her.

'And the best man. What's his story? Why doesn't he have anyone with him? He must be quite a catch.'

'Oh, Jasper's a bit of an enigma.'

'He's not . . .' Henrietta gave one of her eyebrow waggles. 'The other way? I mean, he's *very* well dressed.'

'Not that I know of,' said Clementine. 'But who knows?'

'I wouldn't be surprised.' Henrietta moved along to Elizabeth, who was talking to Freddie and Camilla. 'Honestly, your ma-in-law is *so* glamorous. I'd hate to have to compete with her. How do you cope?'

'I don't. Compete, I mean. We're very different.'

Henrietta sighed. 'I wish I had an ounce of your confidence.'

Clementine gave her friend a squeeze. For all her opinions and endless chatter, Henrietta was quite insecure.

'Are you happy sitting in between Freddie and Ben?' she asked her. 'It took us hours to do the seating plan.'

'Oh, I'll talk to anyone. You know me.'

Poor Ben, stuck between Henrietta and Diana, neither of whom were his type at all. But he would rise to the occasion and everyone could move around after the speeches, when it would all be a bit more relaxed. Clementine moved along the table to check the place names, just as a team of black-clad waiters appeared, bearing the crab beignet on gleaming white plates.

Lunch was served.

*

After the last of the strawberry tart was devoured, Clementine's father stood to give his speech, tinging his fork on the edge of his glass to call attention. Elizabeth braced herself, for she always found the speeches the most emotional part of a wedding.

Jeff Bell was a quiet, unassuming and studious man, but his role as a bursar meant he was good at communicating, and soon everyone was under his spell.

'It is a disconcerting time in a man's life, when he has to relinquish care of his daughter to another man. But as soon as I met Alfie, I knew I didn't have to worry, that she would be in safe hands. In fact, it was Alfie I was more concerned for. Clementine will bring sunshine into any household, but woe betide you if you don't fit into her idea of how things should be. I warn you, Alfie, that ten-year-old Clementine spent much of the war baking special little cakes for Hitler containing deadly seeds gathered from the garden. Her plan was to put on her best dress and proffer them to him should he have the temerity to turn up in Salisbury. She does, I believe, still have the recipe...'

Everyone collapsed with laughter, and Clementine shook her head in fond disbelief at her father's revelation.

Then it was Alfie's turn.

'I can't believe that it was only in April that I turned up here on a Tuesday night to celebrate Nigel and Henrietta's engagement with them.' He raised his glass to his friends in acknowledgement. 'And there I clapped eyes on a girl in a velvet beret with a diamond spider brooch, and I thought to myself: she must be spoken for. But she wasn't, and here we are, with our life mapped out in front of us.

I am so proud to call Clementine my wife today, and to know that I am going to join my father next year at the factory with her by my side. My heart could not be fuller...'

There was a minor commotion as Diana somehow managed to spill her glass of red wine over the table, but Ben leapt to his feet and mopped it all up with his napkin as Alfie went on to thank Clementine's parents.

'Thank you, Jeff, in particular, for the warning. I shall be wary of baked goods going forwards.'

And then it was Jasper's turn, as best man. He stood, then took a while to gather himself, looking down at his notes before looking up again and starting to speak. Elizabeth remembered the last time she'd seen him give a speech. She forgot her resolution not to drink too much and took a gulp of Chablis, reminding herself this was a happy occasion.

'I thought long and hard about whether to mention Edwin today,' Jasper began. 'By rights, it should be him regaling us with indiscreet tales of Alfie's escapades over the years. But I dreamt about him last night, and he said, *You'd better bloody mention me, Jasp. If I can't actually be there, I want to be there in spirit.* I've tried, over the past few years since Edwin has gone, to step into his shoes and be something of a big brother to Alfie. I tried to instil in him a sense of honour and loyalty, though I'm not sure I'm the best qualified person to do that.' At this, he gave a self-deprecating grin, and Elizabeth tried hard not to raise an eyebrow, despite her own complicity. 'But I did introduce him to the best nightclubs and the best wines and his first Joaquin Cuesta cigar. If it's good enough for Winston Churchill...' Everybody laughed. 'Anyway, Alfie is very much his own person, but there is so much of Edwin's spirit in him that will hold him in good stead...'

His voice broke, and he paused for a moment, his head bowed. When he looked up, his eyes were bright with unshed tears. He held up his glass.

'This is a toast from Edwin, wherever he is. Please join him, and me, in wishing the bride and groom the happiest of lives together.'

Elizabeth couldn't find her voice to join in the toast. She was overwhelmed by how perfectly he had woven Edwin in without making it awkward or self-indulgent. She shut her eyes and raised her glass and, next to her, Michael put an arm around her and murmured: 'I know. I'm here and I know.' She leaned against him, and she felt his love and his strength. In that moment, they were united, in both their grief and their joy, such a curious mix.

She realised that this was a turning point. She didn't just owe it to Michael. She owed it to Clementine and Alfie. The stakes were far too high now for her to risk everything. Their obvious happiness helped to lift her heart and calm her mind, giving her confidence that her own marriage could survive, flourish even.

And the courage to tell Jasper it was over, once and for all.

After the speeches, the guests clustered around the cake stand. Daisy had done them proud, and had even piped the Arbutus family crest on the top.

Elizabeth glided up to Jasper. They were standing on the edge of the crowd, slightly apart from everyone else. Her mouth went dry as she gathered the courage to speak.

She watched as Clementine and Alfie held the silver knife in their hands and plunged it deep into Daisy's handiwork, slicing through the white icing, the soft marzipan, the brandy-soaked fruit.

Neither of them took their eyes off the happy couple as they spoke.

'That was a marvellous speech, by the way. Thank you.' Her appreciation was genuine. 'It must have taken a lot of thought.'

'It was from the heart.' Jasper put his hands in his pockets. 'I've missed you.'

'I've been rather busy.'

'Of course.' He paused, cleared his throat. 'You should have more time, now it's all over. Shall we—'

She cut him off before he could make a suggestion. 'I don't think so.'

He turned to look at her, frowning. 'What do you mean?'

'I mean . . .' Elizabeth sighed. If she skirted around the issue, he would only persist. It felt important to do it today. 'It's over, Jasper. I can't do it anymore. There's too much at stake, especially after today. I have to put the family first.'

She could smell his cologne. It brought back so many memories. She had to be resolute.

'So that's it? No explanation? No discussion?'

'There's not much more to say.'

'Eight years, and you just—'

His voice was a little too loud. She put a restraining hand on his arm, smiling in case anyone was looking.

'Jasper. This isn't the time or the place.'

'Well, exactly. Pretty brutal, don't you think? Ditching me right here, in front of everyone?'

'Please respect my decision.' Elizabeth turned and accepted a plate with a piece of cake on it from a passing waiter. 'Oh, how absolutely lovely. Thank you so much. Jasper, would you like some cake? Daisy made it.'

She was making it quite clear the conversation was over.

Jasper stared at the plate offered to him by the waiter. 'No, thank you,' he said crisply, and walked away.

Elizabeth watched him go, her lover of eight years, and lifted the cake to her mouth. She knew it would be perfect. Moist and not too sweet and just the right amount of brandy. She must remember to thank Daisy. She was such a treasure.

But the crumbs turned to sawdust in her mouth, and she couldn't taste a thing.

'I just don't understand. He knows nothing about that factory. Nothing! He's barely stepped foot inside it. You could write what he knows about it on a postage stamp.'

'Diana, calm down.' Rory usually made himself scarce when Diana had one of her rages but they were trapped inside their hotel room, and he wanted to try to quieten her. It would be awful if anyone could hear her.

She'd been impossible during the wedding breakfast, flirting – if that's what you called it; he wasn't sure, for he'd never seen her flirt before and it made him very uncomfortable – with both Jasper and Ben, getting them to light her cigarettes, batting her eyelashes and leaning all over them. At one point she had even force-fed Ben his pudding.

'Come on. Here comes the choo-choo,' she'd said, and

Ben had opened his mouth obediently, he and Jasper laughing their heads off. Rory had felt an absolute chump, sitting there not sure what to do while Diana made a fool of both herself and him. He couldn't remonstrate with her, and tell her to pull herself together, for he knew that would cause a scene. So he ignored them, and tried to make conversation with Clementine's mother, who was very kind, just like her daughter, but they ran out of things to say to each other pretty quickly leaving Rory to stare at his plate.

And now she had worked herself up into a fury.

'Calm down?' she scoffed. 'I'm not going to bloody calm down. I'm livid. I mean, where was Alfie when all the men went off to fight in the war?'

'To be fair, he was at school,' Rory pointed out.

Diana ignored him.

'It was me on the factory floor, keeping everyone's spirits up. But no one gives me any credit for keeping it all going, keeping up morale, churning out gallons and gallons of blackout paint.'

'You're working yourself up.'

Diana snatched up a paperweight from the little writing desk and hurled it at him. Rory, who was the captain of the Breverton cricket team, dodged out of the way and put out a giant paw to catch it. He'd had enough.

'Diana. This is the Savoy, not the backroom of the Trout on a Friday night. Pull yourself together.'

She glared at him. 'Everyone just ignores me and what I did. The war ends and I'm just supposed to slip away quietly and get married like a good girl.'

Rory's face crumpled. 'Well, I'm sorry if it's been such

an ordeal. I've only ever tried to do my best to make you happy.'

At these words, Diana seemed to see him for the first time.

'I'm sorry,' she said. 'I just find it so . . .' She grasped for the word. 'Boring. Not you. You're not boring. But everyone waiting for me to get on with it, to have a baby, looking at me as if I'm a useless lump, when I could be doing something *useful* . . .' She made a sound which was something between a snuffle and a gulp. 'And Alfie gets it all handed to him on a plate. And any minute now *she'll* have a baby, and will make me look even more useless.'

'Diana, you are not useless. Come on. Why don't you get into bed and sleep it off? I think you might have had too much to drink. It always makes you cross.'

'But I'm not cross,' she said in a very small voice. 'I'm just sad.'

She sat down on the bed. She was utterly deflated, all the rage suddenly gone.

Rory wondered why he couldn't make Diana happy. He could never live up to the glamour and charisma of either of the Arbutus brothers, who Diana had grown up with. But he hadn't forced her to marry him. She'd seemed keen enough at the time, and Birch Farm wasn't Foxwood but it was jolly comfortable and she had the whole of the stable yard and he would give her whatever she wanted, she knew that. And he wasn't sure where all this anger about the factory had come from. If that's what she wanted to do, surely she should just tell her father?

Five minutes later, Diana was passed out on the bed, fully dressed. She was lying diagonally, which made it impossible for Rory to get in. He contemplated her for several moments, wondering if he could shift her without waking her up.

He sighed. He wasn't going to risk waking her. He took two of the pillows, found a spare blanket in the wardrobe and curled up on the floor. He'd done his National Service. He could put up with discomfort, and it wasn't as if it was cold. He shut his eyes, thinking what a lovely day it had been, and how content Clementine and Alfie seemed. And he decided that the best thing would be to get Diana in a good mood, somehow, when she was sober, and talk to her, really talk to her.

Was she warm enough? he wondered as he started to drift. He jumped up, took one of the spare blankets he was using and tucked it over her. She gave a little snuffle accompanied by a snort. He patted her gently and headed back to his makeshift bed on the floor, settling down under the remaining blanket to try to get some sleep.

Three rooms along, Michael poured himself and Elizabeth a Scotch. He walked over to the dressing table where Elizabeth was sitting, wrapped in a pale green satin dressing gown. She looked even more beautiful without make-up and her hair down. Less as if she was hiding behind a mask. And younger, somehow. She put up a hand to take the glass.

'Thank you.'

He put a hand on her shoulder. 'That was an unforgettable day.'

She smiled at him in the mirror. 'It was.'

'To be honest, I was rather dreading it. I was terrified about how I was going to feel. You know, with... Edwin not there.'

Her eyes widened in surprise. It was very rare that he spoke his son's name out loud, or discussed his feelings.

'But I felt very happy,' he went on. 'I mean, the sadness was there, of course. I think it always will be. But it sort of... made room for a bit of joy today. For the first time.'

Michael was tracing his fingertips along her collarbone with a featherlight touch that spread a familiar warmth deep inside her. She shut her eyes, relishing the sensation. Michael was right. The wedding had been a joy. It had been magical. It had broken the spell she had been under. She felt as if a huge burden had lifted.

After the cake cutting, after they'd spoken, Jasper had studiously avoided her, and had gone off into the night with Clementine's half-brother, Ben. She didn't want to think about what they might get up to, or who they might end up with, two eligible bachelors with a sense of devilment and no one to answer to. She imagined some darkly glamorous Mayfair club, girls with laughing eyes and low-cut dresses. But that was just as it should be. Perhaps he would meet someone? Once that thought would have twisted her up inside with jealousy, but now she rather longed that Jasper might find someone he could call his own.

Michael was drawing little circles along the length of her spine now, teasing, his touch so delicate she could hardly feel it, but when she did, it sent ripples through her. She tipped her head back.

'Kiss me,' she said, and when he did, she remembered he was a marvellous kisser, ironically much better than Jasper, starting off gently and building up to something more intense, while Jasper had kissed her with a fierceness that sometimes bordered on desperation, which led her to wonder what on earth she found so wretchedly compelling about him. She stood up and pressed herself against him, and he pulled at the belt around her robe until it came loose.

'You know ours is the only room with a balcony?' she whispered to him. 'We ought to make use of it.'

He looked at her in delighted surprise. She reached over to snap off the single lamp that was lighting the room, took his hand, shrugged off her robe and led him through the French door that had been left ajar.

They stayed in the shadows, but making love in the moonlight gave everything a delicious edge, with the whole of London laid out in the distance and the cool night air on their skin.

'Got you,' Michael breathed in her ear as she reached an intense climax, and he was smiling.

'You absolutely have,' she whispered.

They were back, she thought. Somehow the awful distance between them had gone, and they were together again. The two of them. Husband and wife. Michael and Elizabeth.

13

After the wedding, Clementine packed up her things and moved into Alfie's flat in Pimlico – they'd agreed to spend the rest of the year in London while Alfie and Freddie found someone to replace him at Coupe before they moved down to Foxwood in the New Year. And by the end of August, Clementine had been startled to find she was expecting.

'A honeymoon baby,' she told Alfie, looking a little abashed, although they hadn't technically been on a honeymoon yet.

'It is what you want, isn't it?' he asked anxiously.

'Oh yes,' she said. 'It's just a little bit sooner than I expected. Let's not say anything to anyone just yet. I want a little bit of time to get used to the idea and I don't want fuss.'

'I agree. Let's keep the news to ourselves while we still can, and enjoy it.' Alfie was over the moon, and it was all Clementine could do to stop him rushing off to Harrods to buy a Silver Cross pram. Everyone knew you didn't bring a pram into the house until after the baby was born. It was bad luck.

The only thing they couldn't agree on was her continuing to work. Clementine was adamant that she didn't want having a baby to affect her work at the gallery.

'I'll just have to avoid carrying anything heavy. Which is fine, because we don't have another exhibition until the end of October.'

Alfie frowned.

'I don't think you should work at all. I think you should go down to Foxwood and let everyone look after you.'

'Alfie, I'm not ill. I'm pregnant. I'd go mad with boredom. If I get tired, I'll ask Ben if I can go home early. I promise.'

'It doesn't seem right.'

'Don't be so old-fashioned.'

'I'm not old-fashioned,' he bristled. 'I'm just worried. About you and the baby.'

'We are absolutely fine. I promise you. Honestly, I'm starting to wish I hadn't told you.'

'Don't say that. That's awful.'

'And I'm warning you now, I'll be going back to work after the baby is born.'

Alfie looked horrified. 'How?'

'I shall just lug it with me. They're very portable, babies, and Ben won't mind. He's very modern about that sort of thing.'

Alfie felt a little stung, as if he was being compared unfavourably to his brother-in-law.

'Wouldn't you leave the baby with the nanny?'

'Nanny?' Clementine stared at him. 'I'm not having a nanny. That's not the kind of mother I want to be.'

Alfie had no idea how to carry on arguing with her. With a bit of luck, she would change her mind once the baby arrived. So he went along with it all for the time being.

By the beginning of October, they had told everyone, and Clementine agreed to give up work at Christmas, which actually tied in rather nicely, as Alfie was due to start at the factory in the New Year. And she was starting to feel rather tired. Ben had agreed to the exhibition for the Scottish artist she had spotted, and so she had a particular interest in its success. She had underestimated how much it would take out of her, the organising, the entertaining, the late nights. But she couldn't admit to feeling under par, so she battled on. It wasn't too long until Christmas.

The day after the private view, which had been a huge success, red dots spattered all over the paintings, she was feeling drained. She hadn't got home until half past one the night before, and Alfie had been quite cross. Not with her, but with Ben. Alfie thought Ben took advantage of her better nature, but she had assured him he had put her under no pressure.

'Let me get you a taxi,' Ben said now, concerned that she looked rather drawn.

'Don't be daft. The Underground will be much quicker.' Clementine picked up her coat. 'I'll see you tomorrow.'

Ben frowned. 'You should take the day off. You've been doing long days.'

'We'll see.' She smiled. 'I'm sure I'll perk up after an early night.'

Outside, the cold air woke her up a bit. It had been a long day, following up on all the sales, double-checking the paperwork, sending out letters confirming delivery once the exhibition was over, banking all the cheques.

She felt whey-faced and gritty-eyed. All she wanted was a bath, a buttered crumpet and bed.

She was pushing her way through the afternoon crowds at Oxford Circus, when she felt a tug in her belly. She told herself there were bound to be things going on that would feel unfamiliar as the months went on. You couldn't have all that going on inside you without feeling some of it. Perhaps it was a growth spurt or something? Or a little leg giving an experimental kick – how big was it now? No bigger than a ping pong ball, probably. It wasn't a pain, as such, just a dull little ache. She tried to push her concern away as she sat on the journey to Pimlico. There, however, she started to feel a bit shivery and not herself at all. Flu, she decided. That made you ache everywhere. What a nuisance.

She couldn't face the short walk to the flat – she was burning hot now – so she made her way up into the open air and hailed a taxi, wishing she'd taken Ben up on his offer. In the peace of the back seat, without the hustle and bustle distracting her, the dull ache became sharper and more insistent.

Somehow, she managed to get herself out of the taxi, pay the driver, open the front door and pull herself up the stairs by the hand rail. Once inside the flat, she grabbed the telephone and dialled Alfie's office with shaking fingers.

'Are you on your way home?' she asked in a very small voice. 'Only I think something's terribly wrong.'

She lay on the floor, holding her tummy, until he burst through the door just as the clock struck six.

Two days later, she lay in her hospital bed, pinned under a very tightly tucked sheet and two blankets, staring at the sickly green of the ward wall that she thought probably matched her own complexion, for she felt dreadful. Scooped out and hollow and tender and desolate and bewildered. She'd had such a clear vision of their baby, a chubby, jolly little thing that she spoke to in her head on a daily basis, so to discover that it was no longer had come as a shock.

'It's just one of those things,' Sister Milner told her. 'You're not to blame yourself and you're not to worry, because it doesn't mean you can't have another.'

'I don't want another,' said Clementine sadly. 'I wanted that one.'

'I know, duck.' The nurse patted her hand. 'But it's nature's way.'

'Nature's way of what?'

'Making sure everything's just as it should be. If there's something wrong, it's for the best.'

Clementine shuddered. Who decided what was for the best? If she was the baby's mother, didn't she get to make the decision?

'Just take a little time to rest and then ... press on.' Sister Milner gave her a knowing look.

Press on.

If she was devastated, then Alfie was distraught. He sat by her bedside, gripping her hand, raging through his tears.

'I shouldn't have let you carry on working. Bloody Ben.'

'How is it his fault? He wasn't to know.' Clementine's loyalty was staunch.

'Yes, but he's so useless and you convinced me he needed you and if he wasn't so incompetent, he could have managed without you. You shouldn't have been up so late for a start...'

His eyes were red and his skin had come out in blotches. Clementine felt overwhelmed by his grief. She supposed for him it was an emotion that was close to the surface, something that was ready to well up at any moment. Her sadness was small and quiet in comparison. She wanted to curl up and sleep.

Sister Milner saw the situation, whisking back the curtain.

'Mr Arbutus, it's time for everyone to rest now, I'm afraid. We keep very strict visiting hours on the ward, as I'm sure you'll understand. You can come back at six o'clock.'

When he'd gone, Sister Milner came to sit with her, bringing her a cup of tea so strong Clementine thought her teeth would melt away.

'It's often the men who can't manage,' Sister Milner told her. 'We women are born to suffer. We cope.'

For some reason, it made Clementine think of Elizabeth, and how she coped. Was what she was doing the best way through her grief? Everyone found their own way, she supposed. She put her teacup back on the bedside table and burrowed down under the sheets, but she couldn't sleep. For all the nurse's insistence that everyone on the ward needed to rest, there was far too much going on. New arrivals, departures, weeping, arguing, trolleys rattling, emergencies, patients calling out for help, someone falling out of bed, all topped up with the nurses discussing everything and everyone at full volume.

'I want to go home,' she told Alfie when he came back at six.

'But who will look after you?'

'I'll be fine.' The baby was gone. What more could go wrong? 'I can lie in bed at home.'

'I'll take you to Foxwood,' he said. 'My mother is surprisingly good in a crisis. And there's Daisy.'

This time, Clementine didn't protest. The thought of a comfortable bed, Daisy's cooking, the fresh air, the peace... Foxwood would be the perfect place to convalesce.

Three duck-down pillows. An open window with sharp, fresh autumn air. A view over the rolling countryside, fringed with trees turning to flame. A satin eiderdown. Earl Grey tea in a bone china cup covered in green dragons. A hot-water bottle to hug. A freshly laundered Liberty lawn nightdress. A battered Georgette Heyer.

Clementine had never known such comfort and luxury. And the kindness. Perhaps that came from understanding loss, but Alfie's parents had been so openly comforting.

'You poor darling.' Elizabeth had embraced her with a warmth Clementine could feel right in her bones. And even Michael, implacable, reserved Michael, had patted her shoulder and looked her square in the eye as he offered his condolences.

'Whatever you need,' he said. 'Just say the word.'

Not that her own parents hadn't been kind. They simply hadn't known what to do or say. They were bewildered by the news.

'Do come home, of course,' her mother had offered, but Clementine knew her presence would be a worry, would disconcert and agitate them.

Elizabeth took it all in her stride. She knew exactly

what Clementine needed at every minute of the day, and never avoided the subject. People's reactions were strange. Henrietta's, for a start. She hadn't been to see her, as if a miscarriage was somehow catching – she was expecting too, two months ahead. She hadn't even telephoned. She had sent a magnificent bunch of white roses with a stiff little card: 'Get well soon.' Clementine had been irritated. She wasn't ill.

'People are very squeamish,' said Elizabeth, ripping up the card on her behalf. 'You feel as if it's your duty to emerge from the experience unscathed and never to speak of it again.'

'That's exactly it!' exclaimed Clementine.

'I should know. I had several misses. Two before Edwin. One in between him and Diana. Then another before Alfie. So you see, I'm living proof that it doesn't necessarily mean disaster.'

'I'm so sorry,' said Clementine. 'About your babies.'

Elizabeth gave a thin smile. 'You would think it would gird me for what was to come, wouldn't you? But it didn't, actually.'

She gave a little shrug. Clementine's eyes filled with tears. She couldn't even begin to imagine.

'And I'm so sorry,' she said, a catch in her voice. 'About Edwin. You must have been very proud of him.'

It was all coming out in a tumble, but she'd never had the chance to speak about him before. She had no idea if she was saying the right thing. Elizabeth seemed to be in a trance as she listened.

'You would have loved him,' she said at last. 'Everyone did. And thank you.' She reached for Clementine's hand. 'Anyway, the important thing is for you to rest. I put you back in this room because I thought you'd like to have peace and quiet. For the time being, at least.'

Clementine hadn't considered how she would feel about sharing a bed with Alfie again. It was thoughtful of Elizabeth to recognise she might want privacy for the time being, and to put her back in the pretty bedroom she'd had that first night. It would be strange, for she loved being in bed with him, the scent and the heat of him next to her, and they usually made love every night, always before they went to sleep, and often again when they woke, even once she became pregnant. But for now, she was grateful to be treated like an invalid. She needed time to get to know her body again and to decide when she was ready. She had wanted to ask Sister Milner when the time would be right, but she hadn't wanted to seem prurient.

'You'll be seeing the doctor in four weeks, so best keep yourself to yourself until then,' was all the nurse had told her.

And actually, Alfie went back up to town after two days, which was a relief because he'd been following her around like a little shadow, asking her if she was all right every two minutes.

'Darling, don't breathe down Clementine's neck. If anything goes wrong, Dr Boxer can be here in a trice. Go back to work and come home at the weekend.' Elizabeth was very firm with him, and Clementine felt relieved. The last thing she wanted was to push him away when he was so very caring, but she was fine. She needed to be quiet, that was all.

Diana's reaction was the most disconcerting. She had

rushed into Clementine's bedroom, her hair and eyes wild, and grabbed her hands.

'I'm so sorry,' she said. 'I'm so sorry.' She could barely speak, she was crying so much.

Clementine was puzzled. It was strange for her to be so emotional, given that she'd kept Clementine very firmly at arm's length since the wedding. Why was she so upset? Or was she like Alfie, her grief ready to erupt at the slightest provocation? She consoled her sister-in-law, thinking it was as if Diana had lost a baby, not her.

Diana headed back to Birch Farm, staring at the road ahead through the windscreen, her stomach churning. She didn't really believe she'd caused it. But the very fact she'd had such wicked thoughts about the baby, when she'd first heard about it, made her feel sick with guilt.

She'd been furious when she'd found out Clementine was expecting. Though not surprised. Of *course* Clementine had caught straight away. That's the kind of person she was. Lucky. Everything fell into her lap. No doubt Alfie had only had to look at her to get her pregnant. When she'd heard the news, Diana had wondered if she'd already been expecting when they got married. Was that why it had all happened so quickly? Either way it wasn't bloody fair. Maybe she'd lose it, she had thought spitefully, then felt shocked that she could think something so awful.

But she *was* awful. She knew she was, by the way people looked at her. Her mother especially. Elizabeth couldn't hide the irritation on her face sometimes, especially when they rubbed each other up the wrong way. Diana couldn't help provoking her. She could feel herself doing it. She was like that poem from Alice in Wonderland. She only did it to annoy, because it was the only way she ever got any attention. Being nice never got her any.

When had she turned into that kind of a person? She hadn't been difficult as a small child. She had danced through Foxwood like a little sunbeam, delighting everyone. But when Edwin had gone, everything changed. Her world was never going to be the same. Her beloved brother was never going to twirl her around and tell her she looked beautiful. Marrying Rory had seemed the best solution. A neighbouring farmer, pretty well off, easy enough to keep happy. And she'd thrown herself into the horses, because at least they gave her a reason to get up in the morning, at least they needed her, and she could hide behind them, pretend she had a purpose, even though every day she became more and more unsure of the world and her place in it. For after a year, when there was no sign of a baby, she convinced herself that God, or whoever, was determined there should not be anyone else like her in the world because there was enough ugliness already.

And now, whenever Rory lumbered in and asked for a cuddle – his word for *it* – her stomach lurched, not because she found him repulsive, but because she found herself repulsive. And she pushed him away. That wasn't fair on him but she couldn't think what to say to explain herself.

She was a misfit, she thought. Even Clementine fitted into the family better than she did. She tried very hard to hate her but it was impossible, because she was incredibly nice and not in a sickly way either, because you could easily hate someone for being cloying. What was wrong with her? she wondered for the millionth time.

The trouble was, she didn't know what she wanted. She thought about the last time she'd felt happy. During the war, she decided, which was odd, but it had given her purpose, working at the factory, and she'd felt like someone, and her father had taken notice of her, which he didn't now, not really. He wasn't horrible to her, but they weren't close like they had been when they'd worked together, rallying the troops. And she knew that was partly her fault, for keeping her distance and being tricky. She knew jolly well that a baby would solve all that, because they always did, they were like glue, but the thought of deciding that's what she wanted and then trying again and then still not getting pregnant was a horrible prospect. She wasn't brave enough for month after month of waiting and wondering.

She sighed. If only Edwin was still here, she could talk to him. He'd always listened to her, and given her good advice. She certainly couldn't talk to Alfie about anything like that. They weren't nearly as close as she and Edwin had been.

She missed him so much, she thought, tears blurring her eyes again as she turned into the drive of Birch Farm. That was the root of it, of course. How could she ever be truly happy again without Edwin around, teasing her, making her laugh, understanding her? That was when something inside her had broken, the day he died.

14

After a week at Foxwood, Clementine was feeling a little stronger, both physically and emotionally, and a trickle of kindness from various corners had restored her spirits. Ben had sent a cake down from Fortnum's and Alexandra a basket of fruit. *Please let me know when you are next in town*, her note had said. Daisy had embroidered her a little heart on a white handkerchief, and had brought it to her, shyly.

'It's something to remember the baby,' she explained. 'So as not to forget the poor little thing.'

She burst into tears and Clementine went to hug her then burst into tears too, touched by the girl's thoughtfulness.

'It's all right, Daisy,' she said. 'These things happen.' She was echoing Sister Milner.

'They shouldn't though, should they?'

'No.' Daisy's response was heartfelt, and Clementine thought about the fiancé she had lost, and how she looked after them all and never complained. How did grief make some people selfless and others transgress?

Daisy looked at Clementine gravely. 'It's what this house needs. A baby.'

And she hurried away, suspecting she had said too much. Clementine watched after her. She was probably right. Babies put everything into perspective.

Henrietta had phoned her, eventually, in floods.

'I kept picking up the telephone to call you,' she said, 'but I didn't know what to say. Oh, Clementine. It's too awful. I can't bear it. I wish I was nearer.'

'Oh, I'm so pleased to hear from you.' Clementine felt relieved. She didn't want the miscarriage to come between her and her friend. 'I'm coming up to London next week to see Dr Shaw. Let's meet for lunch.'

She spent the afternoon writing thank-you notes on Foxwood notepaper. Cream vellum with a crest of a fox at the top. The black ink flowed beautifully across the thick paper, and it made her feel better, almost as if she was drawing a line under the whole sorry affair. *Thank you so very much for your kind thoughts. It means the world to me and Alfie at such a sad time.*

'There should be some stamps in the bureau,' Elizabeth told her. 'If we've run out, I can get some more when I go to Breverton later.'

Clementine headed into the little sitting room. It was fast becoming her favourite room in the house, so much more cosy than the formal drawing room next door. She loved curling up on one of the sofas, reading a book, watching Joey and Maurice pottering about in the garden. And everyone came here at six o'clock for a drink before dinner. It was clustered with beautiful things, family photographs and mementoes and ornaments, like an Arbutus museum.

The bureau was tucked into a corner underneath a window, a pretty writing desk with an inlaid lid which lifted to reveal one large drawer, inside which were several smaller drawers with mother-of-pearl knobs. She made her way through them. The third was a little stuck, and she had to tug at it. It was full to the brim with pieces of card, stacked so haphazardly that the drawer was jammed, so she pulled them out to make them tidy.

They were invitations. Dozens of them, on thick white card with a gold edge. As she sorted through them she gradually realised they were all different, but all to the same event:

ON THE LONGEST NIGHT OF THE YEAR
THE PLEASURE OF YOUR COMPANY
IS REQUESTED AT
THE SNOW BALL
FOXWOOD
NR BREVERTON
SOMERSET

Each one was illustrated, with the year inscribed in the top right-hand corner. There were garlands of holly and ivy, intricate snowflakes, fir trees, candelabras, a horse-drawn sleigh, a snowman, skaters, robins, a sugar-plum fairy, a plum pudding, each one painstakingly drawn in pen and ink. The very last one was dated 1939, and on it was a jolly Father Christmas sitting with his legs spread out in front of a fireplace, a glass of port in his right hand.

'We never sent that one in the end.'

Clementine jumped. She hadn't heard Elizabeth come in.

'I'm sorry – the drawer was jammed. I was just looking for the stamps –' How awful, if Elizabeth thought she was snooping.

Elizabeth picked up the invitation. 'Edwin drew it in the summer, before war broke out, when we still had hope.' She sighed. 'The Snow Ball's been a tradition in Michael's family for years. They started it before the first war. It was always on the longest night – December the twenty-first...' She trailed off, lost in the memory. 'Edwin started decorating them when he was about twelve.' She leafed through them. 'See – there's his first.'

She showed Clementine a stack of beribboned Christmas presents piled up on a sledge. It was definitely less polished than the later ones, but Edwin's talent still shone out.

'It must have been great fun.'

'Oh, it was. Everybody from around here came, and friends from London, and we dressed up in white and ate and drank and danced and laughed until we collapsed. It was hysterical. Bodies everywhere, tucked into every nook and cranny. It took weeks to get ready but it was worth it, even if it did go in a flash...' She looked down at the last, unsent invitation once again. 'It didn't seem right to hold it that year, once war broke out. And as the war went on, of course, there was rationing and no one wanted to travel, although perhaps it would have done us all good. We could have done something smaller perhaps. We could have made do. But we didn't.'

'That's understandable.'

'If Edwin had still been here, he would have made us revive it, that very first Christmas after the war ended.' She looked at Clementine, her eyes diamond-bright with tears. 'It was his ball, really, by the end. He took over the organising, when he was about eighteen. He loved dressing up, dancing, pretty girls...' Elizabeth was lost in her memories.

'It seems a shame,' said Clementine eventually, 'to stop it for ever. When it was a family tradition.'

'I know. And Edwin would be furious with us. I can hear him now. *What's the point in moping, just because I've gone?*'

Clementine paused for a moment, cautious, because she didn't want to encourage Elizabeth to embark on something she might regret, but the ball had captured her imagination. She pictured fires burning bright, candlelight, tables groaning with food, guests arriving at the door, the pop of champagne corks...

'Perhaps it's time to revive it?'

Elizabeth looked down at the invitation. 'The invitation's here, ready to be printed. We'd just need to change the year.'

'I could help,' offered Clementine. 'I need something to do.'

She had decided she wouldn't go back to the gallery just yet. She still had a tendency to get weepy when she least expected it. And she was rather glad of the break. Clementine was far from lazy, but losing the baby had been a shock. Nothing like that had ever happened to her before.

Elizabeth clasped her hands together, deep in thought for a moment. 'We could start small,' she said. 'Just to see how it goes, to get everyone back into the swing of it. It would be the perfect way for you to meet everyone you haven't met yet.'

Was this a dig at her, for not wanting a big wedding? Clementine didn't think so. Elizabeth wasn't one to take a swipe. She was surprisingly easy-going. And immensely kind. Quite the opposite of what you expected when you saw her, for she was effortlessly glamorous, like an exotic bird flittering through Foxwood. She fascinated Clementine. She seemed such a mass of contradictions, bouncing from warm and caring and concerned to vain and nervy and aloof in the blink of an eye. Perhaps that was what having an affair did to you? Harbouring a secret like that meant you never quite knew how you were supposed to behave.

'How many people, do you think?' she asked her now.

'Let's say ... sixty?'

Clementine blinked. That didn't sound small to her.

'Drinks, dinner, dancing,' Elizabeth went on. 'We have bowls of punch everywhere and a huge buffet, and breakfast before everyone leaves, of course, to send them on their merry way.' Her face clouded. 'I suppose I'd better ask Daisy what she thinks.'

'I expect she'd love it.' Clementine thought Daisy always seemed happiest when she was cooking for a crowd.

Elizabeth nodded her agreement. She tapped the invitation against the palm of her hand. 'I'd better speak to Michael first. Then Daisy. If I get their seal of approval, then we can get going.' She smiled at Clementine. 'Thank you. I would never have thought of it if you hadn't found the invitations. And you're right. It absolutely is time.'

She pulled out another of the drawers and extracted a stamp. And then she was gone, a whirlwind with a mission. Clementine flicked through the remaining invitations, imagining all those years when the house rang with music and laughter. The ball was just what the house needed, to chase away the last lingering shadows and bring the light back in.

'I think it's a terrible idea.'

Elizabeth was shocked. It wasn't like Michael to put his foot down about something. He was usually so easygoing, and went along with whatever she planned. But he almost threw the invitation back at her, flicking it onto the side table next to the sofa. The fire had been lit, and he was three sips into a Scotch and soda before dinner. It had seemed the perfect time to broach the subject, when he'd shuffled off the burden of the working day and was starting to relax.

'What do you mean?'

'Those days are gone, Elizabeth. It won't ever be the same.'

'Of course it won't be the *same*. But we can make it something new, something different. And I think it's what Clementine needs, after losing the baby. It will give her something to do while she's here.'

Michael wouldn't look at her. His jaw was clenched, his frown getting deeper and deeper by the minute.

'I'm not happy about it.'

Elizabeth sighed. 'Well, if you're not happy, then of course we shan't have it.'

He didn't reply. His little finger was tapping on his whisky glass. Was that an indication that he was impatient for her to leave now the conversation was over? Not that it had been much of a conversation. She frowned. They'd been getting on so beautifully since the wedding. He'd seemed much more relaxed, and they'd even talked about

Edwin a few times without him closing up. But this evening, he looked like a stranger.

A sudden chill went through her. Did he know something? He couldn't possibly. There was nothing *to* know, not anymore.

'I'll see you at dinner,' she said, her voice low. He gave a brief nod, and she picked up the invitation and left the room, trying her very hardest not to close the door too hard. She wasn't the sort of woman to lose her temper when she didn't get what she wanted.

She went up the stairs in a daze. By the time she reached her bedroom, and sank onto the cool of the satin eiderdown, she knew exactly what she was going to do, even though she knew she shouldn't. But the urge to see him, to hear him, was overwhelming. He was the one who calmed her jangling nerves, who soothed her, who made all her worries melt away. He was a salve to her troubled soul. Like a secret drinker, she knew it would only be a temporary fix, and that the ensuing guilt would be a bitter hangover, but like a secret drinker, she couldn't resist. More than three months, she'd been without him now, but tonight her need for him was sudden, and sharper than ever.

She picked up the receiver and asked the operator to connect her. Then there was the agony of waiting for him to pick up the phone. He could be anywhere. Abroad even. He often nipped to Paris or Berlin or Florence. It rang and rang.

And then he answered.

'Jasper.' Everything she wanted was in the way she said his name. It was a plea for comfort. A plea to be held. To be taken.

'Elizabeth.' His voice was wary. Perhaps even a little hard.

'I need to see you.'

He sighed. 'You know this isn't fair. You know I won't say no.'

'I know.'

'Is this really what you want? You were pretty adamant last time we met.'

He was hurt. Of course he was. And she wasn't being fair.

'Just lunch. I think I'll go mad otherwise.'

'You've driven *me* mad.'

'Friday?'

There was silence for a moment. 'I'll book a table.'

'Not in public. I'll cry.'

'I'll organise something here, then.'

She needn't go to bed with him. She simply wanted to talk. To try and make sense of the rest of her life.

When she put the receiver down, she felt a sliver of distaste, the same distaste she had once felt for adulteresses. She had never approved of women who had affairs. If things weren't going well, to the point where you couldn't bear it, you did the honourable thing and left your marriage. You didn't have your cake and eat it.

She jumped as she heard a tap on the door and Michael opened it, popping his head round with a tentative smile.

'All right if I come in?'

'Of course.' She sat up, pushing at her hair and rearranging her clothes as if she'd been caught *in flagrante*. Did she look guilty? He came and sat on the edge of the bed.

'I'm sorry about earlier,' he said.

'Never mind.' She shrugged as if it didn't matter, although it did. The tenor of his objection to the ball had shocked her. It was so unlike him.

'I'm a bit preoccupied, that's all. About the factory. Things are pretty tough at the moment. Pretty tight.'

Elizabeth felt a different kind of anxiety tug at her. It had been a long time since he'd said anything like that. He wasn't the kind of man to bring his work worries home. Sometimes she thought she should pay more attention to what was going on at the factory, instead of assuming it was ticking along.

'What do you mean?' she asked now.

'We've got a lot of competition,' Michael went on. 'Lots of new companies with new ideas. And I'm worried we might lose our market share. We can't just rely on our old contracts. We need to shake things up.'

'Surely that's what Alfie's going to do when he comes back? He's been in London. He knows what's what.'

Michael was silent for a moment. Then he spoke.

'I've been wondering about selling the factory.'

'Selling it?' Elizabeth was shocked. She had no idea that Michael was feeling under so much pressure. The factory had been in his family for generations.

'I think we'd get a good price. And I think it could be life-changing.'

'But what would we do? What would you do?'

Michael laughed. 'Nothing. We wouldn't have to do anything. That's the point. There'd be enough for us to live our lives exactly as we wanted.'

'But what about Alfie? And Clementine?'

He shrugged. 'I'm still not sure Alfie's heart is in the factory. I worry he's coming here out of duty. I'd love to give him the chance to do what he wants with his life. There'd be enough for him to invest in his own business. Expand Coupe, if that's what he wanted. I know how much he's loved working with Freddie, and how torn he's been.'

It wasn't often that Elizabeth felt taken aback. She hadn't seen this coming at all. Life-changing, he'd said. A life-changing amount of money. But no matter how much it was, it wouldn't buy her what she wanted. It was the loss of her son that made her so unhappy. Other than having Edwin walk back through the door, there was nothing she would change about her life. She loved Foxwood. She loved Michael, deep down, despite her behaviour. She felt a dart of shame at the phone call she'd just made.

She thought about what Michael had said about Alfie. About him only coming down here out of duty. She'd been so looking forward to him and Clementine moving down to Foxwood, and the prospect of a new baby. She'd been devastated by Clementine's miscarriage, for the two of them, mostly, but for herself too, for the thought of a little one in the house had lifted her heart no end. To be a doting grandmother, she thought, was probably the antidote she needed for her indiscretions. Grandmotherhood and adultery didn't sit well together, she thought. Grandmotherhood was going to save her from herself.

Selling the factory would mean Clementine and Alfie staying in London. Or buying a house somewhere else entirely. She couldn't bear the thought. But was she being selfish? She shouldn't expect everyone to arrange their lives just to do what made her happy. She must put *them* first.

Michael. Alfie. Clementine. Diana. She mustn't forget about Diana.

'What do *you* think?' she asked, to buy herself time while her brain raced over the implications, weighing up the pros and cons.

'I must admit I like the idea of no more pressure. Of doing some travelling, perhaps. With you. A summer in the South of France. Autumn in Italy.'

She could see it in her mind's eye. The two of them, surrounded by matching pigskin luggage, dressed immaculately, checking into an elegant hotel somewhere on the Côte d'Azur. Campari by the pool, lobster for dinner, dancing in each other's arms on a terrace as the moon rose. It was a tempting scenario.

But then what? And why? They couldn't spend the rest of their lives checking into glamorous hotels. It would be meaningless.

'I think we would fall apart, without the factory,' she said. 'I think you underestimate how important it is to this family, to be part of the fabric of Breverton, to have all those people to look after. We've done it for five generations, after all. We can't just cut loose. What would be the point?'

Michael didn't answer for a while. Then he turned and gazed at her.

'I'm touched you feel like that. To be honest, I thought you'd jump at the chance. I thought it might be what you needed. A fresh start. Because don't think I haven't noticed you're not happy.'

'Of course I'm not happy!' Guilt made her sharp.

'I know, I know. But it feels like something deeper, your unhappiness. Not just Edwin.'

'How can anyone expect me to be happy? Ever again?' She was on the verge of tears now.

He took one of her hands in his. 'I know, my darling. I feel the same. But perhaps we should try to bring a little light into our lives. The two of us will always share our grief, but can't we share some hope? Perhaps a change is what we need?'

Elizabeth's eyes were brimming over. 'I don't want a change.' As soon as she'd said it, she knew it was true. The rhythm of life here was what held her together. The familiarity of each season, from chill dark January through to jaunty spring, blowsy summer, mellow autumn and then the comfort of Christmas.

Michael was silent for a moment.

'If that's what you really think, I'll carry on. I do love the factory. I never walk through the door without looking forward to the day ahead, even when times are hard. I love everyone who works for us. And if Alfie really is keen to come on board, eventually he can take on a lot more, so I can slide graciously into retirement when the time is right.'

'That sounds perfect.' By then, hopefully, Alfie and Clementine would be firmly ensconced here with their children.

'And by the way, you're right about the ball. I'm sorry I was such a curmudgeon, but you took me by surprise. It's the right time to bring it back. It doesn't have to be about reliving the past. It's about a new beginning.' He stood up. 'Let's send the invitations out.'

He left the bedroom, and she fell back on the eiderdown and stared at the ceiling. Her hand strayed to the warmth of the satin where Michael had been sitting. Their relationship was taking a turn, she realised. Grief had caused fissures in their marriage – of course it had; what marriage could withstand such devastation without suffering some damage? – but perhaps it was going to become something new, something richer and deeper. By opening up to her, he'd proved he trusted her, she thought. He took her seriously and he wanted her opinion. It was possibly more than she deserved.

And he'd said yes to the ball. Suddenly the weeks running up to Christmas took on a life of their own. Her earlier insecurity had evaporated. She stared over at the telephone. She didn't need Jasper's reassurance now she had so much to think about. She should probably phone him. Call off lunch. But she couldn't now she'd begged him. That would be unkind, and perhaps they did need a chance to say goodbye properly, and thank him, actually, for he had been kind and supportive as well as everything else. She'd have a quick lunch with him – *very* quick – and then head to Liberty on Regent Street to look at Christmas things.

She got to her feet as she heard Daisy ring the gong for dinner below. A crisis averted and a ball to organise. She floated down the stairs, imagining the banisters wreathed in ivy and the hall below filling up with guests.

The Snow Ball was back.

15

The following week, Clementine climbed on board the 8.17 to Paddington at Breverton station and settled down, gleeful to find an empty compartment. She might have it to herself for part of the journey at least. Bliss.

November had taken over from October in Somerset, pushing away the golden days of low, honeyed sun and bringing its own particular grey to the countryside, like a monotonous bore at a party. You had to put up with it until December arrived, with its promise of jollity ahead, and in the meantime, you had to find ways to cheer yourself up.

She took out her notebook to write a shopping list of the things she needed to buy after she'd been to Dr Shaw. Charming though Breverton was, it left a lot to be desired on the sartorial front and wasn't up to much where toiletries were concerned either. And Alfie needed new pyjamas. There were one or two unacceptable holes in his current pairs, and although she could see the funny side they were bordering on the indecent. Not that she was the kind of wife who dictated what her husband should wear, but he would look very enticing in a smart new pair. She'd go to Fenwick, she decided, as that was near Brown's Hotel where she and Henrietta had arranged to meet.

She looked up as the compartment door slid open and a woman and a young boy fell in, laughing and breathless.

'In here, Ted, we've got it to ourselves. Oh!' The woman stopped as she saw Clementine. 'Sorry. Do you mind if we sit here? We nearly missed the train.'

'Of course not.' Clementine smiled at her.

The woman was dazzling, with porcelain skin, pewter eyes and a tumble of red hair that fell halfway down her back. Clementine was intrigued. As the woman settled into the seat opposite, Clementine took in every detail. Her clothes were a little worn, but she had a certain style: a Scotty dog brooch on the lapel of her fitted jacket, a polka-dot dress with a full skirt underneath, high heels. The little boy had a coat on that was too big and trousers that were a little short, and a corduroy cap that swamped him so she couldn't see his face. As he swiped it off and chucked it on the seat next to him, Clementine saw his features and her heart skipped a beat.

Edwin. He was the spitting image of Edwin. Elizabeth kept enough photos of him as a young boy around the house for Clementine to recognise the similarity. The swoop of gold hair across his brow, the straight nose, the full top lip and the slight dimple in the chin. She tried not to gasp but she couldn't help putting her hand to her mouth. Aware that the woman had seen her gesture, she cleared her throat to feign a cough.

'Excuse me. It's the steam.'

She patted her chest. The woman gave a polite nod as

if accepting her excuse, then busied herself getting exercise books out of the bag she was carrying.

'Right, young man. We need to do your spellings, if you're going to miss school today. We might as well do them now as Mr C won't have a clue if you get them right or wrong. He can't spell to save his life. Specially not in English.'

The boy gave a dramatic groan and slumped back in his seat.

'Telephone,' said the woman.

'T-E-L-Y –' the boy began to recite.

'Nope.'

He frowned. 'It must be.'

She shook her head. 'Tel-E-phone.'

He harrumphed. 'T-E-L-E-P-H-O-N-E.'

'Correct! Apology.'

'Why do I have to apologise?'

The woman laughed, a glorious cascade of sound that came from deep inside her. 'Spell it, you nit. Apology.'

'A-P...'

Clementine sat back in her seat and pretended to be looking at her list while they went through the spellings. She was racking her brain to try to find an explanation for the two of them. The Arbutuses had lived in Breverton for generations. Was the little boy a cousin of Edwin and Alfie's she hadn't been told about? Entirely possible, she supposed. Perhaps the son of an estranged brother of Michael's that they never talked about? There was probably a lot she didn't know about the family.

'Muuuum.' The boy had had enough. 'I've done ten. No more.'

'We need to do twenty.' Her voice was firm.

So she was his mother. But who on earth was she? Logic told Clementine the woman must be from Breverton, as that's where she'd got on, but her accent wasn't the soft Somerset burr she'd come to hear in the shops. She was London through and through.

Was there some family secret that they were keeping from her?

After about half an hour, the spellings were finished and put away, an apple was produced and eaten and the boy announced he needed the lav.

'Come on, then.' His mother jumped up. 'Let's go and find it.'

She looked at her bag, then over at Clementine.

'Would you keep an eye on our things?'

'Of course.'

'Ta. Come on, Ted.'

She bustled him out of the compartment. Clementine stared over at the bag, her mind racing. She wondered how long she had got before they returned, if she had time to look in the bag and find a clue.

This was going to be her only chance to get at the truth. Unless she struck up a conversation, but even then she couldn't quite imagine what line of questioning would get her the answers she wanted. She stood up, crossed the space between the bench seats, hooked open the bag with her finger with one eye on the window to the corridor, then looked inside.

A purse. A hairbrush. Another apple. And underneath, a sheaf of paper wrapped up in a red ribbon. It was too dark inside the bag. She'd have to open it wider. It didn't take long for a small boy to have a wee. She had seconds.

She prised it open, letting the light from the window fall onto the page at the top.

The Towpath Gang. Stella Knight.

On the seat next to the bag was the boy's spelling book. Clementine flipped it open. Inside the front cover was printed *Breverton Infants' School* and underneath was a list of the people who the book had belonged to over the years. At the bottom was his name.

E. Knight.

Could his name be Edwin? Was that what Ted was short for? And if so, did that mean what she was wondering? Could he be Edwin's son? A wartime indiscretion? Edwin had been engaged to an American heiress when he died. Stella – Clementine presumed that was her manuscript inside the bag – was not an American heiress. Far from it.

She shot back to her seat and sat down with moments to spare. Ted threw back the door and bounced inside, then headed for the window as Stella gave her a smile of thanks and settled back down. They were about to stop at Newbury station. The train came to a wheezing halt and all along the platform doors clanged open and shut.

'How much longer, Mum?' asked Ted.

'A good hour, love.'

'I'm hungry.'

Stella looked anxious. 'You'll have to wait till we get to Mr C. He'll make you some lunch.'

He gave a melodramatic sigh and flung himself back in his seat, clutching his stomach. 'I'm going to die of starvation.'

'I don't think so,' said Stella with a grin. 'You had a massive bowl of porridge before we left. Here, have my apple.'

'I'm not apple kind of hungry.'

'Well, you can't be hungry at all, then.'

Ted rolled his eyes but he was grinning. He wasn't being a brat, he was just a little boy. Probably a bit bored and probably, yes, a bit hungry. They were gannets at that age.

Clementine opened her own bag. She had a bar of Bournville chocolate tucked in there. She took it out and held it up to Stella surreptitiously, so Ted couldn't see it. She raised an eyebrow, nodding her head towards him and mouthing 'Can I?'

Stella's eyes widened and she smiled. She held up her finger and thumb to indicate a little bit, then nodded.

'I wonder,' said Clementine, leaning towards Ted, 'would you share this with me? I can't possibly manage it all, and it needs eating up.'

Ted stared at the red wrapping with the golden paper. Then looked at his mother.

'Go on, then,' said Stella. 'And say thank you to the kind lady.'

'Cor, thanks!' Ted looked thrilled as Clementine snapped off a chunk and handed it to him.

The train clattered on. Stella stared out of the window, her fingers worrying at a chain around her neck, sliding a ring along its length, backwards and forwards. Clementine looked more closely. She knew that ring. It was an exact copy of Alfie's signet ring. The bloodstone with the pelican engraving. She would know it anywhere. Michael wore one too, so presumably Edwin had had one. Could that be his? Or a copy?

She could hardly start grilling Stella about where she'd got it. She turned over all the clues in her mind. A child the spitting image of Edwin. A ring with the family crest. A stunningly beautiful woman. None of it made sense.

She longed to say something, but she didn't want to crash into their little world. Stella and Ted seemed to have such a special bond. Clementine wondered with a pang if she was ever going to have that experience herself. She tried not to worry about the miscarriage, and whether it would happen again, but seeing the two of them, the way Ted was leaning against his mum, munching his chocolate, and her absent-mindedly running her fingers through his hair, without him seeming to mind – it sent a sharp longing through her. So she stayed quiet.

As the train drew into Paddington, Stella jumped up, grabbing her bag and Ted's hand.

'Come on, love. We need to hurry.' She darted a smile at Clementine. 'Thank you so much for the chocolate.'

And they were gone.

Perplexed, Clementine made her way out onto Praed Street and put her hand up for a passing taxi. It glided to an obliging halt.

'Harley Street, please,' she said, and clambered in.

16

One day, Stella thought, as she and Ted climbed into the Underground carriage beneath Paddington station, she would tell him about London Lives. One day, she would show him the poster, still rolled up and kept in a cupboard in Mr C's shop. One day, when he was old enough – for it was a complicated story – she would tell him how she and his father had fallen in love.

The week war broke out, in September 1939, Stella had joined the Auxiliary Fire Service as a volunteer.

'Ooh, la la.' Monsieur Corbières looked alarmed. 'You cannot argue with fire.'

'I won't be fire-fighting,' she said. 'They don't let women near the actual flames. I'll be manning the phones or making tea or doing a bit of first aid. I won't be in any danger.'

She didn't tell him she was applying for her HGV licence. She could already drive, after all, and was used to a van, as she'd delivered mince and sausages to the schools around Wanstead often enough. They'd need back-up drivers when it all kicked off.

Monsieur Corbières surveyed her gravely and gave her

a nod. She thought she could see the glitter of a tear in his eye. It was the same look her father had given her when she'd gone back home last Sunday and told him what she'd done. Silent acknowledgement of her bravery and spirit. Their saying nothing said it all: they knew they were all in for a rough ride, even if nothing had happened yet and everyone was calling it the Phoney War. It was the ones who babbled on about it all being over by Christmas who were the fools. Silence was chilling, for it was motivated by fear, and the memory of what had happened first time around. Both her dad and Monsieur Corbières had seen things they never talked about. This time around, Mr C was too old, and being a butcher was a reserved occupation, so they wouldn't be called up. Stella wasn't going to stand by and do nothing. That's not how you won a war.

As for thinking it would all be over by Christmas, she'd seen the preparations that were being made: the intense training, the equipment being shipped in, the buildings being taken over to provide extra fire stations... the Government weren't doing that for no reason. It was only a matter of time, and the only answer was to be prepared. They were braced.

A few weeks later, she came into the shop to find Monsieur Corbières and Edwin deep in conversation. Her heart tripped over itself, like a schoolgirl snagging her feet in a game of French skipping. She couldn't pretend she hadn't thought about him ever since the last time he'd been in. Ever since he asked her for dinner and she turned him down. Every time she saw her poster on the Underground she wondered what he'd been thinking about when he'd painted it. And she thought about his invitation, and how she wished she'd had the courage to accept it, only she'd known how it would end if she did. She'd just be a plaything, picked up then discarded when the novelty wore off.

'It feels cowardly, somehow. Prancing about on the side-lines waving a paintbrush. I'm not sure it's right,' Edwin was saying. 'I don't want anyone saying I'm hiding behind a canvas.'

'But it's important,' said Mr Corbières. 'This is how people will know what's going on.'

'I suppose so.' He shrugged. 'And I suppose it's an honour to be asked. Not everyone will be. Sir Kenneth Clarke and his cronies won't invite anyone if they think they're a conchie. Or a communist. Though I don't know why I was chosen, to be honest.'

Monsieur Corbières gave one of his Gallic exclamations. 'Because you are *populaire*. People will flock to see your work. There will be exhibitions. You will be famous.'

Edwin didn't look convinced. Stella had to hand it to him. He wasn't full of himself. He smiled over at her.

'Hello, Angela.' It was the name he'd given the girl on the poster.

Stella rolled her eyes.

'What's happened?' she asked.

Edwin held out a piece of paper. 'An invitation, from the War Artists' Advisory Committee.'

She took it from him and scanned the words. 'That's a real honour. Isn't it?'

'I suppose so. And I like the *idea* of it. Getting up close to the action and getting it down on paper. But there's something about it that feels... ignoble.'

'Ignoble.' Stella had never heard the word, but she

knew immediately what he meant. People were being scathing about signing up to the fire service, making out it was an easy option, a way of dodging the real conflict, so they would be even less impressed by an artist painting pictures of war instead of fighting.

'You've got to show people the truth, though,' she said to Edwin now. 'If they don't see the reality, they start making things up. And that's not going to help, is it? You've got a duty to paint the real picture, so people can see the war for themselves.'

He stared at her, as if he was only just realising the importance of what he'd been tasked with.

'Maybe you're right. Maybe it is my duty.'

'Of course it is. They haven't asked you because they want to keep you safe. They've asked you because they need you.'

'You're sharp, Angela.'

'Don't call me Angela.' She gave him a defiant glare, but her eyes were laughing. 'You know my name.'

'I do.' He stared back at her, his eyes laughing too. 'All right, Stella. I'm only going to ask you one more time if you'll come out for dinner. Just to say thank you. Nothing untoward.' He could see she was hesitating, so he closed in. 'And it would be very churlish to refuse a man who's being sent up to the North of Scotland to paint battleships. We've all got to do things we don't want to for the war effort.'

Stella gave in, laughing. 'If you insist. Never let it be said I haven't done my duty.'

He looked delighted. 'I'll pick you up from here at six o'clock.'

When he'd gone, Monsieur Corbières gave her two ten-shilling notes.

'You won't have time to go home and change. Go and find yourself a dress.'

'Twenty bob! But that's nearly as much as I earn in a week.' She'd never had this much disposable income. She gave nearly all her wages to her landlady for her board and lodging. Anything left over she spent on art materials.

He shrugged. 'You can pay me back one day. When you sell your first picture.'

Stella laughed. He had such faith in her. He was helping her with her drawing when it was quiet in the shop. He would set her a challenge, then make her draw it again and again until it met his exacting standards. It was a frustrating process, but she was getting better. And last week he had actually praised her. She had brought in a sketch she had done of her landlady, sitting at the kitchen table peeling a mound of potatoes.

'That is good,' he said, gazing at it. 'Do not change a thing.'

And for the first time, she wondered if perhaps she did have talent.

She looked down at the money now, uncertain. The thought of going out with Edwin dressed in her dreary blouse and rather shapeless skirt didn't fill her with joy. A new dress would give her confidence. A new dress! She didn't think she'd ever actually been out to buy a new one. She made most of her clothes, or re-modelled other people's cast-offs. To actually walk into a shop and choose one was unimaginable. And it seemed wrong, given what was happening in the world.

Monsieur Corbières could see her hesitation. 'Stella, if

the outbreak of war is to teach us anything it is to live while we can. Get the dress. Go.'

She didn't need telling again. She ran to the Underground, blowing a kiss at herself as she went past the poster, and caught the next train to Oxford Circus, where she headed to the bargain basement at Selfridges. She might have been handed more money than she knew what to do with but she liked to shop clever. She spent half an hour browsing through everything on offer. She didn't want anything too showy. She wanted something she could wear again. She certainly didn't want to look as if she'd rushed out to buy something new. She wanted something that suited her, that made her look as if she was the kind of girl who wore a dress to work that she could go out for dinner in afterwards. Luckily, she'd still been in her coat when Edwin had seen her, so he wouldn't notice she'd changed.

On a sale rail, she found just the thing. It was in deep burgundy crepe with white polka dots, cut on the bias but quite plain, except for ruffled sleeves that swished when she walked. It fitted perfectly. Her shop-girl shoes weren't ideal, but hopefully his eyes wouldn't travel that far down. On the way back, she ran into Boots and bought a lipstick almost the same colour as the dress. Most people would disapprove of a redhead wearing burgundy, but she loved the way her hair looked against the fabric, and her dark lips against the pale of her skin.

Back at the shop, she modelled her purchases for Monsieur Corbières. He nodded his approval, but yet again she thought she saw the glint of a tear. It was the war. Everyone was trying to put on a brave face, but underneath, emotions ran deep.

'He is a good man,' he told her at ten to six, when she reapplied her lipstick. 'A lot of artists are not. They think too much about themselves while they are painting. But Edwin thinks about others.' He paused for a moment. 'He helped me a few years ago, when I was too fond of the...' He mimed drinking. 'He was not afraid to tell me I would lose everything if I didn't change.'

Stella took in his revelation. Monsieur Corbières had always played his cards close to his chest, and although she suspected he had a story to tell, he never gave her much of a clue about his past. Even now, he didn't give much away, except to reassure her.

Although, in fact, it made her more nervous.

'I don't know if I should be doing this,' she said. 'He belongs to another world, Mr C.'

'He will make you his world,' he replied.

Stella was startled by his vociferousness, his belief in the two of them. She wasn't sure he quite understood what she meant. He was French, after all. He probably didn't appreciate the English class system, and how hard it was to move from one to another, especially if you were trying to go upwards. It rarely worked. Maybe they were more open-minded in France, but the English were snobs, and protected their stations in life as fiercely as they were now about to protect their country. Everyone pulled together in times of adversity, but there were still rules. Shop girls didn't belong with posh boys, even if the posh boy was taken by the idea at the time. Edwin might think himself smitten but, in time, the people around him would make life so difficult their relationship would crumble.

In which case, why was she putting herself through

this, if she was so convinced it was doomed to failure? Monsieur Corbières' words of earlier came back to her.

'We have to live while we can,' she told herself. This could be the first and last time she ever went out with Edwin. Who knew what would happen, either to him or to her, in the coming months?

'Do you want to slum it?' he asked her when he arrived. 'Or push the boat out?'

She had no idea what either of those meant. After all, his slumming it was probably her idea of pushing the boat out.

'What about something in between?' she said.

'Good idea,' he said. 'I'm not all that fond of hovering waiters and seventeen knives and forks. We'll go to my new favourite place. It's just opened and it's rather fun.'

The restaurant was dark and wood-panelled with lots of tiny rooms leading into each other. It was noisy and spirited and no one took any notice of them whatsoever as they were led to a table in a shadowy corner. They ate goulash and potatoes roasted in goose fat and red cabbage. The waiters were friendly and slapped everything on the table with aplomb and kept topping up their glasses with wine that made her completely forget her nerves. Edwin was so charming, and funny, and attentive without being suffocating, that she completely relaxed.

'This is as good as my dad's beef,' she said, prodding the melting chunks of meat with her fork. 'I always know when people have cut corners, but this is first rate.'

'That's a great skill to have.'

'I don't have many.'

'That's not true,' Edwin contradicted her. 'Corbières says you're a very good artist.'

'Does he?' She gaped at him.

'And if he says you are, you must be. He's very critical.'

'He is,' she said. 'He makes me do things over and over. To the point where I never want to pick up a pencil or a paintbrush ever again.'

'You're lucky to be taught by him. He's better than going to art school.'

'But that's my dream.'

'Trust me. Stick with him and you won't need to go. He was a very well-respected painter in Paris. His work went for a lot of money.'

'What happened?'

Edwin sighed. 'A woman. She betrayed him. He was painting her in his studio. They fell in love. Well, he thought they did. He lost his heart to her. But her real lover was a bandit. She let him in one night and they stole everything he had ever painted. He never saw her again.'

'Oh, poor Mr C. That's terrible.'

'It broke his heart. He has never painted since. And he left Paris, convinced he was a laughing stock.' Edwin looked genuinely pained. 'He came to London and opened the shop. And if he finds someone he likes, he takes them under his wing. Teaches them everything he knows. And inevitably, they go on to be a huge success.'

'Did he teach you?'

'Sadly not. I discovered him too late. He says I've developed far too many bad habits for him to have any impact.' Edwin laughed, then looked serious. 'But you must stay learning with him. He is a wonderful teacher.'

'Blimey.' Stella took a sip of her wine, thoughtful. No wonder Mr C was so intense, so insistent that she re-do everything, so many times that she lost her judgement and couldn't tell if what she was doing was better or worse. But he usually seemed pleased in the end.

'I probably shouldn't have told you all that.'

'I won't tell him you told me. But I understand him better now. He can be tricky sometimes.'

'Oh yes.'

'Though he's always lovely to me.'

'He thinks a lot of you.'

'Does he?'

'You should show me your work some day.'

'Not yet.' Stella laughed. She couldn't imagine showing Edwin anything she'd drawn.

He was looking at her very intently. Her heart was bashing about inside her chest. She still couldn't believe she was here with him. He was unlike anyone she'd experienced. She'd had a few boyfriends but they bored her quickly, for they never seemed to want much from life apart from football and a few pints and the obvious, and they certainly didn't want to talk about art or books or what else might be out there. Going to a film was as exotic as it got, or maybe the dance hall on a Friday.

Edwin darted from topic to topic, and was interested in her thoughts and opinions. And he seemed genuinely interested in her.

'What do you like to paint the most?'

'Things that catch my eye. I like detail. I found an old sheep skull last time I went to the country. I loved drawing that. And my dad's motorbike. I wanted to paint it so you could smell it. And people. I like painting people.'

He nodded. 'Me too. Which is why I was pleased I got commissioned for the Underground thing.'

'Oh yeah. By the way. You owe me for that.'

'What?'

'I usually charge two bob for a modelling session.'

'I painted you from memory.'

'I don't care. It's still me, so I reckon you owe me at least half a crown. Sixpence extra for not asking first.'

She couldn't keep it up. She burst out laughing at the expression on his face. He looked completely flummoxed. When he realised she was joking, he laughed too.

'Touché,' he said. 'I should have asked.'

'Yeah,' she said. 'It's bloody annoying when people come up to me.'

'Don't you like being sort of famous?'

'I do not,' she said. 'I hate being the centre of attention.'

'But people must look at you all the time.'

She was getting embarrassed now. She didn't know what to say. She wanted him to stop staring at her like that. Yet at the same time she didn't.

'Let's go,' he said.

She nodded, her cheeks burning, and he looked over at the waiter and signalled for the bill. She wondered what was going to happen next. He led her out of the restaurant, taking her arm as he came around to her side of the table, and she wanted to melt into him, here and now. Was it written all over her face, how she was feeling? Could everyone in the restaurant see?

The anticipation was a kind of blissful torture as he led her along Greek Street and into the shadowy silence of Soho Square. A breeze rustled softly in the branches overhead and it sounded like the whispers of a hidden audience waiting to see what happened next. A new moon hung over them, slashing the dark sky with its silvery crescent. He stopped under a tree, turned, and leaned back against the trunk. She was two feet away from him, unable to tear her gaze from his. Her heart was thumping.

'Stella.' He said her name like a sigh. 'There's something I must tell you.'

Instinct told her she wasn't going to like it. 'What?'

'I'm engaged to be married.'

Of course he was. Why on earth had she thought he might be a free man?

'Oh,' was all she could say.

'She's called Meg and she lives in America and I won't be able to see her until the war is over. We were supposed to be getting married this summer.'

It was like a punch in the guts. She wanted to take her fist and drive it into his stomach, so he could feel what she was feeling. 'Why are you telling me this now?'

'I can't lie to you.'

'Then why did you ask me for dinner?' It was cruel, making her feel special, giving her a taste of what might have been.

'It was honestly to say thank you. I knew you were spoken for, so I didn't think anything of it . . .'

'I'm not spoken for,' she said with a sigh. 'I wouldn't have come out with you if I was.'

He turned this revelation over. 'I didn't think it would be like this.'

'Like what?' It was obvious what he was talking about. She could feel it, even now, despite herself, the electric thread of attraction.

'You know,' he said.

He went to touch her, but she stepped back.

'Don't touch me!' she whispered. If he touched her, she'd be lost.

Silence hung heavy between them, for neither of them knew what to say, but neither could pull away.

'We can still be friends,' he said eventually. 'I don't want to lose you.'

She gave a snort of impatience. 'What's the point of that?'

She looked at his beautiful face, those green eyes, those treacherous lips. She should have trusted her instincts. She should have listened to the voice in her head. She'd let down her guard, and now she'd had a glimpse of something she would never be able to forget, and nothing would ever live up to it. What a fool.

'Thank you for dinner,' she said, staring right into his eyes without a smile, then, turning on her heel, she walked away.

Now, as Stella and Ted hurried along Lamb's Conduit Street towards the shop, she recalled Monsieur Corbières' fury the next day when she'd told him what had happened.

'I had no idea,' raged her employer. 'He has never told me of a fiancée. I would never have let you go if I'd known.'

'It's not your fault, Mr C. And it doesn't matter.'

'I will box his ears.'

The little man was puce with indignation and she couldn't help laughing at the thought of him trouncing Edwin, who was a good foot taller than he was.

'Never mind. I'll survive. But you can serve him next time he comes in.'

'I will ban him from the shop.'

'Don't do that. He's a good customer. And it was only dinner. He never made me any promises.'

She didn't want him banned from the shop. She wanted to see him again, even if she couldn't have him.

And here they were now, back at the place that had changed her life. The shop looked just the same as it had done the day she had first gone in there, a hopeful young girl with impossible dreams. And it looked as if her dreams might be coming true, for today she had a meeting with Harriet Banham at a well-known publishing house.

'Here we are, Ted,' she said. The bell pinged as they stepped over the threshold, and there he was, Mr C, so much older, frighteningly so, but still with those bright eyes that missed nothing.

'My assistant is here!' he cried out in delight as Ted flung his arms around his waist.

'I need to go,' she said, knowing she was leaving her son in safe hands. 'Or I'm going to be late. My appointment's in twenty minutes.'

'*Vas-y!*' He waved his hand at her. 'Off you go. Good luck!'

She headed out of the door, knowing that they would be lost in their own world while she was away. The two of them were as thick as thieves when they were together, and she felt guilty that wasn't more often, for Mr C was as close to a grandfather as Ted was ever going to get. But after today, maybe things were going to change.

17

From Lamb's Conduit Street, Stella headed deeper into the streets of Bloomsbury, flanked by gracious buildings either side, until she emerged into Bloomsbury Square. She slowed down, counting the numbers of the houses, looking for the one she wanted. And there it was, with a dark red door, the brass plate on the wall announcing Godolphin Publishing.

Inside, she presented herself to the receptionist and went to sit in the waiting area. She looked around at the framed book covers, in awe of the familiar names, the striking illustrations that made them into bestsellers that would be tucked into bookcases in homes all over the country. Even getting this far was thrilling. She didn't dare to imagine her own name up there some day. This was one small step in the next adventure. Whatever happened, it would have been an experience. She mustn't get her hopes up too much.

The building was much busier than she thought it would be. She'd expected an air of hushed reverence, but there were people running up and down the stairs, in and out of the door, talking and gesticulating, greeting each other with cries of enthusiasm. They all seemed so excited by what they were doing, and she found the butterflies in her stomach had doubled by the time Harriet Banham appeared in front of her. She was incredibly tall, with pale hair the colour of butter cut off at the jawline and wise eyes behind heavy spectacles. She was wearing a blue corduroy dress, with ropes of amber beads slung round her neck.

'Stella?'

Stella jumped up and held out her hand. Harriet took it and squeezed it tight.

'I'm so thrilled to meet you. Did you have a good journey? Did you come on the train? You must be dying for a cup of tea. Annette, could you bring us up some tea?' She called over to the receptionist, who nodded. 'I've got some shortbread too, if you're ravenous. I can't make it to lunchtime without a couple of fingers.'

They headed up the stairs and into a tiny office no bigger than a cupboard. A desk took up more than half of it, piled high with manuscripts.

'I'm the lowest of the low,' laughed Harriet. 'I'm the most junior editor, so they've stuffed me in here. They call it the Broom Cupboard. But never mind. Sit, sit. You get the comfy chair.'

She ushered Stella into a very low armchair that was spilling its stuffing. Outside the window, Stella could see the square, the trees becoming bare, a weak sun trying to push away the dishwater sky. That was how she felt, as if she was trying to push away her own darkness.

Harriet folded herself into a not very comfortable-looking ladderback chair behind the desk and lifted up the sample chapters Stella had sent her a few weeks ago.

She had been astonished to find a letter waiting for her at the post office less than a week later, asking her to come in.

'So.' Harriet waved the chapters at her. 'Tell me more about the Towpath Gang. I love them, by the way. I think I said that in my letter. What inspired you to write about them?'

Stella took in a deep breath. This might be the most important speech of her life. She had to get it right.

'I live on a canal boat. In Somerset. And there's always something going on. I wanted to capture the rhythm. The freedom. The adventure. The unwritten rules. It's another world. There's nothing like it, waking up early in the morning. It's still at first. And quiet. But then when you start listening, all life is there. It's just me and my son on the boat.' Stella paused for a moment. She saw a flicker in Harriet's eyes, but no raised eyebrow. But she knew there would be questions. Inevitably. 'One day I thought – what if there were children living on a boat? What if their parents weren't there, for some reason, and they had to survive? What if they only had each other, a little gang of brothers and sisters. And it's about them finding out how the world works, and how there are good people and bad people, people who judge and people who . . .' She took a deep breath. 'People who don't. People who care.'

As Harriet regarded her with a steady gaze, she hoped she was one of the latter. She ploughed on.

'And what I really want to do is help give children their childhood back. For them to roam free and explore, to build dens and rope swings and roast sausages on an open fire and swim in rivers. I think for a long time we've been led to believe the world is a scary and dangerous place, but it's not. There is so much to discover...' She trailed off, astonished to see Harriet wiping away a tear. She laughed, uncertain. 'It's not supposed to be sad. It's supposed to give hope.'

'I know,' said Harriet softly. 'And that's what's made me cry. Because it's *exactly* what children need. The spirit of adventure. And yours is the first thing to come across my desk that really captures that. I've got a very important job, because by bringing the right books to the next generation I can help mould how they think, and behave, and help them make sense of the world. I think the Towpath Gang would be an incredible influence. They leap off the page. Both the words, and the pictures. You've done something very special.'

'Oh.' Stella hadn't been expecting such a positive reaction. 'Thank you. I've got a few more chapters,' she said, rummaging in her bag. 'I was going to post them, but I thought I'd bring them today.' She pulled out the manuscript and placed it on the desk. Harriet grabbed it eagerly and started leafing through, smiling as her eyes raked across the pages, taking in the words, the hand-drawn pen-and-ink illustrations. Then she looked up, laying her hands over the top of Stella's precious pages as if to stop anyone else from looking at them.

'The thing is, Stella, I could offer you a deal here and now. But as you've only given me a few chapters, it wouldn't be as big an advance as if you'd finished the book, because it would be more of a risk. I need to know you can structure a story, that it would have pace and a satisfying ending.'

Stella's mind was racing. A book deal? Had she actually

said she might offer her a book deal? She had to prove she was up to the challenge.

'I've been doing a serial for a children's magazine for a while now. *The Ditch Babies*.'

'I know. You explained that in your covering letter, so I went and got a copy of the magazine.'

Stella was impressed that Harriet had done her research.

'Your stories are delightful, but a whole book is a very different proposition. Anyone can start a book, but not many people have the stamina to finish. How long do you think it would take you?'

'A month, perhaps two? It's the drawings that take the time.' Was that too long? She couldn't rush it.

'Then I'm going to have to be very patient.' But Harriet was smiling. 'I'm guessing you don't have an agent?'

'No.' Of course she should have an agent. How unprofessional.

'You should get one. It's not really in my interests to tell you that, because they'll probably want to take *The Towpath Gang* to other publishers, to get you the best deal. But I promise you, no one will look after you better than I will. I've got a lot to prove.' A determined look came into her eye. 'I'm new to this job and this would be my first acquisition. I know that's a risk for you, but I have a lot of people with a lot of experience here to give me advice. And I'm horribly ambitious. I'll stop at nothing to make a name for myself.' She laughed. She shuffled the pages back together, lifted them up and held them to her heart. 'I'm not asking you to make me any promises, because I can't make you any, yet. But I hope I'll get first refusal on *The Towpath Gang*.'

By now, Stella was determined that the two of them

would be working together until the end of time. She loved Harriet's openness and honesty, and the way she had completely understood what she was trying to do.

'I'll get working on it straight away.'

'Good. Now, would you like to go for something to eat? We can relax. Chat a bit more.'

The apple on the train had been a long time ago. Stella thought about Ted and Mr C. They would be absolutely fine, she reassured herself. As long as she and Ted were on the six o'clock train from Paddington, all would be well. They'd have to walk home in the dark, but she had her torch. Why not?

18

'Well, I think you're all right to get back on the horse. Back in the saddle, if you're with me.'

Dr Shaw's eyes twinkled at her, and for a moment Clementine thought he was actually going to slap her on the thigh, as if she was a cow at a county show. She swung her legs off the examination table before he could think about it, and sat up.

'Thank you.'

'That'll put a smile on your husband's face, I'm sure.'

'The fact that I'm in good health and there's nothing wrong? Yes, I'm sure it will.'

He gave her a sharp glance, not sure if she was being sarcastic. She smiled sweetly, for she might need Dr Shaw again before long and, in her experience, doctors were all as bad as each other in the way they spoke to you. She preferred a nurse any day of the week. But it was a relief, to know there was no real reason either for the miscarriage or why she couldn't get pregnant again. Alfie would be relieved, for he'd been terrified, treating her like a piece of broken china that had been glued back together but might fall apart again at the slightest touch.

Dr Shaw stepped away and swished the curtain back into place. At least he had the decency to allow her some privacy while she put her clothes back on.

'I shall look forward to seeing you again in the near future.' His voice floated over the top of the cubicle.

'I hope so.' Clementine snapped her stockings back into place. 'Thank you so much, doctor.'

As soon as she left, she felt lighter of heart. She hadn't realised how much worry she'd been holding inside her. She was longing to get back home and tell Alfie the good news, but she had to get to Browns' Hotel to meet Henrietta.

Browns' was Clementine's second home. It was supremely comfortable with a touch of grandeur that made you feel cosseted, a deliciously hushed atmosphere and excellent service. It was where she met her parents whenever they came up to London, and now Henrietta was ensconced in Berkshire it was the perfect place for the two of them, for they could park themselves on a sofa for hours and hours and no one hurried them, but would bring along whatever took their fancy – a cup of Lapsang Souchong, or a pink gin.

Henrietta was already there, in the depths of a sofa the size of the *Queen Mary*, presiding over a large silver teapot, a brace of bone china cups and a cake stand stuffed with dainty sandwiches, scones and a selection of cakes. Clementine flopped down next to her.

'What a day! Feed me. I'm absolutely ravenous.'

'What have you been up to?'

'Oh, not a fat lot.' Clementine pulled off her gloves and reached for the teapot. 'But I did get the thumbs-up from Dr Shaw.'

'Well, you'd better get on with it, then. You need to catch up.' Henrietta patted her own stomach. 'Pass me a ham sandwich, would you? And how's life at Foxwood?'

Clementine knew she had to be careful what she divulged to Henrietta. She loved her friend dearly but discretion was not Henrietta's watchword and she valued gossip over loyalty. Clementine knew this because time and again Henrietta would tell her things she shouldn't, and it wasn't because she knew she could trust Clementine to keep her mouth shut, it was because she lived for the thrill of people's reactions on being told a salacious snippet. She simply couldn't help herself.

And both of the secrets Clementine was keeping close to her chest were potentially explosive. Her mother-in-law's affair, for a start – whether or not it was still going on she couldn't be sure, but she felt the information heavy inside her, and it affected how she viewed Elizabeth. She wished she didn't know, for it tarnished her trust, and that was not what she wanted.

As for today's discovery, she really hadn't had time to mull over what it all meant.

Henrietta would be beside herself with glee at either of the revelations, but Clementine might as well take out an advert in tomorrow's *Telegraph* as confide in her. So instead she told her about the Snow Ball.

'The twenty-first of December? I'm going to be mammoth! I'll be like a snowman,' Henrietta wailed.

Clementine helped herself to a slice of Battenburg. 'Nobody minds. It'll be fun. And I'll make sure you get a room at Foxwood. Everyone will be billeted all around Breverton.'

'Oh, yes please. I certainly don't want to end up at

your sister-in-law's. She's a caution. What on earth's the matter with her?'

'Diana? I don't know. She's very tricky.'

Henrietta made a disapproving face. 'She's so unlike the others. I can't believe Elizabeth's her mother.'

'She's a funny one.' Clementine felt curiously disloyal, discussing Diana behind her back. Despite her sister-in-law's hostility, she felt protective of her. She was such a square peg, and she knew she was. It was almost as if she was proud of it. 'I don't think she's very happy.'

'So tell me more about the ball.' Henrietta was already bored of the subject of someone who held no interest for her. 'Will it be terribly grand?'

'Oh, I don't think grand. Just... fabulous. Everyone's to wear white. There'll be lots of wonderful food – Daisy, the cook, is a marvel. She's the one who did our wedding cake. Champagne, dancing till dawn—'

'So the wedding you didn't have, then?'

Clementine frowned. Henrietta could be so direct.

'You know I didn't want a fuss.'

'Oh, Clem. You need to learn to put yourself first if you're going to survive that family. They're going to walk all over you.'

'*We* didn't want a fuss,' Clementine corrected herself.

Henrietta fixed her with a stern glare. 'I know you. You'll be running around after them all, trying to sort their lives out. Just like you do Ben. Honestly, he's a grown man and he does not need you mollycoddling him.'

'I don't mollycoddle him. I organise him. That's what he pays me for.' Clementine was defiant, but Henrietta had struck a nerve. 'And anyway, I'm not working for him at the moment.'

'People like that know how to use people like you.'

'What do you mean, people like me?'

'You're too good. And kind.'

'You're making me sound like a doormat. And Alfie wouldn't ever use me. He doesn't have a manipulative bone in his body.'

'Just be careful of the women. Elizabeth. Diana. They know exactly how to get what they want.' Henrietta grinned. 'Trust me. It takes one to know one.'

And she bit into a miniature rum baba.

On the way home, Clementine mulled over Henrietta's words. Her friend was very perceptive, but she was also a harsh judge of other people and never gave anyone the benefit of the doubt. She was black and white, whereas Clementine liked to look under the surface, spotting the flaws, the insecurities, the nuances, for life was complicated. And she was very aware that people made mistakes, getting themselves into situations they couldn't control. She could imagine exactly how Elizabeth had fallen under Jasper's spell.

But was it any of her business? No. She felt burdened by the secret though, and guilty for keeping it from Alfie. You should never have secrets from your husband in a good marriage, she thought. Or perhaps you should? Perhaps there were things the person you loved should never know, to protect them. Alfie certainly didn't need to know about his mother's infidelity.

And then there was the mystery of Stella and Ted. What on earth was she supposed to do about them? At the moment, she was working on supposition, but the clues were screaming at her. Ted's likeness to Edwin, his name and the signet ring all suggested a connection – there were too many coincidences. But even if Ted was Edwin's son, what then? Stella obviously didn't want anyone in the family to know, but why not? Did she have the right to keep Ted from them? And if they did find out about him, what would happen?

19

Harriet whisked Stella into a booth in a busy trattoria a few minutes' walk away from the publishing house. A bottle of wine wrapped in raffia was plonked on the table in front of them along with a basket full of bread to gnaw on while they waited. People kept stopping by the table to talk to Harriet and she introduced Stella as her latest discovery.

'So tell me everything.' Harriet was slathering butter onto her bread. 'You're the most intriguing person I've met for a long time.'

'I've told you everything, really. I write and draw while Ted's at school. Or when he's in bed. And that's . . . it.'

She realised it was. She honestly didn't do much else. It was a lonely life in some ways, although she never really felt alone with Ted, they were such a little twosome. But it would probably drive most people mad. She'd trained herself to be stoic and self-sufficient and not want for much.

'Where did you learn to draw? Did you go to art school? You must have done.'

'No. I wanted to but . . . the war.' She gave a wry smile.

'It had been my plan but I was working, and volunteering for the fire service.'

'Golly. That was brave.'

'We all had to muck in, didn't we?'

'I like to think I'd have done something brave if I'd been older, but I was still at school. What did you do?'

'Organising, mostly. Making tea. But I did some driving too.'

If Stella shut her eyes, the chatter in the restaurant could be the buzz inside the school where their local fire service had set up camp. She'd loved the camaraderie, the banter between the fire fighters and the volunteers, the jokes that flew around even while they were preparing for a night of bombardment, the way the energy levels went up even higher when a call came in and it was all hands to the pump. Even if she didn't actually attend the fires, it was dangerous, for the school could take a hit at any time.

'That's incredible.'

Harriet was looking at her in admiration. She was leaning her head in one hand, her wine glass in the other.

'I'm just glad it's over.' Stella took another gulp of wine. She tried not to think about those days. It had been an extraordinary time, with intense relationships, split-second decisions to be made, constant adrenaline alternating with the flat tedium of waiting, waiting, waiting for the next attack, fuelled by tea and biscuits, gossip and snatched sleep. And sadness...

'And it's just you and your son on the boat?'

Stella suspected wine was making Harriet ask questions she wouldn't have asked in the office. Though maybe this was part of the interviewing process? Getting her to let her guard down.

'Ted's father was lost in the war. Towards the end.'

'I'm so sorry.'

'I'm never going to find anyone else like him. So I haven't even looked.'

It was the most she had talked about her private life to anyone for a long time.

Harriet frowned. 'Don't shut yourself away. You're too beautiful, too clever, too talented.'

Stella found herself blushing. She wasn't used to anyone taking any notice of her, let alone paying her compliments. 'I'm used to being on my own.'

'If you become an internationally bestselling children's author, you'll be beating them off with sharp sticks.'

'If...'

'I've got a good feeling.' Harriet clinked her glass gently against Stella's.

As the waiter arrived with bowls of steaming minestrone, Stella felt a surge of warmth. Perhaps all she'd been missing was a friend? Someone to confide in, and laugh with, to go shopping with and to get ready to go out on the town with, to share gossip and hopes and dreams? She didn't have anyone in Breverton, because she kept herself at arm's length from everyone. She supposed she was a recluse, and that wasn't really in her nature. She'd got used to her solitary existence over the years, but now, sitting at a table with someone bright and funny and interesting, it made her yearn for company. Harriet might be a few years younger, but she could already feel a bond between them, a connection.

Perhaps now was the time to spread her wings, climb out of the shadows, and be the person she was always meant to be so Ted could become who *he* was meant to be. And perhaps Harriet had the key. She walked back to Mr C's in something of a daze, full of minestrone and red wine.

'Send it to me sooner rather than later,' had been Harriet's parting words. 'With a fair wind we could publish next autumn, in time for Christmas. Oh, and any ideas for a sequel would really help. I think *The Towpath Gang* could run and run.'

20

When finally Clementine got back to the flat, having stopped off at Fenwick for pyjamas and a new blouse and some decent stockings, the air was filled with the smell of sausages and Alfie was pounding away at a pan of potatoes listening to jazz on the wireless. He dropped everything as Clementine came in.

'How did it go?'

'Dr Shaw's given me a clean bill of health. We've got to carry on as if nothing ever happened and just... see.' She gave a little shrug, and a bright smile.

Alfie pulled her to him, kissing the top of her head. She could feel the relief, flowing from her to him and back again.

'What do you think?' asked Alfie, turning back to the stove and scooping out a spoonful of mash for her to taste.

'Perfect,' she said. 'No lumps, nice and buttery.'

'Though maybe we should go out to celebrate?'

'No. I can't think of anything nicer than staying in with bangers and mash.'

Alfie had been brushing up on his cooking skills since

Clementine had moved into the flat. He'd gone out of his way to turn it from a bachelor pad into something more welcoming. He'd bought some cushions, and a wireless, and new plates and cups, and there was a bowl of rosy apples and he always lit a fire. She loved being at Foxwood but it was rather sweet, being all cosy just the two of them. She still felt a little raw after the baby thing, and didn't want to go out on the town, bumping into people they knew. All she wanted to do was kick off her shoes and flop into a chair. It had been a curious day, and she hadn't realised how worried she'd been about what the doctor might say. Alfie had wanted to come with her but she'd said no, she'd be fine, and had made light of it, but actually she'd secretly feared Dr Shaw might find something terribly wrong, so to know there was nothing awry was a huge relief. It was the first time in her life, as an adult, she'd felt vulnerable and not quite in control.

Over supper at the tiny kitchen table, squashed right up next to each other, they talked about the Snow Ball.

'I was only young for the last one,' said Alfie. 'Me and Freddie drank far too much cider cup and I was sick in the hydrangeas. Mum was furious. I can hold my drink a lot better these days.'

'I think it's a great undertaking for her. She's so excited. She's planning a pow-wow over Sunday lunch so we can delegate who does what. And work out the guest list.'

'That'll be a minefield. They always are. Isn't that why we stuck to a small wedding?'

Clementine laughed. It absolutely was. She finished her sausage and put her knife and fork together. She had to say something now or it would be too late. Maybe there would be an explanation?

'Alfie...' she said, and he looked at her in alarm.

'What is it?'

'I saw something strange on the train on the way up.'

'What do you mean?'

'A woman with a small boy. Alf, he looked just like Edwin. Well, you and Edwin. He was the spitting image of you both.'

Alfie laughed. 'How funny. Lucky boy.' His tone was light. Perhaps too light.

'And he was called Ted.' She paused. 'That could be short for Edwin, couldn't it?'

'Or Edward. Or Edmund. Or Theodore.' Alfie frowned. 'I'm not sure what you're getting at?'

There was a trace of tension in his voice.

'And the woman. She had a ring just like yours.' Clementine reached over and tapped the ring on his little finger. 'It was on a chain round her neck.'

His face gave nothing away as he glanced at the ring. 'Lots of people have signet rings.'

'But it had a pelican on it. That's unusual, isn't it?'

'It's just a coincidence, I'm sure.'

'I don't know. It seems strange. She was very lovely. She had the most incredible red hair.'

Alfie grabbed her plate and piled it on top of his. 'There's some tinned fruit salad, if you'd like it.' He stood up and took the plates over to the sink.

'Don't you think we should try and find out who they are?' Clementine persisted.

'Why on earth would we do that?'

'If you'd seen him—'

'You can't go poking about in people's private lives, Clem. Just because they look like someone.'

He seemed irritated, and definitely wanted the subject closed. Was it because she'd brought up Edwin, or did he know something more? Clementine wondered if she should push it further, then decided not to. For the time being, anyway. This was her and Alfie's first night together after their good news. It would be crass of her to spoil it.

Some up-tempo South American jazz came on the wireless. Alfie started dancing along. 'That reminds me – there's a fantastic band I've seen at the Flamingo Club a few times,' he said. 'The Havana Brothers All Star Jazz Band. I'll see if I can get them to come down for the ball. They'll get the joint jumping.'

Clementine put the train encounter out of her mind and joined in, singing along, and soon they were dancing away together, waving their arms in the air and clicking their fingers. When the song finished they collapsed onto each other, laughing, gazing into each other's eyes. She could feel his heartbeat, and the heat of him.

'We don't have to do anything yet,' Alfie said to her. 'If you don't want to.'

'Do anything?' She frowned at him.

'You know. In bed. We can wait.'

'Wait?' she said. 'Absolutely not. I've missed you. I've missed us. I'm not waiting any longer.'

21

It was gone eleven o'clock that night before Stella and Ted rolled into Breverton station – they'd caught the last train and it was the slow train, stopping off at all the tiny stations. Ted had curled up on the seat and managed to snooze, but Stella's brain wouldn't allow her to doze off. The unaccustomed wine had given her a thick head, so her thoughts felt sluggish as the events of the day played themselves back to her. Her elation was wearing off. Nothing was written in stone, and she had a lot of work to do, with no guarantee that Harriet would like what she had done. Surely if she'd liked *The Towpath Gang* that much she'd have signed her up straight away?

She hurried Ted out of the station and along the high street until they reached the bridge over the canal where they dropped down onto the towpath. As the lights of the town faded behind them, she switched on her torch. The beam was getting weak, flickering half-heartedly, and her heart sank. She'd meant to replace the battery the week before, but in her excitement at the trip ahead she'd completely forgotten.

Five minutes later it gave out altogether. She couldn't

believe how dark it was. Clouds were covering the moon and stars, and it was almost impossible to make out the towpath ahead.

'It's all right, Mum,' said Ted. 'I can see in the dark. I'm like a cat.'

She put her arm around his shoulders and hugged him. Her plucky and kind little boy knew she needed reassurance. They inched forwards along the muddy path, huddling into their coats as an insistent night breeze whipped up, bringing along with it the first few drops of rain. Ted was starting to cough, and she hoped it was just the damp air and not the nasty cough of last winter coming back already. She used the still water of the canal on their right to guide her along the path, hurrying as fast as she could. She needed to get him inside, get him dry and light the fire.

How could she have felt so elated earlier? This was her truth. She was all alone, bringing up Ted, living on a shoestring, only just able to keep them fed, clothed and warm, cutting herself off from anyone who might be considered a friend. She felt a rush of anger towards Edwin. How dare he die and leave her like this? She should have trusted her gut, and not succumbed to him in the first place. She was a fool to ignore her instincts. All her antennae had told her getting involved with a man like him would be bad news for her.

But then she wouldn't have Ted. The true love of her life. And at least on the boat she felt near Edwin, even if he was gone. She had to believe in herself. She had to believe her luck would change, that Edwin hadn't been a mistake, that she'd been lucky to have him in her life, if only fleetingly, those few precious meetings snatched in a time of huge conflict when everyone's lives had been turned upside down.

Finally they reached the boat. The canal was shrouded in a freezing fog that seemed to have made its way inside, and the windows were dripping. Ted was coughing non-stop. Stella told him to get out of his wet things while she lit the stove and put the kettle on top to make him a warm drink and fill a hot-water bottle. Her fingers were so cold she could hardly strike a match. Eventually, she got it alight and helped Ted into his pyjamas. How selfish of her, she thought, to go gallivanting with Harriet when she should have got them both back on an earlier train. She'd got completely carried away thinking she was some bohemian literary type who swanned about Bloomsbury and drank wine at lunchtime. What a fool.

'Keep your socks on and put your jumper back on then snuggle into bed, sweetheart,' she said.

If he got a decent night, he might be all right in the morning, although it was nearly midnight now, and she didn't think the snooze he'd had on the train counted towards the hours of sleep a growing boy needed. She slid the hot-water bottle onto his side of the bed and got herself undressed. She would never normally light the stove this late at night and leave it burning, but this was a one-off.

Somehow, even though it was Arctic, the milk had gone off, plopping into the cups of tea she'd made in rancid dollops. She threw them out. The sheets were like ice when she got into bed. Ted was shivering violently. It was impossible to get warm when you'd got this cold.

Oh God. She missed him so much her bones ached. Or was that the cold? She longed to feel his arms around her, the warmth of him. She shut her eyes tight and prayed for sleep. You can do it, she told herself. You can change things for the better. You've been given a chance. It's up to you to take it.

Edwin had promised this boat would keep her safe, whatever happened.

After Edwin told her he was engaged, Stella kept him at arm's length every time he came into the shop. The first time he visited, Stella had been in the stockroom and had heard Mr C give him a dressing down.

'I had no idea you were betrothed,' he'd stormed. 'I would never have let Stella go for dinner with you if I'd known. That is not the behaviour of a gentleman. You are lucky I am not banning you from the shop.'

Edwin had been suitably shame-faced, and had sent her a long letter from his posting in Scotland, apologising profusely, with lots of funny drawings that made her laugh. So she'd had to forgive him. She wrote back her own illustrated letter, showing him sketches from the idea she'd had for a children's story. His response was enthusiastic, and they fell into the habit of writing to each other by return of post.

She knew she was flirting with danger, for every time she saw his writing on an envelope that landed on the doormat in her boarding house, she felt hot inside, as if she might explode. She would snatch the letter up and run to the bedroom, for she needed to be alone with her thoughts. Very alone. Even though all he wrote about was how cold it was, and how much fun the sailors were, and what he was drawing. Nothing intimate.

The letters brightened the monotony of war. She knew

from the preparations at the fire station that bombing could start at any moment. They were never, ever to get complacent.

'The enemy want to lull us into a false sense of security,' the station master told them. 'Assume, every minute of the day, that a bomb is going to drop.' He pointed up to the sky.

Stella had been living on high alert ever since. She tried to instil the same watchfulness in her fellow lodgers at the boarding house, but they laughed. 'It's a phoney war,' they cried, and she rolled her eyes. Didn't they understand the strategy? Hitler's wiliness? He would want to cause as much damage as possible. Bomb the heart out of London.

Which was why it was important to live each day as if it might be your last.

And then, on 7 September, the Blitz began. Black Saturday. Bomb after bomb dropped on a London that had been braced yet not ready, for how could you ever be ready for such wanton destruction? Dockyards blazed, buildings burned and lives were snuffed out, just like that, with no rhyme or reason as to who was chosen. Soldiers and police and firemen and air-raid wardens and nurses and ordinary members of the public dug deep to drag survivors from the wreckage, to tend to the wounded, to put out fires, to restore some kind of order. Tight-lipped, bewildered, angry and determined not to be bowed, the city picked itself up, night after night. And Stella carried on, working at the shop, turning up for her shift at the fire station. Drawing, and her letters from Edwin, were her only escape.

And then the worst happened. A bomb fell on the butcher's shop, killing both her parents. Stella felt sick with guilt that she had hardly seen them since the war began. The war had been a good excuse for not travelling to the East End, but she knew, in her heart of hearts, that she had avoided going home because she was so determined to build her new life, and she couldn't bear their barbed comments. They obviously thought she thought she was better than they were, which wasn't the case at all, she was just... different. The life she wanted was different. And now they were gone, before she'd had a chance to prove herself and explain to them that all she'd wanted was a window into a new world, not necessarily a better one.

When Edwin came back on leave and heard the news, he didn't hesitate to wrap her up in his arms, in the big black coat that smelled of him.

'I'm so sorry,' he said. 'I'm so, so sorry.'

As Stella nestled into his chest, hot tears pouring down her cheeks, she never wanted him to let go.

Mr C surveyed them both gravely.

'Listen, both of you,' said Edwin. 'I've got somewhere safe in Somerset you can escape to. I'd feel much happier knowing you can get away from the city if you need to.'

Mr C shook his head. 'I am never leaving,' he said. 'They will not hound me out. London is my home.'

'Mine too,' said Stella.

'At least come and look at it,' Edwin pleaded with her. 'Come for the weekend. I'll be going to my parents. You can stay there for the night, see what you think.'

Stella looked uncertain. Mr C looked between the two of them.

'And what would your fiancée say?' he asked Edwin, protective of Stella to the end.

'I'm certain she would understand,' said Edwin, defiant. 'That I can't think of you both in danger without offering you somewhere to hide.'

Stella looked at Mr C for guidance. He shrugged. It was a kind and generous offer, she thought. And there might come a time when she needed to flee the city, and she might be able to persuade Mr C to come too. For them to have a safe place –

'All right,' she said. 'It can't do any harm to have a look, can it?'

Edwin nodded. 'Pack warm clothes. Hat, scarf, gloves. It can be a bit nippy.'

Stella stood outside the station the next morning, underneath where her poster had been. It had disappeared, replaced with something much more ominous. Over a million children had been evacuated from London, but some families were bringing their children home, against all advice. The poster showed a shadowy Hitler urging 'take them back' and a mother wrestling with the dilemma.

Don't do it, Mother. Leave the children where they are, read the slogan.

What would she do? wondered Stella. It would be awful to send your child off to the depths of the countryside to an unknown family, but that was better than putting their lives at risk, surely?

She saw a yellow sportscar pull up in front of her. There he was. She tried not to acknowledge the flip in her stomach. This was a fact-finding mission. An act of kindness. Nothing more.

He tucked her in under a scratchy tartan rug, for it was draughty in the car because of the canvas hood, the wind whistling in where it didn't quite fit. She felt like a queen as they drove up Regent Street to Piccadilly, past Fortnum's and the Ritz, and if you half shut your eyes and ignored the fact that the railings in Hyde Park had been taken down to be sent off to munitions factories, and the air-raid shelters that had been put up near Park Lane, it could be a normal day in the West End, double decker buses trundling along and people out shopping without a care in the world. They flew past Harrods – 'My brother's godmother, Alexandra, lives just behind, and uses Harrods like a corner shop,' Edwin told her – and soon they were on their way along the A4, past Windsor, and onwards down to Somerset.

A weak autumn sun had deigned to come out when they reached Breverton, bathing the little high street in rose-gold. It was Saturday lunchtime, and people beetled in and out of the shops. Stella was enchanted.

'It's like a fairy tale!'

Edwin looked at her quizzically. 'It's just a sleepy Somerset town.'

'I don't get out of London much. To Essex, sometimes. I used to go to the countryside as often as I could, to draw. But it's not like this. Imagine living here!'

He laughed. 'You might get bored. There's no dance halls. Not even a cinema.'

'I would never get bored.' Stella sighed in delight. How little she knew about the world, she realised. The furthest she had ever been was Brighton, with a man who had promised her the world, but only managed to offer her a cold sea, a hard pebble beach and a night of anti-climax in a dreary bed and breakfast. She had ditched him soon after and not ventured out with anyone else since.

Better to be on your own than to sleep with a walking disappointment.

At the far end of the high street, he turned off down a lane that ran alongside the canal. It was lined with tiny houses, and at the far end of them was a small field. He pulled in and parked, then jumped out and grabbed her case.

'We have to walk from here, I'm afraid. It's not too far. Bring the rug.'

She followed him along the towpath, mystified. They must have walked for nearly a quarter of a mile before a brightly coloured narrowboat appeared, painted green and gold.

'My floating palace,' he said proudly.

'That's not what I was expecting,' she exclaimed. 'Is it yours?'

He nodded. 'I bought it last year off a bloke in the Trout who needed some cash. It's my hideaway. No one else knows about it, not even my family. It's where I go when I want to get away from it all. I sleep and paint and watch the canal go by. You should see it in summer. Kingfishers, dragonflies, voles, swans...'

'*Penelope*,' Stella read the name along the side in golden letters.

'It's yours to escape to, whenever you want, if things get too dangerous in London. You and Mr C. Wait till you see inside.' He leapt on board and headed for the door of the cabin, unlocking it. She followed him down some rickety steps, into a long room barely six foot wide. The floor, walls and ceiling were lined with burnished wood, and it was kitted out with everything needed for life on board: a tiny kitchen with cupboards and a pull-down table, a pot-bellied stove, a run of benches covered in cushions, and at the end, a raised platform with a mattress.

'It's like a gypsy caravan!' exclaimed Stella.

'It's a wonderful piece of craftsmanship.' Edwin ran his hands along the wood. 'It might be cramped but there's a place for everything.' He lifted up a cushion on one of the benches and pulled up a lid to show storage underneath.

'Not cramped,' said Stella. 'Cosy.'

'It will be once I've got the fire going.' He pulled open the door of the stove and began to pile wood inside.

She looked around the cabin more closely. The curtains were in striped fabric like a deck chair, and the bed was covered in blankets and cushions, making a very tempting nest. There was a row of books, a shelf stacked with art materials, a cupboard full of tins and a considerable number of bottles – wine and brandy and beer. Some of Edwin's sketches were pinned to the wall. It was the perfect artist's hideaway.

Once he'd got the fire going, he stood up.

'Make yourself at home. Help yourself to whatever you want. I changed the bed sheets last time I left.' He nodded over to the bunk. 'Oh, and there's plenty to eat in here.' He picked up the small basket he'd brought with him. 'Ham. Cheese. Bread. Fruit cake. Tuck in. I'll come back and fetch you in the morning.'

For a moment, she felt as if she was being secreted away, rather, but she told herself it was the boat that was a secret, not her. Although what *would* his family, and his fiancée, say, if they knew Stella was here?

It was perfectly above board, she told herself. It was a kind gesture, to offer this hideaway to her and Mr C, and it was a comfort to know it was here, even if they would probably never take him up on his offer.

It was so quiet once Edwin had gone. Stella had never been somewhere so peaceful. She stepped out onto the deck, looking up at the still, grey sky that was the same colour as the flat surface of the water. She breathed in deeply, sweet air that held not a trace of traffic fumes or smog, just the sharpness of the smoke coming from the chimney. Overhead, the bare branches swayed, almost the only movement on this cold winter afternoon. She could immediately understand why he loved it here. There was nothing to distract you, just a silent beauty. She felt all her worries recede. Usually they were nibbling away at the corners of her mind, but suddenly it was as still as the canal.

She went back inside and pulled a sketch pad off the shelf, and a selection of pencils. Then she sat on the deck and began to draw. She was completely lost in her task, and all she could hear was Monsieur Corbières' voice in her head: *It's not what you put in, it's what you leave out.*

This was the first chance she'd had for a long time to concentrate on her children's stories. She was hopng to see if she could get them published in a magazine, but she needed a decent body of work before she could even think about sending them off. She was going to spend this weekend planning them out. Mr C had encouraged her, helping her work out how much detail to put in each picture to help illustrate the story, how to develop a style that was consistent – she had so much to learn!

As the light began to fade, the sky began to fill with a flock of birds that appeared as if from nowhere, pouring out of the clouds above her head. She had never seen so many, and they seemed to multiply before her very eyes, hundreds of them, swooping and swirling in an elaborate dance, like iron filings twitching around a magnet. Was this a portent? Was it the end of the world? Did they know something? She shivered, realising the temperature had dropped sharply in the past few minutes, but she couldn't tear herself away from the display. Suddenly it was over. They melted into the trees, the last of the light faded, and the world was almost black.

She hurried back inside to find the fire had gone out. With frozen fingers, she lit it again. The silence she had relished earlier was unsettling. The lamps threw sinister shadows onto the walls. She realised she had no idea of the time, for she wasn't wearing a watch, and there didn't seem to be a clock. Panic rose up inside her, and the urge to flee, but the dark outside was too terrifying. If she needed to run for help, where would she go? Back up the towpath to Breverton in the pitch-dark?

She told herself Edwin wouldn't have left her here if it wasn't safe. She found a glass and poured herself an inch of brandy, spluttering as it slid down her gullet and spread its warmth through her chest, then helped herself to a piece of fruitcake from the basket Edwin had brought. As the temperature rose and the brandy slid through her veins, she began to feel calmer. She pulled a book off the bookshelf – *Wuthering Heights* – cut another piece of cake, poured another glass of brandy, then climbed onto the bed, wrapping herself in an eiderdown. Soon she was as warm as toast, and a little bit woozy. The shadows receded and instead the cabin wrapped itself around her. She felt snug – snug as a bug in a rug, as her mum used to say. She felt a pang as she remembered her parents. It was almost the first time she had been truly on her own to grieve. She had been so busy with work and the fire station and the boarding house was so noisy. Besides, grieving almost felt like an indulgence, for there were so many others who had lost people. You were supposed to button yourself up and carry on. But for once, she allowed herself to weep until she felt she had no more tears.

Exhausted, she picked up her glass and her book and began to read, transported to the wilds of the Yorkshire Moors.

She started awake hours later. Edwin was shaking her arm gently.

'Morning,' he said as she opened her eyes.

'Is it?' She sat up, yawning. 'I must have slept round the clock. Must be the country air.'

'Shall I make you a cup of tea?'

'That would be just the job.' She realised she'd fallen asleep fully clothed, but maybe that was a good thing. 'Did you have a good time with your family?'

'Yes. Though I always hate leaving them.'

'Your poor mum.' Stella could only imagine how hard it was, letting your son go.

'She saw me, so she's happy.' He filled the kettle and put it on the stove. 'What did you get up to?'

'I did some drawing. Ate cake. Read.' She picked up the book. She'd lost her place. 'Oh, and I watched the birds. Hundreds and hundreds of birds, circling around.'

'Starlings.' He nodded. 'It's their party trick in winter. They do it before they roost.'

'I've never seen anything like it. I wanted to draw them but they were too fast...'

He made the tea and brought it over to the bunk. They

both sat on the edge, munching on the last of the fruit cake.

'Hey, I want to show you something,' he said, his eyes laughing.

'What?'

He put his tea down and tugged off half his shirt. Her eyes widened as he revealed his right arm, a tattoo emblazoned on his bicep.

'I had to get one, being around all those sailors.' It was a five-pointed nautical star, boldly inked in black and red. 'What do you think?'

'Oh my God.' She laughed in delight. 'You're crazy. Did it hurt?'

'Did it hurt?' He winced. 'Yes, it bloody did.'

'You poor thing.' She pressed a finger onto his skin. The tattoo had absorbed itself completely onto the surface, as if it had been there forever.

'I thought a star was better than an anchor,' he said lightly. 'Or a heart with *Mum* through it.'

'It's beautiful.'

'And it reminds me of you. A star for Stella.'

She drew away her hand. She could feel it, the heat between them, the pull.

'Don't,' she said.

'Don't what?' He widened his eyes, not averting his gaze.

'Look at me like that.' He knew exactly what he was doing. 'It's not fair. On me or her.'

He sighed, nodded, slid his arm back into his shirt and stood up. 'Would you like some scrambled eggs?'

And with that, the spell was broken.

While he cooked, she picked up her book again and

devoured another chapter of *Wuthering Heights*, completely captivated by Cathy and Heathcliff's doomed narrative. She felt safe, wrapped up in her nest, absorbed by the story, listening to the hiss of butter as it hit the pan, smelling the bread toasting.

When the eggs were ready, she put the book to one side with a sigh.

'It's not going to end well, is it?' she asked Edwin.

'I haven't read it,' he admitted, and for a moment she wondered, in that case, who the book belonged to. Who might have left it here? Of course he must have brought women to the boat. Maybe even Meg. But she mustn't allow herself to feel jealous. She had no right. She picked it up again.

'I want to try and finish it before we go.'

After they'd eaten, he got out his sketch pad, and drew her. Eventually she looked up and saw what he was doing.

'Don't draw me! I must look a sight.' She pushed at her hair.

He carried on sketching. 'My manager's badgering me for an exhibition. He says it's important for me to keep my own work going, not just immerse myself in battleships and barrage balloons.'

'He's right. Being a war artist will make you a bigger name. You need to make the most of it.'

He made a face. 'It seems wrong, to exploit something that's an honour for my own good.'

She frowned. 'I don't think you're exploiting it. They chose you because you're brilliant at what you do.'

'Maybe.' He looked down at his work. 'I'll take this home and paint it later.'

She jumped off the bed and came to look at it over

his shoulder. There she was, hair wild, cross-legged in the middle of the bed, holding her book. But she wasn't reading it. She was staring straight out of the picture, and the expression in her eyes told another story. Was that how she'd been looking at him? With naked desire, a half-smile on her lips? She was mortified.

'Oh, blimey. What a heap I look. Don't show it to the public, whatever you do!'

He laughed. 'We'd better start heading back. It's a bit of a drive.'

She packed up her things with a heavy heart. This had been the perfect respite. She had actually relaxed, and realised that she spent her life tense, braced for a bomb. It was good to know that something resembling the world as it had once been was still here, deep in the countryside.

As he locked up the cabin, he gave her the key.

'I'm leaving this with you. You can come here whenever you want. Promise me you will keep yourself safe.'

She took it, smiling her thanks. Why did he care so much? she wondered. But she was very grateful. Just knowing *Penelope* was here made her feel as if safety was within reach.

The next day at work, she showed the key to Monsieur Corbières.

'Perhaps you should go there now,' he said. 'You will be safe on the boat.'

She shook her head. 'That's not going to win us the war, is it? If everyone scarpers. We've got to show them that we all stick together, that they can't bully us. I'm not leaving everyone at the fire station. Or you.'

She stared at him, defiant, and saw there were tears in

his eyes. He reached out and put a hand on her shoulder, but he couldn't speak. She held the key out to him.

'Do you want to go? I know Edwin won't mind. I'll look after the shop for you.'

'*Non.*'

Neither of them spoke for a moment. Then Stella stepped forward and hugged the old man. He was frail beneath his serge jacket, and he smelled of tobacco and last night's wine. There was no need to say anything. It was too terrifying to speculate, because there was no point. They were all at the mercy of Hitler and his determination to bomb them into submission. But he had underestimated his enemy. They might be ordinary souls, but cowards they were not.

Stella put the key on a ribbon and tied it round her neck. It hung next to her heart, and every time she felt it, she thought of Edwin, and how kind he was to her. One day, she thought, she would go to *Penelope*, and he would be there, and they could sit on the deck and draw, then drink wine. And if her mind wandered a bit further, to them curling up in the bunk in each other's arms, well, she was allowed to dream. But for now, everyone had to hold their nerve.

22

At five o'clock the next day, Clementine and Alfie were waiting in the First Class lounge at Paddington. She'd travelled up Second Class, for she thought it was a terrible waste of money to go First, but he'd bought their tickets home.

'Darlings!' The two of them turned to see Elizabeth bearing down on them, a wide smile on her face. She was in a cream bouclé suit, carrying a clutch of shopping bags in her leather-gloved hands. 'I wondered if you might be on this train. I only decided to come up at the last minute. There were a few things I needed. And I wanted to look for something to wear to the Snow Ball. Part of me thinks I should wear one of my old dresses – I have so many from over the years. But it's nice to have something new, don't you think?'

Her voice was too bright, her information too detailed, for Clementine to believe her. Her shopping bags must be a deliberate distraction, no doubt hastily grabbed before or after a tryst with Jasper, for she had the aura of a woman who has spent the day with her lover. There was something wild in her eyes.

'Hello, Mum. Come and join us. Shall I get us all a drink before the train leaves? We've got just enough time.' Alfie looked delighted to see his mother. He reached out to take the shopping bags off her.

'Perhaps a small gin and tonic.' Elizabeth patted her hair once her hands were free, as if checking that it didn't look as if she'd tumbled out of bed.

'Just an orange juice for me,' said Clementine. She was half looking to see if Stella and Ted were anywhere. It was hard to believe it was only yesterday she'd spotted them on the train and become aware of their existence. There was no sign of them. Suddenly she felt exhausted by all the secrets she was carrying. She longed for her little bedroom at Foxwood, then remembered that she and Alfie would be back in their room now she had the all-clear from Dr Shaw. The thought cheered her, and she thought about waking up in his arms tomorrow, the familiar scent of woodsmoke that was beginning to define Foxwood for her drifting in through the window. There'd be bacon and eggs for breakfast.

The journey back to Breverton couldn't go quickly enough.

Once they were on the train, Elizabeth sank into the corner of the carriage and closed her eyes. The afternoon had turned into rather an ordeal, and she was utterly drained.

Jasper had lunch laid out beautifully on a little table in the flat. Ripples of smoked salmon, pale pink on green china, and triangles of buttered bread. Then *poulet anglais*, plump breasts of chicken smothered in a creamy sauce. He had a girl somewhere who came in to cook for him.

Perhaps she shouldn't have come, but it would have been rather cruel, to have phoned him *in extremis* and then cancelled. They'd had a strained hour together, when she'd told him how her family had to come first now, what with Clementine and Alfie coming to Foxwood and the miscarriage, and he had *cried*, which was absolutely awful.

'I'm not sure you realise what you mean to me,' he told her, and she had no idea what to say to console him.

And it was odd, for when she looked at him, she didn't feel a fraction of the attraction that had been so unmanageable for so many years. Once, she'd had an endless compulsion to feed the monster inside her, the lust, that deadliest of sins, the one that could destroy everything she held dear. No matter what she'd done to try and quieten its siren call, it had shouted louder than either her conscience or her common sense.

For years, she'd had two trains of thought in her head all the time. Whatever was going on, on the surface, and *Jasper Jasper Jasper* underneath, with a running commentary of either things that had happened with him or things that might happen, a cocktail of memory and fantasy. It was like being possessed. She had always thought of herself as sensible, and strong willed, but he'd reduced her to rubble inside. Yet to the casual observer, she was a sophisticated woman in control of her life.

She'd excused her behaviour to herself because of Edwin. But she realised now that was despicable, to somehow blame the death of her son for her weakness. There were plenty of bereaved mothers who behaved with decorum and didn't leap into bed with their dead son's best friend.

But it was done. Once and for all. She'd escaped as quickly as she could, bitterly regretting going to see him at all, and had met Alexandra in Liberty. Alexandra had looked at her suspiciously.

'Are you all right?' she asked. 'You seem *agitata*.'

'Oh, fine,' said Elizabeth, picking up a snow globe with a fox inside. 'There's just not all that much time to organise the ball, that's all. I'm out of practice.'

'You could do it in your sleep.'

Elizabeth brandished the snow globe. 'I'm going to get this for the mantelpiece.'

Now, she sighed as she looked at all the shopping bags in the luggage rack. She'd spent far too much money, trying to bury her guilt about Jasper.

'Mum?' Alfie was looking at her, concerned.

'Sorry. I was just thinking about what we need to get in for the weekend . . .' She trailed off. It was exhausting, trying to be normal. She took in a deep breath to try to calm her racing mind.

She looked at her daughter-in-law, her long lashes resting on smooth, pink cheeks as she slept, and her mouth curled into a smile. She had already come to love Clementine, she realised. Her kindness, her sense of fun, her sense of family – even though she didn't have Arbutus blood she felt like one of them. Like the daughter she'd never had.

Elizabeth sat up sharply. How could she have such a thought? She had a daughter! But Diana made such heavy weather of everything. What was wrong with her? she wondered. Diana hadn't been tricky as a child. She'd been quite a sunny little thing. Pony-mad, of course, as she still was – well, horse-mad now – which had made her easy to manage, because Elizabeth could plonk her on the back of Magic and lead her round, or when she got bigger they would go out on a hack together. They'd been quite close, then. And now, she didn't really have any idea what made Diana tick, how she felt about the important things in life. Like children. Elizabeth never dared broach the subject of when Diana and Rory might start a family. That was wrong, surely? She was her mother. They should be able to talk about these things, but honestly she wouldn't know where to begin. She could just imagine Diana's hostile glare if she brought the subject up.

Where had she gone wrong?

Diana had been just nineteen when Edwin died. His death had hit her terribly hard, but they'd all been so wrapped up in their own grief perhaps she hadn't had as much attention as she'd needed. She'd been left to get on with it. And once she'd married Rory, Elizabeth felt a kind of relief that Diana's happiness was someone else's responsibility. But Rory didn't seem to be the answer. Over the past few years, Diana had become more and more confrontational, and there was a bitterness that hadn't been there when she was younger.

She'd try to get to the bottom of it when she got back. It would be a delicate operation. Diana didn't respond well to interference. But it was her duty as a mother to make sure her child was happy. She shouldn't have let things slip so far, but it had crept up on her, the realisation that something must be wrong.

On and on the train sped through towns and villages that were settling down for the night, the street lamps and house lights sprinkling themselves across the countryside. She thought of Michael, who'd be waiting for them on the platform at Breverton in his camel-hair coat, the car outside the ticket office with the engine running so the heater would stay on to keep them all warm. She'd neglected him too, even if he didn't realise it.

She must make life less about her own licentious needs, and more about everyone she loved.

An hour later, as Michael turned into the drive, the two stone foxes gazed down at her with disdain, and the house stood there, honeyed and judgemental, almost daring her to cross the threshold. She stiffened, confused and unsure. *It's not that easy*, she heard a voice say. *You can re-invent yourself as the perfect wife and mother overnight and turn your back on what you were. An adulteress.*

She told herself not to listen. It was her mind playing tricks. The house couldn't possibly have any idea what she'd done. It was her conscience speaking. But the voice was right – she shouldn't forget what she had done.

But why not? It wasn't as if it was something she'd set out to do. She *had* been mad with grief. That awful pain, that was there every morning when she woke up and never left her all day. Even when she was asleep, she dreamt of Edwin. He was always just out of reach, her beautiful boy. No mother should ever have to suffer the loss of a child. It was unbearable. She could feel it now, a grinding ache, somewhere between her heart and her womb, that never dulled. You simply got used to it.

And she'd been so tired. Not put-your-feet-up-with-a-magazine-or-have-an-early-night kind of tired, but deep-down exhaustion from trying to put on a brave face, to smile and pretend that she was coping, keeping her upper lip as stiff as she could while looking after everyone else and making sure they were coping with that awful, awful loss. It was her role and her duty, as a wife and a mother, but it took every last drop of energy from her until she felt there was nothing left but a heap of dried-out bones and skin. She could put on a pretty frock and a painted smile and everyone thought 'How marvellous Elizabeth is', but inside, she was as dead as Edwin.

Had it been so very wrong, to do something that took the pain away?

Perhaps. Only she couldn't go back and change the past. What was done was done. All she could do now was try to make the future better. But was her conscience really not going to allow her to feel renewed? Would it swipe at her every time she felt a sense of achievement? Would it whisper in her ear and remind her she was a traitor? She felt her eyes fill with tears, and her throat tighten, and the ache throb, throb, throb.

No, she thought. She wasn't going to let her conscience destroy her spirit. For Michael. For Alfie and Clementine and the baby she was certain would be here before long. Even for Diana, who she knew deep down needed her, even if she pretended she didn't. Being consumed with guilt served no purpose. She could acknowledge she'd done wrong, but she wasn't going to let regret eat away at her. She would pour her love and her energy into her marriage, into Foxwood, into her children...

Atonement was going to be a long and lonely path, but she was determined not to be cowed. She breathed in until she regained her composure, blinking away the tears and putting on her best smile as the car zoomed in through the gates, cutting through the pale chippings on the drive with a defiant flourish.

23

The table could have been a still life. *Sunday Lunch at Foxwood.* Ox-blood walls adorned with botanical paintings, the table strewn with crumpled napkins, lipstick-stained glasses, plates with smears of blackberry-and-apple crumble and streaks of cream. A bottle of port inched its way around, the perfect accompaniment to the eviscerated Stilton.

Daisy had been called in from the kitchen to brainstorm the menu for the Snow Ball. She came in with her folder of recipes and her battered green copy of *The Complete Illustrated Cookery Book.*

'I could do Poulet Reine Elizabeth,' she was saying. 'It would be a good one for a crowd.'

'That's a lovely idea. A late celebration of the Queen's Coronation.' Elizabeth nodded her approval. 'It's a cold dish, though, isn't it? Surely we need something hot, on the longest night of winter?'

Daisy frowned. 'I could try out a hot version. It would be like a very creamy curry, I suppose. And I could do baked potatoes, instead of the rice salad. Fill everyone up.'

She knew this was going to be important. It was fatal, not feeding everyone properly at a big do.

'In fact, why don't we recreate the whole Coronation menu?' suggested Elizabeth. 'We went to Quaglino's. Do you remember, Michael?'

'Of course! It was wonderful.'

'I've got the menu. I cut it out of the paper, with the recipes.' Daisy had caught Coronation fever, poring over every scrap of detail.

'What was the pudding?'

'Strawberries.' Daisy's face clouded. 'That'll be impossible. They'll be out of season. Even Joey can't grow us strawberries in December.'

'Could we use rhubarb? Though it's not quite the same.'

'What about Queen of Puddings? That's got strawberry jam in it.'

'You're a genius.' Elizabeth clapped her hands in delight.

'Daisy, do you ever not rise to a challenge?' Michael smiled benevolently. 'What would we do without you?'

'I dunno.' Daisy grinned, well aware she was worth her weight in gold.

She was like part of the family, thought Clementine. More than just a cook or a housekeeper. She knew them all, their likes and dislikes and little foibles, and she went the extra mile to keep them happy and comfortable. And in return, Clementine knew, they paid her well. They weren't foolish enough to keep valued staff short. It was a false economy, being tight with wages. If you didn't want to lose good people, you had to make staying worth their while. Michael had the same philosophy at the factory, which was why there was never any shortage of staff on the shop floor. A job with Arbutus Paints could be a job for life, if you played your cards right.

'Obviously Freddie and I will be supplying the drink,' offered Alfie. 'Even though I'll have nearly left Coupe by then. This will be our last hurrah.'

Clementine put her hand on his. She knew he was sad about leaving his old life, especially the thought of being without Freddie, his side kick. It was going to be very different, leaving London for the country, but as Alfie said, Foxwood had always been his destiny.

Clementine had to admit she already felt very at home here. The house was large, and they were in the east wing, which was almost self-contained, with their big bedroom and a smaller one for a nursery for when (hopefully) another baby came along. Until then, she was going to spend three days a week in London working with Ben. And helping with the Snow Ball would keep her occupied until Christmas. She had pored over the old photographs: decades of decadent, glamorous escapades, everyone dressed up in white fur and feathers and velvet and diamonds.

She pulled her attention back to the discussions.

'I'm happy to put people up at Birch Farm,' Diana was saying. 'Don't worry, I'll muck all the bedrooms out.'

This was aimed at Elizabeth, who couldn't help looking mildly alarmed at the offer. Clementine hadn't been to Birch Farm yet but by all accounts, Diana kept her stables immaculate and her home a shambles.

'There's dog hair and half-chewed bones everywhere, and tack hanging off all the furniture and dirty plates in the sink and empty glasses on every surface. And shoes.

Shoes in every corner for some reason,' Elizabeth had confided in her with a wrinkled nose.

'How many rooms?' she asked Diana now, her pencil poised over the notebook she was using to make plans.

'Two at least.'

Clementine quailed inwardly. Would it be up to her to decide who drew the short straw? She felt overwhelmed for a moment. Running the gallery was much less complicated than life at Foxwood. She looked around the table. They had all become so dear to her in such a short space of time, even with their shortcomings. Michael at the head of the table, following proceedings with an amused detachment. Elizabeth, subtly trying to arrange everything to her liking but making it seem as if other people were making the decisions. Darling Alfie, eternally good-natured. Even Diana seemed relaxed today, and when she was happy, Rory was happy.

If it wasn't for the secrets she was hiding, she would be perfectly content. She couldn't ignore them, though.

First of all, she had to confront the issue with Elizabeth. She couldn't carry on living here, pretending she didn't know the truth, for it was compromising her relationship with her mother-in-law. And the presence of Stella and Ted nearby was an unexploded bomb. If she was going to defuse that bomb – or detonate it, by mistake – she needed to know the Arbutus family were watertight. It would be a delicate operation. She had to act with precision timing and extreme care. There was a lot at stake, and everything had to be untangled in the right order.

*

Later, the men all decided to go for a walk down to the Trout for an early evening pint. Diana went back to Birch Farm to feed the horses and Elizabeth announced she was going to sit by the fire.

'Ostensibly to read, but I'm sure I'll fall asleep. I always do.'

This, thought Clementine, was her opportunity. Her stomach flittered with nerves. There'd be no going back, once she'd opened Pandora's box. Was she doing the right thing? The alternative was to mind her own business and turn a blind eye to it all – Elizabeth and Jasper, and Stella and Ted – but that seemed cowardly. She didn't want to live a lie – or be party to anyone else's.

'Would you mind if I joined you?' she asked.

'Of course not, darling. That would be lovely.'

Elizabeth smiled at her daughter-in-law. She wasn't going to be so enamoured of her in a few minutes' time, thought Clementine.

Elizabeth was flipping through *House and Garden* in the small sitting room when Clementine came to join her. The curtains had been drawn against the gloom of the late afternoon, and the fire was leaping about in the grate with the enthusiasm of the newly lit. She settled herself on the sofa opposite, kicking off her shoes and drawing her feet underneath to mirror her mother-in-law. Elizabeth looked up, regarding her with an air of concern.

'I'm so glad it's just us,' she said, putting down her magazine. 'I wanted to ask how you are. Alfie told me Dr Shaw has given you the thumbs-up, but how are you, really?'

'Oh, I'm feeling a little more like myself. Relieved, of course. I didn't realise how much it was hanging over me.'

'Of course it was. It's a rotten thing to happen, but I'm sure all will be well. You just need to give yourselves time.'

She was being so kind and understanding. Clementine felt her nerve wavering. 'We're taking it slowly.'

'Good. Funnily enough, I remember Michael was more worried than I was. About trying again.'

Clementine laughed. 'Alfie too.'

'I suppose that's a good thing. One wouldn't want to be married to a brute.'

'No...'

That was the last thing Alfie was. She felt so safe, lying in his arms at the end of the day, wallowing in that gorgeous feeling that no matter what happened, life would be all right, the two of them together. Was she about to jeopardise that? She couldn't help sighing, and Elizabeth frowned.

'Is something the matter?'

'There is one thing. It's rather difficult...'

'You can talk to me about anything, I hope.'

Clementine looked her straight in the eye. 'I know about you and Jasper.'

Elizabeth held Clementine's gaze. She was expressionless. No panic, no hardness, no fear. 'I see.'

'I heard you talking, in the hallway. The first day I came here. I'm so sorry. I had to say something.'

Elizabeth looked away for a moment while she gathered her thoughts. Silence hung in the air, broken only by the crackling of logs in the grate. Eventually she spoke.

'You must think very little of me.'

'It's not my place to judge. But I couldn't carry on without telling you. I didn't want to compromise our relationship. I know how much you're going to be needed, if and when another baby comes along.'

The mask slipped, and a mixture of emotions danced over Elizabeth's face.

'I'm glad,' she said. 'I'm glad you know. Funnily enough, it makes it so much easier.' She gathered herself up, squaring her shoulders. 'I'm not going to go into the whys. Even if I could pretend it was defensible, it's not, not really. And anyway, it's over. It's been over for some time, actually.' Her voice wavered. 'But now that you know, I can stand firm. Not be at the mercy of my own weak will.' She grimaced at the thought. 'I don't like myself very much. You should know that.'

'Life's been cruel to you. And I'm not sure we should always punish ourselves for mistakes we make.'

'Oh, we have to. Otherwise we'd become monsters.' Elizabeth gave a shaky laugh. 'Anyway, I'm answerable to you now.'

'I don't know that you are. I'm never going to hold it over you. But I needed it out in the open. I couldn't live under this roof with a secret like that between us.'

Clementine felt as if a huge burden had been lifted. One at least. For a moment she was tempted to share the other secret, but stopped herself. That revelation was Stella's prerogative. If her suspicions were true.

'I appreciate your candour. And your generosity.' Elizabeth's eyes glittered in the firelight, and she had a little more colour in her cheeks. 'Now. There's something I'd like to talk to you about. I'm very worried about Diana. I thought you might be able to help.'

The subject was closed. When the men came back some time later, they found Clementine and Elizabeth curled up on the sofa, deep in conversation, the very picture of afternoon bliss.

24

Stella's fingers were flying across the typewriter. As she reached the end of each line, the bell tinged and she whacked the return. Black letters appeared on the white paper as if by magic, pouring out of her mind so quickly she could barely keep up. Sometimes she stopped, for her brain would race ahead to the next part of the story and she panicked she wouldn't be able to remember the words, so she scribbled them down on a notepad next to her.

The characters in *The Towpath Gang* bounced off each other, good-natured, teasing and mischievous. There was the impetuous one, the cautious one, the outspoken one, the caring one, the forgetful one. Sometimes they argued but it was spirited debate rather than rancour. Stella wanted to show her young readers that there could be two sides to every argument.

By lunchtime, she had finished the next chapter. She would go through it carefully this afternoon, making sure every word was the right one. Tonight, she would sit in the lamplight once Ted had gone to bed and draw the illustrations. She had asked Harriet if she would like her to send each chapter as she finished it, but she had said no, she would rather wait to have the whole lot so she could read it in one go.

She poked another couple of logs into the stove and had a look in the cupboard to see what there was to eat for lunch. Writing might be a very stationary occupation but it made you hungry. Bread and jam would do, she decided, thinking longingly of the rich minestrone soup she'd had with Harriet. Perhaps one day soon she'd be able to fill her cupboards with anything she wanted. Big fat sausages from the butcher like the ones she used to make. Sticky ginger cake. A lovely slab of cheddar. Fresh kippers. She was tired of drab, grey food: the stale loaf she got cheap from the baker, thin watery porridge – one day she would make it with the top of the milk and coat it with crunchy brown sugar. At least Ted got a decent hot meal at school, with pudding, and sometimes she got a rabbit from the poacher who lived in a tumbledown shack further up the canal.

A plump chicken to roast. That's the first thing she would buy. Ted had never had roast chicken.

She wondered if she was cruel, to keep him here, living hand to mouth. But the boat was her home – their home – and although life was tough it had a beauty to it. Winters were harsh but come the spring: what joy there was to be had. And this boat was her talisman, her connection to the man she loved with all her heart, and Ted's father. They couldn't cut that tie.

After that first stay on the boat, Edwin had moved from Scotland to more far-flung postings. He brought back drawings and paintings that radiated cold, of a warship floating on a pale icy-blue sea that turned to black when the Arctic sun went behind the clouds, a scene so still everything seemed frozen in time. His work was exhibited all around the country so people could see what England was doing abroad. The reviews were ecstatic:

> *No one takes you to the heart of war like Arbutus. His work is more subtle than the more obvious work of other war artists. On the surface everything seems tranquil, the sun shining on the water, but the unseen looms, ominous. The threat is there, in every brushstroke, underneath the beauty. It is how we live now.*

'I'm so cold. I don't think I'll ever get warm again,' Edwin would say in his letters. And although he was painting, not fighting, she was always afraid for him, for he put himself into the midst of everything, leaping on board aircraft carriers and battleships and into trucks and planes. He was fearless, gung-ho, with a journalistic curiosity and a perspicacious eye that captured the chilling truth.

'There's no point in just drawing the pretty bits,' he told her, although he did that too, with his more intimate portraits of life behind the scenes, men eating, drinking, playing cards, smoking cigarettes, laughing despite the awful conditions and the constant high alert. You were there with them, living their life, feeling their dread, worrying about what might happen to them. Which was the whole point of the war artist scheme. Empathy would win them the war. The ability to put yourself in someone else's shoes.

And meanwhile, London burned and fought the flames and shook its fist at the enemy. Stella did her bit, doing her shifts at the fire station where she veered between the tedium of waiting for something to happen while praying it didn't, to the sheer chaos of an attack when everyone sprang into action, knowing exactly what they had to do even though that was nearly impossible because you never knew when or where or how many bombs would drop. You had to stick together and trust each other, that was all. Pay attention during training and the meticulous planning and do your job. Teamwork, camaraderie, preparation, obedience. The smell of exertion and fear and the heavy canvas uniforms, water turning to steam on hot brick, scorched air. The shouting and screaming, bells and sirens, the crack of overheated glass as it shattered. It was hell on your doorstep.

She was pleased that somehow they had manoeuvred their relationship into a meaningful friendship, even if her heart did a somersault every time he came into the shop when he was on leave. She hid her feelings well, for there was always Mr C's eye upon her, but she lived for his visits, his anecdotes, for his praise when she showed him her work (*The Ditch Babies* were coming along; she nearly felt ready to submit them to a magazine) and his request for her opinion on *his* work.

One night he invited her to a private view at the National Gallery, the opening of a grand exhibition showing the very best war art. He invited Mr C too, so she had felt comfortable accepting his invitation, but at the last minute Mr C had cried off with a nasty cold. She wasn't sure if she had the nerve to go on her own, then told herself there would be lots of people there, so she wouldn't stick out like a sore thumb, and she could slide away after she'd looked at the paintings if she felt awkward. She wore the same dress she had worn for dinner with Edwin, for it was still the nicest thing she had in her wardrobe.

She found the exhibition overwhelming. She moved from painting to painting, spellbound. She watched the reactions on everyone's faces as they were confronted by different versions of the same war that held them all in its grasp. She could see Edwin in front of his work, deep in conversation with the great and the good who had turned out: politicians, public figures, other artists. She absorbed the atmosphere, the reverence, the pure power that art had to tell the truth.

After two hours, she decided she would slip away. She had caught Edwin's eye once or twice, but he was much sought-after, and she didn't want to disturb him. They could talk it all over next time he came into the shop. She was making her way through the front door, heading out onto Trafalgar Square, when he came up behind her and caught her elbow.

'Don't you dare think you're getting away without saying hello. Give me ten minutes. We'll go for a drink.'

He'd seen her. He'd chased after her. He wanted to go for a drink. She wasn't going to argue. She thought it was above board. They'd been to an exhibition and needed refreshment. She sat outside on a bench until he re-emerged a quarter of an hour later. This would be the first time they'd spent time together outside the shop, since their weekend in Somerset. She stood as he bounded down the steps, that familiar big coat flying out behind him.

'Sorry. I had to say my goodbyes. It takes for ever. What did you think? What was your favourite?' He took her arm and hurried her along the pavement. 'I'm in awe of Evelyn Dunbar.' He gave a sigh of admiration. 'Her paintings of the nurses. There's something deeply moving about the humanity in them. The dedication. I think she's marvellous.'

She loved how enthusiastic he was about everyone, and how inspired he seemed by their work. It showed a generosity of spirit. He led her in a zigzag down to Mayfair, where they headed underground into a smoky bar and ordered glasses of thick, dark brown stout. He seemed filled with a strange energy, perhaps galvanised by everything he'd seen. Or perhaps a little drunk? She couldn't be sure. They were tucked away in a corner, their legs pressed together. She could feel the heat of him and her heart thumped, a pulse somewhere deeper echoing its rhythm.

He finished his drink and put his glass down on the table. He slung an arm around her neck, and pulled her towards him. She laughed, then stopped laughing when she heard what he'd murmured in her ear.

'I can't pretend anymore,' he said. 'I've got to do something. I'm falling in love with you, Stella.'

'But you can't!'

'I can't help it. And you can't tell me you're not just a little bit in love with me.'

She felt her cheeks flame. Was it so obvious? She couldn't deny it. But she had to make sure to protect herself. She was not going to be his toy.

'Of course I'm falling for you, Edwin. And it's not just a little bit. But I'm not being your piece on the side.'

'Oh my God, no,' he said, horrified. 'Of course not. That's not what I meant. I want you and no one else, Stella. I've thought about it long enough now. It's not just an infatuation. You mean everything.'

Everything. She felt as if she was being dipped in melted chocolate. Hot, sweet, delicious. But there was still one obstacle.

'What about Meg?'

He dropped his head and rested it on her shoulder, as if in despair. She longed to reach up and caress the back of his neck. Finally, he looked up.

'I have to tell her. But I want to tell her in person. It would be terrible, to tell her in a letter when she's so far away. But I won't be able to see her until this war ends.' He grabbed her hand and held it tight. 'Would you wait for me, Stella?'

He understood that she could never condone any duplicity. She wouldn't carry on with him behind Meg's back. Not even if he had promised to break things off. But she would wait. She would wait until the end of time.

'Of course,' she said, and he leaned in to kiss her. She put up her hands, placing them one on either side of his head to stop him, even though she wanted to feel his mouth on hers more than anything in the world. Their eyes met, and they looked deep inside each other. 'Not yet,' she breathed. 'Not yet.'

Over the next two years, they entered a strange kind of limbo, where they both knew the pact they'd made with each other but couldn't share with the outside world. Stella told no one, not even Mr C. They shared snatched scraps of time when he was between assignments, each of them burning with longing yet holding back. She knew if she kissed him it wouldn't stop there, and was grateful that he kept his distance. She couldn't respect herself if they'd gone behind Meg's back. It would be cruel and spineless. But sometimes she thought that both of them knowing it was only a matter of time was just as bad. Would Meg be grateful for their restraint, if she knew? Probably not.

The lull after the end of the Blitz came to an abrupt end with the arrival of the V1s – the doodlebugs. How could something so destructive be given such a comical name? They were followed by the V2 bombers, with their deadly stealth. You couldn't hear them coming, they couldn't be tracked by radar, they couldn't be shot down. They brought another level of terror. It was a game of cat and mouse. The luck of the draw. A Woolworths store in Deptford was hit. A hundred and sixty dead. A hundred and sixty people who had been minding their own business looking for furniture polish or new pegs to put on the line. Her head felt as if it was filled with brick dust from the collapsed buildings. She was used to walking past people crawling over piles of rubble looking for survivors. She didn't look twice now.

It was Edwin who gave in, under no pressure from her. 'It's never going to end,' he told her one night when he walked her back to her boarding house. 'I can't wait any longer. I'm going to Foxwood tomorrow. I'm going to tell my family that I'm breaking it off with Meg. And then I'm going to write to her. This war might last for ever, after all.'

Stella felt a mixture of fear and elation. This was it. They were going to be together. What would everyone think? Mr C? Would he approve? Edwin's family – what would they make of her? She was hardly an American heiress.

Edwin could see she was uncertain.

'Trust me. This is the right thing to do. For everyone.

Meg will be all right. We'll wait a decent amount of time, and then I can introduce you to my family. They will love you. And eventually we'll live there, Stella. We'll live at Foxwood, you and me.'

He was so certain, she believed him. Yet when he came back from Foxwood, he was in a curious mood. She didn't ask too many questions, but he told her he'd spoken to his father and that he'd written to Meg. All she wanted was to kiss him at long last, but she sensed he was preoccupied. It felt like a bit of an anti-climax.

'Let's go dancing to celebrate,' he said.

Stella hadn't felt like dancing. She felt exhausted by the tension of it all. She was so tired, but she couldn't let him down. An hour later they were out in the West End, at the 400 Club in Leicester Square, drinking gin to blot out reality, letting the music take over their souls. You had to dance each dance as if it was your last. For some people it had been, when the Café de Paris had been hit. They'd literally dropped dead dancing to Snakehips Johnson and his band, their hearts turned inside out from the force of the explosion. You never knew.

Everyone was bent on dancing and drinking and flirting and kissing, living those brief hours at full throttle with a glorious reckless abandon, for they were all in the lottery. You didn't know who might be missing next time you went out, whether they'd been killed in action or the Jerries had made their home or workplace a target.

They were good dancers. She could tell by the way people looked at them with admiration as they spun and twirled. Stella's eyes never left Edwin's, and to look at them you would think they didn't have a care in the world. The music muffled her worries and soon he was laughing too, his low mood evaporating.

And at long last they kissed, and it was everything she had dreamed of. As their lips met, she felt all the clocks in London stop, the Underground come to a standstill, every plane in the sky halt in its tracks as she melted into him and their hearts wrapped themselves around each other. It was gentle, it was fierce. Slow and sweet, like treacle dropping from a spoon.

If she died now, she would die happy.

Afterwards, at his flat, they made love all night long with a feverish energy left over from the dance floor, wrapped up in their own tempo, an invisible conductor driving them on, deliciously urgent and abandoned. They stumbled out onto the street just after dawn, her to go back to the boarding house to change for work, him to head for Iceland, both of them lightheaded from lack of sleep.

'Here,' Edwin said, slipping the signet ring off his little finger. 'I'll get you something proper when I get back. But have this to remember me in the meantime.' He picked up her right hand and slipped it onto her middle finger. Even then it was a bit big.

She looked down at it, at the funny bird pecking at its breast.

'I'll put it on a chain,' she said. 'I don't want to lose it.'

He'd given her his ring. His family ring. He meant it. He really meant it. She was his. He was hers.

It was the last time they saw each other.

Just after two o'clock that afternoon, Stella finished the next chapter. Only three more to go, she thought. She had it all mapped out in a notebook: a page for each chapter, with a brief outline of what happened and the drawing that would go with it. The end was in sight.

What happened next would be out of her control, but she wouldn't be human if she didn't allow herself a daydream. And she didn't get carried away. She just wanted a house. A little two-up-two-down to rent on the outskirts of London somewhere. Nothing grand, just somewhere they could make their own with a decent grammar school nearby for Ted, so he could reach his full potential. They could come to the boat in summertime, when the canal was at its best. It wasn't too much to hope for. A normal life, where she wasn't hiding herself away for fear of someone putting two and two together and starting to gossip. Luckily being a war widow was a respectable cover for a woman on her own with a child, so people weren't too curious, but Ted was looking more and more like his father as he grew up. She could stop living in fear of someone recognising their similarity if they moved back to London.

It was strange, living with Edwin's ghost. She'd thought her sadness would fade, but if anything her dreams of him were becoming more vivid. And during the day, too, she could feel him. If a gust of air rippled through her hair, she thought it was his fingers. Or she would get a drift of something that smelled like him: warm toast and turpentine. And, occasionally, she would hear him whisper or laugh, but it would be the wind whistling down the chimney. Sometimes at night her body would wake, pulsating with longing. She yearned for him as much as ever, and when Ted was at school she would be overcome with grief, burying herself in the nest, weeping into the pillows.

She unwound the paper from the typewriter and laid it on the table top to be read through with the rest once she'd picked Ted up from school. She imagined Edwin congratulating her, urging her on to finish. Their entire future was tied up in these pages, she thought. With luck, it would change everything.

25

Two days later, Clementine stood on the side of the road opposite Breverton Infants and watched the children arrive. It was a traditional little school, just off the high street, built in Somerset stone. In the playground, the boys oafed about, tripping each other up and grabbing each other from behind, while the girls hooked arms and shared secrets. She wondered if perhaps she would be ushering her own children to the gate one day. After all, Edwin and Alfie had gone here when they were small, before heading off to prep school and then Haileybury, and Alfie had said he loved it.

'I was furious to be taken away, but you know how it is. I made lots of friends I still see at the Trout sometimes, and I always had people to play with in the school holidays.'

At last, here they were, Stella and Ted, galloping along the road, hand in hand, Stella with her hair streaming out behind her, the two of them laughing, seemingly not bothered that they were about to be late as the final bell clanged. His satchel bounced along on his hip, and his coat flapped around him. They looked as if they hadn't a care in the world as she hustled him through the entrance marked *BOYS*.

Clementine pulled her hat down over her eyes, aware that she probably looked like someone who was trying very hard not to be noticed. She stood behind a tree for a few minutes, waiting until Stella reappeared and set off back up the road that led to the high street, over the bridge and a little way out of town before disappearing off to the left, along the canal. Clementine hung back a bit, conscious that it would be hard to find a valid reason to be heading down the towpath if Stella turned around. Luckily Stella was walking with purpose, her hands in her pockets. Every now and then she gave a little skip, as if she was excited about something, and for a moment Clementine thought about turning back. Who was she to crash into Stella's world and turn it upside down?

She couldn't turn back. She'd gone over and over the conundrum in her mind countless times since she'd fallen across Stella and Ted the week before. She couldn't do nothing. It would be awful to ignore their existence, carrying on in the heart of the Arbutus family knowing they were nearby. For her own peace of mind, she had to find out the truth.

They'd been walking for a good ten minutes when up ahead she saw a green and gold narrowboat come into view. Stella jumped onto the deck and disappeared inside. Was this where she and Ted were living? Clementine slowed down, and at the same time her heart speeded up. This was it, the moment when she decided what to do. Did she have the nerve to confront Stella? Although confront was too strong a word – she had every intention of going into this as gently as she could. She didn't want to cause Stella any distress.

She told herself if she thought too much about it she would turn tail. She jumped up on the deck and tapped on the window of the door leading down to the cabin. A moment later Stella came to the door and pushed it open. She gazed at Clementine, puzzled, as if trying to work out where she'd seen her. Then her face brightened.

'You're the lady on the train.'

'Yes. Sorry. This is a bit odd. But I wanted to talk to you about something.'

Stella frowned. She was obviously trying to work out what on earth she was doing here, and how she had found her way to the boat.

'My name's Clementine.' It was time to come clean. 'Clementine Arbutus.'

Stella's eyes hardened as she heard the name.

'What do you want?' she asked, her voice wary.

'Just to talk to you,' Clementine replied. 'I don't mean any harm. I promise you. Can I come in? Can we chat?'

Stella shut her eyes, as if she was in physical pain. She had every right to slam the door on Clementine, but, eventually, she nodded, turned to go back into the cabin and gestured for Clementine to follow.

'This is lovely,' Clementine said, looking around. There were pictures everywhere, drawings and sketches and studies, and she recognised Edwin's hand. There were other pictures too, sketches of tiny children peering out from hedgerows and riverbanks. This must be Stella's work.

'It's small. But it's our home.' Stella picked up a copper kettle. 'Can I make you tea?'

'Thank you. Yes.' She tried hard not to be nosy, but she was taking in everything. Their breakfast things still in the sink. Neat piles of clothes. Ted's toy soldiers, and his teddy on the bed. A typewriter on the small table. Their whole life seemed to be in here. 'I'm married to Edwin Arbutus's younger brother. Alfie.'

'I see.' Stella made no attempt to feign puzzlement.

Clementine imagined she was turning everything over in her head, working out what to say. She'd been cornered, but she could tell Stella was someone who was used to difficult situations. She was a survivor, cunning and wily, no doubt, but not, she suspected, devious. She was composed, and had put up a barrier, but that was no surprise. All Clementine had to do was gain her trust.

'When I saw you both on the train,' she began, 'when I saw Ted, there was no mistaking him... He's Edwin's, isn't he?'

Stella was pouring hot water into a stout brown teapot. 'I always knew he'd be the giveaway,' she said. 'He started looking so like Edwin when he started to sprout, when he turned six. Before that he was just a chubby little boy. But now...' She faltered, overcome with emotion. 'He looks so like him.'

Clementine knew it was her turn to keep quiet. Stella pulled two cups down from a shelf and set them down next to the pot.

'Edwin never knew about Ted. When he died, it was months before I realised I was expecting. I was so wrapped up in my grief I didn't notice the signs. But it's not as if I was the only woman having a child alone, thanks to the war. And I was glad, to have something to remember him by...'

'Oh, Stella.'

Stella looked surprised. 'You know my name?'

Clementine blushed. 'I looked in your bag. Sorry.'

She shrugged, as if it was nothing. 'Fair enough.' Her tone was dry.

'So how did you end up here?'

'He gave me the key to the boat – somewhere to run to if things got bad.' She gave a little laugh. 'I never ran here, not during any of the bombing. You have to face up to the enemy, don't you? But I knew this was the best place to bring up Ted.'

'You were together for a long time, then?'

There was a fleeting smile. 'No. For the most part, we were just friends.' She poured the tea out, added milk, then handed a cup to Clementine. 'It was only one night. The last night I saw him...'

Clementine sipped at her tea to give herself time to think. Stella was leaning back against the counter that ran under one window and served as a kitchen area. She really was stunning, thought Clementine – tall, with that wild red hair and pale skin and silver eyes that seemed to look through you. Strength radiated off her – she had an East End carapace that screamed at you not to meddle with her. Yet there was vulnerability too, and a big heart. Her love for both Edwin and Ted shone out of her. She only had to mention them, and it was there in her eyes.

'So how are you managing? Are you all right?'

'We're fine.' Her voice was a little too bright, perhaps.

'It must be hard, on your own.'

'Sometimes it's tough, when it's bloody freezing or when the money runs out.' She seemed to be about to say something else, then thought better of it. 'But we manage.' She put down her cup. 'So what is it you want?'

There was challenge in her voice, and her body language, and Clementine knew whatever she said now, she had to be careful.

'The last thing I want to do is interfere in your life. I completely respect your privacy.'

'Except when you look in my bag.'

Clementine looked shamefaced. 'When I saw you on the train, and put two and two together, I couldn't ignore it. It would have been none of my business, except that I'm married to Edwin's brother.' The next bit was the tricky bit. 'You must understand how terrible losing Edwin was for the whole family. And to know he had a son... I think they have a right to know about Ted, Stella.'

Stella was implacable, her face as still and cold as porcelain, but she was twisting her fingers, winding them round each other.

'I think it would mean the world,' Clementine stumbled on. 'Especially to Edwin's mother. Losing a child is a terrible thing. But to know she had a grandchild. It would bring her such joy.'

There was silence in the little cabin. The temperature seemed to have dropped.

'So are you going to tell them about us?'

'Absolutely not.' Clementine was very definite. 'As I said, I respect your privacy, and your wishes. It's completely up to you. But if you would like to meet them, I can help you.'

'I did think about it,' admitted Stella. 'When Ted was first born. But I thought they wouldn't believe me.

Turning up on the doorstep and claiming the baby was Edwin's. It's an old trick, isn't it?'

'Is it?'

'Course. And if they did believe me, I worried they might take over. Even worse, they might take him off me. People like that have power. They have friends in high places. All they'd have to do is prove I was unfit, and I'd never see him again.'

'Stella, that's a terrible thing to think. Of course they'd never do that.'

Stella gave her a pitying look. 'You've got no idea, have you? How the world works when you're not one of them?'

'Maybe not, but I do know they are decent people who would never take a child away from its mother.'

Stella turned away and crouched down to put more wood in the stove. Her hands were trembling as she tried to relight the fire. Three times, she tried to strike a match, and each time they snapped in half. She dropped the box of matches and put her hands to her face.

'I'm so sorry,' said Clementine. 'I didn't come here to upset you, or cause trouble. But honestly, if you think you'd like to meet the family, if you'd like Ted to meet his grandparents, I can help you. I can make it easy for you.'

Stella picked the box of matches back up and tried again. This time, the match came alight and she held it to the kindling. Once it was aflame, she shut the door carefully. Then she stood up.

'It's been a shock,' she said. 'I've spent so long hiding myself away, and now what I feared might happen, has happened, I'm not sure what to think. And it's not that I don't trust you. I can see that you care. But I'm not sure you truly understand my position. There's a lot that could go wrong if I make myself known to the Arbutus family.'

'But there's a lot that could go right. Foxwood is a wonderful place for a young boy. They could give him—'

'I can give him everything he needs,' Stella cut her off, suddenly angry. 'Ted wants for nothing.'

'I didn't mean to offend you. Or mean that you weren't giving him the very best life. My goodness, I can see what a happy little boy he is, and how much you love each other.'

'Well, maybe we're best left as we are, then.'

Clementine realised she had pushed too far. Stella hadn't had time to come to terms with being recognised. It might take her a while to think it all through.

'Look, let's pretend this didn't happen for now. I didn't feel I could let it go without talking to you, but I promise I won't say a thing to anyone without your permission. You have my word.'

Stella crossed her arms. She was shrinking away from Clementine, as if trying to make herself invisible. It was time to go.

'If you need me, come to Foxwood and ask for Clementine. Otherwise, you won't hear from me again.'

'All right,' Stella said gruffly, but that was all Clementine was going to get out of her, so she buttoned up her coat and made her way to the door. Moments later she was out in the cold November air. She stood for a moment on the deck, looking down at the still water of the canal, at the clumps of mistletoe in the bare branches overhead, breathing in the smell of damp leaves on the path. What was it like here for Stella, living out here on her own? It must be so dark and silent at night. Yet inside the boat had been a little haven – once the fire got going it would be warm and snug and cosy, so perhaps she felt quite happy there. Either way, Clementine admired her spirit and her courage, bringing up Ted on her own when she must be bereft at losing Edwin. Clementine wasn't sure she would be so brave in the same situation.

She had no idea if she had done right or wrong, trying to bring Stella and Ted into the family fold. But action was always better than inaction. Of that Clementine was certain. She set off back down the towpath, wondering if Stella might call after her, but she didn't.

After Clementine had gone, Stella lay on the bed, staring at the wooden ceiling that was only a couple of feet above her. She felt both sick and resigned. She couldn't pretend that she hadn't envisaged something like this happening one day, even though she'd done her best to stay out of the limelight. Being in Breverton had been dangerous, but she'd cut off all her hair when she'd come here, to avoid the slim possibility of someone recognising her from the Underground posters and linking her with Edwin Arbutus – although even if they had, what of it? Eventually she'd become complacent, letting it grow full length again, for the posters had become a distant memory, so she'd thought it very unlikely anyone would make a connection. But in the past couple of years, Ted's similarity to his father had unsettled her. She didn't move in Arbutus circles, she was careful and watchful when they shopped together, she was cautious about who he befriended at school – it would only take a brush with a member of staff at Foxwood for someone to ask questions. Perhaps she should have moved them, but the boat was their home, his home, and she didn't see why they should be uprooted. She had done nothing wrong. Nothing but love the wrong man.

A week after their night together, as she had crossed the threshold into the shop one morning, Stella had known immediately, by the way Monsieur Corbières looked at her, that the worst had happened. He had heard on the artists' grapevine, for it wasn't in the news yet. A sunken boat. Edwin on board, eager to capture the excitement of a reconnaissance mission. It had plunged into the icy sea, no bodies recovered and no survivors.

She slumped into Monsieur Corbières' arms. He held her tight but it was he who shook with sobs, burying his face in her shoulder as he wept. She felt numb, not a tear inside her. She was rigid with shock, wondering how many times she had imagined this very moment, and now it was here, she had no idea what she was going to do. How could she live without him? She wanted to slide into the depths of the freezing water and join him.

She shivered now, at the memory. Clementine's visit had unnerved her. She looked over at her typewriter. That was the key. She must press on, finish the rest of *The Towpath Gang*, and hope and pray that it would give her the means to escape, to allow her and Ted a new life somewhere with independent means and a bright future. She sat down and wound a fresh new piece of paper into the typewriter, rubbed her fingers to warm them up a little and began to type.

26

Elizabeth drove to Birch Farm through a milky morning mist that was gradually being dissipated by the sun. It was nestled in the next valley, amidst rolling pasture dotted with Rory's Belted Galloways. He was a good farmer who looked after both his land and his cattle well. His hedges, walls and fences were immaculate, his fields beautifully tended, his animals plump and content.

It occurred to Elizabeth that she didn't know her son-in-law all that well. He was always good-natured, perhaps not brimming with personality or imagination, but perhaps she should try to dig a little deeper. After all, her mission today was to get to the bottom of what was troubling Diana, and to see if she could do something to help. And Rory was probably key to some, if not all, of the solution. All she wanted, really, was for Diana to be happy, and it was apparent by her behaviour these days that she wasn't.

The trouble was, when people started turning into monsters, everyone tiptoed around them and they ended up getting away with it. Diana didn't deserve to be a monster. She was better than that and enough was enough. Elizabeth had been so wrapped up in her own grief and her own obsession to see what was happening, but now she had dealt with Jasper, it was time to do what she should have done a long time ago.

She parked the car in front of the farmhouse and made her way round to the stable yard. She heard the ring of hooves on concrete and saw Diana lead a handsome grey hunter towards his stable. She was always up at the crack of dawn to exercise, and she went out with the West Somerset Vale twice a week. Perhaps she should take up riding again, thought Elizabeth. They used to ride together when Diana was small.

Once she'd put the horse back in its stable, Diana strode across the yard, hands in her pockets, hunched up inside her hacking jacket, her eyes half closed against the wind that was whipping its way across the valley. She came to a halt in front of her mother.

'To what do I owe the honour?' There was open hostility in her face.

'I just wanted to come and see how you are.'

'Really?' Her tone was dry. 'Let's go inside. It's brass monkeys out here.'

She led her through the back door and into the farm kitchen. Elizabeth was shocked. It was even worse than the last time she'd been; an absolute rat's nest. Washing up everywhere, paperwork all over the table, dog bowls, dog hair, horse blankets, bits of tack, bits of equipment that Elizabeth was too nervous to enquire about but looked as if they might involve chopping off an extremity. It seemed at odds with the way Rory kept the land or Diana kept the yard, but perhaps they had less respect for themselves than they did their animals, or simply didn't see the mess.

Maybe that was Diana's fatal flaw? She simply didn't see the mess she made.

'Tea?' said Diana, picking up a kettle.

'Actually, I won't. I've not long had one,' Elizabeth lied, not able to see a cup she could bring herself to drink out of. 'The thing is, darling. I'm terribly worried about you. You don't seem happy.'

'No. I'm not, particularly. But I'm not sure what anyone can do about it.'

Diana lit the gas burner with a match but her hand was shaking. She was obviously more unsettled than she was making out, thought Elizabeth. She took in a deep breath.

'Well, I'd like to try and help. If I can.'

'What's brought this on?'

'I'm your mother.'

'And you want to know why you're not a grandmother yet?'

'Absolutely not!' Elizabeth was horrified Diana might think that.

Diana sank into a chair with a sigh. 'I just don't see the point of myself anymore.'

'That's an awful thing to say.'

'Tell me, then. What the point of me is? Who actually cares?'

'Please, darling, try not to—'

'Oh, I'm so sorry if you find the truth upsetting.'

Her voice was harsh and Elizabeth flinched. It was very tempting to change the subject, but she knew she had to try to persevere.

'Everyone cares, darling. Daddy and I do, very much. And Rory, of course.'

Diana gave something between a tut and a humph, with a roll of her eyes.

'Don't dismiss him. He's your husband, and he loves you.'

'Does he, though? I wouldn't love me if I was him. I'm horrible to him.'

'But why? He's so kind. Isn't he?' Perhaps he wasn't? Perhaps she really didn't know the real Rory.

Diana stared at her. 'Of course he is. And I don't know why,' she said, a crack in her voice. 'And you and Daddy only love me because you have to.'

'That's simply not true.'

'And Alfie definitely doesn't give a monkey's about me. Not now he's got Princess Clementine.'

'Of course he does. You can love more than one person, you know.'

'Can you?' There was so much sarcasm in Diana's voice that Elizabeth knew exactly what she was driving at, and she couldn't help her cheeks colouring. She wasn't going to be blown off course by one of Diana's barbed remarks.

'What would make you happy?' she said.

'What would make me happy?' Diana looked up at the ceiling. 'Let's see. How about... Edwin walking back into the room?'

Elizabeth put her face in her hands. This was going to be even harder than she'd thought. When she looked back up at her daughter, there were tears in her eyes.

'That's not fair,' she said. 'We all want that.'

Diana had the grace to look shamefaced. 'I know. But I miss him so much.' Her face crumpled. '*He* made me feel like somebody. When we were out on the horses, flying across the fields, over the fences... I can't even think about him, it hurts so much.'

'Come here.' Elizabeth stood up, walked around to her and opened her arms. Diana fell into them, and all her grief came pouring out, years of sorrow and abandonment and bewilderment. And although Elizabeth felt torn apart too, and at any given moment could be subsumed by her own grief, for once she had to be strong. The pain was intense, but she would walk through fire for her children, even now they were grown up, even if they behaved as badly as Diana had been behaving. She held her until she stopped sobbing, then detached herself gently to make the tea that had been forgotten, putting a cup in front of her daughter.

'I don't like seeing you like this,' she said, heading for the biscuit tin and pulling out a few digestives. She put them on a plate and set them on the table. 'It would be wrong of me, as your mother, to watch you torturing yourself. Because you're not yourself, Diana. You've always had a sharp tongue, but you used to be funny. Now you can be rather cruel. And I don't think you mean to be. So let's find a way to get you back.'

Diana picked up a digestive and stared at it. 'I don't know how to be me. That's the awful thing. Because I don't know what I'm *supposed* to be. My life doesn't fit anymore.' Her voice was desolate. 'We're supposed to be trying for a baby. But I just can't face... *it.*' She gave an exaggerated shudder. 'Because I'm scared, about bringing someone into the world, when I don't even like myself. And poor Rory. I know he thinks it's him I don't like, when it comes to the bedroom. But it isn't.' She snapped a bit of biscuit off and put it in her mouth. 'I've been so worried, that he might go off with the barmaid at the Trout, or something. Because you can't just ignore men, can you? Isn't that where the trouble starts?'

'Oh dear,' said Elizabeth. 'We have got a lot of untangling to do.'

Elizabeth thought this was probably the first time Diana had told anyone how she truly felt. And she had to be very gentle with her. No doubt Edwin's dying was at the root of it. She hadn't come to terms with it, not at all.

'You've been through so much, losing Edwin, and I don't think you, or anyone, has realised how much it's affected you,' Elizabeth told her now, reaching across the table to stroke her hand, and Diana gave another little sob. 'You've spent so long fighting your feelings, and it's all become so much worse than it needs to be. Not that it wasn't awful. Of course it was. But you can't carry on thinking these terrible things, about yourself and everyone else.'

'I know. It's all just a muddle in my head.' She looked over at her mother, and although she looked awful, red-eyed and bedraggled, she managed a smile of appreciation. 'Thank you.'

'I'm your mother. It's my job. But you must trust me. Now.' Elizabeth tapped the table with her Chair of the Village Fête authority. 'I think one of the problems is you're bored. You've got no sense of purpose. I think once we give you something to think about, you might feel better about everything.'

'Maybe.'

'How would you feel about going back to work?'

'Work?'

'At the factory. I know your father's struggling to keep

apace at the moment. And you and he were so brilliant together during the war. You ran that place like clockwork. He always said he couldn't have done it without you.'

'He couldn't,' Diana said stoutly. 'Those women were all over the place until I licked them into shape.'

'Exactly. So why don't we see if you can go back? Even if it's only for a short time.'

'But what about Alfie? He's the one destined to take over. The son and heir.' There it was again, that bitterness.

'There's plenty of room for both of you.'

'I don't think he'll like it.'

'Why not? And even if he doesn't, it's not up to him.'

Diana set to work on her second biscuit. 'I loved working at the factory.'

'Well, there you are.'

'Will you ask Daddy for me?'

'I think you should ask him.' Elizabeth had never believed in spoon-feeding her children. 'I think he'll welcome you with open arms. I'm sure you could be a great help.'

'I'll go up there this afternoon.' There was a sparkle in Diana's eye she hadn't seen for a long time.

'Good,' said Elizabeth. 'Now, there is one other thing.'

'What?'

'This kitchen.' She looked around her. 'Honestly, darling, there are no words. It's disgusting. It's like Cold Comfort Farm.'

'Cheek!'

'I didn't bring you up to live like this. And once you've sorted it out, I guarantee you'll feel better. Anyone would feel down in the dumps coming down to this every morning.' She might be pushing it, but there was no point in mincing her words.

Diana looked thunderous, and for a moment she thought she might have gone too far. Then Diana started laughing.

'You're right,' she said. 'It's a pigsty.'

'Come on,' Elizabeth jumped to her feet. 'I'll give you a hand. We'll have it ship-shape in no time. Then you can get changed and go and see your father.'

It took them all morning. The clutter on the surfaces was restored to its rightful place, the washing-up done, the floor mopped, the windows cleaned and the cooker scrubbed. When Rory came in for his lunch, he did a double-take to see Elizabeth arranging a vase of late chrysanthemums and placing them in the middle of a fresh tablecloth.

'What's going on?' he asked.

'A new broom.' His mother-in-law smiled.

Rory beamed his gentle approval, then did another double take as Diana swept into the room with her hair freshly washed, wearing a skirt and cardigan and high heels. He hadn't seen her in a skirt for years.

'It's not Christmas already, is it?' he asked, and Diana gave him a fond cuff around the head.

He carried on looking around in amazement.

'Oi. Where's my Ritchey nipper?' he demanded, looking at the empty table.

'On the shelf in the lean-to.'

'I don't want to know what that is, do I?' asked Elizabeth.

'You do not,' chorused Rory and Diana. Diana did a

snipping motion with her fingers near Rory's flies, and Rory winced.

Laughter rang around the kitchen walls. Elizabeth smiled. Being a working farm, this kitchen was never going to have the finesse of the one at Foxwood, but it was already lighter and brighter, as was the atmosphere. A good morning's work, she thought.

Elizabeth got back to Foxwood to find that the invitations to the Snow Ball had arrived from the printer. They looked stunning, Edwin's artwork on the front and the details on the back, on thick white card with a gold edge. She spent the afternoon at her desk, addressing all the envelopes. They were all done, in a neat, towering pile. There was just enough time to take them to the post office before it closed.

She was heading into the hall for her coat when the telephone rang. She nearly ignored it for she might miss the post, but you never knew who it might be. Hopefully someone with an offer of more beds. She picked up the receiver.

'Breverton six four two.'

'Elizabeth.' His voice trickled like honey down the line.

Jasper. She curled her fingers round the telephone cord.

'What are you phoning for? You're not supposed to phone.'

'I've got something important to tell you.'

'It had better be life and death.'

'It is. I've made a decision. You can't resist torturing me, so I'm doomed to a life of on/off, on/off, which is unfair. Unless you leave Michael, which you won't, will you?'

He paused long enough for her to know he was giving her one last chance. She sighed. She had been very clear it was over for good at their last meeting, but she didn't blame him for trying. It had been intense.

'No,' she said, for there was no point in giving him false hope.

'I thought not.' His voice only wavered slightly. Although Jasper seemed rather hard and a bit superficial, she knew he wasn't, for she'd seen his emotions unwrapped, in bed, and during his eulogy to Edwin, and his wedding speech. He felt *so* deeply he had to cover it up with his playboy persona. And although he pretended not to mind when she kept her distance, he needed to know he was irresistible. 'I'm moving to Paris.'

'What?' This was an unexpected development.

'It's the perfect place for me. Art. Women. Sex in the afternoon. All that food and that delicious *froideur*. I don't know why I didn't think of it before.'

She could see him there, trailing along the streets of St Germain, a life of bohemian decadence peppered with artists and writers and singers and . . .

Her? She imagined them in a ritzy hotel, sipping champagne.

Stop it.

'That's an excellent idea.' Her voice was crisp. If he went to Paris, she couldn't ever be tempted to pick up the phone and arrange a rendezvous. 'When are you off?' She realised she sounded rather abrupt.

'Not until Christmas. I need a chance to say goodbye to everyone.'

Was he hinting at some sort of farewell meet-up? That was a bad idea. And for the first time since they'd embarked upon their affair, Elizabeth's mind didn't jump to how she could manufacture a meeting.

'Well. Bon voyage, I suppose.' She gave a small laugh, impressed by her own composure. A few months ago, she would have fallen apart at the thought of him going away for a mere fortnight.

'Thank you. I think.' He sounded a little bit hurt. Jasper was vain. He would have been expecting histrionics. She relented.

'Thank *you*. You were a good thing for me, Jasper. Well, a bad thing but a good thing, if that makes sense.'

'That's me. A mass of contradictions.'

'The French women will love you.'

'I do hope so.'

She could see him in her mind's eye, lounging on his sofa with a drink at his elbow, his silk shirt unbuttoned, his hair tousled. Paris would suit him. Late nights, even later mornings, bitter coffee, long lunches –

'Send me a present, would you? Something terribly chic to remind me of you. Us.'

'Steady.' His voice held a warning. 'You're not to tease.'

She sighed. 'Old habits.' She knew him so well, it was hard not to fall into familiar ways. And she couldn't help tantalising him, now she knew he was to be out of reach.

'Goodbye, Elizabeth.'

She could hear the front door opening. She had to get him off the line.

'Goodbye, Jasper,' she said, and hung up. For a moment, she gazed at the little face in the grandfather clock. *Well, you got away with it*, it seemed to be saying. She was still staring at it when Michael came in with a rush of cold air.

'How are you, darling?' He came forwards to kiss her on the cheek.

'Very well. That was the vicar, about the choir.' He didn't need to know that. She was over-explaining. 'You?'

'Very good. I had a surprise visit to the factory this afternoon. Diana.'

'Oh,' she said. She'd almost forgotten, she'd been so distracted by Jasper's call. 'And?'

'She's coming back to work for us. I've tasked her with co-ordinating our stand at the Ideal Home Exhibition.'

'That's marvellous.'

'I never thought she'd be interested. Once the war was over, I thought she'd be wrapped up in married life and horses.'

'I think Diana needs more. She's always been bright.'

'It's going to be wonderful to have her back. She was my right-hand girl at one point.' Michael looked genuinely delighted.

Running a family was like a game of chess, thought Elizabeth. You had to be strategic when you moved the pieces around.

'Where are you off to?' Michael was asking her now.

'Oh. I'm taking the invitations to the post office, but there's someone I've forgotten.'

She rushed back into the sitting room to her bureau, took out the last invitation and wrote Jasper's name and address on the front of the envelope. Up until now, she'd left him off. But if he was going to be safely in Paris for the foreseeable, she could reinstate him. He was a family friend, after all. Of course he had to be there.

27

A week later, Diana swept into the boardroom at Arbutus Paints. Around the table were her father Michael, Colin the sales director, the head of production and several of the reps. And although she could sense a few raised eyebrows and glances being exchanged, she felt no trepidation.

She had been barely sixteen when she had kept morale and turnover high on the factory floor, galvanising the women of Breverton who had stepped in to take over from the men who had gone off to fight. By sheer force of personality, she had made it a place where people were proud to work. There was banter and camaraderie, a sense of teamwork as well as pride, along with endless cups of tea and music on the wireless.

Standing here now, she realised what it had meant to her. When she'd married Rory, it hadn't occurred to her to carry on working, for that wasn't what was expected of women of her class except in extremis, and once the war was over, she had felt there was no place for her at the factory. She had drifted away into the role of farmer's wife, even though it held no thrall for her and she wasn't terribly good at it. No one had forced her into it, it was simply convention. She supposed she was following in her own mother's footsteps, playing second fiddle, although running Foxwood was a full-time job, together with all the unspoken duty that came with being mistress of the big house.

She had spent several afternoons up at Foxwood with her mother, picking her brains for inspiration. They spent hours leafing through magazines, talking about what it was women wanted, and how to make Arbutus the paint they all turned to. Diana was determined to make her mark, and help turn the factory around. They'd done it in the war, after all, and now peace reigned once more, it was time to help the country rebuild, to make the houses they lived in homes.

And the factory had definitely gone back to being a male enclave. Gradually, the women on the shop floor had disappeared once the men returned from war. Now there were only a few at the factory – a couple of secretaries and the odd cleaner. That balance would have to be redressed, in time, thought Diana. Women definitely brought a vibrant energy to a workplace that was lacking at Arbutus Paints these days.

Now, standing at the foot of the table, Diana held up the pieces of card painted with sample colours that were used during sales pitches.

'The first thing we need to do to make us stand out is to give our paint colours evocative names. At the moment, they are numbers. What does Blue Thirteen conjure up in your mind?' Diana held up a card painted pale blue. Everyone looked blank. 'Absolutely nothing, I can see. But what about Daybreak? I can see the colour immediately in my mind's eye, and everything it conjures up: the first light of day, with a vibrant freshness, a blue that is both pale but bright at the same time. Who wouldn't want that on their walls? And this.' She held up another card. 'This is called Red Seven. But what if it was called Fireside? You immediately want to be there, toasting crumpets – it's warm and cosy and atmospheric.'

The men stared back at her. They didn't seem to have a clue what she was on about.

'Surely they can see the colour for themselves, just by looking at the card?' This was Colin. Excellent at his job but set in his ways, and not a man who liked to be told how to think by a woman. Diana gave him a gracious smile.

'They can *see* it but they can't *feel* it. In short, you're telling the customer a story they want to step into. A story they can have in their own home.'

'I reckon my wife would swallow that guff, hook, line and sinker,' said one of the reps. 'They love everything dressed up, don't they? Women?'

'Of course they do,' said Diana. 'Women love creating a fantasy world around them. Because reality is hard. They lived through the nightmare that was the war, and now they want a new beginning. Arbutus Paints can feed that fantasy by capturing the customer's imagination and making them believe our paint is the one that will create their dream home. Where they can lead their dream life.'

She had no idea she had it in her to be so articulate, but she believed in what she was saying. At the moment, Arbutus Paints was depending on its reputation for good quality and practicality, a paint that covered well and went a long way. They needed to push harder to be market leader. Throw a little bit of magic into the mix. They had an excellent reputation, a fantastic product, a good team. And she thought she could help them broaden their vision, for Arbutus Paints to be able to change your world to one you wanted to live in.

Standing in the board room, she couldn't believe how elated she felt. It was wonderful to have a sense of purpose at long last. The kitchen table at Birch Farm had turned into her office, spread with cuttings from magazines and notebooks and lists of ideas. Rory was bemused but intrigued by her new persona as her confidence grew and her days took on a momentum they had been lacking. She even dressed differently, changing out of her jodhpurs after exercising the horses each morning, putting on make-up and brushing her hair, before heading up to her office in the factory.

By eleven o'clock, the board had agreed she should go through the entire Arbutus catalogue and rename the paints. It was a little daunting, for there were almost a hundred different shades.

They moved on to discuss their stand at the Ideal Home Exhibition, a huge event at Olympia where firms showcased their new products: everything from a three-piece suite down to an orange juice squeezer. Things were changing fast now the memory of war was fading. Art. And music. And food. And the way people were using their homes was different. Every month there was some new-fangled contraption. A lockable refrigerated box to be set into the wall by the front door, for the milk delivery. A kitchen stool with a spring in its seat, which would move up and down to the height you wanted. Everything you could possibly want to make your life easier.

The exhibition was where all the big deals were done, so it was important for them to make an impact. April wasn't so very far away, with Christmas around the corner, and after that, time would fly. Competition was fierce, and the exhibition was getting more and more popular.

'We need to do something different. Something eye-catching that will bring the customers to our stand,' said Colin.

He was stating the obvious, rather, thought Diana, but at the same time a flash of inspiration came to her as she remembered playing in the nursery as a little girl.

'What about a doll's house?' she suggested. 'A replica of Foxwood, each room painted differently to show off all our colours.'

Michael nodded his approval. 'I think that would be a fantastic draw. I could definitely find someone to knock us one up.'

'Everyone loves a doll's house,' went on Diana. 'And it would be a real novelty. We could even raffle it off as a prize at the end. Perhaps raise some money for a charity. That would get us publicity.'

Where was all this inspiration coming from? She supposed it had been lying dormant. She'd been wallowing in her own self-pity for years, drowning in grief and bitterness and a little bit of fear for her own future, pushing all the people who loved her away. She felt ashamed when she looked back on it, but she also felt grateful that it was not too late to build bridges and make amends. Spending time with her mother had opened her eyes to how life could be. She and Elizabeth had actually *laughed* together for the first time in years.

And Rory. He had been so loyal and steadfast, even

though she'd been rotten to him. She was lucky to have found someone so endlessly forgiving. She wasn't sure how to express her gratitude. Maybe she didn't need to. He wasn't one for deep and meaningful conversations. He was a straightforward farmer who wanted an easy life, whatever it took.

She hoped this would make her a better wife, in the long run.

She felt re-invigorated as she made her way back to Birch Farm that evening. She hadn't anticipated that thinking up ninety-two names for paint colours would bring meaning to her life, but her brain was whirring as she drove home thinking of gloriously evocative words and phrases inspired by the countryside around her.

Evenfall. Toadstool. Chimney Pot. Jackdaw. Cloche. Woodsmoke. Conker...

28

Stella stared at the words on the page in front of her. *The End*. She couldn't believe it. And the most wonderful thing was, she thought it was good. Her characters had lifted her up and carried her along with them on their funny little adventures, had led her to places she didn't know she was going to take them, yet somehow it had all made perfect sense, as if she was writing down something that had really happened. And the ending had felt like an ending, but at the same time full of new beginnings, and she'd jotted down ideas for a sequel as they came to her, to convince Harriet this could be a series.

She only had to do one more drawing, for the last chapter. She would do it when Ted was in bed tonight, then wrap it all up and send it off to Harriet tomorrow. She'd had two postcards from her – jolly little pictures with Mabel Lucie Attwell drawings on the front, with '*Good luck!*' on the first one, and '*Keep going!*' on the second, and they really had spurred her on, for they had made her realise Harriet believed in her. It was a tiny gesture, but so thoughtful, and she sensed she would be in good hands if she did end up being published by her.

They'd go to the shop when she picked Ted up from school, she decided, and get some ginger nuts to celebrate. That was their favourite biscuit, dunked into tea while they sat by the fire. The trick was to get them soft, but not so soggy they broke off and your cup was filled with biscuit crumbs. She grabbed her coat and ran out of the door – she'd been so wrapped up in the thrill of finishing that she was going to be late if she didn't hurry.

Every time Ted came out of the school gate, she felt a rush of love, but it seemed even more overpowering today, for a brighter future was almost in her grasp. Clementine's visit had unsettled her for a few days, but she trusted her not to betray her confidence, and in the end, it had spurred her on to finish *The Towpath Gang*, for Stella valued her independence over everything. If she ever was to meet Edwin's family, she wanted to be in a much stronger position than she was now. She was vulnerable, living from hand to mouth on the boat, and she didn't trust the Arbutuses not to take advantage of that.

'Ginger nuts?' she said now as Ted scurried over to her with a big grin. One day, she thought, he might not be so eager to be with her, and would become his own person, standing on his own two feet, but for the moment she was going to make the most of her boy and his big, open heart.

'It's not ginger nut day, is it?' He frowned, for they usually had them on the Thursdays her money went in from the magazine.

'Not officially, but I finished *The Towpath Gang* this afternoon, so I think we should celebrate.'

'Yay!' He gave a little punch of triumph. She'd told him all about the book, spent time discussing the characters and what they got up to with him, for she was writing it for boys and girls his age. He'd been very useful, even coming up with some good ideas. As they walked along the high street towards the shop, she thought about the dedication she would put at the front of her manuscript. *To Ted. Head of our own little Towpath Gang.*

They procured the biscuits, and she bought a small bag of mint humbugs too, and they wandered back over the bridge, sweets lodged in their cheeks. As they dropped down onto the towpath, she frowned. She could see a plume of smoke in the distance. She couldn't work out where it might be coming from. The canal bent slightly to the left just after Breverton, so it wasn't possible to see straight ahead to the boat from the bridge. But theirs was the only boat on this stretch of canal at the moment. And there were no buildings. Nothing else it could be. The smoke could only be coming from *Penelope*.

She grabbed at Ted's arm. In her mind's eye, she saw herself open the stove door and put in an extra log earlier. Had she forgotten to shut it? She can't have done.

'Ted,' she said, trying to keep her voice steady. 'I want you to run back to the shop and ask Margaret to call the fire brigade.'

She saw his eyes swivel round and focus on the smoke. 'Is it the boat?'

'I don't know. I'm going to go and see. But stay at the shop, please.' He seemed mesmerised by the sight. 'You need to hurry, love.'

He nodded and shot off back towards the high street. There was no time to waste. She broke into a run. If the boat was on fire, there wasn't going to be much she could do. The whole thing was made of wood. It would go up pretty quickly. Within seconds, she could feel her heart bursting, a mixture of panic and exertion. She couldn't run fast enough. Her legs were like jelly. It was like the most awful dream – she'd had enough of them, desperate nightmares as she ran away from burning buildings. Only this time she was running towards the fire.

She was coming up to the bend. Her mouth was dry with fear as it became more evident what she was going to find. She raced around the corner, dread in her heart, and there she saw it, her beloved *Penelope*, the cabin already engulfed in thick, greedy flames. She could feel the heat on her face, hear the almost gleeful crackle as they made their way along the deck. She stood at a distance, for it was too fierce for her to get any closer, tears pouring down her face, as it destroyed their home, their lives, everything they owned, her and Ted, from the teddy he'd had from birth, all the things Edwin had left behind, her belongings. And the manuscript of *The Towpath Gang*. Those precious pages would be charred beyond ruin.

She sank to her knees in despair, powerless to do anything. She was taken back to the war, to the seemingly endless conflagrations she'd witnessed from a distance, the almost carefree way a fire would take hold and destroy everything it its path, showing no mercy. She knew, from experience, that there was no hope. That, even if a fire engine could get down the towpath, *Penelope* was too far gone to be rescued, that now she would just have to burn herself out. She heard shouts from behind her, people running to her side, someone lifting her up and drawing her away from the scene.

'Come on, love, there's nothing you can do.'

She slumped against a man she recognised from the

ironmonger's. There were half a dozen people now, some with buckets, but as they gathered on the towpath it became obvious that any attempt to put out the fire was futile.

'Where's Ted?' she asked, panicking. The last thing she wanted was for him to see *Penelope* like this. It would be far too traumatic for him.

'Margaret's got him at the shop.' Everyone gathered around her, protecting her, offering reassurance. All she could do was stare out across the canal as *Penelope* disappeared, flame by flame, wrapped in a pall of black smoke. Someone was trying to persuade her to head back into Breverton but she shook them off.

How could this have happened, just when she felt so sure her luck was going to change? A new life had been almost within reach. What was she going to do? She had nothing, literally nothing except the clothes she stood up in. As *Penelope*'s name disappeared, eaten up, the gold letters turning to black, she turned away in defeat and stumbled back along the towpath.

At the shop, she clung to Ted, who was white-faced and silent. Margaret made hot, sweet tea but Stella couldn't even hold her cup. She was trembling with shock, and her bones felt as cold as ice. There were crowds of people in there, offering help and reassurance, but most of what they were saying drifted in and out of her consciousness. She was here and she wasn't here. Nothing made any sense. All she could smell was scorching fumes. All she could hear was the crackle of flames. Dr Boxer came and offered her something for the shock, a sleeping draught, but she didn't want to take it. She needed her wits about her. Besides, she had nowhere to sleep. She sifted through her trains of thought, desperate to find something in there that would make sense. Monsieur Corbières – he was too far away, and he didn't have a phone, or a car, and he was too old to deal with a crisis like this. Harriet? She couldn't contact her. She wasn't even her publisher yet.

And then a face appeared amidst the muddle in her mind. A pair of kind blue eyes and a gentle smile. And she heard a reassuring voice. 'Ask for Clementine.'

Right now, it was the only option she had.

'I wonder if you could give us a lift?' she asked Dr Boxer, surprised at the clarity of her voice as she took Ted's hand. 'To Foxwood.'

29

It was dark by the time Dr Boxer pulled in through the gates of Foxwood. The stone statues looked down in surprise at this new arrival. They hadn't been expecting anyone. There were so many windows, thought Stella, looking at the facade. Some blank with blackness, some glowing warm amber, giving away the whereabouts of the inmates. The house was even more impressive than she'd imagined. Edwin had played it down to her, describing it as 'just a comfy family home, really.' But it was elegant. Impressive. And a little intimidating. Not the kind of house you turned up at unannounced.

'Just leave us here,' she told the doctor.

'Would you like me to come in? I know Mr and Mrs Arbutus.'

'No. It's fine. Thank you so much.' She opened the car door and slid out onto the gravel, Ted scrambling out after her.

'Would you like me to come back tomorrow?'

She was touched by his concern. 'I'll let you know if we need you. If that's all right.'

He nodded his agreement. 'Do look after yourselves. You've had a shock.'

Despite the awfulness of their situation, Stella couldn't help smiling at the understatement. 'We will.'

As he drove away, she took Ted's hand. 'This is the house where your father grew up,' she told him. She had always been honest with him about who his father was, a famous artist who died in the war before he was born, and had explained that as she had never met his parents while he was alive, she had never got to know them. And because her mum and dad had died before he was born, he'd never really queried it. He'd never felt the lack of grandparents.

'Crikey,' he said as they walked up the steps to the front door. 'Does that mean we're rich?'

'We're not, sweetheart, no. But I hope they might help us.' She tugged on the bell pull, and heard it jangling inside the house. Who would come to the door? And how would she explain herself?

Eventually, the door opened. It was the young woman Stella had seen in Margaret's shop that summer, the cook who had been making the wedding cake. She gave Stella an uncertain smile which widened when she saw Ted.

'I'm here to see Clementine,' said Stella. 'If she's in?'

There was a puzzled frown. 'Who should I say is calling?'

'Stella. Stella Knight.'

'If you don't mind waiting, I won't be a moment,' said the cook, and she shut the door.

She didn't blame her, thought Stella, for shutting the door on them. An unlikely couple turning up out of the blue couldn't be brought inside a house like that without further investigation. She shivered a little in the night air, a typical dank November, chilly and mean. For a moment, she imagined the remains of *Penelope* sinking into the depths of the canal, giving herself up to whatever lay underneath – weeds and eels and bicycle wheels, no doubt – and their blackened belongings sinking into the mud. And then she heard voices, and the door opened and there, there was Clementine, her face alive with excitement, the cook three steps behind her.

'Stella! This is a surprise. A lovely surprise. It's wonderful to see you. And Ted.'

She reached out and tousled the little boy's hair. To her horror, Stella found herself completely overwhelmed, mostly by relief at Clementine's warm welcome. She tried to speak, but all that came out was a choked sob.

'Whatever's the matter?'

Somehow Stella managed to find the words. 'It's the boat. Our boat. It caught fire. This afternoon. There's nothing left . . .'

'Oh, Stella.' Clementine didn't hesitate. She stepped forwards and wrapped her up in her arms. 'You poor girl. I'm so sorry. This is awful. Come in, both of you. Quickly.'

She ushered them over the threshold and into the hall. Stella gasped at the sight of the paintings. All of Edwin's work, plastered all over the walls.

'Now listen,' said Clementine. 'I'm going to ask Daisy to take you into the kitchen and get you something to warm you up. I need to go and speak to Edwin's parents and explain everything to them. Would that be all right?'

'Of course,' said Stella. 'I suppose it will be a shock.'

'Leave it to me.' Clementine gave her a reassuring smile.

Daisy was staring at them both, wide-eyed. 'He's a dead ringer for Mr Alfie,' she said, nodding at Ted.

'I know.' Clementine bent down to Ted. 'Do you remember me from the train?'

He nodded. 'You gave me chocolate.'

'Well, there might be some more in the kitchen, if you're lucky. There's definitely a tin of biscuits, because we had some earlier. Daisy, look after them, would you? I'll be as quick as I can.'

Clementine knew that Elizabeth and Michael would be in the small sitting room having drinks, for she and Alfie had been about to join them as was their habit before dinner. Alfie wasn't going up to London until the morning, and she was glad he was here. She was nervous as she headed to the drawing room, and she hoped they would have open minds and open hearts, and most of all wouldn't think her duplicitous. She stopped for a moment outside the sitting room, wondering how best to explain, feeling grateful that Elizabeth hadn't come out to see who was at the door, praying that her revelation would end in Stella and Ted being made welcome. How awful, she thought, to lose their home. It was up to her to make sure they were made at home here, after such a terrible thing. She put her hand on the doorknob, took in a deep breath, and headed inside.

Elizabeth and Michael were deep in conversation. Michael was standing by the fire, while Elizabeth was in the same place on the sofa she'd been when Clementine had spoken to her about Jasper – her favoured spot. It was the perfect English country house scene, thought Clementine, with a soft glow from the well-placed lamps, a vase filled with orange and yellow chrysanthemums on the coffee table, thick silk curtains drawn against the night outside, a hint of Elgar spilling out of the gramophone. And through it all, Oscar snoozed on the rug in front of the fire, oblivious to everything. Shameless Joyce was out in the stables, banished for the time being with a litter of mystery puppies, the result of a careless open door the last time she was in season.

'Who knows where she got to?' Elizabeth had said. 'The father could be a chihuahua or a St Bernard. I suppose we'll never know. But they're here now, so we have to look after them.'

Clementine hoped that she would feel the same way about Stella and Ted.

They both smiled as she came in, and Michael automatically headed to the drinks trolley, picking up an empty glass and brandishing it.

'Clementine. What can I get you? We're having brandy and ginger to warm us up. It's so damp . . .'

'That's sounds lovely.' Her voice sounded high, pinched with nerves. 'But I've got something I need to talk to you about.'

She went and sat down opposite Elizabeth, who looked concerned.

'Is everything all right?'

'I'm not sure where to start. But I think the easiest way to explain is . . . I met a woman on the train a few weeks ago, when I went up to London.' She paused. 'With her son. He looked just like Edwin and Alfie. I've seen pictures of them when they were small.' She nodded over to the piano in the corner of the room, which was smothered in photo frames of the Arbutus family over the years.

Elizabeth and Michael glanced at each other, then back at Clementine. Elizabeth reached for Michael's hand.

'What do you mean?' she asked, her voice a little tight.

'When I got back, I did a bit of detective work and found out where they lived. On a narrowboat, on the canal. I went to see her.'

'And?' Elizabeth was stiff with wariness. Michael seemed much more composed, as if he was ready for what was to come.

'She and Edwin fell in love, towards the end of the war. After he died, she found out she was expecting his baby.'

Elizabeth's grip tightened on her glass.

'So was he the little boy? On the train?'

'Yes. His name's Ted. Named after Edwin, of course. And they're here, tonight. There was a fire on their boat today. They have nothing left. Nothing.'

There was a stunned silence, broken only by the grandfather clock in the hall striking seven.

'But why didn't we know about her?' Elizabeth was bewildered. 'Why did he never tell us? And how could she have kept the boy from us?'

Clementine knew this was going to be difficult to explain, and that she had to be careful not to make Stella the villain. To elicit Elizabeth and Michael's sympathy, not anger.

'Edwin never knew about his son. And Stella always felt that she wouldn't be welcome here. Which is terrible, of course. But she worried that she wouldn't fit in at Foxwood. That she was too ordinary. Or that's what she thinks. She's not ordinary at all. Far from it.'

Elizabeth shook her head in disbelief. 'This is too much to take in. You mean he's been here in Breverton all the time? Our own grandson?'

Michael hadn't said anything at all during this exchange, but suddenly he stood up. His face was grim.

'Clementine, would you leave the two of us alone for a moment?'

Clementine blinked, a little taken aback by his abruptness. 'Yes. Of course.'

She stood up, not sure what was going to happen next. Michael didn't look happy, and she prayed he wasn't going to banish Stella and Ted from the house without even meeting them. She hurried from the room, closing the door behind her. Michael turned to his wife.

'I knew about her,' he said. His face was white.

'What do you mean?' Elizabeth was finding it hard to take it all in.

'I knew there was another woman. Apart from Meg.'

'How?'

Michael's voice shook as he tried to explain.

'The last time he came here. The last time we saw him. He came to see me, to tell me he was breaking off his engagement. He told me he'd met someone else, and he wanted to marry her. I was furious. I felt he'd let us all down. The Engadines, and poor Meg. We had an awful row...' Michael's voice broke. 'He accused me of only being interested in Meg's money. He told me he was writing to Meg, and he was going to marry whoever this girl was, and if I didn't like it, then he wouldn't come back and work for the factory.'

'But you never said anything. And he never told me any of this.'

'I told him not to. I told him to go back to London and think very seriously about what he was doing. I told him he was a fool and he'd been dishonourable...' Michael sat down on the sofa and put his face in his hands. 'It was the last thing I ever said to him. My wonderful son. It was only because I thought he was making a mistake. That he'd had his head turned because of the war, and was being rash...'

He looked up, anguished.

'Oh, darling.' Elizabeth came and sat next to him. 'He would have known you didn't mean it. That you were just trying to protect him.'

'But would he?' Michael looked at his wife. His face was as pale and drawn as it had been when they'd heard the news of Edwin's death, and there were tears in his eyes. 'It haunts me, to think he died thinking I didn't love him.'

'Darling, he absolutely knew you loved him. The last thing he said to me was "Look after the old so and so".' She could remember it so clearly, standing in the hall, Edwin dropping a farewell kiss on her head then heading out of the door. She'd had no idea he and Michael had had a row. And why hadn't Edwin told her of his plans? They'd often talked about affairs of the heart. She would have been the obvious confidante. But perhaps he thought it was a formality, to tell his father about breaking off his engagement.

Poor Meg. That's how everyone referred to her. Elizabeth had thought the girl charming, but, on reflection, perhaps she and Edwin were never kindred spirits. They had, after all, met and got engaged before Edwin had made his name, before he had become a war artist. Both of those things would have changed him.

'Every morning, when I wake up, all I can remember is my last words to him,' Michael said. 'It's the worst mistake I've ever made. It's a father's duty, to love his son unconditionally...'

Elizabeth couldn't bear watching her husband's heartbreak. She wrapped her arms around him and held him as tightly as she could. Her noble husband, who had kept this revelation from her for all these years, so she could preserve her memory of her son. And it explained so much. Grief was not measurable. One person didn't suffer more than another after a tragic loss. Yet she had often felt that Michael had worn Edwin's death more heavily than she had; that there had been something weighing him down, yet he had never wanted to talk about it. And she felt ashamed, that her solution had been not to try to heal him, but to turn to someone else for comfort.

She shut her eyes for a moment to work out the best thing to do. This was what she was good at. Weighing up what everyone needed, and the best plan of action. She didn't need to think too hard. It was obvious.

'Darling,' she said, 'you know what we must do. For Edwin. We must make this girl of his welcome, and our grandson. We must look after them. It's what he would have wanted.'

Clementine hurried upstairs to find Alfie. She was conscious of Stella and Ted waiting in the kitchen, but Alfie needed to be told what was happening. She found him in their bedroom, getting changed into a clean shirt for dinner.

'What is it?' he asked, when he saw her face.

'That girl,' she said. 'That girl I saw on the train, with the little boy.'

He frowned. 'What about her?' There was wariness in his voice.

Clementine swallowed. She was going to have to confess, that she'd been to visit Stella behind his back. And that her hunch had been correct. She explained it all to him, as quickly as she could.

'So they're here?' he said.

'In the kitchen. With Daisy. Your parents are talking it over. They seemed rather shocked. Of course...' She frowned. Alfie was staring at her, but the look on his face wasn't what she'd expected. It was... guilt?

'I knew,' he said softly. 'I knew about her all along.'

'Stella?' Clementine tried to take in what he was saying. 'You knew about Stella? But when I told you about her, you got angry. As if you didn't believe me—'

Alfie put his hand up. 'I know. And I'm sorry, but I was only trying to protect Edwin. I didn't want anyone rummaging in his past. I didn't want my parents to be upset.'

'But *how* did you know? What did you know?' Clementine was trying not to let this revelation rankle. 'Were you trying to put me off the scent?'

'No.' He sighed. 'Jasper and I went to clear out the flat after Edwin's death. To make sure there wasn't anything there that might upset Mum or Dad. It's the worst part of the job, when someone dies, to see evidence of the last thing they were doing when they were alive...'

'Oh, Alfie.' Clementine softened immediately. How terribly sad for him.

'We put everything in order. His clothes. Tidied up. You know. The last coffee cup he'd used. His shaving brush. Jasper was an absolute brick. I couldn't have done it without him.'

Clementine didn't say anything, but this made her think a little more kindly of Jasper.

'Anyway, I was hanging up his blazer and I found a letter in the pocket. It was addressed to Meg. He must have meant to post it. Anyway, I opened it. I wanted to see what it said before I forwarded it to her. I thought it might have been of some comfort, but it was lucky I checked.' He took in a deep breath. 'He was breaking off his engagement to her. Of course, being Edwin, it was the most beautiful, gracious letter. Explaining how the past few years had changed him, and how he didn't think he was the right person for her any longer.'

'Oh,' said Clementine. This was heartbreaking.

'I burned it. Of course. Meg knew he was dead – my mother telephoned and spoke to her, but because of the war she wasn't able to come over. And I wanted her memories to be intact. I never wanted her to know Edwin didn't want to marry her.'

'Of course not. And it was the right thing to do.'

'I didn't tell anyone. Even Jasper. And then I found the painting.'

'What painting?'

'The painting that explained it all. Of a girl, with red hair, sitting on a bed, reading *Wuthering Heights*. There was a little pencil sketch with it. I knew everything when I looked at it. This girl was the reason for the letter. I could feel Edwin's adoration in every brushstroke. And the look in the girl's eyes as well – they were laughing, but there was . . . something else in them.' He managed a smile. 'You know, that look when you know you've fallen head over heels with someone, even if you haven't admitted it even to yourself.'

Clementine nodded. 'Do you still have it?'

'I hid it away. It's at the flat, in an old portfolio of sketches. I didn't want to destroy it, but I thought if I mixed it up with other stuff it wouldn't seem so important. She could have been anyone from any time.'

'And you never told anyone?'

'No. I never felt any of it was mine to share. It would all cause too much hurt and speculation. And I never knew that she'd had a child. That Edwin had a son.'

'I wish you'd told me,' said Clementine. 'I wish you'd trusted me, when I told you I'd seen her. You must have known it was Stella.'

'I was afraid, of upsetting people. I wanted his memory to stay intact. For everyone to have their memory of him untainted . . .' He trailed off, looking miserable. 'I never wanted to be the keeper of his secret.'

'I understand,' said Clementine. 'It was complicated. And confusing.'

'I'm sorry if you feel as if I didn't trust you.'

'It doesn't matter. Because she's here now. And Ted is all the proof anyone needs. Let's go and find your parents. We can't keep them waiting in the kitchen all night. It's unkind, after what they've been through.'

Alfie gazed back at his wife. 'I love you so much,' he said. 'I can't wait to meet him,' he paused, his voice wobbling. 'My nephew.'

She walked over to Alfie and put her arms around him. 'Oh, wait until you see him, Alfie. He's a dear little boy.

He's going to mean the world to your parents. Their first grandson.'

He squeezed her hand, knowing what that word meant to her. He was in awe of how she could be so overjoyed about finding Ted, after losing their own baby so recently. How lucky he was, he thought. How lucky they all were, to have Clementine in their lives.

In the kitchen, Stella was getting agitated. Fifteen, then twenty minutes went by. Ted had finished his cocoa and had polished off half a dozen biscuits from a tin of Carr's – there was a pile of wrappers next to his plate. He was falling asleep at the table. Daisy was trying to keep up a conversation, but it was obvious she wasn't quite sure of her role in all of this, except to keep them fed.

'Can I make you boiled eggs?' she asked. There were pork chops waiting for the family dinner but she wasn't sure she should offer those up.

'I'm not really hungry,' said Stella. The rich cocoa had made her feel slightly sick. 'I think Ted just needs to sleep. I'm wondering if perhaps we should go. If you could telephone Dr Boxer...' He was the only person she could think of to help. Tomorrow she would try to get in touch with Monsieur Corbières. They could travel up on the train. He would organise something for them. He might know someone who would have a room amongst all his artistic contacts. Her heart sank slightly at the thought of falling on London's mercy, but perhaps there would be more opportunity to start again.

'Oh, don't go,' said Daisy, alarmed.

At that moment the door opened and Clementine appeared, looking apologetic.

'I'm so sorry to have kept you waiting for so long. It's awfully rude. But there was a lot of explaining to do.' She sat down at the table next to Stella, looking concerned. 'Would you like to come and meet everyone? I know it's probably a lot to take in, after everything...'

Clementine was right. Stella wasn't sure if she was ready at all. Here she was, the outsider, about to meet the parents and brother of the man who had meant so much to her. She supposed she had little choice. They knew about her now. More importantly, they knew about Ted. They were unlikely to let him slip through their fingers.

He deserved to have some family, she thought. He deserved to have a chance to share in this life. The kitchen at Foxwood had wrapped itself around them, with its warmth, its enticing smells, its larder stuffed with munificence. Already, they'd had a taste of a better future.

'Ted,' she said gently, and he roused himself. 'Come on. Let's go.'

In the small sitting room, Michael, Elizabeth and Alfie tried to arrange things to look welcoming. They switched off the overhead light and snapped on a few more lamps, threw another log on the fire and turned off the rather portentous Elgar. Michael and Elizabeth sat on one sofa with Oscar between them, while Alfie stood by the fireplace. The sense of expectation was palpable. Elizabeth could hear her own heart pounding in her ears, and Michael reached out his hand to hold hers. She squeezed his fingers to reassure him, and was taken back to the wedding, to them waiting for the ceremony to begin.

And then the door opened, and Clementine ushered in a tall woman with a mane of red hair. Her face was astonishingly pale, like fresh milk, and her eyes were as silver as sixpences. And she had her arm around a small boy, about eight years old, who looked around the room wide-eyed.

'This is Ted,' said Clementine. 'He's eight years old and he's jolly good at spelling. And this is Stella.'

Michael jumped up and strode across the room with his hand outstretched. Oscar poured himself onto the floor and followed, eager to investigate the new arrivals.

'Stella. I'm Michael. Welcome to Foxwood. And this must be Ted. Oscar, down. Honestly, he has no manners. I'm so sorry.'

Ted fell on his knees and put his arms around Oscar's neck, burying his face in his fur. Oscar, of course, loved the attention, wallowing in it shamelessly.

'Ted loves dogs,' said Stella, holding her hand out to shake Michael's. 'But we couldn't really have one on the boat.'

'I'm so sorry to hear what happened. Of course, you must stay here for tonight at least.'

Elizabeth was approaching too. She only had eyes for her grandson. The moment she saw him, her heart burst with something even more than love. It was an overwhelming desire to protect, a fierce rush of maternal instinct combined with the joy of seeing someone connected to the son she had lost. She came and crouched down in front of him so her eyes were level with his.

Those clear green eyes the colour of the marbles he used to roll along the corridor outside the kitchen. The lock of hair that stuck up at the front – she would endlessly pat it down only for it to spring up. The little dent in his chin. The more she gazed at him the more similarities she found. But there were differences too. Ted's eyebrows were arched where Edwin's had been straight. His nose was more of a button where Edwin's had been aquiline.

'I'm very pleased to meet you, Ted.' She longed to hold him, but not yet perhaps. She didn't trust herself not to cry.

'Is this your dog?' he asked.

'Ted!' said Stella. 'Say hello properly.'

'It's all right,' said Elizabeth. 'Yes, this is Oscar, and there's Joyce too. You can meet her tomorrow.'

The puppies, thought Elizabeth. All small boys need a puppy, to tell their woes to. She was jumping too far ahead. She stood and held out her hand. 'Stella. I'm Elizabeth. I'm so sorry to hear what happened.'

Stella took her hand. 'It's awful,' she said. 'Everything's gone. I'm not sure Ted's taken it in yet. Actually, I'm not sure I have.'

'Well, we're very happy to have you here, although I'm sorry it's under such difficult circumstances.'

'Thank you.' Stella managed a smile. 'We don't have anywhere else to go. Well, we could go back to London. But I don't even have the train fare. I've got my purse, that I took to the shop. That's it.' She held out her arms and looked down at her clothes – a brown jumper, a pair of woollen slacks and lace-up shoes.

'I don't want you to worry about anything for the time being,' Elizabeth said. 'I can find you some things.'

Stella could only nod her appreciation. Elizabeth saw she was exhausted, and was barely taking anything in. Her eyes never left Ted, and were filled with anxiety. But she smiled as Alfie came over.

'Alfie,' she said, before he'd even had time to introduce himself. 'Edwin told me so much about you.'

Alfie had been going to offer his hand, but instinct made him open his arms to embrace her. The two of them held each other, so much waiting to be said, but it felt so right. Stella found herself burying her face in his shirt, breathing him in, her hands tightening on the arms that held her, and he patted her on the back. He knew. He understood.

Elizabeth saw the shadows under Stella's eyes were purple, and she had begun to shiver. This must all be overwhelming. Elizabeth had so many questions about so many things, but she sensed now was not the time to ask. If they took things slowly, there would be all the time in the world. She wasn't going to interrogate the girl about why she had kept hidden for all this time. Or pry into her relationship with Edwin. She certainly wasn't going to query the veracity of her story. She needed no more proof than the boy with his arms around Oscar.

'You both need to sleep,' said Elizabeth. 'Let me ask Daisy to get you a room ready. I expect you'd like to be together for tonight, after everything.'

Stella wrapped her arms around herself and nodded. Her teeth were chattering. Michael looked at her thoughtfully.

'I think,' he said, 'we should get Dr Boxer back. Just to check you over.'

It was nearly midnight before Stella crawled into bed. Ted was already fast asleep. Dr Boxer had given her a little something to put in his bedtime drink.

'We don't want him having nightmares,' he said. 'And

there's something here for you too. I'd recommend taking it. Sleep is a great healer.'

She didn't tell him she already knew that. Sleep was all she had done after Edwin died. Work, eat and crawl into bed to find oblivion for as long as she could, for while she was awake only one thing circled around in her mind: how was she going to live without him? Somehow she had survived, even with the shock of finding out, eventually, that she was expecting, but Ted had been the saving of her, because she'd been to some very dark places in her head before she knew he was coming along. She'd stayed at the boarding house in London to have him, feeling safer in the hands of a city hospital than a rural one, but when Ted was four months old she'd packed everything up and headed down to Somerset to live on the boat, for Edwin's solicitor had contacted her and told her Edwin had left a confidential letter of wishes for the boat to be hers. In Breverton, she did as she pleased and no one interfered, although she was under no illusion that they didn't speculate, or have opinions. But it was easy to keep herself to herself, the eccentric widow who lived on the canal.

What was everyone in the town going to say when they knew the truth? She'd seen Margaret's eyes gleam with interest when she'd asked the doctor to take her to Foxwood. No doubt gossip would be flying around the little town already, but she felt safe here, protected from prying eyes and loose tongues. She sank into the softness of the mattress, pulling up the smooth linen sheets and the wool blankets and the satin eiderdown, luxuriating in the warmth. She and Ted had both had a long hot bath each, and she had felt some of the horror of the day float away.

She was overcome by the welcome the two of them had been given. She had felt reassured as soon as she met Elizabeth and Michael. Yes, Elizabeth was terrifyingly glamorous in a yellow crêpe dress and discreet diamonds, and Michael was a typical country gentleman – though not the red-faced, port-soaked variety, thank goodness – but they had been immediately welcoming and kind and warm. If only she'd had the courage to approach them sooner. But she simply hadn't had the confidence. She had worried she was no replacement for an American heiress, that they might resent her for displacing Meg. She'd had nothing to bring to the table. But it seemed her fears were unfounded.

'My family will love you,' Edwin had always said, and she should have believed him.

Sleep was floating in, courtesy of Dr Boxer, a warm tide gathering up her thoughts and carrying them away. The bed was enormous, but she reached out to pat Ted's back as he lay curled up beside her. And then blackness fell, extinguishing every last worry, and she slept.

30

The next morning, when Stella woke, she could hear the chime of a grandfather clock in the distance, but lost count of the chimes in her fug so she had no idea what the time was. She pulled back the curtain: it was light outside. The bedroom looked out onto swathes of velvet lawn encircled by oak trees. A gardener was tidying away the flower beds for winter, gathering up all the dead leaves and cutting back the bare rose branches. Ted was still asleep, snuffling gently.

She headed for the door to go to the bathroom. There was a neat pile of clothing on the landing outside. A selection of blouses, jumpers and skirts for her that, judging by the quality, must be Elizabeth's, and another pile of clothes for Ted. Someone must have been to Purkiss and Son, the outfitters in the high street. There were vests and pyjamas, and a smart pair of corduroy trousers and a checked shirt. He would look like a mini Michael, thought Stella, and for a moment she felt a flicker of concern. She didn't want them to be moulded into something they weren't. But then she told herself to be grateful, and not so touchy.

This was a country house, and she supposed these were the clothes you wore for an aristocratic country life.

Ten minutes later she was washed and dressed. She was taller than Elizabeth, so her clothes were a little short in the arm and leg, but it was interesting to wear someone else's choice: a lambswool cardigan in cornflower-blue, and a pleated skirt in a heathery tweed with flecks of the same blue in it. She gave herself a fleeting grin as she looked in the mirror – quite the lady of the manor. She sat on the edge of the bed for a moment to see if Ted might stir, but he was out for the count and she thought it was best to let him sleep on. There was a lot to think about. A lot to decide.

How did you start again, when you'd lost everything?

There were people to contact. The school, to say that Ted might not be in for a few days. Monsieur Corbières – she must tell him what had happened. He was her constant, her adviser, the one who understood more than anyone about love and art and life. And Harriet. She would have to tell her that her story had been lost, that it was going to take some time before she could rewrite it. She thought of her poor typewriter, that had served her so well. How was she going to afford a new one?

She sighed, covered Ted over with the eiderdown, and headed downstairs, not quite sure of the etiquette or how she was going to make herself known. Should she go to the kitchen? She stood at the foot of the stairs in the hall, looking more closely at Edwin's paintings – the still lives, the portraits, the landscapes – and it was as if he was in the next room, for all of his outlook on life was here, his eye for detail, his sense of beauty, his sense of awe, his sense of humour. Oh God, how she missed him. She sat down on the bottom step and put her head in her hands, feeling all her hope drain away. It had been hard enough, building a new life when he'd died. Could she do it again?

She heard footsteps, and looked up to see Elizabeth looking at her with concern.

'Stella. Is everything all right?'

Stella looked up wearily.

'I miss him so much.' She waved a hand at all the paintings.

'I know,' sighed Elizabeth. 'Oh, I know.'

She came and sat down beside her on the step, reached out for Stella's hand and held it tight. They sat there, the two of them, until the sheer utter misery of their grief passed through them.

'It knocks you off your feet sometimes,' said Elizabeth. 'But you get up eventually. You have to.'

'Thank you,' said Stella. 'For everything.' She was still holding on to Elizabeth's hand. 'The clothes. Ted's clothes.'

'I nipped into Breverton first thing. I hope I chose well. And I hope it all fits. We can alter anything that doesn't.' She looked at her approvingly. 'But that looks lovely. I chose things I thought might go with your hair.'

'Oh gosh,' said Stella. 'I've given up trying to make things go with my hair. But thank you.'

The grandfather clock stirred into action, chiming out the half-hour. Stella looked at it and realised the time.

'Half past ten! I'm usually up at six.'

'You needed the sleep.'

'Mum?'

They both turned round to see Ted standing at the top of the stairs in his vest and pants.

'Teddy! You must be freezing. Let's get you into some clothes.' Stella jumped up.

'Hello, Ted,' said Elizabeth. 'Did you sleep well?'

'I don't know,' he said, looking confused.

'In that case you must have. You'd better come and have some breakfast. Daisy will make you poached eggs on toast. Are you keen on eggs? We have chickens, so it could be your job to collect them every day, if you like.'

Stella eyed Elizabeth with interest. She was sliding into her unexpected role of grandmother with consummate ease. She was a natural. A sliver of guilt rose to the surface, but she batted it away. She didn't have room for guilt on top of everything else.

Michael was dealing with the practicalities of the situation with a quiet authority. He disappeared into Breverton after Elizabeth came back, heading to the bank to put twenty pounds in Stella's account to tide her over so she didn't have to ask for money. He went to see the headmistress of Breverton Infants, securing assurance that Ted needn't go back to school until he was good and ready, and a promise that thereafter they would keep an eye on him. He spoke to the head of the local fire brigade, who informed him the fire had most probably started from a build-up of creosote in the chimney.

'It does happen,' he said. 'Especially if you've been using wet wood. You can only be grateful they weren't on board. That would not have ended well.'

Stella was overwhelmed by his generosity.

'I don't want you to have to go cap in hand to anyone,' Michael told her. 'Use it to get yourself back on your feet.

And if you need anything else, please don't be afraid to ask.'

'I'm going to need a typewriter,' she said. 'I've got my magazine stories to write, or I'll never be able to pay you back.'

'Leave it with me,' he said.

She sat down later that morning to write to Harriet.

> *The most dreadful thing has happened. I finished The Towpath Gang yesterday afternoon, and went to collect Ted from school. When we got back, our boat was on fire. We've lost everything, including the manuscript. I'm staying with Ted's grandparents, and I'm hoping to be able to rewrite everything as soon as I can. But I fear it might not be this side of Christmas...*

She prayed that Harriet would understand her position, and wouldn't think her unprofessional, or imagine she was making excuses.

She wrote to Monsieur Corbières too, for she wrote to him at least once a month to keep him up to date with what they were up to. The old man would write back in his flowing French script, often including some money which she put aside for Ted. That had all gone up in flames, she thought sadly. It wasn't a fortune but it might have bought him something to remind him of Mr C one day.

Lunch was late, for breakfast had been. Daisy made leek and potato soup and there was delicious home-made bread and a slab of craggy Somerset cheddar with apple chutney. Ted ate with relish, and Stella was relieved that he seemed to have his usual chirpy spirit. This was an adventure for him so far, and she was glad he hadn't actually seen the fire. She herself couldn't bear to think back on it, and kept remembering things that she would never see again, especially all her reminders of Edwin, for the boat had been full of his belongings: his pen knife and a long woollen scarf and his favourite cup. And the pictures. Especially all the silly little sketches he'd been going to turn into paintings. They had reminded her of him and had given her comfort every day.

'They're only things,' she told herself, for she had shuddered when Michael had told her what the fireman had said. What if they'd got back to the boat with their ginger nuts and had been sitting there, happily dunking, when the chimney caught fire?

Things only went sour when lunch was nearly over, and Diana arrived, bursting into the dining room with Bingo in tow. She stopped short when she saw strangers at the table.

'Oh,' she said. 'Visitors. Are you going to introduce me?'

'Diana!' Elizabeth looked at her daughter. 'Gosh. Um – this is Stella and this is Ted. Stella was a friend of Edwin's.'

'A friend?' Diana raised an eyebrow.

There was an awkward silence.

'More than a friend, actually,' Stella said. 'Edwin is Ted's father.'

Ted was eating one of Daisy's brandy snaps filled with cream. He was sitting to the right of Michael, and the family resemblance was striking.

'You don't say.' Diana managed a glimmer of a smile. 'Well, it would have been nice if you'd all telephoned me with the good news. It's not every day you turn up and find a lost... a lost...' She frowned for a moment, as if working it out. 'Nephew.'

'We were going to tell you. This afternoon. But it's been a bit chaotic, to say the least...' Elizabeth was gabbling. She knew she'd made a mistake. She'd been trying to keep things calm and she'd kept thinking of telling Diana, but Diana would bring another layer of drama that no one needed, especially Stella, so it was about finding the right moment.

'It's my fault. We've been taking up a lot of everyone's time. But it's very nice to meet you,' said Stella.

Diana looked at her. 'So what's brought you out of the woodwork?'

'Diana.' Michael shot her a stern glance.

Stella didn't baulk. 'It's a fair question. We lost our home in a fire yesterday.'

'Oh. Sorry to hear it.' She didn't sound sorry. She turned to her mother. 'Can I have a word?'

Elizabeth put down her napkin and stood up. It was obvious that the sooner Diana was out of the room, the better. Her daughter turned on her as soon as they got out into the hall.

'I can't believe you didn't tell me straight away.' Diana was trembling. 'I'm that little boy's *aunt*. Didn't you think to ring me?'

'Diana, darling,' Elizabeth said. 'Please calm down and realise this has been a shock for us, and if we handled things wrongly, I'm very sorry.'

Diana didn't say anything for a moment. Her face was expressionless. Elizabeth braced herself for a riposte. When it came, it ripped her heart out.

'Well, at least you've got the grandson you've been

wanting for so long. Given that neither Clementine nor I have managed to produce one.'

Elizabeth leaned back against the wall, weak with despair. It was still there, Diana's ability to say something completely eviscerating.

'Although are you sure he's Edwin's son?' Diana went on. 'It's like something out of Dickens. I mean, it would be very easy to pretend. I bet there are people who read obituaries and—'

'He's definitely Edwin's,' Elizabeth cut her off. 'He's got a whorl of hair on his head exactly the same. And his eyes are identical. Even his knobbly knees are Edwin's.'

'You think that because you want to believe it. I'd be very wary.'

'And she's got his signet ring.'

Diana flinched. They had all presumed he had been wearing the family signet ring when he'd been lost.

'Oh. Well. She could have pinched it.'

'And Clementine saw all his sketches on the boat.'

'What boat?'

Elizabeth explained how Clementine had seen her on the train, had put two and two together, and had found Stella living on a boat that had apparently belonged to Edwin. Diana raised an eyebrow.

'Clementine's probably in on it too. They've cooked it up between them. They've wormed their way into Foxwood and they'll get us knocked off, one by one. Until whatever-his-name-is inherits the lot. Presumably he'd be the heir if we all died?'

'Ted. His name is Ted and you're being ridiculous.'

'I'm looking out for you. You can be naïve.'

'I don't think so.'

'Oh, come on. You think no one knows about you and Jasper, for a start.'

'What?'

'Have you ditched him yet?'

Elizabeth swallowed down her panic. And her irritation.

'Diana. I don't want us to come to blows over this. I'm very sorry I didn't tell you straight away. It's actually been rather a shock for me. What I'd really like is support.'

For a moment, Diana didn't reply. Everything had been going so well. She was the happiest she'd been for a long time, now she was back at the factory. She had felt closer to both her mother and her father than she had ever since Edwin died. She couldn't help feeling threatened by this new arrival, this cuckoo in their nest. But what was the point in kicking up a fuss? She could see Stella and Ted had won over everyone's hearts and had their feet under the table.

Her mother took her hands. This time, her voice was soothing.

'It's important that we stick together. We've all got a bit lost over the past few years. Perhaps some of us have made mistakes. We are only human.' Her voice wavered a little. 'I'm certain that Stella's story is true. Edwin told your father about her the last time he was home. And Alfie told us about a letter he found, from Edwin to Meg, breaking off their engagement. And there's a painting, that Edwin did, of Stella. I'm quite certain that he loved her, and that she was his world. So for Edwin's sake, I'm going to do everything in my power to make sure that she and Ted are looked after. They are going to be part of this family whether you like it or not. Now, you can either be gracious and welcoming or difficult. It's up to you.'

Diana didn't answer for a long time. 'I don't actually have a choice, do I?'

She walked back into the dining room with her mother and went round to greet Stella.

'I'm so sorry. I was taken unawares rather. I'm sure you understand. Welcome to Foxwood.' She crouched down to speak to the little boy, a smile growing across her face. 'And to you too, Ted. I'm so happy to meet you. Are you keen on horses? We could organise something if you are.'

Elizabeth felt a mixture of relief and pride. Diana had risen to the occasion. And it had been thoughtless of her, to leave her out. After all, Diana had been closer to Edwin than any of them, at times.

Later that afternoon, Elizabeth took Ted out to the stables, where the four puppies were installed in a wire pen, Joyce splayed out amidst them, longsuffering but proud of the results of her midnight rendezvous with nobody knew who. She tolerated their shenanigans with a bemused detachment, batting them occasionally with a paw if they got too boisterous. They were ridiculously appealing, with their ginger fur, black button noses and fat feet.

Ted dropped in amongst them and talked to them all. Was there anything more joyful than watching a small boy writhing amidst a litter of puppies?

'We'll be keeping one of them,' she heard herself saying. They'd had no intention of keeping any of them to start with, as they weren't pure breeds, but how could she not let him have one? 'And it can be yours, to keep here. So we'll look after it, but technically it will belong to you.'

Ted stared at her in disbelief. 'Do you mean it?'

'Of course I do. It will always be here for you, whatever happens.'

He was shaking with excitement. 'Thank you,' he said, and Elizabeth wanted him to keep them all, forever, and for her to keep the whole lot of them, Ted and the puppies, safe at Foxwood until the end of time.

'They'll be ready to leave their mum in about a week,' she told him now. 'And we can start training. It's hard work, but it's important. There's nothing worse than a badly behaved dog. Is there, Joyce?' she said meaningfully, but Joyce stared back, unashamed.

She loved the little boy already, with a fierceness that surprised her. It wasn't just because he was Edwin's. It was his immense spirit, even in the face of disaster. She liked to think it was an Arbutus trait, for they all showed it, Michael and Edwin and Alfie, an ability to push through the hard times with a smile on their face and without making a fuss. Although she had to admit, Stella set a pretty good example herself. She had shown nothing but grit, albeit with a few moments of despair, but that proved she was human. And that must have been what attracted Edwin to her. Both her boys had found strong women, interesting women, women who rose to the occasion but without having to prove themselves in an overbearing fashion. It was important, thought Elizabeth, to have a softer side when you were female, and that in itself could be a weapon.

That evening before dinner, Stella listened to Ted wax lyrical about his afternoon.

'It's the smallest, so it's sort of the runt, but Elizabeth'

– Elizabeth? Who had told him he could call his grandmother Elizabeth? – 'agrees he's got the most character, so I'm keeping him. Well, they're keeping him, but he's technically mine. For ever. And he's called Paddy, because she says my dad had a friend at school called Paddy who was Irish, like they are. Well, half Irish, because nobody knows where Joyce got to.'

'That's wonderful.' There was a lump in her throat. There was so much kindness going on. It was almost *too* much, after the horror of the day before. They'd been thrown from hell into heaven. And the price of heaven was guilt. Guilt that she had never trusted Edwin's assurance that she would be made welcome at Foxwood, that his family wouldn't look down on her, that she wouldn't be made to feel like an outsider. Her own stupid pride and insecurity had stopped her from being part of what she realised now was a wonderful family – well, apart from Diana, maybe, but she seemed highly strung, and a bit of an outsider herself. Feeling alienated made you hostile, Stella knew. It closed your mind and forced you to keep people at arm's length. Mistrust was a bad master. An open heart was a much better guide to life.

For proof, she only had to turn to the little desk in the corner of the bedroom. She had come back this afternoon to find a portable typewriter on it, along with a fresh ribbon and a pile of paper. She had no idea how she was going to thank Michael. How had he done it, produced a typewriter out of thin air? The gesture had given her so much faith in human nature, so much confidence, that she almost felt she could start writing straight away. The stories were still fresh in her mind, after all. She would have to tease them out, pin them down, and they might not come out exactly as they had first time around, but she thought she could do it, and the illstrations too. If Harriet hadn't given up on her, that is. For a moment, she regretted sending the letter off earlier. Harriet might put her out of her mind, and get excited about another project. She didn't suppose she would wait forever. Tomorrow. She would start tomorrow.

A few days later, a taxi trundled up the drive to Foxwood, and a young girl got out staggering under the weight of a large hamper from Fortnum and Mason. It was Elizabeth who answered the door, for it was Daisy's day off – she'd left sausages and peeled potatoes for mash for supper. It was their tradition, when Daisy wasn't there, to eat in the kitchen, and it would be much better for Ted to eat early as he'd gone back to school the day before.

'I'm Harriet Banham,' said the girl. 'Stella's editor. I wonder if I could see her?'

'Oh,' said Elizabeth, eyeing up the hamper. 'Of course. Come in. She'll be in her room but I'm sure she'd love to see you. Let me take that.' She took the hamper off Harriet and stood to one side to let her past. 'If you wait here, I'll nip upstairs and get her. I'll be two minutes.'

She set the hamper down. This must be good news. No one turned up with a Fortnum's hamper if it was bad news. She ran up the stairs, tapped on Stella's door and heard the sound of the typewriter stop. She'd been typing away for what felt like days.

'There's a girl to see you. Harriet Banham?'

'Harriet?' Stella's face was a mixture of delight and puzzlement. 'What on earth's she doing here?' She started to tidy up her hair and rearrange her clothes. Today she was wearing an olive-green shirt dress of Elizabeth's that tied at the waist, and it suited her to perfection.

'Get yourself ready. I'll go down and show her into the sitting room, if you like.'

'Thank you. I won't be long. I just need to make myself look presentable.'

Elizabeth headed back down the stairs, where she found Harriet looking around at Edwin's paintings in fascination, peering at every last detail through her spectacles as if she was looking for woodworm.

'Are these all by Edwin Arbutus?' she asked.

'Yes.' Elizabeth felt a burst of pride. 'Do you know him? Or of him? He is... was my eldest son.'

'Of course I know him. His paintings are wonderful. My mother took me to an exhibition at the National Gallery during the war. We both agreed his paintings were far and away the best.'

'Thank you. We think so too, though we're not allowed to say that.' Elizabeth gave a little laugh.

'I've only seen his war work in real life. These are glorious. The detail is incredible. And the colours...' Her eyes swept over the collection from top to bottom. She pointed at the picture of Clodagh. 'That dog! She looks as if she might jump out of the frame. Sorry, I'm gushing rather. But I don't often get to see work like this up close. He was a genius.'

Elizabeth tried hard to feign modesty on Edwin's behalf. 'I don't know about genius, but he was quite talented. These are just the things he painted when he was here. We got everything framed after he died and put it all up. It seemed the perfect memorial.'

'You must be very proud.'

'I am. I'm very proud.'

'And I'm so sorry. That you lost him. I remember reading about it in the paper. I cut out his photo. I was sixteen...' She blushed a little. 'I've never been a film star sort of a girl. More writers and artists.'

'He'd have loved that.'

They looked up as Stella came down the stairs. She looked a little uncertain.

'Harriet. This is such a surprise...'

Harriet rushed forwards and threw her arms around her. 'I had to come and see you. As soon as I got your letter I wanted to make sure you were all right, but I've had meetings and lunches and launches and I couldn't get away until today. I've brought you a hamper – just some treats. For everyone, really. There's champagne in there too. Champagne does very well as commiseration as well as celebration. Stella, I'm so sorry. About the boat...' She finally drew breath.

Elizabeth could see Stella was lost for words.

'Why don't you both go into the sitting room? I'll bring in tea. Daisy's not here but she's left flapjacks so I think we'll manage.'

She could see Harriet was bursting to find out the connections, and she thought it was best if she made herself absent while Stella explained.

Stella could tell that Harriet was no stranger to grand houses, but nevertheless she exclaimed over the charm of the small sitting room, as everyone did. Stella settled her into one of the sofas and sat opposite her, being careful not to steal Elizabeth's favourite spot.

'So tell me,' said Harriet. 'Is Knight a pen name? Or

are you an Arbutus? Were you trying to hide it from me, because you didn't want to use the name to get a book deal?'

'If I'd known that's all it took...' Stella laughed. 'But actually, I'm not an Arbutus. My son is. Though he uses my surname.' Harriet looked confused, so she decided to put her straight. 'Edwin was his father.'

Harriet's eyes widened behind her glasses.

'So that's who he was,' she said softly. 'You said you had lost someone in the war. I didn't want to invade your privacy by asking any more, but now I understand. What a talented couple you must have been.'

'Not really,' said Stella. 'I mean, he was, of course. I'm nothing in comparison. Though he taught me a lot.'

'I'm so sorry. That you lost him. Your great love. It's too awful.' Harriet sighed. 'And the boat too. But I'm very glad to see you being looked after.'

'I've been incredibly lucky. His parents have been wonderful.' It seemed crass to mention that she had never met them until the day of the fire. Harriet didn't need to know that yet.

Harriet sat forwards excitedly, clapping her hands together.

'Anyway, I've come for two reasons. First to make sure you're all right. And second, I've got some good news. Before I go any further, I have to tell you, you don't have to accept this offer. Because, as I said when we met, there are probably other publishers who would snap you up.' She paused to draw breath. Stella was gradually coming to realise that all Harriet's thoughts came tumbling out of her in a torrent. 'When I read your letter, I went straight to Upstairs. To the publishing directors. I told them your story, told them how completely wonderful I think you are and how much I believed in you. I showed them what you'd given me so far, and they gave me permission to give you an advance on the part-manuscript.'

'What?' said Stella. 'Say that again?'

'I've got permission to give you an advance,' repeated Harriet. 'I'm hoping it will get you back on your feet and you'll be able to deliver the rest before too long, but the important thing is I don't want you to worry, about money or about when to deliver, because *The Towpath Gang* is so brilliant I would wait for ever to get it in my paws.'

Stella sat back in astonishment. 'Do you mean it?'

'Just say the word, and I'll get the contracts drawn up. You're incredibly talented, Stella, and I feel lucky to have found you. Although I suppose you found me. Not that it matters, who found who. Either way, we are going to have a bestseller. I shall make sure of it.'

That night, when Harriet had taken a taxi to the station to catch the train back to London, Elizabeth suggested that Ted might like to move into Edwin's old bedroom, up on the third floor, now the initial shock was over.

'I moved all Edwin's bits and pieces into the attic when he went off to art college,' Elizabeth told her, trembling slightly at the memory. It was hard for any mother when a child left home, but even harder when there was no hope of them ever coming back. 'But there's a decent bed and a chest of drawers and we can get him a desk. Or whatever he needs.'

The room was perfect for a small boy, tucked into the eaves, with wonky wooden floors and a window onto the garden, and an Egyptian carpet that looked as if it might fly if you shut your eyes and made a wish.

As Stella stood in the doorway, she imagined Edwin in here at Ted's age, lining up toy cars on the windowsill. What would Edwin say if he could see Ted there now? Would he point out the big oak tree, with the owl that taunted you with his plaintive hoots if you happened to be awake at three in the morning? Would he tell him to look out for foxes in the shadows? Or explain to him all the phases of the moon – she remembered him showing her the Cold Moon one December, which was certainly aptly named.

'It's also called the Moon before Yule,' he'd told her. She must get Ted a book on astronomy. And perhaps a telescope. The dormer window was crying out for a telescope.

Stella didn't allow herself to feel any guilt that he could have had his own room all these years, if she hadn't been so determined to be independent. He'd been happy on the boat. And she reminded herself that they wouldn't be here for ever. With today's news, she might be able to find themselves a place of their own sooner than expected. Who knew where they might end up?

31

'It's not a formal ball,' Clementine explained to Stella the following weekend. 'More an excuse to dress up and have fun. Though all the men will be in white tie, of course. It just makes it easier.'

Stella smiled. *Of course.* Imagine living in a world where it was assumed you had white tie. But then she reminded herself that's exactly the world she was living in at the moment. Not that Clementine or any of the Arbutus family rubbed it in. They wore their privilege lightly, but it was still there, undeniably, a protective ring of gold flung around the house.

'I remember Edwin talking about the Snow Ball, especially at Christmas,' she said. 'Didn't he once collect the guests from the station in a white pony and trap?'

'Did he?' laughed Clementine. 'I don't know. This is my first one too. Elizabeth would know. They take it very seriously. There's weeks of preparation, usually, but we've got a bit behind, what with one thing and another.'

'What with long-lost children turning up on the doorstep.' Stella gave a wry smile.

'Nobody would have it any other way,' said Clementine.

'Do you know, everyone seems so much happier now you're here. Ted's brought light into the house.'

It was true. He brought energy, and momentum, and everyone loved being part of his life. Michael had taken him up to the factory and given him a tour of the paintworks. Alfie took him and Paddy around the grounds, showing him all the secret places where he and Edwin had made dens and forts. And Elizabeth had the boys' old train set brought down from the attic to put into his room, and some new rolling stock had been ordered from Hamley's to arrive in time for Christmas.

Was he being spoilt? Stella worried. Perhaps not. Perhaps it was making up for everything he hadn't had so far. She'd done her best to indulge him when she could, but money had been tight. And he was always very grateful. How awful it would be if he started boasting at school, or lording it over the others, but she didn't think he had it in him. In the same way that neither Edwin nor Alfie were show-offs. They knew exactly how to treat people. Edwin had always been charming to waiters when they went out, chatting to them as if they were friends.

'It's how you know a good egg from a bad egg, how they treat staff,' Edwin told her.

Stella, Clementine and Daisy were sitting at the kitchen table, waiting for Elizabeth and Diana, for today they were making a definitive list of what needed doing.

'Two weeks today!' Daisy looked alarmed. If anyone was going to crack under the pressure, it was her, although Elizabeth had been down to the Breverton Arms and was borrowing three of their waitresses to help with the food. The family had insisted that Daisy should be a guest, although she wasn't all that happy about it. She didn't trust anyone else to do the job properly.

Elizabeth swept in, carrying that day's shopping.

'Sorry to have kept you all waiting. The butcher is always so busy on a Saturday. They've run out of kidneys, Daisy, so we'll have to find something else for breakfast tomorrow. I thought a kedgeree? I got some smoked haddock instead. Now.' She settled down in the remaining chair with a sigh. 'Where are we with it all?'

Clementine looked at her lists. 'I suggest next weekend we borrow some muscle from the factory to move furniture around, put up the Christmas trees and help with lights. All the boring practical stuff. It does mean living in chaos for the following week, but perhaps we can eat in the kitchen, if Daisy doesn't mind? Then when everything is where it should be, we can do the decorating over the next week.'

'That sounds an excellent plan.' Elizabeth looked at her daughter-in-law with admiration. 'And can we find Diana something to do? I want her to feel part of it all. She's supposed to be coming this morning.' She looked at her watch.

Stella tensed slightly at the thought of Diana pitching up. The two of them had reached an uneasy truce, but she still felt on edge when Diana was around. This was so cosy, the four of them, plotting away together. She thought how lucky she was to have these three women in her life. Elizabeth had been so warm and welcoming and they talked a lot about Edwin, in quiet moments, sharing things about him that the other didn't know, crying sometimes. It had really helped Stella, to share her grief with someone who understood what she was missing, and she hoped it helped Elizabeth too.

Clementine was becoming a close friend too. Although she was younger than Stella, it didn't matter. She was thoughtful and observant and headed off problems before they presented themselves, being acutely aware of people's feelings.

As for Daisy, who was a little older, Stella felt closer to her than any of them, for she was an ordinary person just like her, and had lost her fiancé. She never spoke about him much, but one day, when Stella was helping her with some baking, she opened her heart.

'He never thought twice about joining up. The moment war was announced he was off. I was so proud of him. He joined the RAF at Charmy Down. But he died in a training exercise. He was in a Westland Whirlwind and it crashed into another one. He never got to actually fight, and that would have annoyed him.'

'It doesn't make him any less of a hero, Daisy.'

'I know. That's what I'd tell him if I could.'

She pressed her lips together and patted the pastry she was making into a round ball. Stella put her arm around her shoulders. There was no need to say any more. Daisy relaxed for a moment, melted into her and allowed herself the comfort of Stella's warmth. For a split second, the ghosts of the two men they loved were in the kitchen with them, and there was a glimmer of what might have been, four spirited young people with their future ahead of them, full of laughter and hope. Then Daisy pulled away and took the pastry to the fridge. The moment had gone.

As they went through the final plans for the food, Daisy

was wondering, inspired by Elizabeth's change of breakfast menu, if kedgeree would be the thing to fill everyone up at midnight, when suddenly Diana appeared, red-faced and flustered.

'I'm sorry. One of the horses lost a shoe so I had to put it in the stable to wait for the farrier. What have I missed? What's my job? Just don't ask me to cook. But I'll do anything else.'

'You could help me with the decorations?' Stella suggested. She was going to cut giant snowflakes out of leftover wallpaper from the factory.

'But I don't have an artistic bone in my body.'

'If I traced the shapes out carefully, anyone could cut them out. We just need sharp scissors.'

'All right,' said Diana, looking pleased. 'That sounds easy enough.'

She was making an effort, thought Stella, and noticed the relief on Elizabeth's face that her daughter was being co-operative. The five of them spent a very jolly hour eating biscuits and batting ideas backwards and forwards, and actually Diana was quite funny when she relaxed, telling them stories of what she and Edwin had got up to when they were young, and only allowed to go to the Snow Ball for an hour before being escorted upstairs by the nanny. Stella was starting to warm to her. Of course she'd been miffed about not being included the day she and Ted arrived. It was horrid, feeling left out. But now she was in on the act, she was as happy as anything.

'God knows what I'm going to wear,' Diana said now.

'I haven't a clue either,' said Daisy, looking anxious.

'Nor me. I was going to make something. I could make

you both something to wear,' said Stella. 'Is there a sewing machine?'

'Yes. In the laundry.' Daisy looked excited. 'Oh, would you?'

'I've always made my own clothes.' Before the war, Stella had been expert at copying the latest fashions, plundering jumble sales for dresses to remodel and altering hand-me-downs by changing the buttons or taking up the hems or adding some lace to a collar. 'Although there's not much time, if I've got to make us all something.'

'Don't panic,' said Elizabeth. 'I've got years of dresses upstairs. I always had something new, which seems an awful waste now.' The war had taught them all to be careful, and although she hadn't quite got the hang of frugality, she was much less extravagant, much more inclined to see where a saving could be made. 'You're welcome to have a look through them all and see what fits. In fact,' Elizabeth jumped up, 'why don't you come upstairs now and try them on? I'd love to see them used. There's no point in them sitting there.'

And so the five of them spent the next hour going through Elizabeth's collection of ball dresses. Swathes of velvet and silk, embellished with beads and feathers and lace. Stella and Daisy and Diana tried them all while Clementine and Elizabeth looked on, offering their opinions. As Stella ran around with a mouth full of pins – 'Do whatever you need to. They were only bits of fun run up by a local dressmaker, not *haute couture*,' said Elizabeth – a sense of anticipation for the ball started to fizz.

Daisy stood on a chair while Stella took up the hem of a 1920s-style flapper dress. Her eyes were shining with excitement.

'I can't remember the last time I danced,' she said. 'It would have been when Roy was still alive.'

'Oh, Daisy,' said Stella. 'We must always remember to dance.'

She thought how much younger Daisy looked out of her usual drab pinafore, the cream silk reflecting onto her skin. Daisy always seemed happy with her lot, quite content to be cooking away, looking after everyone. But she deserved a second chance at happiness. She wouldn't find that stuck in the kitchen.

Diana was staring at herself in the mirror. She was swathed in white velvet with long sleeves, trimmed with swansdown. She looked puzzled, as if she didn't recognise herself. Elizabeth pulled her daughter's hair out of its usual ponytail and fluffed it up.

'Look at you,' said her mother. 'You look marvellous.'

'I can't remember the last time I wore a long dress,' said Diana. She seemed a bit emotional, as if it was a revelation that she could put one on and the world wouldn't come to an end.

Stella found a white devoré dress with a halter neck, cut daringly low at the back. Because she was so tall and slim, it looked breathtakingly elegant. She imagined a warm hand on her bare skin guiding her to the dance floor. She shook herself out of it. Now was not the time to look backwards.

The dresses were put to one side, ready for Stella to do the final alterations.

Here we all are, she thought, five women brought together under the same roof at Foxwood, all touched by war, as everyone had been, determined not to be bowed, determined to make the Snow Ball a night to remember.

*

It was nearly one o'clock when Stella went off to find Ted and get him to wash his hands for lunch. She couldn't find him anywhere, or Paddy. The puppy had barely left his side since he'd been old enough to leave his mum, and Ted spent hours trying to train him – 'Sit!', 'Lie down!', 'Heel!' – with a trail of snipped-up cold sausage he'd begged from Daisy. Ted was extremely patient, and Paddy extremely eager to please, so it was a match made in heaven.

She looked in the stable yard, and all around the garden, but they were nowhere to be seen. She ran upstairs to his room, but apart from being awfully messy – how could he have made such a mess already? – there was no sign of him.

She had run out of ideas as to where he might be. Could he have gone over to the factory to find Michael? It was only half a mile away, and already he worshipped his grandfather. But she could hear Michael's voice in the hall downstairs, and presumably he'd have brought Ted back with him if he'd ventured that far. Stella hadn't worried about him roaming around, for she firmly believed in a long rein and Elizabeth had reassured her that Edwin and Diana and Alfie had wandered for miles and never come to any harm. But Ted was on his own and hadn't been brought up here, so should she have laid down some stricter rules? He wasn't a reckless child. Inquisitive, perhaps, but not foolhardy.

No one had seen him since breakfast.

Half an hour later, he still hadn't turned up and Stella felt panic start to rise in her chest, a cold, hard lump that was stopping her breathing. He must be hungry by now, and he knew they were strict about mealtimes at Foxwood. What if he'd jumped off a gate and broken his leg and was lying somewhere? Or been hit by a car? There wasn't much traffic around the lanes, but people did drive fast if they happened to be passing.

After an hour, Michael phoned the factory and sent out a search party to comb the fields between the factory and Foxwood. Alfie and Rory got in the car and drove to Breverton – maybe he'd got it into his head to go and visit a friend? There was no football today because the ground was frozen hard, but perhaps he'd fancied a kickabout.

Stella stood at the gates to Foxwood, looking up and down the road. It was cold and silent, the sky glowering above, the trees bare. There were no clues – no trail of footprints or pawprints. She tried to listen to her gut, her motherly instinct, but nothing told her where he might be, whether he might have gone right or left. All she knew was he wouldn't have disappeared like this on purpose. He wasn't a thoughtless child, and he wouldn't willingly cause her distress. As the hands of her watch swept round, she felt a wave of despair. Michael strode out to find her and bring her back inside, but she collapsed against him, sobbing.

'I can't bear this. I just can't.' She could take losing Edwin. She could take losing the boat. But not Ted. Michael took her arm and walked her back to the house. He was white with worry himself.

'I'm telephoning the police,' he told her, and she had no idea if this was supposed to reassure her, but it didn't.

Dr Boxer arrived, and wanted to give her a sedative, but she refused, even though Elizabeth tried to persuade her. She needed to be alert, just in case. Daisy brought her hot sweet tea and hugged her.

'He's going to be all right. I know he is,' she told her, and Stella was grateful for her certainty, for no one else was able to give her any. She could see no one knew what to think, and they were beginning to fear the worst. Only something terrible could have stopped him from coming back by now.

Four hours. Five. It grew dark. The police arrived and interviewed everyone. There was talk of searching the river, at which Stella became completely hysterical. Clementine and Elizabeth surrounded her, held her tight, so tight, until she ran out of energy and collapsed onto a chair, weeping quietly. What if she never found out what had happened to him? What if he disappeared, leaving her to wonder for the rest of her life?

The men were out searching the nearby woods. Elizabeth, Clementine and Stella sat together in the small sitting room, occasionally making a comment or a suggestion, on high alert for any noise that might suggest news. Daisy brought in more tea and sat with them, visibly distraught. Stella sat with her eyes shut and her hands twisting in her lap, her jaw clenched, rigid with tension.

Just after six o'clock, the telephone rang, an insistent drill into the hushed silence. Everyone froze, staring at each other. It could be Alexandra phoning for a gossip. Or the vicar. Or it could be—

Elizabeth flew to the hall and everyone followed. She picked up the receiver. She was quiet for a moment, then cried out and sank into the chair by the phone.

'Oh, thank God!'

She smiled, but her face crumpled as she finally broke down, holding out the phone to Stella, unable to speak.

Stella grabbed the receiver off her. 'Who is it?'

'He's run away to London, your boy,' said a familiar voice.

'Monsieur Corbières!' Stella reached her hand out to hold Elizabeth's. She was smiling. The relief. The hot, sweet relief. Was there a better feeling in all the world, as you felt fear and panic recede, pulling in their claws and crawling back into the shadows. 'Where are you? Is he there? Can I speak to him?'

'I am at the pub, using the telephone. He is here, with the puppy.'

'How did he get there?'

'The train, and the Underground, of course.'

'But he's got no money. That I know of.'

Monsieur C chuckled. 'He's cunning.'

Stella wasn't quite so amused. 'Keep him safe, Mr C. We'll come and get him straight away.'

Clementine stepped forwards. 'Alfie can drive you.' The men were due back in half an hour, reporting in reguarly. 'Daisy, go and pack some sandwiches, would you? And a flask of tea?'

Daisy nodded, beaming. 'I knew he'd be all right. But bloody hell – the little monkey. All the way to London? He's got more nerve than me, I'll give him that.'

'But why did he do it?' asked Elizabeth, bewildered. 'Why did he run away?'

'I suppose we'll find out,' said Stella. Anger with Ted was starting to creep in, even though she hated the idea of being angry with him. But did he have any idea of the agony he'd put them through?

The next hour passed in a whirl of euphoria as they prepared to go and fetch Ted. Luckily the Alvis had enough petrol to get them there, just. Elizabeth found blankets and cushions to keep them warm on the journey. And Daisy packed up the hamper Harriet had brought, with cheese sandwiches and pork pie and cake and squash.

'That's enough to feed an army. We're hoping to be back by morning,' said Clementine, who had decided to come too. Moral support would probably be needed, and she wasn't sure Alfie would appreciate quite how high Stella's emotions would be running. Being a man, he thought the drama was over, but there was a chance it had only just begun. *Why* had Ted run away, for a start? There were a lot of questions.

She telephoned Ben. She'd phoned him a few days before and told him about Stella and Ted. Now, she asked him to go round to the shop to check up on the two of them. Monsieur Corbières had sounded quite calm, but he was getting on and might not be on the ball with what Ted needed. Stella was a bit anxious about Mr C's ability to look after him, having been taken unawares, and worried he'd be giving him absinthe and oysters. He would definitely have been well into his first bottle of wine by the time Ted had reached him. Ben was the sort of person who could procure piping-hot fish and chips at a moment's notice, or pie and mash – suitable fodder for the end of an adventure.

'I was about to go out on the razz,' Ben said. 'We're off to the Sunset Club later. Maybe you could come on after?'

'No, Ben. We're coming to fetch Ted, not having a night on the town.' Clementine rolled her eyes, but she was smiling. 'Can you pop round and see how they are? We'll be there with Stella as soon as we can.'

*

Stella tucked herself into the back of Alfie's – Edwin's – car. It was strange being in it again. It smelled the same, of damp canvas and oil and leather, and brought the memories flooding back of him whisking her away to Somerset that weekend to stay on the boat. She remembered swishing out of London in it, feeling like royalty.

She could never have predicted that she would be sitting in it again, this time on a rescue mission to get their son, the son he never knew existed.

Why had Ted run away? He'd been perfectly chirpy at breakfast. Saturday was bacon and egg, his absolute favourite, and he'd devoured his helping and had three slices of toast. There had been nothing to suggest that anything was amiss. But Dr Boxer had warned there might be some kind of belated reaction to the fire.

'It's a big shock, to lose your home, so keep an eye on him. Of course he might take it all in his stride, but if there's anything you're worried about, just let me know.'

She racked her brains for any clue. Ted was settled at school, quite happy to head off there every morning, although he did hate leaving Paddy. But he knew the puppy would be looked after, and would be there when he got home. He'd been thrilled with his new bedroom. And there was lots to look forward to. He was excited about the Snow Ball, and was going to be allowed to stay up for the first couple of hours, handing around hors d'oeuvres. And of course straight after the ball was Christmas. Their first Foxwood Christmas.

She huddled into the corner of the back seat and pulled the blanket more tightly around her. There was hardly any room, and the seat was rock hard, and it was freezing cold. She slept fitfully on the journey up, only waking as they made their way down the A4 into Hammersmith. London was such a different place now, the street lamps glowing and lights on in all the houses, not like during the war, when it kept itself as dark as it could.

She remembered coming home from a shift at the station, blundering around streets that were familiar in daylight but hostile at night, not giving away any clues. You had to be so careful, not to trip and fall over a kerb or a loose paving stone, feeling your way in the pitch-black, hoping against hope that this wasn't going to be the night it was your turn in the deadly game of cat and mouse. You couldn't do anything but keep quiet and pray, for the enemy delighted in lack of warning. When the war ended, it took years to get used to the idea that a bomb wasn't going to drop any minute. Even now, as they entered the city, she found herself looking up at the sky, eternally watchful. She never did that in Somerset.

They pulled up at the shop on Lamb's Conduit Street just before midnight. Stella rushed to the door to find it locked, so rang the bell to Monsieur Corbières' flat. She was startled when a stranger opened the door. He was tall and slender, with laughing eyes set in a thin face, heavy glasses, wild dark hair and a full mouth which gave her a welcoming smile.

'You must be Stella.'

'You must be Ben.'

Clementine had told her she'd sent her half-brother over, but Stella had been expecting someone rather more conventional, not this rather intriguing creature, part scarecrow, part dandy.

'Come in, all of you,' he said. 'I'm afraid Ted's fallen asleep, but he'll be so glad to see you.'

Stella needed no second telling. She rushed through the shop, breathing in the scent of pencil lead and paint, straight through the door behind the counter and up the stairs. She burst in through the door to find Monsieur Corbières sitting with Paddy on his lap, and Ted curled up in an armchair. She took in the familiar chaos, the bookshelves groaning, the walls crammed with paintings, the empty bottles and glasses and the smell of coffee and cigarette smoke and dust. She'd spent so many hours in here, being tutored by him, looking at artwork in his extensive collection of books, dissecting why a painting worked and why it didn't.

Monsieur Corbières put his finger to his lips, and she crept in quietly, heading straight to her son, kneeling beside him, feeling the tears rush into her eyes as she touched his shoulder as if to make sure he was real and not a mirage.

Ted's eyes snapped open, and he sat up. 'Mum?'

'Oh, sweetheart.' She put her arms round him and pulled him in until she could feel his very heartbeat, his breath, his warmth. 'What on earth have you been up to? What happened?'

Ted ruffled his hair and looked over her shoulder. 'Oh, hello, Alfie. Hello, Clementine. What's everyone doing here?'

The others had followed in behind her, all of them crammed into the tiny flat.

'We've come to fetch you. You had us worried sick.'

'We had a little chat about that,' said Ben, who was bringing up the rear.

'*Oui*,' agreed Monsieur Corbières. 'He promises he will not run away again.'

'But how did you *get* here?' asked Stella.

'On the train,' said Ted. 'It was easy. I sneaked on at Breverton. And told the guard that Paddy had eaten my ticket. He laughed and gave me another one.'

'What? The brass neck of you!' Despite herself, Stella was impressed.

'I did the same on the Underground. I remembered the way from last time we came. When you left me with Mr C.'

The day she'd been to meet Harriet. She couldn't help but look at him in admiration. 'I'm going to have to watch you. You're like the Artful Dodger.'

'I couldn't believe my eyes when he walked into the shop.' Monsieur Corbières shook his head in amazement. 'I tell him, it's not good to give an old man a shock.' He patted his heart.

Stella put her hand on his shoulder.

'Clementine. Alfie. This is Monsieur Corbières. He introduced me and Edwin.'

'Forgive me. I am being held prisoner.' Monsieur Corbières nodded down to the puppy on his lap.

'It's lovely to meet you,' said Clementine, bending down to stroke Paddy. 'I've heard so much about you.'

'My brother often spoke about your shop. He loved it here,' added Alfie.

Monsieur Corbières nodded. 'He was a good friend. He always took the time to stop and talk to me. So many artists are in a world of their own, in a hurry, only interested in their work. But he was interested in people. I think that's why his paintings were so wonderful.'

Alfie nodded his gratitude for the man's kind words, and was obviously moved by what he had said.

'I have Chartreuse or wine or coffee,' Monsieur Corbières offered. 'But no tea. I know you English like your tea in a crisis.'

'We brought a flask,' said Clementine, producing it with a flourish.

'Good old Clem. Always prepared,' said Ben. 'I stopped off at Federico's and they gave me a dish of macaroni cheese, so we've had a good supper.'

'But Ted,' Stella knelt down and took his hand so he wouldn't feel frightened, 'we need to know what happened. Why did you run away?'

Out of the corner of her eye, she saw Ben and Monsieur Corbières look at each other. Ted scratched his head, obviously reluctant to divulge the truth.

'Go on, mate,' said Ben. 'It'll be all right. You've done nothing wrong.'

'It's everyone at school.' Ted looked bewildered as he told his story. 'They've been teasing me. Calling me Lord Muck. They don't want to play with me anymore.' He shrugged, confused. 'They laughed at my new clothes. *Haw haw haw...*' He gave an imitation of them imitating someone posh. 'I don't want to go back, Mum.'

Stella felt sick. How could anyone be so cruel to a little boy? A little boy whose home had just gone up in flames? She knew exactly why, of course. They were jealous. Or their parents were – they would have heard the speculation, the assumptions, and being children, they would have fed on it. Gossip would have been flying around Breverton ever since the night of the fire, and no doubt there would be malice from certain quarters. It was dispiriting, but that was small-town life. She'd already felt a change in how people perceived her. They looked at her with new eyes, unsure how to speak to her, even though she was still the same person and treated them no differently. Margaret in the shop had been flustered and pink-cheeked when she came in, and the headmistress had been curiously officious.

'Oh, Ted,' Clementine was saying. 'Give them a week and they'll have forgotten. They'll get bored with teasing. I promise you.'

Stella looked at her gratefully. 'Clementine's right, darling. Sometimes people say things they don't mean because they don't understand.'

She put her arms round Ted and let her head drop onto his shoulder, feeling hot tears fall onto her cheeks. Why was it so hard to keep her boy safe? She seemed to be lurching from one awful crisis to another. Maybe they shouldn't go back? Maybe they should stay here, in London, where people were too busy with their own business to worry about who and what you were. You could be anonymous here, without any fear of judgement. She could go back to her old boarding house, perhaps? They'd often had rooms available. They could squirrel away in there and start again.

Then she thought of Elizabeth, and her joy at seeing Ted for the first time, and how quickly they had become close. She thought of Michael, and his quiet kindness to his grandson. She thought of Edwin's bedroom, and how it had been the first time Ted had space of his own. Alfie and Clementine, too, had been so welcoming and thoughtful and were always such fun. And Daisy, who always went out of her way to make Ted special things and slip him a chocolate biscuit when she thought no one was looking.

She thought how happy she was at Foxwood too. Hours at the typewriter while Ted was at school, walking in the woods, the fire in the little sitting room in the evening, making cocoa in the kitchen. And then there was the ball. The excitement of the ball, and all the things she'd promised to do. Make dresses and decorations and help Daisy with the cooking.

For now, it was where they belonged while they adjusted to their new life. Things would settle; people would get used to the new status quo, and she could take her time working out what was best for her and Ted without worrying about how to keep a roof over their head.

'Come on,' she said to Ted. 'Go and get your coat. Let's go home.'

32

The Snow Ball was nearly upon them. Mid-December brought sparkling frost and crisp mornings, and the short days gave everyone a sense of urgency, hurrying to get everything done before dusk fell. Foxwood turned itself upside down as furniture was rearranged. Elizabeth winced as the grand piano was scraped across the elm parquet in the big drawing room and the sofas were pushed back to make room for the band. The tuner arrived and the air was filled with a dissonant plink-plink. Two hours later he gave a virtuoso performance of a Chopin nocturne, every note perfectly in tune.

'We must use the piano more,' said Elizabeth to Michael. It was lovely to hear music floating around the house.

It would be wrong, she thought, to say she felt like her old self. She could never be that again: there were too many scars, too many mistakes, too much pain. But she was gradually coming to like her new self. Being a grandmother was pure bliss. The prospect of Alfie and Clementine here full-time in the New Year was exciting. She and Michael had settled back into themselves since he had opened up about his hidden guilt over Edwin. They had talked for hours, and there had been tears, but they had been the kind that make you feel better, and she felt closer than ever to him now. As for Diana, she was transformed, positively dynamic, and was practically running the factory, she was so full of ideas.

'I'm not sure you need me,' Alfie had joked to his father.

'Please. I definitely need you. I need an ally. She's terrifying,' Michael quipped back, but he was delighted by his daughter's drive and determination.

Elizabeth turned her attention back to her list. She was the mistress of lists and delegation but also had an iron nerve. Whatever happened, it would be a night to remember, and if something was forgotten, it was unlikely anyone would notice. Everyone was contributing however they could, even Ted, who had been out chopping logs with Maurice and trundling them into the house in a wheelbarrow to fill the log baskets.

The day before the ball, Elizabeth supervised Joey harvesting huge balls of mistletoe from the tops of trees in the nearby orchard. He had his ladder propped up precariously against the highest branches, and handed them down, one by one. She wanted one hanging from the centre of each room: the hall, the small sitting room, the drawing room and the dining room, tied with white ribbon to match the milk-white berries.

When she got back, she found Alfie and Freddie had arrived with a van loaded up with bottles of champagne and wine, and a curious drink that looked like cream.

'It's advocaat,' said Alfie, with pride. 'There's a new

cocktail in town called a Snowball. It's all the rage. What could be more perfect?'

He made a jug full, with advocaat and extra cream, eggs, sugar and brandy, and everyone declared it delicious.

'We'll have that at midnight,' decided Elizabeth.

'I can't believe it's tomorrow,' said Clementine, thinking of the afternoon she'd found the invitations. 'So much has happened.'

She was right, thought Elizabeth. So much *had* happened, and although some things had been under the surface and nobody needed to know about them, this year's Snow Ball represented a fresh new start for everyone. The perfect way to close the year and look forward to the next.

Before dinner that night, Alfie knocked on Stella's bedroom door. He was carrying a package wrapped in brown paper which he handed to her with reverence.

'This is for you,' he told her. 'I took it to Ben to get it reframed, which is why it's taken a while.'

Intrigued, Stella peeled back the paper. As the picture revealed itself, she gave a gasp. There she was, sitting on the bunk in the boat, her hair wild, sitting in the clothes she'd slept in, reading *Wuthering Heights*.

'I remember him doing a sketch,' she breathed. 'I had no idea he'd done a painting. Oh, Alfie. This means the world.'

She grabbed him and held him tight. She was so grateful to him for the gesture, for apart from the signet ring, which she had always worn on a chain round her neck and never taken off, it was the only thing she had that connected her to the man she had loved so much. And she remembered that day so well. It was the day they had fallen in love, even if they hadn't admitted it either to themselves or to each other. But the love had been there, in that boat, and here was the proof.

'It's very special,' said Alfie, feeling choked. If he needed any evidence that Edwin had truly loved Stella, that she had meant the world to him, then this was it.

Later, after supper, which was shepherd's pie in the kitchen because the dining room was completely upside down, Stella stood at the head of the table and held it up for everyone to admire. She was touched by how moved they all were.

'Can we put it in the hall, with the others? In pride of place?' asked Elizabeth. 'Or would you prefer to have it in your room?'

Stella hesitated. In some ways, she wanted to keep it to herself. But if anything proved that the Arbutus family had welcomed her into their midst, it was to have her portrait hung high in the hall, so she agreed. And first thing the next morning, the perfect place was found, a nail was driven into the thick plaster, and there she was, Stella Knight, smiling down, ready to welcome all the guests who were going to come over the threshold at Foxwood.

The night of the ball was a clear, bright evening, with a sprinkling of stars, as if someone had flung a handful of diamonds across the sky. The house itself glowed from inside, all the lights on the ground floor ablaze, the curtains swathed just so. There were lanterns burning along the drive and up the steps to the front door, which was surrounded by tangles of ivy. In the hall, Edwin's paintings, with Stella in their midst, were each topped with a sprig of holly. By the staircase stood a towering Christmas tree, decorated with white glass baubles like giant pearls. And from the ceiling hung the biggest ball of mistletoe, spinning gently.

Elizabeth and Stella were sweeping through the house, double-checking every flower, every ornament. In the drawing room, the Havana Brothers were warming up, and the rafters rang with the golden notes of the trumpeter, a little bit of Cuba in the Somerset countryside. The grand piano winced a little at the over-enthusiastic fingers of the pianist, but it was nice to have it used again.

In the kitchen, Daisy was talking through the menu with the waitresses.

'The first trays to go out will be the oysters, to be served with champagne as everyone arrives. When they're gone, you go out with the angels-on-horseback and sausage rolls. These are warm so you need to be quick so they don't go cold. And then there are the devilled eggs and the vol-au-vents.'

She was worried that there wasn't enough food. She was worried about how on earth they were all going to manage without her in charge because she was supposed to be enjoying herself as a guest. In the end, Elizabeth had to calm her down.

'Daisy, you've been slaving away for weeks making sure everything is perfect. And when have you ever let us run out of food? And the girls know what they're doing.'

Daisy eyed the three of them doubtfully. She wasn't sure the Breverton Arms worked to her standards. She would just have to keep popping in and out to check they were doing everything correctly. The dining room had been set up for the buffet, and there would be silver chafing dishes filled with her hot Poulet Reine Elizabeth, followed by queen of puddings and pavlovas topped with chestnut cream. There would be kedgeree at midnight to send everyone on their way at one o'clock, back to their billets or the Breverton Arms or the spare rooms at Foxwood which had been aired and polished and the beds made up with fresh linen.

The stage was set, and the house had never looked more beautiful.

And nor had its inmates. Now was the time for them to disappear off and put on their glad rags, ready for the family portrait to be taken by the fire in the drawing room, before the first guests arrived.

In the master bedroom, Elizabeth slipped into the dress that had been earmarked for the ball that never was. She wondered if it was bad luck, then told herself there was no such thing. It still fitted perfectly. Worry and rationing had made sure that she'd put on no weight in the intervening years. She remembered buying it at Fenwick two months before war broke out. What if Chamberlain's negotiations with Hitler had been more successful, and he hadn't uttered those now famous words: 'This country is at war with Germany'?

But he had, and what had happened had happened, and she was proud of her son for taking on the challenge he'd been given. And she knew Edwin would be cheering her on, pleased that finally she had revived the family tradition. The Snow Ball. She couldn't believe it was fifteen years since the last one. Sometimes it felt like yesterday.

All in all, she felt much calmer than she thought she

would. She was much calmer, full stop, these days. Once, she would have been rushing about, panicking, double-checking, driving everyone mad. This time, though, Clementine, Stella, Daisy and even Diana had shared the burden, and she felt positively serene. Her only worry was that she might get emotional. But who cared? She was allowed to shed a tear or two.

'I'm looking forward to this evening,' said Michael, doing up his dress studs. 'I never thought I would. When you first mentioned the idea, I was appalled. But you were right. I think this is important for us. It's steering us on. And it's brought us all together, hasn't it?' He chuckled. 'I've just been to tie Ted's tie for him. He's about to pop with excitement. There's no way you're going to get him to go to bed.'

'Well, the boys never went to bed, did they? Or Diana. They were always up and down the stairs until after midnight with one excuse or another.'

Elizabeth sat down to finish off her make-up now that she was dressed. She watched Michael behind her, in the mirror. He was taking a small package out of his chest of drawers. She frowned as he walked over and put it on the dressing table in front of her. It was a red leather jewellery box, the name of her favourite jeweller embossed on the lid.

'What's this?'

'Call it an early Christmas present,' he said, smiling. 'I thought you deserved something special for tonight.'

'You shouldn't have,' she said, as that was what one was supposed to say, but she was intrigued as she flipped open the lid. Inside was a pair of diamond earrings, two snowflakes that glittered and flashed in the lamplight.

'Oh, my goodness,' she exclaimed, completely taken aback. 'They're perfect.'

'Snowflakes for the Snow Ball,' he said as she hurried to take them out of the box and put them on, screwing the backs on as tightly as she could. She gazed at her reflection in the mirror. Her eyes were sparkling, as if the diamonds were reflected in them.

'I'm not sure I deserve them.'

'Of course you do,' he said. 'You keep this house together. All of us. And this is your night.'

Stella felt as if she was becoming someone else as she wriggled into the dress she had chosen. Was it too much? Or actually, not enough – she was conscious that most of her back was bare as she did up the clasp at the neck. Her hair was piled onto her head in a rather sophisticated arrangement – Elizabeth's hairdresser had been up to tend to them all earlier – and the red lipstick she'd bought in the chemist in Breverton stood out against her pale skin. She looked very noticeable, and she wasn't sure how comfortable she was about it. She would rather slink into the background.

For a moment she imagined Edwin coming into the room and admiring her. What would he think? She'd never really had the chance to dress up like this with him. Is this what their life would have been like, if things had gone according to plan? Fancy dinners and balls and cocktail parties and private views? All they'd really had was a few clandestine outings, under the shadow of the war. They'd never really had a chance to live life to the full.

She wasn't going to let it bring her down. She might be standing there in a borrowed dress, in a room that wasn't hers, but she had done her best to make the best life she could for her and Ted. And she felt excited about the future. *The Towpath Gang* was coming together, different but in some ways better, and she was hoping to deliver it to Harriet in the New Year. And then she could start to make plans to stand on her own two feet. She could never repay Elizabeth and Michael for what they had done, but she understood that they didn't expect to be repaid. And with every day that passed, she began to feel more like a member of the family.

Most important of all, Ted was flourishing. She'd declined Michael's offer to intervene at the school – he'd been furious when he found out about the bullying – and she'd been to see the headmistress herself. She'd been met with profuse apologies and a reassurance that it wouldn't happen again. Two days ago, she and Elizabeth and Michael had been to the school Nativity play, and they'd all beamed from ear to ear watching Ted throw his heart into his role as a donkey, and afterwards, when they'd gathered in the hall for mince pies, they'd watched him mucking about with his peers as if nothing had ever happened.

She looked at her watch. It was nearly time to go and greet her guests. Both Mr C and Harriet were staying at the Breverton Arms, and were sharing a taxi over to Foxwood. She couldn't quite imagine the conversation, but she thought they might get on together. She couldn't wait to see them both.

Clementine was putting on her wedding dress. She had always intended to wear it again, and the Snow Ball had presented itself as the perfect opportunity. Elizabeth's hairdresser had smoothed her curls into a sophisticated roll, so she looked different from her wedding day, when they'd been loose and under a veil.

She was a little nervous about this evening. After all, it had been her finding the invitations that had sparked it all off. But she had to admit it had been the perfect way to bring everyone together, and the excitement had reached fever pitch. It had even infected her parents, whom she'd booked into the best room at the Breverton Arms. They were coming for lunch tomorrow, so she could spend some proper time with them before they drove back to Salisbury.

'He*llo*, Mrs Arbutus,' said Alfie in his teasing voice as he came into the bedroom in his white tie and tails. 'Will I do?' He held out his arms to the side.

Would he do? He would more than do. She'd known as soon as she saw him that he was the person she'd been waiting for. He was strong and kind and funny. That was all you needed in a man. The perfect recipe.

'You look very handsome,' she told him.

'I'm wearing Edwin's cufflinks,' he told her, and there was a slight catch in his voice. 'Mum gave them to me. He got them for his eighteenth.'

He showed her the flat, pale gold discs engraved with Edwin's initials. *EMA*.

'Oh, darling,' she said. 'He's here with us. I'm sure of it.'

'He absolutely is,' said Alfie. 'I can tell you, he'd be downstairs already with a glass of champagne in one hand. This was his favourite night of the year.'

'Well, let's go and do him proud.' Clementine pinned her diamanté spider onto the front of her dress. 'Let's make this a night to remember.'

*

At first, Diana hadn't wanted the hairdresser anywhere near her, but her mother had talked her into it, and she had been right, as Elizabeth annoyingly always was. Her hair was loose from its usual scraped-back ponytail and was in shiny waves around her face. She was staring at the reincarnation of the girl she remembered from the first Snow Ball she'd been allowed to stay up all night for, when she had danced until dawn.

She didn't like to think about the intervening years too much. The bloody war had been too much for all of them. Then Edwin's death had turned her sour, like old milk. But tonight, she was proud to look in the mirror. She'd reached inside and found her old spirit, and now she woke up every day with a new zest for life, a sense of purpose, that she had never thought she would have. Of course, the sadness was still there, as it was for all of them, but you couldn't wallow. There was no point.

'Would you do my tie?' Rory came towards her in his dress shirt and underpants, his sturdy legs pink from his recent bath, his tie dangling around his collar. She felt a rush of fondness. Those big hands of his were no good at fiddly things. They were made for pulling calves out of their mothers when things were getting difficult.

'Of course,' she said, turning away from the mirror and walking towards him. His mouth dropped open at the sight of her.

'Wow,' he said. 'You look...'

He stopped, reddening. She could see he didn't know what to say. She could see he was frightened, in case she thought he was after something more, or was implying she should make an effort more often.

'Very nice,' he managed in the end.

What a beast of a wife she had become, that her own husband was afraid to pay her a compliment. She mustn't let him feel like that a minute longer. After all, her horrible sense of self-loathing had evaporated; the one that made her behave so badly. She *liked* herself.

She didn't say anything for now, just tied his tie with a flourish, just as she used to tie Edwin's, for she had the knack. She was good at fiddly things. It was all those manes she plaited. She stood back and smiled at Rory, at his eager, slightly confused, dear face.

'You look very nice yourself,' she said, and kissed the tip of his nose. He couldn't have looked more shocked. It was the most intimate moment they had shared for a long time. And it made her feel happy. It was a very unfamiliar but very welcome feeling.

'Come on, get your trousers on,' she said, smacking his bum playfully. 'Or we're going to be late.'

Just before seven, the photographer jostled them all into position in front of the fireplace in the big drawing room. Michael and Elizabeth in the centre, Diana and Rory to their right, Alfie and Clementine to the left. In front of them all, Stella was seated in an armchair with Ted perched on her lap. Bingo and Paddy and Oscar and Joyce were at their feet, and the photographer had to be quick sharp to take a picture before the dogs bolted.

It was time for the Snow Ball to begin.

Streams of guests trickled through the door over the next hour, resplendent in their finery. Taffeta and chiffon and diamonds and fur; black patent shoes and moiré cummerbunds and twenty-four-carat dress studs. There were shrieks of excitement as trays and trays of champagne were brought around, the crystal glasses winking in the candlelight. Alexandra arrived, looking like Marie Antoinette in swathes of white satin, then Henrietta swept in, a ship in full sail, followed by Nigel and Freddie and Camilla. Freddie remembered the last ball, for he'd been with Alfie in the hydrangeas, swigging illicit cider cup.

And then the smallest member of the Breverton choir walked in through the front door, holding a candle, and began to sing the opening verse of 'Once in Royal David's City'. Everyone fell silent, and there was barely a dry eye as he made his way through the hall, down the corridor and into the drawing room, where the pianist from the band joined in the second verse, along with the rest of the choir.

'We mustn't forget about Christmas,' Elizabeth had thought two weeks earlier, and had telephoned the vicar to arrange it, glad that she had overcome her prejudice and invited him. He was here now, in his white surplice, and he'd told her he would be slipping away before too long. People who said that were usually the last to leave.

Elizabeth had wondered if Jasper would actually come. He had scrawled an *RSVP* in black ink on the back of a postcard saying he would, but she couldn't be sure. Once she would have worried for days whether he'd turn up, but when he did she felt nothing more than mild pleasure, the kind you had on seeing an old friend after a brief absence. It was nothing like the torrent of lust he'd once ignited in her, that sweet rush through the veins that left her almost mad. Addictive though that feeling had been, it was a relief for it to be gone, for it had complicated her life far too much, she realised now, and led her into a dangerous place where her decisions were predicated on desire, not common sense.

He was, of course, the kind of man white tie was made for. He looked dashing in a midnight-blue tailcoat as favoured by the Duke of Windsor. She went to kiss him, a brush on each cheek, and this time his fingertips were cool on her skin, where once they would have set her on fire.

'You look ravishing,' he told her, dark eyes eating her up.

She smiled her thanks. 'Remind me where you're staying?' She hoped he wasn't expecting a bed here. The guests were going to be stuffed in like sardines.

'Oh, I'm not. I'll drive back tonight. I fly to Paris on Christmas Eve, so there's much to be done.'

'Wonderful,' she said. 'Paris at Christmas.' Once she would have felt sick at the thought of him leaving.

'That's what I thought. I'll wake up in the Georges Cinq and Paris will be my oyster.'

He was still holding on to her arms. Looking into her eyes. She knew what he was after from her. He wanted protest. Regret. Longing. She wasn't going to give him an inch.

'Well, I hope Father Christmas can find you. Or should that be *Père Nöel*?'

'I'm sure he will.' He let his hands drop. She wasn't being cold as such, just cool. She felt so much stronger, not being controlled by that terrible urge inside her.

'Jasper.' Michael appeared at her side, and held out his hand for Jasper to shake. 'Merry Christmas. Elizabeth tells me you're off to Paris.'

'A new adventure.' Jasper nodded.

'Well, perhaps we'll come and visit. Elizabeth and I have plans to do more together now Alfie and Diana are at the factory.'

Did he know? wondered Elizabeth. Had he suspected? Had he seen the signs of her obsession? If he had, he'd never said anything, and the strategy had worked, for now, given the choice, she would choose Michael over Jasper every time, for his quiet strength, his dignity, his unshowy handsomeness, his sense of duty and family. Jasper, by contrast, was flighty, probably unfaithful – though how could you expect fidelity when you were breaking your own marriage vows? – capricious... though he had been fun.

You are my past, thought Elizabeth now. And there you must stay.

After dinner, Stella escaped the midst of the throng, after she'd introduced Harriet to Freddie and Camilla and Monsieur Corbières to Clementine's parents, and slipped into the hall. She needed a moment to herself, and this was the quietest place now everyone had arrived. Most people were either in the dining room, where a bar had been set up, or in the magnificence of the drawing room, where there was a pianist and a huge cauldron of mulled wine for those who preferred it. She could hear cries of delight as people greeted each other, roars of laughter, the popping of champagne corks. It all felt a bit overwhelming, and she realised she hadn't really been to any kind of social event in all the years she'd had Ted. It was exhilarating and exhausting in equal measure.

She wasn't quite sure how to behave. She wasn't shy, she'd never been shy, but she wasn't really used to polite chitter chat or laughing politely at someone's terrible joke. Ted was racing about the place with Paddy in tow, lapping up all the attention, which made her happy, though she must make sure he wasn't going to become a nuisance.

She jumped as she felt a hand on her shoulder. She turned and looked into huge grey eyes behind heavy spectacle frames and a lopsided smile in a thin face. The wild hair she remembered had been slicked back. Clementine's half-brother.

'Ben!'

'Stella.' He feigned a double-take. 'My God, you look as if you're about to step onto the stage and accept an Oscar.'

She laughed. 'I'm not quite as dishevelled as I must have been that night. You didn't see me at my best. Thank you so much again for your mercy dash. I love Monsieur Corbières dearly but he's not necessarily reliable after six o'clock.'

'I was talking to him earlier. He's enjoying himself enormously.' Ben mimed raising a glass to his lips.

'Oh dear. I'd better go and find him in a moment. Make sure he doesn't have too much champagne.' She was so pleased Mr C had come, but he looked older and frailer than ever, and she hoped the journey and the excitement weren't too much for him.

'Ah, he's having the time of his life. And how's Ted? I saw him flash past earlier.'

'Full of beans. I think he's going to be a party boy like his father.'

She was trying not to stare at him while taking in as much of him as possible. He must be older than he looked, for although he had a boyish demeanour the laughter lines around his mouth and eyes were quite deep. She remembered Clementine saying he was awfully clever, that he'd been in the Intelligence Corps in the war. She found that hard to align with the person in front of her, his face alive with mischief. His white tie was askew, and he had a fringed silk scarf slung around his neck.

He held up his glass, indicating the paintings on the wall. 'I came out to have a closer look at these. They're astonishing.'

'Oh, I know. I look at them every day and I never tire of them.'

He was looking at the picture of her, frowning.

'I was quite a bit younger there,' she told him, thinking he was wasn't sure if it was her.

'You've hardly changed. It's extraordinary. It's so... alive.'

She looked at it again, remembering how she'd felt that day. 'I'd never felt so alive.'

He put a hand on her elbow. 'I'm so sorry. That you lost him.'

'Thank you.' She smiled her appreciation. His fingers felt warm on her skin. She was sorry when he took his hand away.

There was silence for a moment.

'Clem told me the story, you know,' Ben began. 'About seeing you on the train. She's not usually an interfering sort of person, so it bothered her, whether she'd done the right thing, coming to find you on the boat.'

'We wouldn't be here now if she hadn't. Though at the time, I was... terrified, to be honest. I trusted her, but I wasn't sure what to do. We'd been on our own for so long.'

'I'm sorry about the fire, too. It must have been hard, losing everything.'

She nodded. 'It was losing his stuff that was the worst. Especially all the drawings and sketches. They were like having him with me.' She hadn't told anyone this before, but somehow, Ben was easy to talk to.

'I can imagine. I can almost feel him here now.' He looked around at the paintings again. 'I can tell I'd have liked him.'

'Oh, you would,' she agreed. 'And I think he'd have liked you.'

He looked surprised, but pleased. She wasn't sure why she'd said it, for it was quite an intimate observation, but she meant it. Ben was intriguing. More serious than Clementine had led her to believe, for she had complained of his antics with a fond exasperation. Or perhaps serious was the wrong word. Thoughtful? Certainly not as flighty as you might think, given his flamboyant dress.

'I'm so glad,' he was telling her now, 'that Clem found Alfie. I was getting worried about her. I was dreading her settling for second best. But the minute I met him, I knew he was right. A safe pair of hands, but not a stuffed shirt.'

'Alfie's wonderful,' she said.

'It's hard, isn't it, getting the right balance in people?' he said. 'If someone's too much fun, they can end up being a nuisance.'

He sighed, and she wondered who he was thinking about. 'Is that the voice of experience?'

He gave a wry smile. 'I've as good as given up. I'm a terrible picker when it comes to women. I think I want fun and then I end up picking up the pieces, and then they think I'm trying to *spoil* their fun.'

'Oh dear,' she said, teasing. 'Well, you'll have to try for someone a bit more sensible.'

'Sensible,' he said, looking at her. 'I'm not sure about sensible. All shirt-waisters and flat shoes. There must be a happy medium.'

She took a sip of her champagne.

'Do you think the family would ever consider doing an exhibition?' he asked eventually.

'You mean of these? I don't know.' She raked her eyes over them all again. It was an impressive collection.

'Everyone knows his war art, and, of course, there's London Lives...' He looked at her again, then frowned. 'Was that you? The girl with the red hair?'

It was a long time since she'd been recognised.

She laughed. 'It was. I was furious with him.'

'I always wanted to be the man in the poster. He captured it so perfectly – that overwhelming *need* to be near someone that you get when you first meet...'

'Yes,' she said, remembering.

Their eyes were locked, and eventually she looked away.

'Anyway,' he said, 'I think it would be wonderful for people to see these. Get a feel for the real Edwin, and what his life was like. But of course, it would be a big decision. They might not want the intrusion.'

'I could ask them.'

'Oh God, that's not what I was getting at.' He looked horrified. 'Please don't think that. I can write to them. Don't say anything.'

They stood side by side, looking at the paintings again. The silver teapot flanked by bone china cups. A silk shawl left on the back of a wicker chair. A tennis racket leaned up against a wall. And her own favourite: a painting in a round frame of a tiny mouse peering out of a hole.

The minutiae of English country life.

Stella could see the exhibition in her mind's eye. It would be the talk of London. The reviews would be ecstatic. It would make every other painting soar in value.

It was not her decision to make.

From the drawing room, the triumphant tootle of a trumpet ripped through the air, followed by a drum roll and the clash of cymbals. The band had begun.

'Would you like to dance?' asked Ben, giving her that wonky smile.

She hesitated. She hadn't danced since that last night. She wasn't ready. She wasn't ready to dance with someone she wanted to dance with so much.

'Perhaps later. I must go and find Mr C. Excuse me.'

Her heart was pounding as she melted away from him. She could feel Ben's gaze on her back as she left the hall, leaving ripples on her skin.

Half an hour later, Clementine made her way into the drawing room where the nine-piece band were blasting out an up-tempo version of 'Takes Two to Tango'. The dance floor was crammed with guests, old and young, letting their hair down to the infectious beat as the trumpeter threw his golden notes up to the ceiling. She stood watching for a moment, admiring the costumes, the men universally handsome in their white tie and tails, the women swathed in silk and velvet, the air filled with perfume and cigar smoke. The Snow Ball was in full swing.

There were Diana and Rory, jiggling away together, Diana surprisingly nimble, Rory a flat-footed farmer who had more enthusiasm than rhythm. They danced a few feet apart, though occasionally he would reach out a hand to take hers and twirl her around and she would end up in his arms, laughing. Something had shifted in Diana. There was a newfound confidence in her. A lightness too. The wariness in her eyes had lifted.

And there were Elizabeth and Michael. They reigned over the dance floor, indisputably the King and Queen of Foxwood, her hand on his shoulder, his hand on her waist, moving in perfect time. On the edge of the crowd, Clementine saw Jasper and Alexandra. An unlikely pairing, but it seemed that the usual animosity between them had evaporated. They looked good together, she thought, both of them flamboyant in their dress. They were both attention seekers. They would, she thought, have made a much better couple than Jasper and Elizabeth. Much more of a match for each other, although there was no chemistry between them. They were just having fun.

Elizabeth had told her earlier that Jasper was going to live in Paris. He was better off out of reach.

As the band struck up a new tune and the crowds shifted, she saw another couple. Her mouth dropped open in disbelief and delight. Of course! There they were, unable to take their eyes off each other, talking and laughing while they moved to the beat. Stella and Ben. How absolutely perfect. She'd been longing for the right girl to come along for him for ages, someone who would love him for his ebullience and his firefly mind, but keep him on his toes. She'd known it would have to be someone special, for Ben was easily bored. He seemed spellbound by Stella, and she smiled. He might be a handful, but underneath he was deeply caring and loyal, and Stella had enough grit to be able to manage him. She didn't put up with nonsense.

'A new beginning, perhaps?' said a voice at her elbow, and she turned to find Monsieur Corbières, a glass in one hand and a cigar in the other.

'Perhaps,' she said.

It suddenly occurred to her that she had played no small part in all these outcomes, and she felt a rush of pleasure. Clementine was never self-important, nor did she seek approval or praise, but she gave herself a pat on the back. Although she hadn't manipulated anyone. Just... encouraged.

The band slowed down to a more leisurely time signature, gliding into 'Hold Me, Kiss Me, Thrill Me'. Clementine turned to find Alfie behind her, holding out his arms. She walked into them as he led her onto the dance floor, and she laid her head on his shoulder and moved with him as everyone else faded into the background. It hadn't even been a year since the night she'd first met him, and a few weeks later he had invited her to Foxwood. An invitation she couldn't refuse.

'When you know, you know,' Alfie murmured in her ear, and she looked up at him, smiling.

At midnight, Stella fled to her bedroom, like Cinderella. She wondered if perhaps she'd had too much champagne, because that could give you feelings you shouldn't have, if you weren't careful, and make you say things you didn't mean. Or did it simply reveal the truth? Either way, she had felt tiny bubbles inside her as she danced with Ben

– she hadn't been able to say no, when he asked her again – and that ping of electricity when you touched someone for the first time, and she felt afraid. So she'd murmured her excuses – thank goodness for Ted; she was able to say she was putting him to bed – and she ran up the stairs to gather her thoughts.

Now Ted was firmly tucked up, fast asleep under his blankets with Paddy on top of him. Not usually allowed, but all the rules were being broken tonight. And she wasn't sure what to do with herself. Should she go back down for kedgeree and simply keep out of Ben's way? She was over-excited, that was all. This was the first ball she'd ever been to, and there had been such a build-up, so much anticipation and excitement, so it was probably a natural reaction to her being in close proximity to an attractive man for so long. But it wasn't just that he was attractive – in his inimitable, slightly bohemian way. He seemed to understand everything, how she felt about things.

She heard a tap on the door. Her heart leapt.

'Come in!'

It was Clementine. 'I came to see if you are all right. You've been gone a while.'

'Sorry. I felt a bit woozy.'

'Are you going to come back down? Alfie's making Snowballs for everyone. And there's kedgeree.'

It would be rude not to reappear, she thought. Everyone had probably noticed. And it was unkind to Ben. He'd done nothing to deserve being abandoned. They had danced. Nothing more. And maybe she'd imagined it all. Now the champagne was wearing off, she felt less fizzy.

'Give me five minutes.'

Clementine looked at her. She seemed about to say something, then thought better of it.

'What is it?' asked Stella.

Clementine hesitated. 'It is all right, to love someone else, you know,' she blurted out. 'No one will mind. And I can vouch for him. I've known him all my life.'

Stella was flustered, and had no idea what to say. 'Is it so obvious?'

Clementine smiled. 'It's adorable,' she said. 'Everyone is longing for something to happen.'

Stella patted her cheeks. 'Oh God. How embarrassing.'

Clementine made her way back across the room. 'Don't keep yourself on ice for the rest of your life,' she said, and the door closed behind her.

Stella could hardly breathe. Everyone had noticed. It must be real. She hadn't imagined it. She wasn't sure she had the nerve, to go back down when everyone would be scrutinising her – their – every move. And did Ben really feel the same way she did? She thought so, because there had been a certain wonder in his eyes, a smile on his lips...

She touched up her lipstick, rearranged her hair, took in a deep breath and headed for the door.

As she came down the steps, she saw him. He had on an overcoat, and was obviously about to leave.

'Ben.'

He looked up and saw her, halfway down the stairs, her hand on the banister. He put his hand to his heart, as if it was about to stop.

'Don't leave,' she said. 'Not yet.'

He walked to the bottom of the staircase as she came down. She stood on the last step, and put her hands on his shoulders, feeling the soft warmth of his coat beneath her fingers.

'It's been lovely to talk to you tonight.'

He blinked. Swallowed. Smiled. Nodded. Shut his eyes. He was overwhelmed, with no idea what to say. She stepped down onto the floor, so they were level. He opened his eyes and looked deep into hers. She put her arms around his neck and had just enough time to see the surprise in his eyes before she kissed him.

His kiss felt very different. It didn't feel like kissing Edwin at all. Ben was more urgent. More intense. It felt like setting off on a wild adventure. He was trembling under her fingertips, and after a few moments, she felt his hot tears on her own cheeks.

'You're crying.' She kissed his face, brushing away the tears with her lips.

He couldn't speak. He held her head in his hands, burrowing his fingers into her hair, pressed his forehead to hers, gazed into her eyes. He bent to kiss her collarbone, ran his hot mouth over her bare skin. She gasped, feeling Catherine wheels spinning inside her, pushed herself closer to him.

Eventually they broke apart, breathless, laughing, wide-eyed. She put up her hands and he laced his fingers in between hers.

'I hope you weren't going anywhere,' she whispered.

He shook his head. 'Absolutely not.'

Behind them, Harriet and Monsieur Corbières appeared in the doorway, wrapped up ready for the cold air.

'Oh,' squeaked Harriet. 'Sorry. I think our taxi might be here. Quarter past midnight, it was coming.'

Stella and Ben disentangled themselves, and for the

next few minutes, busied themselves helping Mr C out to the taxi with Harriet two paces behind.

'It's been wonderful, Stella. Thank you so much for asking me. And I'll look forward to hearing from you in the New Year. You're going to be a star, I just know it. She's going to be a star,' she said to Ben, as if he might not believe it.

'I know,' he said.

Soon the two of them were installed safely, the doors were shut, and Ben and Stella watched as the taxi headed off down the drive. They turned back towards the house, and Stella looked at Foxwood, at the bright lights glowing behind its windows, at the silhouettes of the guests inside. The sound of 'Ain't Misbehavin'' floated in the air, mischievous, irresistible.

'Let's go and dance.'

She felt Ben's fingers wrap themselves around hers, and as they walked up the steps, the stars shone a little brighter above and the very first snowflakes began to fall, like kisses on the ground.

33

Four months later

Elizabeth didn't think she had ever been so tired. Diana had made her get up at five o'clock to get to Olympia and help get the stand ready. It was all hands on deck for the Ideal Home Exhibition. She had been on her feet all day and hadn't stopped talking to visitors. The doll's house had been a roaring success, with each room decorated in a different colour scheme showing off their newly named range of household paints. Stella had even done miniature versions of Edwin's paintings to hang on the walls.

Hordes of visitors had crowded around. They'd sold hundreds of raffle tickets, and orders were at a record high. And just after midday, the crowds had parted, standing back to let Princess Margaret onto the stand. Dressed in a luxurious fur coat and a matching hat, she'd shown great interest, and had talked about Queen Mary's doll's house at Windsor Castle, which she'd been very fond of as a child.

The day could not have gone better. Michael was almost beside himself.

'I might have to give you a job too,' he joked to his

wife. 'Though at this rate, Diana will be taking over from me.'

Diana had done more for Arbutus Paints than anyone could ever have imagined. She had secured editorial slots in several magazines featuring Elizabeth, who let readers into her secrets of how to decorate the perfect country home. The next thing in line was a new range of Arbutus wallpaper, which Stella was helping to design – it was intricate and inspired by nature, influenced by some of Edwin's paintings of the landscape around Foxwood.

Life, thought Elizabeth, was as good as it could possibly be. She and Michael would never be the same – you never were, after losing someone – but their love had grown deeper and more meaningful, with a newfound respect. She'd had one postcard from Jasper, of Rodin's *The Kiss*, with a scrawled message saying *Paris is waiting for you*. She'd tucked it into her dressing-table drawer as a souvenir, nothing more.

Now, she was longing to get back to the flat before they headed off to the Savoy for dinner with Alfie and Clementine. For two pins she'd have stayed in with baked beans on toast, but no doubt she'd get a second wind after a bath. A cube of Yardley, a change of frock and she'd be ready for anything.

Ben had painted the walls of the gallery a dramatic grey-black. An Arbutus paint, of course, that was named Church Roof. Stella hadn't been sure at first, she had thought it might be too overpowering, too gloomy, but in fact now all the pictures had been reframed in dark blood-red, she could see it was perfect. Every one of Edwin's paintings stood out against the dramatic backdrop. It made the colours even more striking. And the centrepiece, the one that had its own wall, was the painting of Stella.

The painting was on the front of the catalogue too: *EDWIN ARBUTUS: THE FOXWOOD COLLECTION.*

'What do you think?' asked Ben.

'You were so right,' was all she could say.

He'd written to Elizabeth and Michael after the Snow Ball. A passionate but carefully worded letter, asking them to consider letting him exhibit their private collection.

> *I would guard each one of the paintings with my life. It would be such an honour to show them to the world, to let them see his genius extended beyond what we all already know and love. And, of course, you would have Clementine's eagle eye over everything. They could not be in safer hands...*

Dozens of people had replied to the invitations Clementine had sent out, including Sir Kenneth Clarke. They had finished hanging earlier that afternoon, aided and abetted by Monsieur Corbières, for Ben declared there was no one with a better eye for juxtaposition: the two of them had become firm friends, and had spent hours moving the paintings around, deciding on the best place to hang each one.

It made Stella realise that despite his ebullient exterior Ben was someone who thought and cared about things very deeply. She had been careful to take things slowly, after that first kiss at the Snow Ball. She hadn't wanted either her heart or his to be bruised by a too-swift entanglement. He had respected her wish for caution. He teased her, they bantered and flirted, she teased him back, and something powerful simmered beneath the surface providing a delicious tension every time they met.

And now, looking around her at all the love and care and thought he had put into displaying Edwin's work, she knew what she was about to do was the right thing. She'd been to look at a little flat in Bloomsbury earlier. It was small, but with two bedrooms, one for her and one for Ted. There was a lovely little school nearby, and the headmistress there had assured her that they were very good at preparing their brightest pupils for the grammar school.

She had thought long and hard about the move. It was what she needed, for her career, which was the most important thing to her, for it represented independence. And although Elizabeth and Michael had been sad at the thought of them moving back to London, she and Ted would come to Foxwood every holiday, and his grandparents would see him every time they came to stay at the flat.

And she would be near to Ben. She was ready, she thought, to take the next step and embark on something more serious, and her living in London meant they could get to know each other properly. She had given the landlord a deposit, and agreed to move in the next month so Ted could start at his new school during the summer term.

'We need to go,' she said now. 'We're due at the Savoy in ten minutes.'

He groaned. 'Do we have to go? Can't we just go for supper somewhere quiet?'

'You know we have to. Clementine's organised it,

remember?' She knew he would never do anything to upset his sister. 'And I've booked a room.'

'What?' He looked startled.

'There's no space for me at the flat because the whole family are up for the Exhibition. And my advance came through today. So I thought I'd treat myself.'

'Well.' He looked pleased for her. 'You deserve it.'

She looked at him, her eyes sparkling with mischief. '*We* deserve it.'

His eyebrows shot up. 'Oh,' he said. 'Oh! I see.' He looked pleased. 'Well, in that case, let's get our skates on.'

She was a little bit nervous, but it was a delicious kind of nervous. It had, after all, been a very long time, but she'd had to be sure. And what could be more perfect than a room at the Savoy to celebrate Harriet's approval of *The Towpath Gang*, and the fact that everyone was so confident about it they'd signed her up for a sequel? She couldn't make a habit of splurging on a swanky hotel, but she'd wanted to do something to mark her success, and how far she'd come. She had lost so much – her parents, her lover, her home, her work – and gradually, she had rebuilt her life. She couldn't have done it without help, of course, but she didn't think anyone would begrudge her one night of indulgence.

With the gallery door firmly locked, they wandered together through the streets of Soho towards the Strand, holding hands, hardly speaking, both wrapped up in the glory of what was about to happen, the absolute thrill of it. And when they walked in through the revolving door of the Savoy, and up the stairs to the American Bar, it was obvious to anyone who saw them that they were deeply, irrevocably in love with each other.

*

Here they all are, thought Clementine, as the waiter brought a tray of cocktails to the table. All the people I love. People I wasn't expecting to love. People I didn't even know this time last year. Unexpected arrivals. And twists in the tale. She'd smiled to herself as Stella and Ben arrived, starry-eyed. Elizabeth and Michael had exchanged amused glances. She was glad they didn't mind that Stella was having a second chance at love. Of course they didn't. It was no reflection on her love for Edwin. That would never die. But she deserved to be happy, and she knew Ben would worship the ground she walked on.

She picked up her French 75. She only took a sip, then put it down, but she'd wanted to order one. It felt right, for it reminded her of the night she'd first met Alfie, when he'd handed her one as part of his rescue mission. She picked up the long-handled silver spoon the waiter had left for mixing their drinks, and tapped it on the side of her glass. Everyone looked up in surprise.

'Alfie and I have an announcement. We wanted to make sure everything was all right before telling anyone. But I've been to see Dr Shaw today, for a proper check-up. And I'm glad to tell you, there's another baby Arbutus on its way. Due in September. And all is well.'

'Oh, darling,' Elizabeth leaned in and kissed her cheek, 'I couldn't be more thrilled.'

'That's wonderful,' said Stella.

'Well done, sis,' said Ben, his eyes glistening.

'A Snow Ball baby,' laughed Diana, who had swiftly counted backwards. 'You made that a night to remember.'

Michael ordered champagne.

It was all perfect timing, thought Clementine. The

war was firmly behind them, gradually becoming a dim memory. Alfie, Diana and Michael were steering Arbutus Paints into a bright new future. Stella had her book coming out, and there was Edwin's exhibition. And dear little Ted would have a cousin for Elizabeth to spoil.

Foxwood was ready for the next generation.

Author's Note

As this is a work of fiction, I curated the exhibitions that appear in the book myself, picking work by my own favourite war artists to hang at the Imperial War Museum and the National Gallery.

If the subject interests you, please go along to the Imperial War Museum where there is an exceptional collection of wartime art, although sadly Edwin Arbutus won't be on the wall.

Discover your next uplifting read from
Veronica Henry

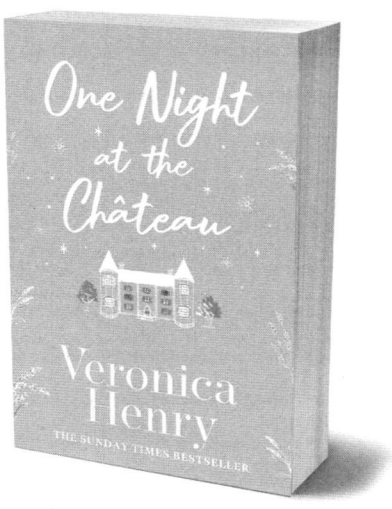

**One night to fall in love.
One summer to change everything...**

Over the last few months, Connie's whole world has fallen apart. Her husband's run off with an older woman, the magazine she works for has gone bust and she's having to sell the family home. So when her beloved godmother, Lismay, begs her to help run the beautiful Château Villette, it couldn't come at a better time...

No one knows the château quite like Connie. She spent a blissful summer there in her twenties, learning to cook delicious French food for the guests, ironing the lavender-scented sheets – and trying to resist the very handsome neighbour, Remy.

As soon as she arrives, it's clear that the château is close to crumbling and Connie knows she's going to have her work cut out. Could it be the fresh start she didn't even know she needed – and will she find a way to save the château, before it's too late?

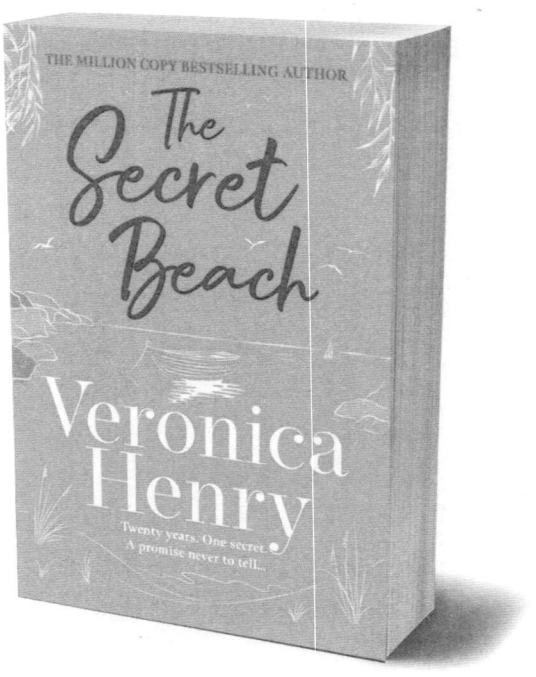

***Nikki kept her secret safe for twenty years.
Now the tide is about to turn...***

Nikki finally owns the little coastguard cottage of her dreams – and it's a few steps away from the hidden beach that means so much to her.

But when a handwritten note lands on her doorstep, she realises it's only a matter of time before the heartbreaking truth of her past is uncovered.

Twenty years ago, her whole world was turned upside-down when a terrible storm rolled into the small seaside town of Speedwell.

Ever since that night, Nikki has been keeping a secret. One she knows has the potential to destroy the lives of those she loves most.

Because as sure as the tide turns, there are no secrets in a small town ...

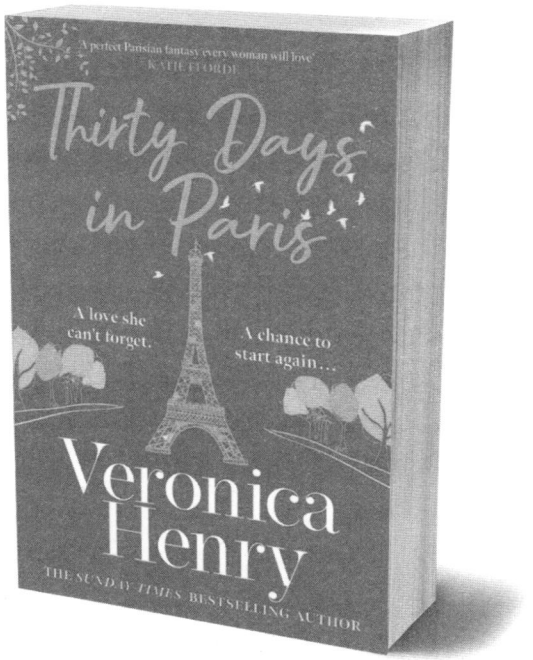

Because Paris is always a good idea . . .

Years ago, Juliet left a little piece of her heart in Paris – and now, separated from her husband and with her children flying the nest, it's time to get it back!

So she puts on her best red lipstick, books a cosy attic apartment near Notre-Dame and takes the next train out of London.

Arriving at the Gare du Nord, the memories come flooding back: bustling street cafés, cheap wine in candlelit bars and a handsome boy with glittering eyes.

But Juliet has also been keeping a secret for over two decades – and she begins to realise it's impossible to move forwards without first looking back.

Something tells her that the next thirty days might just change everything . . .

Credits

Veronica Henry and Orion Fiction would like to thank everyone at Orion who worked on the publication of *The Invitation* in the UK.

Editorial
Charlotte Mursell
Sanah Ahmed

Audio
Paul Stark
Louise Richardson

Contracts
Rachel Monte
Ellie Bowker

Editorial Management
Charlie Panayiotou
Jane Hughes
Bartley Shaw

Design
Heike Schüssler
Charlotte Abrams-Simpson

Finance
Jasdip Nandra
Nick Gibson
Sue Baker

Marketing
Lynsey Sutherland
Lucy Cameron

Production
Ruth Sharvell

Operations
Jo Jacobs

Sales
Dave Murphy
Sammy Luton
Victoria Laws
Rachael Hum
Ellie Kyrke-Smith
Frances Doyle
Georgina Cutler

Publicity
Leanne Oliver
Sian Baldwin